A HANNAH SWENSEN MYSTERY
WITH RECIPES

CHERRY CHEESECAKE MURDER

JOANNE FLUKE

KENSINGTON BOOKS
KENSINGTON PUBLISHING CORP.
http://www.kensingtonbooks.com

KENSINGTON BOOKS are published by

Kensington Publishing Corp.
850 Third Avenue
New York, NY 10022

All Kensington titles, imprints and distributed lines are available at special quantity discounts for bulk purchases for sales promotion, premiums, fund-raising, educational or institutional use.

Special book excerpts or customized printings can also be created to fit specific needs. For details, write or phone the office of the Kensington Special Sales Manager: Kensington Publishing Corp., 850 Third Avenue, New York, NY 10022. Attn: Special Sales Department. Phone: 1-800-221-2647.

ISBN-13: 978-0-7582-0295-6
ISBN-10: 0-7582-0295-4

First Hardcover Printing: March 2006
First Mass Market Paperback Printing: February 2007
10 9

Printed in the United States of America

Savor the Praise for Joanne Fluke's Wickedly Tasty Hannah Swensen Mysteries!

"Mm, mm, Fluke's fans can't wait for the next confection in the series to be served up."
—*Winston-Salem Journal*

"For an enjoyable cozy mystery and lots of new recipes, readers need look no further."
—*Mystery News*

"Fluke has the recipe for appetizing mysteries."
—*Long Beach Press-Telegram*

"The realistic and delightful characters make this a lively read."
—*Mystery Scene*

"With all the cooking and investigating, what more could you want?"
—*I Love a Mystery*

"This series may remind some of another well-known series that includes recipes, but it is better!"
—*Cozies, Capers and Crimes*

"Wacky and delightful characters, plus tempting recipes make this lighthearted offering sure to please the palate of any cozy fan."
—*Publishers Weekly*

"Joanne Fluke imparts a feeling of fun in her books that makes reading them a delight. The addition of mouthwatering recipes throughout the story clinches the popularity of this series."
—*Times Record News*

"An always tasty series."
—*Library Journal*

"Her expertise in creating yummy recipes and believable characters will have dessert lovers and mystery fans feeling like part of the crew that helps Hannah solve her latest case."
—*Romantic Times*

Books by Joanne Fluke

CHOCOLATE CHIP COOKIE MURDER

STRAWBERRY SHORTCAKE MURDER

BLUEBERRY MUFFIN MURDER

LEMON MERINGUE PIE MURDER

FUDGE CUPCAKE MURDER

SUGAR COOKIE MURDER

PEACH COBBLER MURDER

CHERRY CHEESECAKE MURDER

KEY LIME PIE MURDER

Published by Kensington Publishing Corporation

This book is dedicated to my best friend, Shiva.
It's not the same without you, girl.

Acknowledgments

In Memory Of:
Ikuko, a lady I wish I had been fortunate
enough to meet.
Bob Rogers, talented friend.
And Little Al and Betty.

For Ruel, who's always there when I need him.
And for the kids, even when they ask, "Are we eating
another experiment?
Or can we have a ***real*** dessert?"

Thank you to our friends and neighbors:
Mel and Kurt, Lyn and Bill, Gina and the kids,
Adrienne, Jay, Bob M., Amanda, John B., Trudi,
Dale C., Dr. Bob and Sue, Laura Levine and Mark,
Richard and Krista, Nina, the princess of cheesecake,
and Mark Baker, who's been hoping for this title.

Thank you to my editor's parents,
Mr. and Mrs. Scognamiglio.
Without you, John wouldn't be here.
And without John, Hannah Swensen wouldn't be here!

Thank you to Hiro Kimura, my cover artist, who truly
outdid himself with those scrumptious cherries on the
cover, and thanks to Lou Malcanji for putting it all
together in such a delectable dust jacket.
Thanks also to all the other talented folks at

Kensington who keep Hannah sleuthing
and baking up a storm.

Thank you to Dr. Rahhal and Trina for all you do.

Many hugs to Terry Sommers for proving that you can bake every single cookie and dessert recipe in this book and go on to live a normal life.

The Mini Cherry Cheesecake recipe is from Jane at Mysteries To Die For in Thousand Oaks, CA—
Thanks, Jane!

Thanks to Marcy for suggesting the All-Nighter Cookies, and to Betty for the Double Flake Cookies.

Thank you to Jamie Wallace for her superb work on my Web site
MurderSheBaked.com

Thanks to Lois Hirt, who knows almost everything about dentists, and a hug for Kamary, who came all the way from Michigan to meet me.

A big thank you to everyone who e-mailed or snail-mailed.
In a perfect world, The Cookie Jar would be just around the corner and we could all meet for coffee and cookies.
(I've got dibs on the Mock Turtles!)

Prologue

Lake Eden, Minnesota—Wednesday, the Second Week in March

"Cut!"

Dean Lawrence had directed at plenty of locations, but Lake Eden was the worst. These yokels raised boredom to a whole new level. The chubby broad who ran the bakery made a great cherry cheesecake, and that was the only good thing he could say about Podunk Central.

Nothing was working today. They were never going to get this scene. The local lethargy must be catching, and it was time to kick some butt.

"What's with you, Burke? You're supposed to make people weep for you! Get up. I'll show you what I want here." Dean pushed Burke out of camera range and got ready to play the scene himself.

Midway through the scene, he noticed that the redhead who baked his cheesecakes was staring at him with new respect. Maybe she'd be a little more receptive, now that he'd impressed her with his talent. He opened the center desk drawer, pulled out the prop gun, and stared at it while he waited for Lynne's line.

"I love you, Jody! Don't do this to me!"

It was a perfect reading of the line and Dean was glad he'd decided to use her in his next movie. He put on a tortured expression as the camera came in for his close-up, and gazed at Lynne with tears welling in his eyes. "I'm not doing it to you, Li'l Sis. I'm doing it *for me*."

He raised the gun to his temple. Lynne looked horrified, exactly as she should, and he gave her a last, sad smile. Then he squeezed the trigger.

The gun went off and Lynne screamed for real. Their director was dead.

Chapter One

Two Weeks Earlier

Hannah Swensen did her best to convince her sleep-logged mind that the insistent electronic beeping she heard was in the soundtrack of her dream. A huge semi tractor-trailer was backing up to the kitchen door of her bakery, The Cookie Jar, to deliver the mountain of chocolate chips she'd ordered for the gazillion Chocolate Chip Crunch Cookies she'd promised to bake for her biggest fan, Porky Pig, who'd finally overcome his stutter with the help of a voice coach and was now being sworn in as president of the United States . . .

The dream slipped away like the veils of Salome, and Hannah groaned as she clicked on the light. No doubt her dream was the result of watching Cartoon Network until two in the morning and eating two dishes of chocolate ice cream with a whole bag of microwave popcorn. She silenced the alarm and threw back the covers, sitting up in bed in an effort to fight her urge to burrow back into her warm blankets and pull them up, over her head.

"Come on, Moishe," she said, nudging the orange-and-white lump that nestled at the foot of her bed. "Daylight in the swamps, dawn in the desert, and sunrise in Lake Eden, Minnesota."

Moishe's yellow eyes popped open. He looked out the window into the darkness beyond, then swiveled his head to stare at her accusingly. While most people didn't think cats could understand "human-speak," Hannah wasn't most people. This was primarily because Moishe wasn't most cats. "Sorry," Hannah apologized, backpedaling under his unblinking yellow gaze. "It's not really daylight in Lake Eden, but it will be soon and I have to get up for work."

Moishe seemed to accept her explanation. He opened his mouth in a wide yawn and gave the little squeak in the middle that Hannah found endearing. Then he began to stretch.

Hannah never tired of watching her previously homeless tomcat go through his morning calisthenics. Moishe rolled onto his back and gazed up at the bedroom ceiling. His right front leg came up in a fascist salute and after a slight pause, his left front leg shot up to join it. Then his back legs pushed toward the foot of the bed and spread out in a tensely inverted "Y," like the handholds of a witching rod. Once his whole body was stretched taut, he began to quiver like the proverbial bowlful of Jell-O.

The kitty quiver lasted for several seconds and then Moishe flipped from back to stomach. This was the position Hannah called "shoveled," because it was about as flat as a cat could get without the aid of a steamroller. All four legs were stretched out to the max and Moishe's chin was perfectly parallel to the worn nap on the chenille bedspread Hannah had rescued from Helping Hands, Lake Eden's only thrift store.

The part that came next was Hannah's favorite. Moishe's back legs moved forward, first the left and then the right, in what her first grade friends had called "giant steps" in their games of *Captain, May I.* This continued by awkward measure until Moishe's rear was up in the air, his hips so high it turned him into a kitty teepee. Once the apex had been reached, he gave a little sigh, a little shake, a little flick of both ears simultaneously, and then he made a big leap to the floor to follow Hannah down the hallway.

"Hold on," Hannah said, hopping from foot to foot as she pulled on her fleece-lined moccasin slippers. "You know you can't open the Kibble Keeper by yourself."

After a short trip down the hall spent dodging Moishe's efforts to catch the laces on her slipper, Hannah reached the kitchen. She flicked on the bank of fluorescent lights and winced as the walls shimmered dazzling white to her sleep-deprived eyes. Perhaps it was time to paint her walls a darker color, a color like black, especially if she kept operating on three hours of sleep. Last night had been another night in a long string of nights spent in her living room, stretched out on the sofa with a twenty-three pound cat perched on her chest, watching television until the wee small hours of the morning and wrestling with a decision that would have stymied even Solomon.

An indignant yowl brought Hannah back to matters at hand and she opened the broom closet to lift out the Kibble Keeper. It was a round, gray, bucket-type container with a screw-on lid that was guaranteed to keep out even the most persistent pet. Hannah had found it at the Tri-County Mall after Moishe had defeated every other means she'd tried to keep him from helping himself to his own breakfast. It wasn't that she begrudged him food. It was the cleanup that made feline self-service dining unfeasible. Hannah had swept up and dumped out the last kitty crunchy she was about to sweep and dump, and the salesclerk at the pet store had assured her that no living being that lacked opposable thumbs could open the Kibble Keeper. It was made of a resin that was impervious to biting and scratching, knocking it over and batting it around had no effect at all on its sturdy exterior, and it had been tested on a tiger at the Minnesota Zoo and come through with flying colors.

Even though Hannah knew that Moishe was physically incapable of unscrewing the lid, she still concealed her actions from him. It wasn't wise to underestimate the cat who was capable of so much more than the ordinary tabby.

"Here you go," she said, scooping out a generous helping and dumping it into his bowl. "Finish that and I'll give you some more."

While her feline roommate crunched, Hannah poured herself a cup of steaming coffee and sent a silent message of thanks to whoever had invented the automatic timer. She took one sip, swallowed painfully, and added a coffee ice cube from the bag she always kept in the freezer. A regular ice cube would dilute what her grandmother had called "Swedish Plasma," and that was why Hannah kept one ice cube tray filled with frozen coffee. She needed her caffeine full-strength in the morning.

Several big gulps and Hannah felt herself beginning to approach a wakeful state. That meant it was time to shower and dress. The lure of a second cup of coffee would make her hurry, and she was awake enough not to doze off and turn as red as a lobster under the steaming spray.

Hannah reentered the kitchen eleven minutes later, her red hair a damp mass of towel-dried curls, and clad in jeans and a dark green sweatshirt that proclaimed CHOCOLATE IS A VEGETABLE—IT COMES FROM BEANS in bright yellow script. She'd just poured herself that second cup of coffee when the phone rang.

Hannah reached for the bright red wall phone that hung over the kitchen table, but she stopped in midstretch. "What if it's Mike? Or Norman?"

"Rrowww!" Moishe responded, looking up at the phone as it rang again. "Yowwwww!"

"You're right. So what if they both proposed? And so

what if they're waiting for me to choose between them? I'm thirty years old, I run my own business, and I'm a sensible adult. Nobody's going to rush me into a decision I might regret later . . . including Mother."

As Hannah uttered the final word, Moishe's ears flattened against his head and he bristled like a Halloween cat. He despised Delores Swensen and Hannah's mother had a drawer full of shredded pantyhose to prove it.

"Don't worry. If it's Mother, you don't have to speak to her."

Hannah took a deep breath and grabbed the phone, sinking down in a chair to answer. If it was her mother, the conversation would take a while and there were bound to be unveiled references to her unmarried state. If it was her younger sister, Andrea, the conversation would include the latest about Hannah's two nieces, Tracey and Bethany, and it would also take a while. If it was Michelle, Hannah's youngest sister, they were bound to have a discussion about college life at Macalester College and that would also eat up the minutes Hannah had left before she had to go to work.

"Hello?" Hannah greeted her caller, hoping mightily that it wasn't either of the two men in her life.

"What took you so long? I was almost ready to give up, but I knew you wouldn't leave for work this early."

It was a man, but it wasn't either of the two in question and Hannah breathed a sigh of relief. It was Andrea's husband, Bill, the only other early riser in the Swensen family. "Hi, Bill. What's up?"

"I am. I'm out here at the sheriff's station and we've got a problem."

Hannah glanced at the clock. It was only five-fifteen. Bill kept regular hours now that he was the Winnetka County Sheriff. He never went to the office until eight unless there was an emergency. "Is there anything I can do to help?"

"You bet there is. And you're the only one who can fix this mess!"

"What mess?" Hannah had visions of homes burglarized, motorists carjacked, public buildings vandalized, and murder victims stacked up like cordwood. But if crime was running rampant in Lake Eden, she certainly hadn't heard about it. And how could she possibly be the only one who could fix it?

"It's Mike. You really did a number on him, Hannah. One minute he's on top of the world, telling everybody that you're bound to choose him. The next minute he's all down in the mouth, absolutely sure that you're going to ditch him and marry Norman."

Hannah did her best to think of something to say. It wasn't *her* fault that Mike couldn't handle the stress of waiting while she made up her mind which proposal to accept. It had been only a week. A girl, even one whose mother thought her old enough to qualify as an old maid, was entitled to all the time she needed for such an important decision.

"Look, Hannah. I know it's not totally your fault, but I've got a dangerous situation here."

"Dangerous?"

"That's right. Mike's supposed to be my head detective, my right hand when it comes to solving crime. The way he's acting right now, he couldn't catch a perp even if the guy stood in front of his desk holding a sign that said, I DID IT. I mean, what if we have a real murder, or something like that? What'll happen then?"

Hannah let out her breath. She hadn't even realized she'd been holding it. "So what do you want me to do?"

"Make up your mind so Mike can get back to work. Fish, or cut bait . . . you know?"

"But I can't rush my decision. It's just too important."

"I understand," Bill said with a sigh, "and I'm not really trying to influence you. I just know it'll be Mike in the long run. If you love him as much as I think you do, you'll accept his proposal today and put him out of his misery. He's the right one for you and that's not just my opinion. Everybody in the department thinks so, too."

"I'll . . . uh . . . think about it," Hannah said, settling for the most noncommittal reassurance in her arsenal.

"Think fast. And keep your fingers crossed that we don't need Mike for anything until you give him a yes."

Hannah promised she would and hung up the phone. She could understand Bill's point. A week was a long time to keep anyone on hold, but she was no closer to making a decision than she'd been on the day both men had proposed. Mike was handsome and exciting. Norman was dependable and endearing. Mike made her stomach do flips when he kissed her, and Norman's kisses made her feel warm and tingly all over. She wished she could have both of them, but she couldn't. And there was no way she could give up one for the other.

Before Hannah could take another swallow of her coffee, the phone rang again. She grabbed it in midring, certain that it was Bill who'd forgotten to tell her something. "What did you forget, Bill?"

"It's not Bill, it's Lisa," Hannah's young partner replied. "I just wanted you to know that you don't have to hurry to work this morning."

"Why not?"

"Because I'm down here at The Cookie Jar already."

Hannah glanced up at the clock. It was five-thirty and Lisa wasn't due at work until seven. "Why so early?" she asked, hoping that Lisa hadn't had a fight with her new husband.

"Herb had to get up at four and after he left, I couldn't go back to sleep."

"Why did he have to get up at four?"

"He's driving to Fargo for the Traffic Tradeshow."

"What's that?" Hannah asked, although she suspected that if she'd remained silent, Lisa would have gone on to tell her.

"It's everything to do with traffic and parking, like signs, parking meters, and traffic signals. Mayor Bascomb called us at home last night and he wants Herb to check out the price on parking meters."

"Parking meters?" Hannah was shocked. Parking had always been free in Lake Eden.

"That's right. He told Herb to find out how much it would cost to put them up on Main Street."

"On Main Street?"

"Yes, but Herb thinks it's a smokescreen."

"A smokescreen?" Hannah repeated, feeling more and more like an obedient mynah bird.

"There's a group that wants Lake Eden Liquor shut down. They say the city shouldn't be making a profit on the sale of alcohol."

Hannah gave a little snort. Every few years someone organized a group to close down the municipal liquor store. "I wish people would learn that you can't legislate morality. Closing the liquor store isn't going to cut down on drinking."

"I know, but this time they're really serious. They're collecting signatures to get it on the next ballot. Herb's sure that's why Mayor Bascomb wants an estimate on those parking meters."

Hannah took another slug of coffee, but she still didn't see the connection. "What do parking meters have to do with the liquor store?"

"Herb thinks the mayor's going to give them a choice. Close the liquor store and put parking meters on Main Street to make up for the lost revenue, or keep it open and forget about the tax increase they'll have to pay to get the parking meters installed in the first place."

"That ought to work," Hannah said with a smile. The mayor was almost as devious as her mother.

"I think so, too. Everybody wants to park for free and nobody wants to pay more taxes. Anyway, I'm here and you don't have to come in until you want to. You need some time to think."

"Think?"

"About Mike and Norman. Mayor Bascomb asked Herb if you'd made up your mind yet."

"He did?" Hannah was surprised. "I didn't know he cared one way or the other."

"Well, he does. He wants you to marry Norman. He says it's your civic duty."

"What!"

"That's exactly what Herb said, but Mayor Bascomb explained it. He said that they can always hire a new detective, but finding a dentist to take over the clinic will be a lot harder."

"Wait a second . . . the mayor thinks the man I don't marry will leave town?"

"Yes, and he's not the only one. Herb says Mike's not going to stick around and feel like a loser if you end up marrying Norman. He's too proud to eat crow in front of the whole town. And Norman's not going to stay here and watch you live happily ever after with Mike. He really loves you and it would be too painful for him. Not only that, if Norman leaves, Carrie will probably go with him, because he'll be all depressed and she'll think he needs her. And then your mother will end up losing a partner."

"Oh, boy!" Hannah groaned under her breath. This was a whole new set of problems to consider. She'd been thinking about how her choice would affect her own happiness, but now it seemed it could have ramifications on the whole town of Lake Eden!

"Anyway, take your time about coming in. I'll see you when you get here."

Hannah said goodbye and turned to look at Moishe. "I wish I'd known sooner. Turns out we could have slept in."

"Rrrow!" Moishe replied, and Hannah thought he looked disappointed. Sleeping in while nestled at the foot of the bed, half buried in the fluffy comforter, was one of Moishe's favorite activities.

"Oh, well. I guess I might as well carry out the garbage and . . ."

Before Hannah could finish telling an uninterested feline her plans, the phone rang again and she snatched it up. "Hello?"

"Hi, Hannah. It's Barbara Donnelly. I know it's early, but I wanted to catch you before you left for work."

"Hi, Barbara." Hannah grabbed the steno notebook she kept on the kitchen table. Barbara was the head secretary at the sheriff's station and she always ordered cookies for the staff meetings she held on Monday afternoons. "Do you want cookies for this afternoon?"

"Yes. Give me three dozen Black and Whites. I'll send one of the girls in to pick them up. On second thought, better make it four dozen. They're our favorites. But that's not the reason I called. I need a favor."

"What's that?" Hannah asked, wise enough not to agree before she heard what Barbara wanted.

"I'm begging you to put an end to this whole thing today."

Hannah was 95 percent certain she knew what Barbara meant, but she went for the remaining 5 percent. "What whole thing is that?"

"The whole thing with Mike. He's driving us all nuts. I had to assign three different secretaries to him in the past week."

"Why so many?"

"Because after a day with him, they come to my office and ask for reassignment. It's just too stressful working for a boss that's walking around whistling one minute and chewing his fingernails the next. Of course I hope you choose Mike, but that's up to you. I just want you to make a decision today and put my secretaries out of their misery."

"I'll try," Hannah promised and signed off. She'd no

sooner hung up the phone than it rang again. "Okay, okay," she plucked the receiver from its cradle. "Hello?"

"It's Doc Bennett, Hannah."

In one fluid motion, Hannah stretched out the phone cord, poured herself another mug of coffee, and sat back down in her chair. "What's up, Doc?"

"Wery funny," Doc Bennett responded in his Elmer Fudd voice, the same voice that had taken the fear out of going to the dentist for so many Lake Eden children. "Seriously, Hannah, what's up is Norman."

"What do you mean?"

"That poor boy isn't getting any sleep and he called to ask me to fill in for him again today. It's a real pity, Hannah. I don't know how much more of this Norman can take. So far, he hasn't made any dental mistakes that I know of, but it's only a matter of time before he fills the wrong tooth, or something even worse. What's taking you so long, anyway? If you love Norman as much as I think you do, you should accept his proposal today and let him get some sleep!"

Hannah was stymied. She didn't know what to say. "I . . . I'm . . ."

"I know it's an important decision, but you've taken long enough. Will you try to decide today?"

"I'll try," Hannah agreed, doubting that she'd be successful.

"Good. I've got to go. Mrs. Wahlstrom is coming in early for a cleaning and I haven't even had breakfast yet."

Doc Bennett hung up abruptly and Hannah was left holding a dead line. As she hung up on her end, she uttered a phrase she'd never use within Tracey or Bethany's hearing, even though Bethany was too young to understand it and Tracey had probably heard it before, and then she turned to Moishe. "They're ganging up on me. What am I going to do?"

Moishe gave her a wide-eyed look that Hannah interpreted to mean he didn't have the foggiest idea. She reached down to pet him, but before her hand connected with his orange-and-white fur, the phone rang again.

"Uh-oh," Hannah breathed as Moishe's ears flattened against his head and he started to bristle. Her kitty caller I.D. wasn't infallible, but nine times out of ten that bristle meant her mother was on the phone. When Moishe's tail started to switch back and forth like a metronome, Hannah reached for the phone. Her mother was nothing if not persistent. If she didn't reach Hannah at home, she'd wait and call her down at The Cookie Jar. "Hello, Mother."

"You really shouldn't answer the phone that way," Delores gave her standard greeting.

"I know, but you'd be disappointed if I didn't."

"Perhaps," Delores conceded. "I need to talk to you about something important, Hannah. And I want you to know that normally I'd never interfere . . ."

But, Hannah provided the next word. She knew it was coming, although she chose not to say it aloud.

"But Carrie just called me and we have a situation on our hands. Do you know that Norman's down at Hal & Rose's Cafe right now, slogging down coffee as fast as Rose can pour it?"

"No," Hannah answered truthfully.

"Well, he is. Rose called Carrie to tell her. She said she tried to get Norman to go easy on the coffee, but he said this could be the most important day of his life and he wasn't about to sleep through it."

Hannah groaned. "Norman thinks I'm going to give him an answer today?"

"It's not just today. Carrie says he's been like this every day since he proposed. And to make matters even worse, Mike's down there too. He's sitting right across from Norman in the back booth, matching him cup for cup."

"At least it's not beer for beer," Hannah commented, grinning slightly.

"Shame on you, Hannah Louise! That's not one bit funny and you know it. I've done my very best to keep mum, but this time you've gone too far. I didn't raise you to be cruel!"

"Cruel?" Hannah was shocked.

"What else would you call it? I'm serious, Hannah. Enough is enough and it's time for you to stop dithering. You should choose which man you want to marry, tell him so, and let the other down gently. That's what a lady would do under the same circumstances. Drawing it out the way you've done is unkind to everyone concerned."

Hannah was silent for a long moment, considering what her mother had said. Delores did have a point. "You're right, Mother."

There was a crash as Delores dropped the phone. And then a scrabbling noise as she picked it up again. "I'm sorry. Did you say I was *right?"*

"That's what I said."

"Well . . ." Hannah's mother sounded slightly breathless and extremely shocked. "Does that mean that you agree to settle this once and for all?"

"Yes, I'll settle it."

"And you'll do it today?"

"I'll do it right now. Talk to you later, Mother."

Hannah hung up the phone to cut off any further questions, filled Moishe's food bowl one last time, grabbed her coat and car keys, ignored the phone that was frantically ringing again, and headed out the door to keep her date with destiny at Hal & Rose's Cafe.

Chapter Two

Twenty minutes later, Hannah skidded around the corner of Third and Main in the candy-apple red vehicle the Lake Eden kids called the "cookie truck," and nosed up to the snowbank that Hal had left when he shoveled the sidewalk in front of the café. The plate glass window was steamed up and she couldn't see inside, but Mike's Hummer was parked on one side of her and Norman's sedan was on the other. Since there was a layer of ice on both windshields, Hannah surmised that they must have arrived the moment Rose unlocked the door for the DelRay employees who stopped for breakfast before their early morning shift.

Hannah got out of her truck and headed for the door. She pulled it open with a clean jerk and marched right in. The first thing she saw was a blackboard hanging on the back wall by the curtained poker room. It said, NORMAN VS. MIKE—BETS CLOSE AT NOON TODAY.

Hannah hadn't thought she could get any angrier, but she'd been wrong. One glance at that blackboard made her blood boil. She gave a most unladylike snort as she spotted Norman and Mike sitting in the back booth and she imagined she could hear the strains of theme music from *Jaws* as she headed across the floor.

Mike nudged Norman as he spotted her. Norman looked up and began to frown. Hannah figured that was because of her thundercloud expression. It was too early in the morning to assume a poker face and she didn't care if the whole town of Lake Eden knew that she was steaming mad. She didn't appreciate receiving five phone calls before six in the morning from people who were dead set on giving her unwanted advice. This was *her* life, these were *her* proposals, and *she* was the one who'd have to live with her decision. There was no way she enjoyed being the subject of a very public betting pool at Hal & Rose's Cafe, and it was long past time to put an end to the speculation.

Hannah strode forward with purpose, her rubber-soled boots thudding against the floor. She was unaware that the other patrons in Hal & Rose's had swiveled around on their stools to watch what they assumed would be a spectacle. She didn't hear the whispered comments or see the money that quickly changed hands. She was concentrating on the two men in the booth and what she was going to tell them.

"What's wrong, Hannah?" Norman asked as she arrived at their booth and stood there in front of it, her hands on her hips.

"Everything," Hannah said, deciding not to mince words. "Why did you have to ask me to marry you anyway?"

"Because I love you," Norman was the first to respond.

"And I love you, too," Mike said.

"Well, that's just great, because I love you."

"Who?" Norman asked.

"Yes, who?" Mike added.

"Both of you. But that's not the biggest problem. I'm sick and tired of people telling me that I have to choose between you! And I really resent the fact that everyone in this whole town is urging me to make a decision right now!"

Mike held up his hand. "But, Hannah . . . "

"Quiet!" Hannah interrupted. "Just this morning, I got calls from Bill, Lisa, Barbara Donnelly, Doc Bennett, and Mother. I even got an ultimatum from Mayor Bascomb! They all want me to make my decision right now, but they've got it all wrong. I should be the one to decide when to decide!"

"Huh?" Norman asked, looking confused.

Mike wore the identical expression. "What was that, Hannah?"

"Never mind. I know what I mean and that's good enough for me. Do you still want to marry me?"

If it had been raining, both men would have drowned as they looked up at her with their mouths open in surprise. Mike was the first to recover. "I do."

"So do I!" Norman added.

"Good." Hannah gave them both a tight smile. "That means I'm going to turn both of you down. You're off the hook. You can stop moping around and waiting for the other shoe to drop. There's no way I'm going to bow to peer pressure and choose between you."

"Hold on," Norman said, looking dismayed. "Does that mean you're not going to marry either one of us?"

"That's what I just said."

"But . . . is there someone else?" Mike asked.

"No, there's no one."

"Then why . . ."

Norman started to frame a question, but Hannah interrupted. "It's a matter of principle. Who decided that the man had to be the one to propose, anyway?"

Both men shrugged and Norman finally answered, "I don't know, but I think it's always been that way."

"Well, I don't like it and I'm changing the rules. I'm taking back my own life and following my own timetable. Nobody's going to push me into anything I don't want to do. I'll decide when I want to get married. And when I do,

I'll ask the man of my choice if he wants to marry me. Is that clear?"

Mike and Norman exchanged glances. Then they both turned to her and nodded.

"Perfect. Now can we all stop acting like characters that escaped from a soap opera and get back to a seminormal life?"

"Yeah," Mike agreed, smiling for the first time since Hannah had come in the door.

"You bet!" Norman said, but he didn't smile. "I don't want to open a can of worms here, but will you still go out with me, Hannah?"

"Absolutely."

"And me?" Mike asked.

"You, too. Let's just forget about marriage and go back to the way we were."

"You're on," Mike said.

"Deal," Norman concurred, smiling at last.

"I'm really glad we got that settled." Hannah was smiling as she turned to Norman. "Would you please go get me a chair? If I'm not sitting next to either one of you, the customers that are staring at us from the counter can't speculate on what that might mean."

"Sure thing," Norman said, and slid out of the booth.

"And would you go tell Rose I'm as hungry as a bear and I want two eggs over easy, bacon extra crispy, and toast?" Hannah asked Mike.

"Of course."

Mike slid out of the booth, but Hannah grabbed his hand as he was about to walk away. "Just a second," she said. "Do you think you can pretend you're on duty for a minute?"

"I guess. Why?"

"I'd appreciate it if you'd remind those guys at the counter that gambling's illegal in Minnesota. And then you can tell Hal that I'm not going to marry either one of you and that he should donate to charity every cent of the money he's holding."

When Hannah came in the back door at The Cookie Jar, Lisa gave her a thumbs-up. "You were absolutely right to turn both of them down."

"Thanks, but how did you hear about it so soon?"

Lisa pointed to the wall next to the sink and Hannah turned to look. The cord from the wall phone was stretched out to its limit and the phone attached to the end of the cord was out of sight, shut tightly in the drawer that held the dishtowels. "Too many calls?"

"You said it!" Hannah's petite partner gave a little laugh. "Everybody in town who doesn't know wants to pump me for information. And everybody who *does* know wants to be the first to tell me about it. I couldn't get the baking done and answer the phone at the same time, so I took it off the hook."

"And you hid it in the drawer so you wouldn't see it on the counter and feel guilty?"

"You know me too well."

"Well, I'm here now. I'll take care of the calls." Hannah opened the drawer, retrieved the phone, and hung it back on the hook. There was a moment of breathless anticipation and then it began to ring.

"Your turn," Lisa declared, slipping into her coat and heading for the door. "I'm running over to the school with the cookies for the faculty meeting."

"Put on your gloves. It's cold out there," Hannah called after her. Then she reached for the phone, hoping the person on the other end of the line was someone comfortable, someone friendly, someone from out of state. "The Cookie Jar. Hannah speaking."

"Hi, Hannah!" A familiar voice reached Hannah's ear. "I figured you were there when I couldn't get you at home."

"You were right," Hannah said, giving a big sigh of relief. It was Michelle, her youngest sister, calling from the house she rented with friends and fellow students just off the Macalester campus.

"I heard you turned both of them down."

Hannah sputtered slightly. Michelle was over sixty miles away. "How did *you* know?"

"It's not like I live in a vacuum. Lots of people keep me up to date on what's happening in Lake Eden."

"Mother!" Hannah breathed.

"Mother," Michelle confirmed. "You did the right thing, Hannah. It's a whole lot better than saying yes to one of them and changing your mind later."

"You're right. Is that why you called?"

"That's part of it. The other part is to tell you that I spent a whole week talking up Lake Eden and saying what a great town it is."

"It *is* a great town."

"I know that, but Mr. Barton didn't."

"Who's Mr. Barton?"

"The producer of the Indy Prod."

Hannah felt like she was running around in circles. "What's an Indy Prod? And what does it have to do with Lake Eden?"

"Mr. Barton was a guest in our drama class and he's the producer of an independent production. That's what Indy Prod means."

"You're talking about a movie producer?" Hannah cut to the chase.

"Yes. He's almost through shooting a film set in Minnesota and he said he was looking for a small town close to a lake, with a church, a school, and a park."

"That's practically every small town in Minnesota."

"I know. I told him that, and then I recommended Lake Eden."

Hannah hoped that Michelle didn't have her heart set on seeing her hometown on the big screen. While Lake Eden was a very nice town, there were other, more picturesque settings for movies. "That certainly would be interesting, Michelle, but I doubt that . . ."

"That certainly *will* be interesting," Michelle interrupted to correct her.

"*Will* be? You mean . . . ?"

"That's right! My drama professor called to tell me this morning. Mr. Barton sent a scout to check out Lake Eden. You met him, Hannah. He came into The Cookie Jar."

"He did?"

"Yes. Do you remember a guy named Mitch who asked about the name for the lake and the town?"

"A couple of strangers asked me that," Hannah said, not mentioning that almost every nonlocal who stopped at The Cookie Jar wanted to know why the town was called Lake Eden, and the lake was called Eden Lake. The answer was that the lake had been named first, almost thirty years before the town had been built, and the town fathers had wanted a name that tied in with the lake, but was different. Tired of answering the same question over and over, Lisa's cousin, Dianne Herron, had suggested a solution. Hannah had ordered cards printed up with the answer and they set them out on the tables in the summer during the tourist season.

"Well, Mitch said you were really nice about explaining it to him, and he was crazy about your Molasses Crackles. He wrote up a glowing report and once Mr. Barton did a drive-through, he decided to talk to Mayor Bascomb and find out how much it would cost to rent Main Street for a week."

"Rent Main Street?" Hannah was amazed. "But what will that mean for our businesses?"

"You'll all get compensated. That's the way these production companies work. Mitch told me that Mr. Barton usually pays last year's gross revenues for the same period plus ten percent for the inconvenience. And they always use locals for extras. Isn't that exciting?"

"Exciting," Hannah repeated, not sure what effect a movie company would have on her sleepy little hometown. "Does Mayor Bascomb know about this?"

"Not yet, but he will. The producer is going to call him this morning. I just wanted to give you a heads-up before it happened, and to tell you the best news of all."

"You're getting married?" Hannah quipped, knowing full well her youngest sister was doing no such thing. Michelle had made it abundantly clear that she was going to finish college before she even considered walking down the aisle.

Michelle laughed. "Of course I'm not and you know it. But the producer hired me as a production assistant and I'll be coming home for a week. I'm getting paid and I'm getting college credit for the job."

"Good for you!" Hannah did an abrupt reversal. She'd been half-hoping that the movie company wouldn't disrupt life in Lake Eden, but now she was all for it. Michelle would enjoy the experience and it would be wonderful to have her home again. "Would you like to stay in my guest room?"

"I'd love to, you know that, but I'd better stay with Mother, especially after all the trouble she had with Winthrop and all. She's bound to be lonely. And speaking of Mother, the producer promised me that he'll hire Mother and Carrie to help locate props. And when I told him how they decorated Granny's Attic to look like the first mayor's house, he said he'd have his set decorator look at it and maybe they'd use it as a set in the movie."

"Too bad the movie's not set in Regency England," Hannah mused. Both Carrie and Delores were founding members of the Lake Eden Regency Romance Club and the producer would have to look far and wide to find anyone more familiar with the period.

"I know, but this is almost as good. The part of the movie they're filming in Lake Eden takes place in the nineteen-fifties. That should be a snap for Mother and Carrie since both of them were around back then."

Hannah gave a little chuckle. "Yes, but neither of them will admit it."

After a few more minutes of chatting about the advance crew that would be arriving next week, and the full cast and crew the week after that, Hannah said good-bye and attempted to hang up. But the phone rang again the moment she settled it in its cradle. Since she didn't feel like talking to anyone, there was only one thing to do.

"This is Hannah at The Cookie Jar," she said in the flattest voice she could muster. "I'm sorry I can't answer your call right now, but if you'll leave your name and number, I'll call you back just as soon as . . ." There was a click, and Hannah stopped speaking. Her caller, assuming Hannah wasn't available, had hung up.

She was about to hang up on her end when she reconsidered. It was time to take a lesson from Lisa. Hannah stretched out the cord, opened the drawer, and hid the phone under the dishtowels again. Then she hurried through the swinging restaurant-style door to the coffee shop.

Hannah's first task was to put on the coffee and she made short work of filling the thirty-cup urn and plugging it in. She set out cream, sugar, and artificial sweetener on each table and wrote the daily cookie specials on the blackboard behind the front counter. She had just gone back into the kitchen to fill the glass canisters they used to display the day's cookies when Lisa came back.

"I'll help," she said, shedding her coat and heading for the sink to wash her hands. "Everybody at the school wanted to know why you turned both of them down."

Hannah just shook her head. It was barely eight in the morning, but there were no slackers on the Lake Eden Gossip Hotline. "What did you say?"

"I told them I hadn't asked you because it was none of my business."

Hannah eyed her diminutive partner with new respect. "Being married is good for you. You've picked up some of Herb's assertiveness."

"That's not *all* I picked up!"

"What do you mean?" Hannah asked and then wished she hadn't as all sorts of dire possibilities ran through her mind.

"I picked up all of Great-Grandma Beeseman's recipes. They were in boxes up in Marge's attic, and she said I could have them. She couldn't read them because they're in German."

"You read German?"

"No, but Herb found an Internet translation service and a woman from Germany is helping me." Lisa reached out for a cookie on the baker's rack and handed it to Hannah. "Try this. They're called *Kokosnuss Schokolade Kekse*."

"Coconut chocolate cookies?" Hannah asked, seriously draining the small cache of German words she'd picked up over the years.

"That's right! Do you speak German?"

"Not unless you count *Volkswagen* and *sauerkraut* as vocabulary. I was just reacting to the cognates." Hannah took a bite and smiled her approval. "These are good."

"I know. Do you want to add them to our cookie list?"

"Absolutely, but let's think of another name. The German is too hard for customers to remember and the English translation isn't catchy enough."

"How about Cocalattas?" Lisa suggested.

"I like it. It sounds like coconut and chocolate, and that's what they are. Write it on the board and we'll give them a trial run today."

Lisa nodded and grabbed the steno pad Hannah kept handy for notes about supplies. "I'd better write down flaked coconut. We're almost out."

"Good idea. And while you're at it, make a note to order Jujubees and Milk Duds."

"Are we going to the movies?" Lisa quipped, looking up with a smile.

"No, the movies are coming to us. Just as soon as we carry in these canisters, we'll take a coffee break and I'll tell you all about it."

COCALATTAS

Preheat oven to 350 degrees F., rack in the middle position

1 cup melted butter ***(2 sticks, ½ pound)***
¾ cup white ***(granulated)*** sugar
¾ cup brown sugar, firmly packed
1 teaspoon baking soda
2 teaspoons coconut extract ***
½ teaspoon salt
2 beaten eggs
1 cup finely chopped coconut ***(from approximately 2 cups coconut flakes)***
2¼ cups flour ***(don't sift—pack it down in your measuring cup)***
1 cup chocolate chips ***(6 oz. package—I use Ghirardelli's)***

****** It's not absolutely positively necessary that you use coconut extract, but the cookies will be much more delicious if you do. If you can't find it, or you're making these in the middle of a blizzard and you can't get to the store, just use vanilla.***

Melt the butter. ***(Nuke it for one and a half minutes on HIGH in a microwave-safe container, or melt it in a pan on the stove over low heat.)*** Mix in the white sugar and the brown sugar. Add the baking soda, coconut extract, and salt. Add the eggs and stir it all up.

Chop the coconut flakes in a food processor. ***(Most people like the coconut chopped because then it doesn't stick between their teeth, but you don't have to go out and buy a food processor to make these cookies. Just find the finest, smallest flakes you can in the store, spread them out on a cutting board and chop them up a little finer with a knife.)*** Measure the coconut **AFTER** it's chopped. Pack it down when you measure it, add it to your bowl, and stir thoroughly.

Add half of the flour and the chocolate chips. Stir well to incorporate. Finish by mixing in the rest of the flour.

Let the dough "rest" for ten minutes on the counter, uncovered. Drop by teaspoons onto **UNGREASED** cookie sheets, 12 cookies to a standard

sized sheet. If the dough is too sticky to handle, chill it slightly and try again. Bake at 350 degrees F. for 9 to 11 minutes or until golden brown around the edges.

Let cool for three minutes, then remove cookies from the baking sheet and transfer to a wire rack to finish cooling.

Yield: Approximately 6 dozen depending on cookie size.

Lisa's Note: Herb's great-grandmother's recipe calls for chipped chocolate, so I used chocolate chips. Hannah says that if chocolate chips had been available when Herb's great-grandmother was alive, she probably would have used them.

Hannah's Note: These are Herb's new favorite cookies. He says they taste like a crunchy Mounds bar. The Pineapple Right Side Up Cookie Bars that I made especially for him are still his favorite bar cookie.

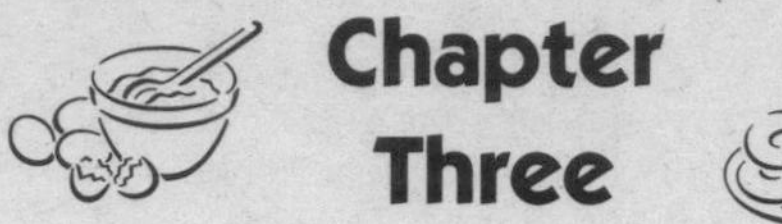

Chapter Three

Hannah was just finishing her last sip of coffee when the phone rang. They'd put the receiver back in the cradle and Lisa had promised to answer it. In less than a minute, her partner was back, grinning from ear to ear.

"That was Mayor Bascomb," Lisa announced. "He's going to stop by in a couple of minutes. He said he's got breaking news that'll rock Lake Eden to its foundation. Do you think it's about the movie?"

"It must be. We don't live in earthquake country."

Lisa groaned. "I wish I'd thought to say that. Of course I couldn't have said it, since he's theoretically Herb's boss and he might have taken it wrong. I'd better set out some PBJs for him. You know how crazy he is about peanut butter."

In less than five minutes there was a tap on the door and Mayor Bascomb came in. He wiped his boots on the rug inside the door and sniffed the air appreciatively. "Do I smell peanut butter?"

"Right here, Mayor Bascomb." Lisa pointed him toward the plate of cookies that sat in the center of the work island and the mayor pulled up a stool.

"No sugar for me today," he instructed Hannah as she headed for the table with his mug of coffee. "Steffie says I put on a couple of inches around the middle and I'm trying to cut down."

Hannah didn't say anything as the mayor reached for a cookie. She watched it disappear in two gulps, followed by a second and then a third. If that was *cutting down*, she wanted to go on Mayor Bascomb's diet!

"So what's this breaking news?" Hannah asked, hoping that she could look appropriately surprised when the mayor told them what they already knew.

"I just got a call from a guy named Barton. He heads up some movie company in Minneapolis. They want to shoot part of a movie right here on Main Street."

"That's wonderful!" Hannah said, hoping she sounded surprised enough not to raise suspicion. "But won't it interfere with business?"

"Yes, and the movie company is prepared to pay for that. I want every business owner to check revenues for the second week in March. That's when they're coming. I had to do some fancy talking, but they're going to pay us last year's gross profits for the week plus ten percent for the inconvenience."

"You drive a hard bargain, Mr. Mayor," Hannah complimented him, hiding a grin as he cited the exact figure Michelle had said the Indy Prod usually paid.

"Well, I'd better go," the mayor stood up and pushed back his stool. "I've got to talk to all the other business owners and give them the good news."

Lisa rushed to put the rest of the PBJ Cookies in a takeout bag for the mayor while Hannah walked him to the back door. Then Hannah collected the mugs they'd used and put them in the dishwasher while Lisa wiped down the work counter.

"He must have forgotten something," Hannah said, reacting to a loud knock at the door. "I'll get it."

Hannah pulled open the door to find her niece, Tracey, holding an empty baby carrier in one hand while her mother brought up the rear. Andrea was juggling the baby, Bethany, in one arm and speaking on her cell phone.

"I said I understand," Andrea's voice quavered a bit and it was clear that she was upset, "but that doesn't mean I have to like it!"

Hannah watched as her sister clicked off the phone with one perfectly manicured nail and stepped into the warmth of the kitchen. She gave a long sigh that Hannah might very well have labeled as theatrical if she hadn't heard the quaver in her sister's voice, and handed the baby to Hannah.

"You take her," she said, passing the baby over like a football. "Coffee! I need coffee!"

"I'll get it," Lisa responded, heading for the kitchen pot.

"She's stressed," Tracey explained, setting the baby carrier on the work island. Hannah's oldest niece could have posed for a cover photo on a children's fashion magazine with her baby blue winter coat, dainty white boots, and white cap with a pom-pom on top. The only thing that stopped her from being absolutely adorable was the frown that furrowed her forehead. "Just put Beth in her carrier, Aunt Hannah. I'll rock her if she wakes up."

Hannah put the baby in the carrier without incident. Her pretty new niece was sleeping so soundly, not even her mother's frantic call for coffee had awakened her.

Tracey sat down on a stool and pushed the mug of coffee that Lisa brought in front of her mother. "Have some coffee. And eat one of those cookies. They're chocolate and the endorphins will help. Right, Aunt Hannah?"

"Absolutely," Hannah said. She would have been amused at the way her oldest niece had picked up on one of her favorite culinary remedies, but this situation sounded serious.

"Do it, Mom." Tracey nudged her mother. "And then tell Aunt Hannah."

"Tell me what?" Hannah prompted, once Andrea had taken a big sip of her coffee to chase down a bite of Lisa's great-grandmother's-by-marriage creation.

"Bill's leaving us!"

"What?"

"What part of *leaving us* don't you understand?" Andrea retorted. And then she promptly burst into tears. It was obvious that it wasn't for the first time that morning, because her eyelids were swollen and the tissue she pulled from her pocket was damp and bedraggled.

Hannah turned to Tracey who, at almost six years of age, seemed to be the most rational person in the small family group. "What's going on, Tracey?"

"It's not as bad as it sounds." Tracey snagged a cookie from the plate and took a quick bite. "Daddy's going to a conference in Miami, and Mommy's all upset because she can't go. It's not like they're getting a divorce, or anything like that."

"Well, that's a relief!" Lisa said, giving Tracey a little hug as she passed out napkins and placed a box of tissues in front of Andrea. "What kind of conference is it?"

"It's about fitness in law enforcement," Andrea answered the question. She still sounded stressed, but at least she'd stopped crying. "The only problem is, *she's* going too!"

"She who?" Hannah asked. She was almost certain there was a better and clearer way to ask the question, but she didn't want to bother with that now.

"They'll pay for *her*, but they won't pay for me!"

"Her who?" Hannah asked again, changing the pronoun, but not the intent.

Andrea turned to look at her oldest daughter. "Tracey? Why don't you go . . ."

"Away," Tracey interrupted, picking up the glass of orange juice Lisa had poured for her and using a napkin to grab two more cookies. "I'll just go have my breakfast in the coffee shop so you can tell Aunt Lisa and Aunt Hannah what I'm too young to hear. I can always ask Bethany what you said later."

Hannah burst out laughing and so did Lisa. A moment later, even Andrea ventured a small laugh.

"That's better," Tracey said, looking proud. "I've been trying to get you to laugh ever since Daddy told you he was going."

Once the swinging door had closed behind Tracey, both Hannah and Lisa spoke up. "Who?" they both asked, within seconds of each other.

Andrea stared at them for a moment and then she gave a giggle that sounded more than a little hysterical to Hannah. "You two sound like a flock of owls."

"Parliament," Hannah corrected her. "A flock of owls is called a parliament, but that's not really important. Who's going to the fitness conference with Bill?"

"Ronni Ward, that's who! Remember when Bill hired her to hold exercise classes for the deputies?"

"I remember."

"Well, her official title is *fitness instructor* and that means she's qualified to go along, all expenses paid by the department."

Hannah reached out to pat her sister's arm. She could understand why Andrea was upset. Escaping the frozen tundra for a tropical climate, all expenses paid, was a collective Lake Eden fantasy during the winter months.

"The conference is in a hotel that's right on the beach," Andrea continued. "And you know what *that* means!"

Hannah didn't bother to respond since all three of them already knew that the beach meant bikinis and Ronni Ward was the three-time winner of the annual bikini contest. "But surely you don't think that Bill . . ." Hannah stopped speaking as she read the look on her sister's face. "Have some more chocolate. It'll help."

"I know exactly how you feel," Lisa said, pushing the plate of cookies closer to Andrea. "I'd feel the same way. But maybe Ronni will find a really handsome fitness instructor and they'll . . . they'll do exercises together, or something."

Andrea gave Lisa a halfhearted smile and Hannah could tell she wasn't convinced. She took another cookie, though, and ate it before she spoke again. "It's just making me a little crazy that I can't go, that's all. It's so boring in Lake Eden this time of the winter."

Hannah exchanged glances with Lisa. "When is Bill leaving?"

"The second week in March. And you know as well as I do that nothing ever happens in Lake Eden in March."

"Well, this year is an exception to the rule," Hannah stated, sharing a smile with Lisa. And then she proceeded to tell Andrea why Ronni Ward was going to wish she'd stayed home in Lake Eden instead of flying off to Miami with Bill.

PEANUT BUTTER AND JAM COOKIES (PBJs)

Preheat oven to 350 degrees F., rack in the middle position

1 cup melted butter ***(2 sticks, ½ pound)***
2 cups brown sugar ***(firmly packed)***
½ cup white ***(granulated)*** sugar
1 teaspoon vanilla extract
1½ teaspoons baking soda
1 teaspoon baking powder
½ teaspoon salt
1 cup peanut butter
2 beaten eggs ***(just whip them up with a fork)***
½ cup chopped salted peanuts ***(measure AFTER chopping)***
3 cups flour ***(no need to sift)***
approximately ½ cup fruit jam ***(your choice of fruit)***

Microwave the butter in a microwave safe mixing bowl for approximately 90 seconds on HIGH to melt it. Mix in the brown sugar, white sugar, vanilla, baking soda, baking powder, and salt. Stir until they're thoroughly blended.

Measure out the peanut butter. ***(I spray the inside of my measuring cup with Pam so it won't stick.)***

Add it to the bowl and mix it in. Pour in the beaten eggs and stir it all up. Add the chopped salted peanuts and mix until they're incorporated.

Add the flour in one-cup increments, mixing it in until all the ingredients are thoroughly blended.

Form the dough into walnut-sized balls with your hands and arrange them on a greased cookie sheet, 12 to a standard sheet. ***(If the dough is too sticky to form into balls, chill it for an hour or so, and then try again.)***

Make an indentation in the center of the dough ball with your thumb. Spoon in a bit of jam, making sure it doesn't run over the sides of the cookie.

Bake at 350 degrees F. for 10 to 12 minutes, or until the tops are just beginning to turn golden. Cool on the cookie sheet for 2 minutes, then remove to a wire rack to finish cooling.

Yield: approximately 7 dozen cookies, depending on cookie size.

Hannah's Note: If you happen to run out of fruit jam and you have cookies left to fill, put a few chocolate chips in the indentation. You'll have to call those cookies PBCs, but they're wonderful!

Tracey likes her PBJs with strawberry jam, Andrea prefers apricot, Bill's wild about blueberry, and Mother loves them with peach. I prefer to eat one of each, just to test them of course.

Chapter Four

The next two weeks passed much too slowly, as winter weeks often do, but at last the big day arrived. Everyone who wasn't engaged in business of the utmost necessity turned out to watch as the movie crew rolled into town. Lisa and Hannah were no exception. The Cookie Jar wasn't open. It was never open on Sunday, but both partners and their extended families sat at tables in front of the window, watching the cars, motor homes, tractor trailers, and smaller cube trucks turn the corner by the lumber yard at First and Main, and drive down Main Street to Sixth, where an area had been set aside for them to park.

"That's the wardrobe truck," Michelle explained, as a truck pulling a long, narrow trailer came down the street. "The inside looks just like a closet with two long poles and hangers that lock so they don't jiggle off the poles."

Hannah smiled at her youngest sister. Michelle had arrived the previous night on the bus, and this morning she was holding court at a table with Delores, Carrie, Andrea, and Lisa. Norman, Mike, and Herb were at a separate table and they were wearing almost identical *I couldn't care less* expressions designed to convince everyone else that they weren't at all interested in spotting the actors and actresses as they drove by the plate glass window.

Hannah, herself, was perched on a stool between the two tables, watching the clock over the counter. In a few minutes, she'd head out to the community center to help Edna Ferguson with the brunch Mayor Bascomb had arranged so that the movie crew could meet the residents of Lake Eden.

"That's Dean Lawrence's car," Michelle said, drawing everyone's attention to the black limousine that rolled past the window. "He's got his own driver."

Delores looked envious. "That must be nice, especially in the winter."

"You said it!" Carrie agreed. "I'd love to have a driver who'd warm up the car before he came to get me."

"A driver would be great," Lisa said. "You'd never have to worry about getting a good parking spot. If there wasn't anywhere to park, he could drop you off right in front of wherever you were going."

"That's what I do now," Herb groused, but his loving smile told his new wife that his complaint was far from serious. "I guess that makes me your chauffeur."

"Maybe it does. I'll look around for one of those cute little hats with the stiff brim."

"Dean Lawrence's chauffeur isn't *just* a chauffeur," Michelle spoke up. "His name is Connor and he's listed on the credits as a production assistant, just like me, but he's really a combination driver, bodyguard, and secretary."

Hannah turned to smile at her youngest sister. "I'll bet he makes more money than you do."

"Lots more." Michelle gave a little laugh. "Connor makes scale for extras, too. He gets a walk-on part in every movie Mr. Lawrence directs."

"D. L. is practically a household name in Hollywood," Andrea informed them. "*Variety* just did an article on him."

"D. L.?" Hannah turned to her sister in surprise.

"*Variety*?" Michelle asked, picking up on another part of Andrea's comment.

"D.L. is how *Daily Variety* refers to Dean Lawrence," Andrea explained to Hannah. Then she turned to Michelle. "And yes, I read *Variety* every day. I subscribed right after you told us that they were shooting C.I.C. here."

"What's C.I.C.?" Hannah asked, wishing her sister wouldn't use so many initials.

"*Crisis in Cherrywood*. That's the name of the movie. What I want to know is how a little Indy Prod like this landed such a big-name director. After *Three Minutes to Paradise*, everyone thought he'd go on to another big box office success."

"Connections," Michelle answered Andrea's question. "It's all about who you know and who owes you. I asked one of the prop guys about that and he said there's some sort of family connection between Mr. Lawrence and the man who financed the film. He didn't know the details, but he said that's why Mr. Lawrence signed on."

"I wonder if there's been any trouble yet," Andrea mused. "In the article I read, they called D. L. the *Bad Boy Director*. He's got a huge ego and last year he was named the director that most actors love to hate."

Michelle laughed. "Mr. Barton told me that, but he said there's an upside. Mr. Lawrence is really hard on his actors, but he makes them look good because he always gets great performances out of them."

"As interesting as this is, I've got to go." Hannah glanced at the clock and slid off her stool. "I promised Edna I'd be at the community center in less than five minutes."

Andrea got up from the table. "Do you need any help? I have to go home to pick up Tracey."

"Not really. The food's already down there, and the only things I need to bring are napkins and tablecloths."

Hannah said good-bye to everyone and hurried through the kitchen, grabbing her parka coat on the run. Once she'd successfully negotiated the ruts in her alley, she rolled down her window and took a deep gulp of air. The breeze was ice cold, but it felt fresh, full of promise and new beginnings. Almost everyone in town was looking forward to a brush with celebrity and a tiny taste of fame if they were lucky enough to be chosen as extras. The size of the part didn't really matter. They just wanted to appear in the film. And when it was all over and Lake Eden had been captured forever on film, they would exercise bragging rights with friends and relatives who lived more humdrum lives in less fortunate places.

There was a parking spot in front of the community center and Hannah took it. She went around to the back of her truck and opened the rear doors, eyeing the stacks of tablecloths and napkins she'd picked up from her condo neighbors, the Hollenbeck sisters, who'd washed and ironed them in honor of this special occasion. It had taken her three trips to load them in her truck and it would take that many to deliver them to Edna at the community center kitchen.

Hannah stacked up her first load, the widest brown paper-wrapped bundle on the bottom and smaller paper-wrapped bundles on top. When she had a pyramid of five packages, she picked them up and started for the door.

"Hold it!" a female voice called out, and Hannah stopped in her tracks. The top bundle was blocking her view and she peered around it like a kid with a periscope to see who'd halted her forward progress.

"Hi, Pam," Hannah greeted Jordan High's Home Economics teacher.

"Girls?" Pam addressed the half-dozen high school seniors who'd volunteered for waitress duty and were following in her wake. "Don't just stand there. You know what to do."

Beth Halvorsen, one of Hannah's favorite high school seniors, led the charge to Hannah's cookie truck and soon the packages were being loaded into younger arms. One of the girls veered off to relieve Hannah of her burden and before she could do more than say thank you, Pam's students had disappeared inside the building and Hannah was left as free as a bird, with nothing but her purse to carry.

"It's times like this that I wonder if I should have been a teacher," Hannah said, falling into step with last year's teacher of the year.

"Maybe. My girls adore you."

"Don't let that fool you. It's because I bring cookies every time I visit your class."

"You've got a point," Pam said, as they stepped inside and headed for the stairway that led down to the community center banquet room.

The two friends parted ways at the bottom of the stairs. Pam went to help her student teacher, Willa Sunquist, supervise the girls, who were draping tablecloths over the tables and setting out the centerpieces they'd made in class.

"Hannah!" Edna called out as Hannah pushed open the kitchen door. "I'm so glad you're here early!"

"There's a problem?" Hannah asked, guessing that something besides blusher must have caused the high color in Edna's normally pale cheeks.

"You can say that again! What can we make to take the place of Loretta Richardson's Sausage and Egg Casserole?"

"I'm not sure. Why do we have to think of something to replace it?"

"Because Loretta slipped on a patch of ice on the way out to the garage and all three pans spilled in the snow. We need something else and we need it in less than two hours."

Hannah thought fast. Since Edna had been planning to put three pans of Sausage and Egg Casserole in the oven, she had extra oven space. "I could make Fruit Pocket French Toast."

"What's that?"

"It's something my Grandma Ingrid used to bake for breakfast on Christmas morning."

"Then it's a holiday dish and it's bound to be good. How long does it take to make it?"

Hannah added up the cooking time of forty-five minutes, preparation time of ten minutes, and standing time of twenty minutes. "If I can get all the ingredients I need in ten minutes, I can have it ready to serve in about an hour and a half."

"Perfect." Edna looked around for Florence Evans and beckoned her over. "Can you open up the Red Owl? Hannah's going to pull off a miracle and she needs supplies in a big hurry."

"No problem. Give me a list."

Hannah scrawled a quick list and gave it to Florence. "Can you be back in here in ten minutes? Time's going to be a factor."

"I'll be back in five," Florence promised, grabbing her coat and heading out the door to the parking lot.

While Florence was gone, Hannah and Edna prepared the pans. They'd just finished heating the butter, brown sugar, and maple syrup they'd found in the community center kitchen when Florence came back carrying two sacks of groceries.

"Here, Hannah. I brought you canned peaches, pears, and apricots," she said, setting the cans out on the counter.

"Thanks, Florence. What kind of bread did you get?"

"One loaf of raisin bread, one of egg, and another called country potato. They're all sliced. And here's your chopped pecans, whipping cream, eggs, and butter. What can I do to help you?"

"Open the cans of fruit and dump them in strainers," Hannah instructed. "And then you can soften half of the butter in the microwave."

"I'll do that," Edna said, grabbing the butter and starting to unwrap it.

While the two women set about their assigned tasks, Hannah poured the heated syrup, brown sugar and butter mixture in the bottoms of the pans. She sprinkled the chopped nuts over the top and was just opening the first loaf of bread when Edna came back with the softened butter.

"What do you want me to do with this?" Edna asked, holding the bowl aloft.

"Make fruit sandwiches. We'll do one pan at a time so we won't get mixed up. Butter six pieces of bread and put slices of drained fruit on top. Then cover the fruit with another six slices of buttered bread."

"I'll slice the fruit and put it on," Florence volunteered. "It's just like making sandwiches for the grandkids. I always lay out the bread in pairs and do it like an assembly line."

"That'll work just fine. When you're through with a sandwich, cut it in half and put it in the pan on top of my syrup mixture. We can't have any more than one layer in each pan. You can crowd them together, but don't overlap them or the recipe won't work."

"Okay. What next?"

"We beat the eggs with sugar and cinnamon, and then we mix in the cream. Is there any vanilla in the pantry? I forgot to add it to the list."

"I brought some, just in case," Florence told her, dropping several thin slices of pear on a buttered piece of raisin bread. "It's still in the bag."

Hannah found a large bowl and started to crack eggs. When the eggs were beaten with the sugar and cinnamon, she handed the bowl to Edna, who mixed in the cream and added a generous slug of vanilla.

"How are you coming?" Hannah asked, glancing over at Florence.

"All done." Florence added the last sandwich to the pan, and then she headed for the sink to wash her hands.

"You can pour the egg mixture over the sandwiches now," Hannah told Edna. "Then we'll cover the pans with plastic wrap and leave them out on the counter for twenty minutes while the oven preheats."

"And then we take off the plastic wrap and bake them?" Florence asked.

"Not quite. We melt the rest of the butter first, and pour it over the sandwiches. Then we bake them."

"That's a lot of butter!" Edna commented.

"True, but that's what makes them so good. They have to sit for a couple of minutes when they come out of the oven to set up. Then we'll sprinkle them with powdered sugar and they can be served. Tell whoever does it that a half-sandwich is one serving."

The three women had just settled down to a cup of Edna's excellent coffee at the large round booth that had been especially designed for the kitchen workers, when the kitchen door opened and Winnie Henderson marched in.

"Here!" she said, setting a box on the round table in the center of the booth with such force that the spoon in Edna's cup rattled. "A promise is a promise so I brought 'em. Six-dozen homemade doughnuts, half powdered sugar, and half cinnamon and sugar. But if I'd known what I know now, I never would have promised!"

"Wait!" Edna reached out to grab Winnie's hand as the raw-boned farmwoman turned to go. "Are you mad at me, Winnie?"

Winnie shook her head so hard, the salt and pepper hair she wore in a no-nonsense cut swung across her face. "Not you, Edna. It's him! He sold us out just like Judas, excepting this time it wasn't for pieces of silver. He got a part in that movie and that's why he's sitting back and doing nothing to keep our town from getting ruined!"

"Who's sitting back and doing nothing?" Florence asked, eyeing Winnie with some trepidation. Although Winnie didn't weigh more than a hundred pounds and she was at least a decade past the mid-century mark, she'd worked hard all her life and she was as strong as an ox. "That is . . . if you don't mind saying, of course. You don't have to say if you don't want to."

"Don't mind at all! The more people that know, the better. They ought to find out the truth about the man they vote for year after year. He's a wolf in sheep's clothing, that's what he is!"

"Mayor Bascomb?" Hannah guessed, since he was Lake Eden's most important elected official and she'd heard he had a part in the movie.

"That's him! I'm glad you said it, girl. I don't even want his name to pass my lips. And now I got to get going, 'cause if I set even one of my eyes on him, I'm going to kick his you-know-what to kingdom come!"

FRUIT POCKET FRENCH TOAST

½ cup butter ***(1 stick, ¼ pound)***
1 cup brown sugar, firmly packed
½ cup maple syrup
1 cup chopped pecans ***(optional)***

Loaf ***(at least 12 slices)*** of sliced bread ***(white, egg, raisin, whatever)***
½ cup butter softened ***(1 stick, ¼ pound)***
2 cups canned or fresh fruit ***(any kind except melon or grapes)***

8 eggs, beaten
¾ cup white ***(granulated)*** sugar
2 teaspoons cinnamon
2 cups heavy cream ***(whipping cream)***
2 teaspoons vanilla extract

½ cup butter ***(1 stick, ¼ pound)*** melted

Powdered ***(confectioner's)*** sugar to sprinkle

Leave one stick of butter out on the counter to soften it, or unwrap it and nuke it for a few seconds in the microwave.

If you're using canned fruit, open it and dump it in a strainer now.

Heat a second stick of butter, the brown sugar, and the maple syrup in a microwave-safe bowl on HIGH for 2½ minutes ***(I used a quart measuring cup)*** or in a pan on the stove, stirring constantly, until the butter is melted. Spray a 9-inch by 13-inch cake pan with Pam or other non-stick spray and pour the syrup mixture in the bottom. Sprinkle with the chopped pecans, if you decide to use them.

Lay out twelve slices of bread—you're going to make fruit sandwiches.

Spread softened butter on one slice of bread. Top it with well-drained fruit cut in very thin slices ***(Berries or pineapple can be crushed.)***

Spread butter on a second slice of bread and use it to cover the bread with the fruit. Cut this fruit sandwich in half and place it in the pan on top of the syrup mixture. Make 5 more sandwiches, cut them in half, and put them in the pan. You can crowd them a bit, but do not overlap the bread.

Press the sandwiches down with a flat metal spatula. Squish that bread!

Beat the eggs with the sugar and the cinnamon. Add the cream and the vanilla, mixing thoroughly. Pour this mixture over the bread in the pan.

Cover the pan with plastic wrap or foil and let it stand out on the counter for a minimum of twenty minutes. ***(If you're having a fancy breakfast, you can also make this the night before and keep it in the refrigerator until it's time to bake it.)***

Preheat your oven to 350 degrees F., rack in the center position.

Take off the plastic wrap. Melt the third stick of butter. Drizzle it over the top of the sandwiches.

Bake the Fruit Pocket French Toast at 350 degrees F. uncovered, for approximately 45 minutes, or until the top has browned. Let the pan cool on a wire rack for at least five minutes.

To serve: Sprinkle the top of the pan with powdered sugar before you carry it to the table. This will make it much prettier. Dish out the Fruit Pocket French Toast with a metal spatula, and offer more syrup and butter for those who want it. A half sandwich is one serving.

Yield: 12 half-sandwich servings.

Hannah's Note: If you want to make this and you're really in a pickle because you don't have any fruit, try spreading the bread with a layer of fruit jam or marmalade. I haven't tried this, but I'll bet you a batch of my best cookies that it'll work!

Chapter Five

Naturally, Hannah had been elected to serve the Fruit Pocket French Toast and she was glad she'd worn the pale lavender silk blouse Claire Rodgers had assured her would dress up any outfit, even a pair of black jeans and a black turtleneck sweater. The blouse had been expensive, but Claire had given Hannah her usual good-neighbor discount since Claire's boutique, Beau Monde Fashions, was right next to Hannah's shop.

"This is a wonderful brunch dish, Hannah," Delores came up to compliment her. "Have you made it before? It reminds me of something, but I'm not quite sure what it is."

"Grandma Ingrid's Fruit Pocket French Toast, except she made it with apple slices."

"Of course!" Delores reached out to pat Hannah's shoulder with one perfectly manicured hand. "It was always my favorite, but so rich! And extremely fattening, with all those carbs." Delores leaned a little closer. "Better watch it, dear. I think you've gained a little around the hips. That blouse hides it really well, but still . . . when a woman gets to be a certain age, she has to be more conscientious about her diet."

Hannah managed to keep her polite smile in place, but she had the urge to upend the nearly empty pan with its residue of sticky caramel-maple syrup on top of her mother's impeccably styled coiffeur.

"Well! Enough about that. You've heard it all before."

Hannah looked up at her mother in surprise. Delores actually sounded a bit apologetic about her previous comment. But her next statement shattered that illusion.

"You really ought to change to shoes, Hannah. Those boots don't go with your outfit at all. And a little lipstick and makeup wouldn't hurt."

"I don't like to wear makeup."

"I know you don't, but men notice things like that. They want a wife who's well groomed, someone they can be proud to be seen with."

"You're forgetting that two men proposed to me and I wasn't wearing a lick of makeup at the time."

"Oh." Delores frowned slightly. "Well . . . there *is* that. I'm sorry, dear. Truce?"

"Truce," Hannah agreed with a smile, squelching the nasty little voice in her head that whispered, *I wouldn't take your advice about men on a bet, Mother. Just look where it got you with Winthrop!*

Hannah had just filled her own plate and slid into a chair directly across from Mike and Norman when Michelle came rushing up. She was followed by a thirty-something guy with dark hair, and Hannah assumed he was one of the movie crew. He wasn't leading-man handsome, but he was certainly good-looking in an intriguing way. His eyes were a bit too close together, but they were a brilliant blue that more than made up for the former defect. And they were framed with long, dark lashes that most women could achieve only with long minutes in front of the mirror and the very best lash-lengthening mascara. His mouth was generous, wide enough to match his nose, and his clean-shaven chin was strong. Definitely an attractive man, Hannah decided. Not really conventionally handsome, but eye-catching all the same.

Michelle arrived at Hannah's side and turned back to face the man who was following her. "This is my sister, Hannah. She owns the cookie shop that Mitch couldn't stop talking about. And Hannah?" Michelle swiveled to give her oldest sister a smile. "This is Mr. Barton, the writer–producer of *Crisis in Cherrywood*."

Hannah gasped as the man smiled. He looked very different from the last time she'd seen him almost four years ago, but there was no mistaking the distinctive dimple in his left cheek. "Ross Bartonovich?"

"It's Barton, now. Makes it easier for me to spell." He swept Hannah up in his arms and whirled her around in a circle. "You look even better than you did back then."

"I don't," Hannah quickly denied it, but she started to laugh as Ross lifted her in a giant bear hug and her feet came up off the floor. And she laughed harder still as she saw the expression of total disbelief on her sister's face.

"You . . . you two know each other?" Michelle asked.

"We're a blast from the past. Twenty-two forty-seven Muskrat Lane, second floor in the rear. Right, Hannah?"

"Right. And we should have knocked a hole in the wall because we were always together. Is Linda here?"

"She's here, but it's not Linda anymore. Now it's Lynne, Lynne Larchmont."

"Larchmont? But I thought you two were getting marri . . ." Hannah stopped speaking and the color crept up her cheeks. She'd never been very good at small talk, and she was especially handicapped now with her foot stuck firmly in her mouth. "I'm sorry," she said at last. "I shouldn't have asked."

"That's okay. It just didn't work out, that's all. A lot of things changed when you left school and we weren't the Three Muskrateers anymore."

"So you went to college together?" Michelle asked, saving Hannah from replying.

Ross turned to her and nodded. "That's right. I should have told you, but I wanted to surprise Hannah."

"Well . . . you did!" Hannah managed.

"I interrupted your brunch," Ross said, glancing at Hannah's barely touched plate. "How about if I get another cup of coffee and join you while you eat? We can talk about old times."

"I'll get it, Mr. Barton," Michelle offered quickly. "Just sit down and I'll bring it right over."

Ross held out Hannah's chair and then he grabbed another from a nearby table and slid in next to her. Hannah glanced quickly at Mike and Norman. They'd been talking to each other, but now they were silent. Both of her suitors looked wary as they stared at Ross Barton, almost as if they'd been taking a leisurely stroll through the woods and were suddenly face-to-face with a bobcat.

Hannah tried to think of something to say, anything to get everyone talking. But Ross didn't seem at all disconcerted by Norman's and Mike's wary gazes. He held out his hand in a gesture of goodwill to Mike.

"Ross Barton. I'm the writer–producer. And you're . . . ?"

Mike had no choice. He reached out to shake Ross's hand. "Mike Kingston. Acting sheriff of Winnetka County."

"Glad to meet you," Ross stared hard at Mike, and Hannah knew he was sizing him up. "Ever done any acting?"

"Me?" Mike looked surprised. "Nope, never have."

"I've got a walk-on part that would be perfect for you."

"Oh, yeah?"

"As a matter of fact, it's right up your alley. We need to cast a small-town sheriff. He's a professional, but he knows everyone in town and he's got a heart. He comes in right after the suicide scene, and he's got a few lines. Are you interested?"

"Maybe." Mike was noncommittal, but Hannah knew him well enough to see that he was intrigued.

"You could do some security work for us, too. After hours, of course, so it wouldn't interfere with your regular duties. We're a small company and the pay's not all that great, but you'd get screen credit."

"Well . . . I guess I could give it a whirl."

Hannah glanced over at Norman and thought she detected a bit of envy in his demeanor. *Was everyone in town with the exception of Winnie Henderson and yours truly being seduced by the bright klieg lights of movie fame?* she wondered.

"I'd like you on the crew, too." Ross held out his hand to Norman.

"Me?" Norman gulped slightly. "But I'm not in law enforcement."

"I know that. Michelle told me that you're the town dentist and we need you to be on call. You never know when somebody's going to break a cap and need a quick fix to go on with a scene. It would mean a screen credit for you, too."

"Count me in," Norman said, shaking Ross's hand and looking pleased.

Hannah looked at Ross with new respect. He'd effectively diffused a tense situation and suddenly he was Norman's and Mike's new best friend. But was he really? Hannah gave a little shiver as Ross's arm brushed hers. Had their chairs been this close together when they'd sat down? Or had Ross inched over so that he could be closer to her?

Michelle came up carrying a cup of coffee. "Here you go, Mr. Barton. Is there anything else I can do for you?"

"Not right . . . yes, there is." Ross obviously changed his mind in midsentence. "I've just cast Mike here as the Sheriff of Cherrywood and Norman's going to be our crew dentist. Why don't you introduce them to the rest of the cast and crew? That'll save time later, at the auditions."

It was no sooner mentioned than it was accomplished. Mike and Norman stood up and Michelle led them away to do the introductions. The moment they had left, Ross turned to Hannah. "So? What do you think of the new assertive me?"

"It's a big change," Hannah said honestly. The Ross she'd known at school had been content to sit back and wait for someone else's suggestions. This older, more mature Ross had morphed into someone who led, not followed.

"Do you like me the way I am now? Or was it better the way I was back then?"

"What a question!" Hannah said with a laugh. "I liked the old you just fine. But I don't know the new you well enough to say."

"Well . . . we'll have to remedy that," Ross said, slipping his arm around Hannah's shoulder and giving her a squeeze. "It's wonderful to see you again, Hannah. I never said anything, but did you know I had a terrible crush on you in college?"

Hannah, who'd just taken a bite of scrambled eggs, swallowed with difficulty. She would have died rather than admit it, but Ross's crush on her had been reciprocated in spades! "I . . . but . . ." Hannah stopped and regrouped. "You were living with Linda!"

"I know, but a guy can dream. I always thought we were better suited. She never laughed at my jokes or picked up on my drama quotes."

"Come on, Ross. That's not really fair. I had to know my

plays. I was taking a seminar on American Theater. Linda majored in art history."

"But she had a minor in drama. And you've got to admit that my quotes weren't obscure. *Pop, I'm a dime a dozen and so are you.*"

"Biff in *Death of a Salesman* by Arthur Miller," Hannah answered, and then she drew a deep breath. Ross was right, the lines he'd quoted had been so well known that any drama student should have recognized them. But there was no way she'd say anything negative about Linda, especially since she wasn't here to defend herself. Hannah looked around for the old friend in question, but she didn't spot her. "You said Lind . . ." Hannah stopped to correct herself. "You said Lynne was here, but I don't see her. Where is she?"

"She's sitting right over there with Burke Anson. You recognize him from those Surf 'n Turf commercials, don't you?"

Hannah nodded. According to the financial column in the *Lake Eden Journal*, Surf 'n Turf, the national chain of steak and seafood restaurants, had tripled their business after hiring Burke as their spokesman. "But . . . Lynne is the *blonde?"*

"Right. You probably don't recognize her, because she had some work done."

"Work? Like in plastic surgery?"

"That's right. A new nose, some nips and tucks, a couple of enhancements, liposuction, cosmetic dentistry, a good hair stylist, and the best personal trainer in L.A."

Hannah didn't say anything. She couldn't. She was too surprised. Lynne didn't look at all like the slightly plump, brown-haired girl with the gap between her front teeth. Now, she was thin and glamorous, with a nose that looked much straighter and teeth that were white and even.

"I never would have recognized her," she said, shaking her head. "Is Larchmont her stage name?"

"Yes, but it's also her married name. After we split up, Linda changed her name to Lynne and went out to California to try to make it in the biz. She was there for over six months and almost ready to give it up and catch the next Greyhound home when she got lucky and landed a small part in a TV drama. That led to another, slightly bigger part in a made-for-cable movie, and that's when she met Tom Larchmont. She always says that being Tom's wife is the best part she ever landed. He's rich, a lot older than she is, and he's totally crazy about her."

Hannah could hear the sincerity in Ross's voice. "You don't sound at all bitter."

"I'm not. Tom's a nice guy and I'm glad Lynne found someone. It worked out great for me, too. Tom's financing this whole project because Lynne read my script and she told him she wanted to play the lead."

"What's the movie about?" Hannah asked him.

"Lynne's character, Amy, is haunted by memories of her father. He's dead, a suicide, but she just can't come to terms with it and it begins to break up her marriage. Then her aunt dies, the aunt that raised her, and her shrink tells her to go back home for the funeral and try to lay the ghost of her father to rest. Amy goes back to Cherrywood, stays in her old family home with her older brother, Jody, and starts to have flashes of memory that don't mesh with the explanation he gave her the night of their father's death. Are you with me so far?"

"I'm with you." Hannah said, clearly fascinated by the story that was unfolding. "So the story the brother told Amy was a lie?"

"That's right. Amy realizes that she's been brainwashed by Jody and her fraternal aunt, the woman who came to live with them after their father died. The aunt knew Jody killed his father, but she perpetuated the lie because she didn't want her nephew to go to jail."

"A circle of lies," Hannah commented.

"Right. During the cocktail party that Jody hosts for her on the last evening of her visit, Amy relives the night of her father's death, which took place right before a big cocktail party. It all comes back to her with startling clarity, and she finally realizes that Jody killed their father, why he did it, and how."

"Sounds fascinating. Does she confront Jody when the memories come back?"

"Yes, and it's the pivotal scene in the movie. When Amy tells Jody she remembers, he kills himself with the same gun he used to kill their father."

"You mean right there at the party in front of the guests?"

"That's right."

Hannah frowned slightly. "That's awfully dark."

"That's true. There are a couple of cheerful scenes of Amy as a child and as a teenager that lighten it up a little, but it's still the story of a fatally flawed family. The only thing that saves it from complete tragedy is that Lynne's character goes back to her husband and family at the end."

Hannah glanced over at Lynne again, wondering if her college friend could handle such a demanding part.

"Oh, she can do it," Ross said, answering Hannah's unspoken question. "She was always a pretty good actress and she's gotten even better over the years. When she married Tom, he sent her to a top-notch acting coach and she worked one-on-one with him for almost two years."

"Good for her. How about Burke Anson? Does he play her husband?"

Ross shook his head. "He's her brother, Jody. This is his first movie role. Burke's a better actor than you'd think from watching his commercials."

"Really?" Hannah gave a little laugh. "You mean he can do more than hang ten?"

"A lot more. You probably think of him as an empty-headed surfer, but he's capable of showing a surprising depth of emotion."

Hannah nodded, but her face revealed her doubts. Burke was in his late twenties, a deeply tanned actor with sun-bleached hair who looked strangely naked without his surf-board. There was no way Hannah could imagine him playing a tortured young man with a traumatic past.

"I saw your shop when we drove past. It looks like you, Hannah."

"It *is* me. I bought it, I decorated it, and I ran it alone until I found a perfect partner. Are you going to use it in your movie?"

"Just the outside, but I'd like you to keep on baking cookies, if that's all right with you. We'll pay you extra if you'll cater coffee and cookies for the cast and crew. Our meals are taken care of. We're staying out at the Lake Eden Inn and Mrs. Laughlin's providing a breakfast buffet and dinner. She'll pack box lunches for everyone and most of the crew will be eating lunch right here. I just thought it would be nice if the senior staff and cast could eat our lunches at The Cookie Jar, since it's midway between most of the locations we're using."

"That's fine with me," Hannah said quickly. It would be nice to be in the thick of things and Lisa would be thrilled to hear the latest movie news.

Hannah glanced over at Lynne again. She didn't seem all that interested in her handsome costar, but she was certainly mesmerized by the rugged-looking man sitting across from her at the table. "Is that Dean Lawrence?" she asked, remembering the picture Andrea had shown her in the back issue of *Variety*.

"In the flesh. I still can't believe how lucky I am that he agreed to sign on as director. Dean has all sorts of contacts for distribution and we're sure to pick up a deal at Sundance. He's already talking about Cannes and even a possible Oscar nomination!"

Hannah was dubious. "That's impressive, but are you sure it's not pie in the sky?"

"Pretty sure. Dean's a big name in the business and any project he works on gets tons of prerelease publicity. Of course everyone tries to get a little buzz going, even Dean."

"And you?" Hannah teased.

"Me, too."

Hannah remembered what Andrea had said about Dean's signing on because of family connections. Perhaps it was true, but she'd ask the source. "How did you get such an important director?"

"Tom Larchmont arranged it. Dean's wife, Sharyn, is Tom's niece, and I worked out a deal with them."

"Can you tell me about it?"

Ross leaned closer, even though there wasn't anyone close enough to hear. "All I have to do is keep Dean productive, sober, faithful, and happy."

"That doesn't sound too hard," Hannah commented.

"It is, though. The productive part is easy. Dean never misses a day of work. Directing is his life. He loves to play God and intimidate people. But that's only one out of four."

"There's still keeping him sober, faithful, and happy." Hannah stated the obvious.

"Precisely. Dean loves to drink. And when he has one too many, he also loves to . . . well . . . let's just say that he's been known to exercise poor judgment when it comes to women."

"But what can *you* do about that?"

"I'm keeping an eye on him. I've been his best buddy for the past six weeks, keeping him on the straight and narrow, but it hasn't been easy. At least that part of the job's almost over. Sharyn and Tom are flying in on Tuesday night and they're staying for the wrap party on Saturday. Sharyn will keep Dean honest."

"And she'll also take care of the fourth thing? Keeping him happy?"

"Not necessarily, but you might be able to help on that one. Do you make cherry cheesecake?"

Hannah was a bit disconcerted by this new tangent. She figured Ross didn't want to talk about the relationship between Dean Lawrence and his wife. But rather than quiz him on something that was none of her business, something that she could probably find out anyway from another member of the cast or crew, she responded quickly to his query. "If you want it, I can bake it."

"Good. If you can make it the way Dean likes it, it'll do a lot to take care of item number four. He loves cherry cheesecake, and having one delivered every morning makes him happy and puts him in a good mood for hours. Do you think you could do that?"

"Sure."

"You're a doll, Hannah." Ross gave her another little hug. "We paid forty dollars a cake plus ten dollars delivery at the last location. And Dean said that cheesecake was all right, but not special. How about fifty if you deliver it to the Winnebago he's using as his office every morning? It'll come straight off the top of the production budget."

"Deal," Hannah said quickly, not mentioning that she'd been about to quote him a price that was less than half of what he'd offered. Ross was paying way too much for a simple cheesecake, but that was what he'd paid before and she didn't want to sell her baked goods short. Now all she had to do was find out what qualities Dean Lawrence liked in a cheesecake and make sure the cherry cheesecake she baked had every one of them.

Chapter Six

Lake Edenites, or whatever the proper collective noun was for citizens of Lake Eden, Minnesota, believed that dessert was the best part of a brunch. Hannah and Edna had just finished bringing every dessert they'd made out to the serving table, turning it into a true groaning board, when Andrea rushed up to Hannah.

"I've got great news! Do you have a minute?"

"Sure. Just let me get a cup of coffee."

"I need one, too."

"Okay, I'll get coffee for both of us. You go stake out a place at one of the tables."

When Hannah, a cup of coffee in each hand, looked around for her sister, she found Andrea sitting at one of the overflow tables, a small two-person round pedestal affair that was barely large enough for two plates and two cups of coffee. As she headed over, Hannah assumed that her sister's news wasn't for public consumption and she'd deliberately found a place to talk where they wouldn't be overheard.

"Where's Tracey?" Hannah asked, setting her sister's coffee down in front of her.

"With Mother and Carrie. And I left Bethany home with Grandma McCann," Andrea named her live-in babysitter. "She was sleeping like a little angel when I left."

Andrea waited until Hannah had settled into her chair, and then she leaned forward for a private conversation. That was overkill on her part because even though there were two long tables on either side of them, they were completely empty. Everyone who'd sat there for the first part of the brunch was off getting dessert and there was absolutely no one within earshot. "Michelle just told me that you *know* him!"

"Ross?" Hannah guessed. It was an educated guess based on a process of elimination since Ross Barton was the only movie man she knew.

"I took Tracey over to meet him when he pulled into the lot. We just happened to be getting out of the car."

"How long did you have to sit there freezing?" Hannah asked, not believing a word of it.

"Only a little over a half hour, and we ran the heater every ten minutes or so. Anyway, we walked in with Mr. Barton, and he invited us to the auditions this afternoon. Isn't that fantastic?"

"Yes, it is," Hannah said, impressed with her sister's ambition. Only a truly dedicated stage mother would sit in a parked car in the winter so that she could waylay a producer in the parking lot. "Is Tracey going to try out as an extra?"

"Only if she doesn't get the part of Amy as a child. I think she looks just like her, don't you?"

"Who?"

"The female lead. She's the gorgeous blonde in the aquamarine dress. Another actress is playing her as a teenager, but they need someone for the child's role."

Hannah glanced across the room, where Lynne was holding court with several of Lake Eden's most personable would-be Romeos. "You're right. I didn't notice it before, but Tracey looks a lot like Lynne."

"Lynne?" Andrea looked surprised at her sister's use of the star's first name. "Don't tell me you know her, too!"

"Of course I do. I went to college with Ross and Lynne. We lived in the same apartment building, right next to each other."

"Oh, Hannah!" Andrea reached out to clasp her sister's hand. "I'm so glad you went to college!"

"I take it that the knowledge of English Literature I brought back to Lake Eden with me is *not* the primary reason."

The color rose in Andrea's cheeks and she looked slightly embarrassed. "That's not fair, Hannah. Of course I'm proud of you because you know a lot about books and things like that. But what I really meant was . . ."

"That's enough," Hannah interrupted her, and smiled a bit to take the sting out of her words. "I know *exactly* what you meant. You want me to use what influence I have with Ross and with Lynne to get the part for Tracey."

"That's true. I know it might sound a little cold-blooded, but everyone uses the contacts they make, and their contacts use them right back. That's one of the first things I learned in real estate college."

"Right. I'll do what I can, Andrea. I think Tracey would be perfect for the part. How about the teenager who's playing Amy? Does she look like Tracey, too?"

Andrea glanced over at the table where most of the cast was sitting. "I think she does, but judge for yourself. Her name is Erica James and she's sitting right next to Dean Lawrence."

Hannah looked over and gave a little gasp.

"What's wrong?"

"She's giving Dean Lawrence a very steamy look and he's giving it right back to her. And on top of that, she's practically sitting in his lap! How old is this Lolita-in-training anyway?"

"Lolita?"

"It's a novel by Nabokov."

"Oh, *that* Lolita. I think we had to read it in high school."

Hannah's eyebrows shot up. She doubted that very much, but she didn't bother to correct her sister.

"Anyway, you asked about how old she is," Andrea picked up the thread of their conversation. "I asked Michelle and she said fifteen. See that woman sitting next to her?"

"I see her," Hannah said, eyeing the attractive woman sitting next to the wayward nymphet.

"Well, that's her mother," Andrea went on with her explanation. "Her name is Jeanette, and Michelle says she's here to supervise Erica and make sure she doesn't get into any trouble."

"Big job," Hannah commented and as she watched, Jeanette James grabbed her daughter's arm and pulled her closer to whisper something in her ear. The burgeoning sex kitten pursed her lips in a pout, but she pushed back her chair and dutifully changed places with her mother. "Jeanette James looks tired. Maybe it's a good thing her watchdog role is almost over."

"What do you mean?"

"Sharyn is flying in on Tuesday night."

"Who's Sharyn?"

"Dean Lawrence's wife."

Andrea looked completely astonished. "Don't tell me you know *her*, too!"

"No, I've never met her. All I know is, Ross said they were flying in on Tuesday night for the last few days of shooting and they'll stay for the wrap party on Saturday."

Andrea looked envious. "That's *so* exciting. I guess

you'll be going, especially since you know Ross and Lynne. I saw him with his arm around you and he'll probably ask you to be his date. I don't suppose I'll get invited."

"I'll make sure you get an invitation," Hannah promised, 99 percent certain that Ross would grant her that small favor. "Besides, if Tracey gets the part, you'll both be invited."

"You're right. I didn't think of that. Uh-oh!"

"Uh-oh what?"

"I'm being summoned."

"Who's summoning you?"

"Mother and Carrie. They probably want me to take Tracey. I'd better go."

"I'll go with you. I haven't said hello to Tracey yet."

The two sisters got up and walked toward the table where their mother and Carrie were sitting across from each other. Tracey was nowhere in sight.

"Where's Tracey?" Andrea asked, pulling out a chair and sitting down next to her mother.

"With Mr. Barton. He asked if he could take her over to his table and introduce her to the actress playing the lead."

"Oh boy!" Andrea breathed, and then she turned toward Hannah, who'd just taken the chair next to Carrie. "That's got to be good, doesn't it?"

"It couldn't be bad. I don't think he'd introduce her to a member of the cast unless he was interested."

"Interested in what?" Delores asked.

"Using Tracey in the movie." Andrea beamed from ear to ear. "We ran into Mr. Barton on the way in, and he invited us to the auditions this afternoon."

"Do you have a copy of the script?" Carrie asked, leaning closer to Andrea, even though no one else at the table was paying the least bit of attention to them.

"No. Do you *have* one?"

"Of course we do," Delores opened her tote bag so that

they could see the script inside. "Mr. Barton sent it to us right after we agreed to collect all the props his man couldn't find and check everything for authenticity. Take the whole tote, dear. There's a copy machine in the library. You can get the key from Marge and run upstairs to make a copy."

Andrea took the tote with a smile. "What a great idea! Then Tracey can rehearse before we go to the audition. Thanks, Mother. You and Carrie are the best!"

Once Andrea had rushed off to find Marge and get the key to the library, Hannah stood up to go. "I guess I'd better see if Edna . . ."

"Aunt Hannah!" a small voice interrupted her and Hannah turned to see Tracey and Ross heading their way. "Hi, Honey"

"Hi!" Both Tracey and Ross spoke at once and then they turned to each other and laughed.

Hannah laughed right along with them. "Not you, Ross. I was talking to my niece."

"And here I thought you were really warming up to me." Ross gave her a slightly crooked grin.

Tracey glanced from her aunt to Ross, and then back again. "You're probably going to tell me it's none of my business, but are you two flirting?"

"No," Hannah said, overlapping Ross's reply of "Yes."

"I see," Tracey said, giggling. "Just let me know when I should stop calling you *Mr. Barton* and switch to *Uncle Ross*, okay? I'm going up to the buffet table to get some dessert."

Ross waited until Tracey had left and then he mopped his brow with his handkerchief. "Whew! She's a real pistol. I bet you were just like her at that age."

"Not at all. I was a shy, retiring child."

Hannah's smile belied her words and Ross laughed. "Right. I just can't get over how bright Tracey is. When I introduced her to the head of the makeup department, she asked about the differences between stage makeup, movie makeup, and street makeup."

"That's Tracey," Hannah replied, proud that her niece could phrase intelligent questions. "Did Lynne like her?"

"Lynne was crazy about her. They talked for a couple of minutes and then Lynne said if she ever had a daughter, she'd want her to be just like Tracey."

"What did they talk about?"

"Lynne's career. Tracey said she'd seen her in one of her TV dramas and she wanted to know if Lynne was really crying in one scene. Lynne said no, she was acting, and Tracey could hardly believe it. She said it looked so real to her that she started to sniffle."

Smart move, Hannah thought, but she didn't say it. Actors always loved to hear their work praised.

"Then she asked Lynne to please not mention it to her mother, because the program was on after her bedtime and she sneaked downstairs to watch it."

"And Lynne promised?"

"Of course."

Hannah just shook her head, remembering a psychology class she'd taken in college. The professor had said, "Get someone to do a favor for you, and their opinion of you will rise." At first that hadn't made sense to Hannah, but then she'd thought long and hard about it. She believed that she was a good judge of character and if she took the time and the trouble to grant a favor to someone, then that someone must be worthy. Asking for a promise from Lynne was a favor, and Lynne had granted it. That meant her opinion of Tracey had risen. Tracey might not know the psychology behind manipulating people, but she'd accomplished it with amazing acumen. Of course she'd learned from a master, her mother. And also from the grand master of manipulation, her grandmother Delores.

"So Tracey charmed everyone?" Hannah asked, certain that Ross's answer would be in the affirmative.

"Even Erica and her mother, and they were sitting there glaring at each other before Tracey came on the scene. She had both of them eating out of her hand and smiling at each other within two minutes. If she does a good job of reading for the part, I'm going to cast her."

"You won't be disappointed," Hannah promised. "Tracey's a talented girl with a sunny personality, and she gets along with everybody."

"I can see that."

Hannah smiled as they walked over to the table where Delores and Carrie were sitting. As coincidence would have it, she'd watched a documentary about stage mothers on television last night and they'd mentioned several who'd been positively spiteful when the demands they made for their child stars weren't met. And as Ross greeted Delores and Carrie, Hannah couldn't help thinking, *I just hope Andrea isn't like that!*

"Just between the four of us, I think she's perfect for the part," Ross said, glancing over at Tracey, who sat two tables away with her friend, Karen Dunwright. "I wish I'd brought a copy of the script with me. Her mother could read it to her."

"You mean, *she* could read it to her mother," Hannah corrected him. "Tracey reads on a fifth-grade level."

"I thought Tracey was in kindergarten!"

"She is. She taught herself to read about a year and a half ago, and she's been checking out library books ever since."

"Maybe I should run back to the trailer and get her a copy of the script."

"You don't have to do that," Delores said, and a bit of

guilty color rose in her cheeks. "Carrie and I gave Andrea our script. She's upstairs in the library, copying it."

Ross didn't look upset at this news, and Hannah figured he didn't mind at all that Tracey's family had banded together to give her an edge at the auditions. "How are you ladies coming along with the props?"

"Just fine," Delores answered for both of them. "We've spent the past several weeks going through farmhouse attics and storage sheds. I think we have everything on that list your prop man gave us. We have to talk, though. We found a couple of discrepancies for something that's set in the fifties."

"Like what?"

"Your prop man wanted us to find a period cable box for the television set. Small towns in Minnesota didn't have cable in the fifties."

"Good for you for catching that!"

"That's not all, but we can go into it later," Carrie spoke up. "Delores and I were around back then, and we remember what it looked like."

Delores flashed Carrie a dirty look. "What Carrie means is, people in Lake Eden don't redecorate until things wear out. That means the fifties look stayed around for at least twenty years."

Good save, Mother! Hannah thought silently, hiding a most unladylike snort of laughter by coughing into her napkin. Delores was an expert at thinking on her feet, and she'd crawl through a field filled with cow pies before she'd divulge her true age.

Ross exchanged a glance with Hannah and she thought she saw an amused twinkle in his eyes. Then he turned back to Delores. "Michelle told me how you decorated your store to look like the first mayor's house for the Winter Carnival."

"That's right. We didn't have pictures, of course, but there were letters from the first mayor's wife to her sister back east and she didn't stint on words describing the new house that her husband built for her. With a little more research, Carrie and I were able to replicate that house. It was a showplace for its day, built shortly before the turn of the century." She gave a little laugh. "The *last* century, that is. Eighteen ninety-three, to be exact."

"Very impressive. I know it's a lot to ask, but Michelle thought you might be able to do it again, but this time make it a house in the nineteen fifties."

"We could do it, Delores!" Carrie spoke up excitedly.

"Well . . . I'm sure that we could, but . . ." Delores stopped to give a little sigh, but Hannah, who was watching her mother closely, saw the gleam of avarice in her eyes. "It *would* be a lot of work. And we'd have to store the antiques from other periods."

"I have a whole crew at my disposal and my carpenters can build you a temporary storage facility. Actually, we could do it according to code and make it permanent. That way, you'd be able to keep it for future use."

"That *would* be nice. We could always use more storage."

"Of course my crew would be at your beck and call for painting, wallpapering, moving furniture, whatever you'd need. It would be a matter of just dressing the downstairs. Michelle showed me pictures of the inside and we won't need any structural changes. We might have to take out a window or two to get a particular shot, but naturally we'd replace those."

"How long would we have to decorate it?"

"That's part of the problem. I'd need it by Wednesday afternoon."

Ross turned to look at Carrie, who was wise enough to realize who was running the show. "That's up to Delores," she said.

"Delores?" Ross gave her a smile. "Did I mention that you'd be paid very well for your trouble? And that after we're through shooting, my crew will put everything back exactly the way it was?"

"No, you didn't mention that."

Cut to the chase, Hannah thought, but both Ross and her mother remained silent. Perhaps it was time for her to take the initiative and get this thing settled before the whipped cream on top of Edna's Jell-O parfait turned into a milky lake.

"How about screen credit?" Hannah threw out her suggestion.

"Good idea! Screen credit for both you and Carrie. And there may be a part in the movie for you. Just a small walk-on with one line apiece, but that might be fun for you. Do we have a deal?"

Delores glanced at Carrie, who was nodding like one of the old-fashioned dipping birds that Doc Bennett used to set up on his windowsill to keep his young patients occupied while he drilled.

"We have a deal," Delores said.

"Thank you all for inviting us here this afternoon," Ross stood in front of the crowd at the podium Mayor Bascomb usually used to open town meetings or call everyone to the table at potluck dinners. "You've shown real hospitality by inviting the cast and crew to brunch. I've got to tell you that if this movie is half as good as the food we had here today, it'll be a huge box office success."

There was laughter and Ross waited until it had died down. Hannah was impressed. When she'd first known him, he'd been shy around people, but he'd certainly gained a lot of self-confidence in the years they'd been out of touch.

"Michelle Swensen is my local production assistant, and she tells me that in a town the size of Lake Eden, all you have to do is mention something to one person and before the day's out, everybody in town knows about it. Does everyone know that we need extras for the crowd scenes and we're hoping you'll help us out?"

There was more applause and a couple of whistles from some of the high school crowd. "And do you know that we're holding auditions at the school this afternoon for some walk-on parts in the movie?"

"We know!" someone shouted out, and Ross laughed.

"I figured you'd know all about it, because Michelle said if I told one person that would do it. And I told Michelle."

This time the whole room exploded into laughter, and Michelle stood up and took a bow.

"Auditions are at Jordan High auditorium from two to four. There'll be sign-up sheets for extras, and a half-dozen or so walk-on parts we need to fill." He turned to Michelle to confirm it, and she shook her head. "Okay, I'm wrong. How many parts, Michelle?"

"Twelve, counting the plumber."

"I stand corrected. It's twelve parts. I hope you'll all drop by to sign up to be an extra in the crowd scenes and to try out for the bigger parts. We need . . ." Ross stopped speaking and held out his hand to Michelle. "Do you have that list?"

Michelle walked up to the podium to hand it to him, and Ross began to read. "We need a plumber, two waitresses for a cocktail party, a grade school teacher, a florist, a caterer, a bus driver, a party planner, a pianist, a filling station attendant, a mailman, and . . ." Ross paused to let the tension build, ". . . a really lousy driver who's just been in an accident. But don't go out and wreck your cars or anything like that. We never get to see this person drive on screen. All he has to do is go to makeup so our talented team can outfit him with fake bruises, a couple of bandages, and a pair of crutches."

Ross referred to the sheet again. "There are also a couple of larger parts we need to fill. We need two policemen, two local women who come for the cocktail party, someone to play the female lead as a child, and a mayor. That's it, except . . . we also need a cat."

"A real cat?" someone asked.

"A real cat. Does anyone know someone who has a big orange and white tomcat, about twenty-five pounds or so, blind in one eye, and with a torn ear?"

Hannah's mouth dropped open in surprise as everyone in the room swiveled to look at her. "I . . . you just described *my* cat!"

"I know," Ross said, and everyone laughed. "Your sister told me and we thought we'd like to use him in the movie. You don't have to bring him in to the high school to audition. I know cats aren't fond of traveling. Have dinner with me tonight out at the inn and you can tell me all about him. And then, if everything's a go, we'll go back to your place so I can take a look at him. Is that all right with you?"

"That's fine," Hannah said, smiling at him. And then she happened to spot Mike's scowling face. She turned slightly to glance at Norman and saw that he was scowling every bit as hard as Mike.

"Uh-oh," Hannah breathed, gulping slightly. Unless she was terribly mistaken, Ross had just asked her for a date in front of the whole town, and she'd accepted.

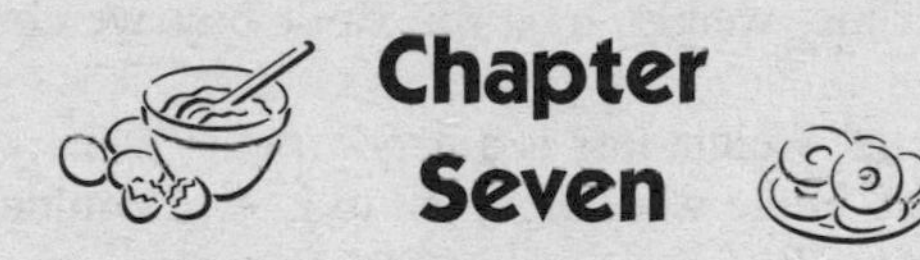

Chapter Seven

The auditorium at Jordan High was crowded, but Hannah found a spot in the back row. The acoustics weren't good here, because of the balcony overhang, so most people knew to avoid it. Hannah figured the back row would be perfect for her, since she was only here to watch Tracey. When it was her niece's turn to audition, she could stand up and move out to the aisle where she could hear better.

"Hannah Fandana!"

Hannah whirled around as a well-known voice from the past greeted her. "Hi, Linda . . . except Ross told me not to call you that anymore. He said you're Lynne Larchmont now."

"I'm still Linda to you. It's really great to see you, Hannah! You haven't changed a bit."

"You have. You were always pretty, but now you're glamorous."

"I'd better be!" The new, glamorous Lynne gave a little laugh. "I spent a lot of money to get this way. My dental bill was astronomical, not to mention what I paid to my plastic surgeon, and my makeup and hair stylists. You can purchase glamour, you know."

"But you lost weight, too. You can't buy weight loss with money."

"That's true. Weight loss is a perk you get when you're poor. I was so broke when I got out to L.A., I couldn't afford to buy food."

"What did you do?"

"I asked my dates to take me to all-you-can-eat buffets, and I lined my biggest purse with a plastic bag. When the guy wasn't looking, I shoveled in the food and then I went back for more. I don't think I spent more than a dollar on food until I landed my first part. And by then, I'd lost twenty pounds."

Hannah laughed, but she felt a little stab of envy as Lynne slipped into the seat next to her. They'd been able to borrow each other's clothes when they were in college, but now Lynne was Andrea's size. Instead of dwelling on the twenty or so pounds she should lose and probably wouldn't anytime soon, Hannah decided to switch subjects. "I'm sorry you broke up with Ross. I always thought you two were a perfect couple."

"So did I, for a while. But people grow up and they change. Ross and I wanted different things out of life and we grew apart."

Hannah was silent. It didn't seem like they'd wanted different things way back then. Lynne had wanted to be an actress and Ross had wanted to write and produce. And since that was what they were doing now, where did the bit about wanting different things come in?

"I'm really sorry about Bradford," Lynne reached out to put a hand on Hannah's arm as she mentioned the name of Hannah's college boyfriend, the assistant professor who'd started to date her without mentioning that he was already engaged. "I know your father died and that's the official story you gave for leaving college, but Ross and I figured that Bradford had something to do with it. He's divorced now, in case you're interested."

"Not even on a very lonely night," Hannah said, leaving it at that. "What did you think of my niece Tracey?"

"She's absolutely adorable! Talking to her is like talking to a little adult, and that's exactly the quality we need in the actress who plays Amy as a child. I told Ross I thought she was perfect for the part."

Hannah felt a big smile spread across her face. She loved to hear people sing Tracey's praises.

"They should be holding tryouts for the speaking parts any minute now. Ross's down to the last couple of walk-ons, and then he'll probably do Amy."

"How many kids are trying out?"

"Three. Ross introduced them to me and, you can trust me, Tracey doesn't have any competition. For one thing, she has just the right demeanor. The other two are pretty and charming, but they don't sell serious little girl. You know what I mean?"

"I'm not sure I do."

"Okay. Let me explain it another way. You should get the feeling that there's a brain working away behind those pretty blue eyes. The face might be laughing, but the brain behind it is always thinking, always planning, always very careful."

"You just described Tracey to a tee, except for the last part. That sounds a little paranoid."

"It is. Don't forget that Amy lives with a manic-depressive father. And when he's manic, he has anger issues. Amy and her brother are the only ones who see that anger. Amy's just a child, but she's very careful to assess her father's mood and act accordingly. He's never lashed out at her, but that's because she's careful not to antagonize him when he's in anger mode."

"Why doesn't she tell someone about it?"

"She's afraid that no one will believe her."

"That sounds like a very bad situation."

"It is. Anyway, those are the family dynamics and they're

just fascinating. I spent some time talking to Tracey, and I'm sure she can handle the part. I'll stay and watch her audition with you. And then I'll put in another good word with Ross." Lynne stopped speaking and sighed dramatically. "Oh, look! There's that gorgeous detective!"

"Mike Kingston," Hannah told her, watching as Mike walked across the stage. He was in full uniform and he turned from side to side in response to an instruction they couldn't hear from their position in the back row.

"You *know* him?" Lynne asked, and then she gave a little laugh. "Of course you know him. You're bound to know him. Lake Eden is a pretty small town and you probably know everybody. I tell you, Hannah . . . if I didn't love my husband, I'd be all over him."

Hannah was about to make a wisecrack, something about how Lynne would have to get him on the rebound because he'd proposed to her and she'd just turned him down. But Hannah didn't say that. For one thing, it would sound like bragging. And for another thing, they weren't best college buddies anymore, and her love life, or lack of it, wasn't any of Lynne's business.

When Mike left the stage, Lynne turned to Hannah. "They'll take a break now, and then they'll audition for the speaking parts. That's the way they always do it."

"Maybe now would be a good time to meet Mr. Lawrence," Hannah suggested. "Ross asked me to bake for him and I need to know what kind of cheesecake he likes."

"Cherry."

"I know that, but there are different kinds of cherry cheesecakes. Does he like the light and fluffy type with cherry swirled all the way through? Or would he prefer it dense and heavy with the cherries only on the top?"

Lynne shrugged. "I really don't know. Let's go ask him."

A moment later, Hannah was being introduced to the most theatrical looking man in the room. Dean Lawrence wasn't that tall, but what he lacked in stature, he more than made up for in rugged good looks. He reminded Hannah of a Bantam rooster, posturing next to the stage. The fact that his hair was tousled and stuck up slightly on the top of his head added to the rooster illusion, and the ascot he wore around his neck had a pattern that looked a bit like neck feathers.

"Nice to meet you, Mr. Lawrence," Hannah said politely, after Lynne had introduced them.

"It's Dean, Lovey. Only my enemies call me Mr. Lawrence."

Lovey? Hannah did her best not to bristle. She really didn't care to be tagged with pet names by someone she'd just met. "I'm baking your cheesecakes, Mr. . . . er . . . Dean. And I'd like to know your preferences."

"Preferences?"

"Yes. Do you prefer your cheesecake light or dense?"

"Light or dense?"

"A light cheesecake is fluffy. A dense cheesecake is heavy."

"Oh. I see what you mean. I like a dense cheesecake, very heavy. And it should be very smooth, too. When you take a bite, it should almost melt in the mouth."

"Okay. Do you like it with a sweet crust, or a crust that tastes like toast crumbs?"

"Sweet. I have a sweet tooth, Lovey."

There it was again, the unwarranted and unwanted term of endearment. Hannah did her best to ignore it and asked the next question. "How about the cherries? Would you prefer your cheesecake to have cherries all the way through, a swirl of cherries mixed in for color and flavor, or just cherries on the top?"

"Cherries on the top, with cherry sauce running over the sides. And I like the kind of cheesecake with sour cream spread over the top under the cherries. I think it's called New York cheesecake. Do you think you can bake it?"

"I'm sure I can."

"That's the attitude, Lovey! Never say you can't do it until you try, isn't that right?"

"Right," Hannah agreed. "I'll deliver it to your trailer by nine tomorrow morning."

"That's just fine, Lovey. I'll be waiting for you with a fork in my hand." Dean switched his attention from Hannah rather abruptly and waved at Ross, who was just taking his seat in the front row. "Ready to roll, Duckie?"

"Ready," Ross said, with no apparent reaction. Since Michelle had mentioned that they'd been in production for almost two months now, Hannah figured that Ross must be used to Dean's nicknames.

"So . . . " Hannah said to Lynne, delaying the rest of her thought until they were out of earshot. "Does Dean give everyone nicknames?"

"Oh, yes. He calls all the women Lovey and all the guys Duckie. I don't know why he does it. He's not even English!"

"I think I know why."

"You do?"

"It's just a guess, but I'll bet it's so he doesn't have to bother remembering their names."

Chapter Eight

"Just wait until you see what's on the dessert cart," Hannah said, watching as Jordan High senior, Amber Coombs, pushed the lusciously laden serving cart their way. Even from this distance, Hannah could see Sally's towering Neapolitan cake, a six-layer concoction with alternating layers of chocolate, vanilla, and strawberry cake, each layer affixed to its neighboring layer with a matching frosting.

Ross gave a theatrical whimper as he eyed the contents of the cart, and Hannah knew exactly how he felt. It was close to impossible to choose one dessert when they all promised to enchant the taste buds

"I want one of each," Ross said.

"Me, too. But if we do that, Amber's going to have to roll us out of the dining room."

"We should have skipped the entrée and come straight here," Ross remarked, pulling his gaze away from the decadent delights to smile at her. "I can still remember your motto in college. Always . . ."

"Eat dessert first," Hannah joined in as he recited it.

"How about if we get two desserts and split?"

"That sounds perfect to me. It's almost as good as getting two desserts apiece." Hannah smiled up at Amber Coombs, who was trying not to laugh at their antics. "I'll have a piece of Sally's Flourless Chocolate Cake. With two forks."

Ross had drawn a bead on the bowl of Apricot Bread Pudding, and he spoke without lifting his gaze. "And I'll have the bread pudding. I've been dreaming about Hannah's bread pudding ever since she packed up her recipes and left college. This looks a lot like one you used to make, Hannah."

"That's because it is," Amber spoke up. "Mrs. Laughlin uses Miss Swensen's recipe."

"Well . . . that changes everything!" Ross said with a smile. "If it's Hannah's bread pudding, I'll have a double helping."

"Would you like that warmed?"

"Oh, yes."

"With heavy cream, sweetened whipped cream, or vanilla ice cream?"

"Oh, yes."

Amber cracked up, but she quickly sobered. "Would that be with all three of them, sir?"

"No, I'll have the heavy cream. That's the way Hannah used to serve it." Ross glanced at Amber, who looked very pretty and trim in her flattering waitress uniform. "I wish you'd been at the auditions this afternoon, Amber. I would have cast you as one of the waitresses in the cocktail party scene."

Amber, who up to this point had been the quintessential waitress, dropped her newfound maturity right along with her jaw. "Really, Mr. Barton?" she squeaked.

"Absolutely. Of course waiting on us tonight was just like an audition, wasn't it?"

"If you say so, Mr. Barton," Amber said, barely managing to hide her excitement.

"Then you've got the part if you want it. Do you think you can work it into your schedule?"

"Oh, yes!" Amber breathed. "Mr. Purvis, he's the principal at Jordan High, told us we could take time off class if we got a part in the movie. All we have to do is make up the work later."

Hannah watched Amber as Ross told her about the release form her mother would have to sign and when to report to wardrobe. Amber couldn't seem to stop smiling and by the time she pushed the dessert cart away, she was practically dancing across the dining room.

"Maybe that was a mistake," Ross said, watching the excited girl push the cart into the kitchen.

"You mean . . . you don't want to use her in the movie?"

"Oh, no. I want to use her. It's just that she's so excited, she might forget about bringing my bread pudding."

An hour later, Hannah was unlocking her condo door. Amber hadn't forgotten Ross's dessert and they'd devoured both of them with gusto.

"You'd better stand back," Hannah said, her hand on the doorknob.

"Okay, but why?"

"Moishe has a greeting ritual when I come home at night."

"Greeting ritual?"

"He jumps up into my arms. And since he weighs over twenty pounds, it knocks me back a step or two . . . especially if I forget to brace myself."

"Forewarned is forearmed," Ross said, moving closer and placing his hands against Hannah's back. "If he knocks you over, I'll catch you.

"Deal," Hannah agreed, surprised at the reaction she had to Ross's touch. Just this totally impersonal gesture even through his gloves and her coat made her heart beat a bit faster.

Ross gave a startled chuckle as Hannah opened the door and an orange-and-white ball of flying fur hurtled through the air directly at them. Hannah caught her cat expertly, resisted the urge to lean back against Ross even though she wasn't one bit off-balance, and stepped forward into her living room.

"Meet Ross," she said, giving Moishe a little scratch behind the ears before placing him on the ledge at the back of the couch. "If you act cute, Ross might make you into a movie star. Then she turned to Ross, who was smiling. "This is my roommate, Moishe."

"Lucky cat," Ross said with a grin.

Moishe stared at Hannah for a moment, as if he were digesting the information she'd given him about being a kitty movie star, and then he arched his back and went into his Halloween cat pose. He held that position for a moment or two, and then he relaxed his whole body and did what Hannah thought of as his *kitty toupee*, tucking his tail under his body and stretching out flat over the back of the couch like a miniature throw rug.

"He's going through his paces," Hannah told Ross. "Do you think he's auditioning for you?"

"Without a doubt. He must have understood what you said about being a kitty movie star, and he wants his paw prints at Mann's Chinese."

"Not to mention his own star on the Hollywood Walk of Fame." Hannah's smile turned into a laugh as Moishe lifted his head and yawned widely, showing them a full set of sharp white teeth. Then he swiveled his ears, first together, like twin satellite dishes receiving the same signal, and then separately, one ear turning forward and the other backward.

"I still can't do that," Ross said, glancing over at Hannah. "Can you?"

Hannah shook her head. She knew exactly what Ross was talking about. When they were all in college, Lynne had learned to simultaneously move her right hand in a circle going forward, like a miniature Ferris Wheel, while her left moved in a circle traveling in the opposite direction, backward toward her chest. Both circles had to be started at the same time and they had to be of the same size and speed. "I tried for months and I still couldn't do it. I think it takes more than practice."

"I know it does. I practiced, too. Lynne didn't. She got it right the first time she tried it. I'm sure there's some sort of psychological measure we could devise about the differences between the people who can do it and the people who can't, but we probably shouldn't get into that now."

Hannah turned to give Ross a sharp look, but he was staring at Moishe. Ross had claimed he wasn't bitter about the breakup with Lynne, but she'd heard an undercurrent in his voice that told her it hadn't been all sweetness and light. It wasn't really any of her business and she certainly wasn't going to ask him about it now, but that curious bone in her body began to tingle. "Do you want coffee?"

"I'd love some, if you're not in a hurry to get to bed, or anything like that."

What a line! Hannah thought, but it probably wasn't and she wasn't sure if she was disappointed, or not. "Coffee's no trouble at all. I usually stay up until at least ten on nights before work, and it's only a little after nine."

"Okay. You're the boss. What time do you open your shop?"

"We've been opening at nine. When the tourists are here in the summer, we open earlier."

"Well, I don't need you to open before ten, so that'll give you an extra hour."

"Not really. I promised to deliver Mr. Lawrence's cheesecake at nine and I still have to bake it. That'll take me about two hours."

"Do you want company while you bake it?"

"Sure," Hannah said, hoping Ross would be content to spend most of that time sitting at her kitchen table drinking coffee. Now that he was a big-time movie producer, he might have different ideas about what behavior was appropriate between two friends who hadn't seen each other for years, but he was a guest in her home and that meant she defined the terms.

By the time Hannah came back with two mugs of coffee, Ross was sitting on the couch and Moishe was on his lap. "He must know it's a casting couch," she quipped, and then wished she hadn't when Ross gave her a devilish smile.

"Well, he's got the part so he doesn't have to extend himself any further. His owner, however, could . . ."

Right on cue, Moishe yowled, interrupting what Hannah was fairly certain had been an opening gambit from her old college chum. Then her overprotective feline undraped himself and settled down on the couch between them, discouraging any possible intimacy.

"Does he do this with everyone?" Ross asked, just as the phone rang.

"Only men," Hannah answered, reaching out to pick up the receiver. "Hello?"

"Hi, Hannah." Hannah frowned as she recognized Mike's voice. "I just wanted to tell you that someone drove through the wooden arm on your entrance gate again."

"I know. It was broken when we came in. It happens almost every weekend. People put their gate cards next to their credit cards and the little magnetic strip gets corrupted. And then, when it won't open the gate, they get mad and drive right through."

"You're probably right, but you don't know for sure," Mike sounded very serious. "Someone could have broken in and I thought I should warn you."

"Okay, I'm warned. Thanks for calling, Mike."

"Don't hang up, Hannah! I was just thinking that maybe I should come over so you're not alone. I mean, you shouldn't be alone when someone could be out there roaming around with an eye to a possible break-in."

And the only thing you're concerned about is my safety, Hannah thought, but instead of saying that, she said, "That's okay, Mike. I'm not alone."

"You're not? But it's almost ten o'clock and you always go to bed at ten on work nights. I mean, you have to get up early to open the shop tomorrow, don't you?"

"Not really. Ross just told me that I don't have to open until ten," Hannah said, not mentioning that she still had a cheesecake to bake. "Isn't that just great?"

"Great," Mike repeated, sounding massively insincere. "So . . . maybe I'll take a run out there and do a little patrolling on foot. You know . . . just to make sure and all. That broken gate has been nagging at me ever since I saw it."

Gotcha! Hannah thought and started to smile. She'd suspected from the beginning that Mike was calling because he was jealous of the time she was spending with Ross, and now she knew it for a fact. "Ever since you *saw* it?"

"Yeah. Uh . . . it's like this, Hannah. I had to take a run out your way earlier. Somebody thought they spotted a guy on one of those *Most Wanted* programs. And since I was so close anyway, I decided to drop by to see if you were home. That's when I noticed the gate."

"I see," Hannah said, seeing much more than Mike had hoped she would. "Well, you don't have to bother. Everything's perfectly all right out here. Thanks for being concerned, though. I appreciate it. See you tomorrow, Mike."

"So Mike's jealous?" Ross asked the moment Hannah hung up the phone.

"You could say that. I might not say it because it wouldn't be nice, but *you* could."

Ross laughed. "He's jealous, all right. It's probably because you turned him down."

"How do *you* know about that?"

"Michelle told me. I asked if you were dating anyone, and she gave me the lowdown."

"It seems that everybody knows my business," Hannah said, trying not to sound churlish.

"Life's like that a lot. I'll give him five minutes. How about you?"

"Who?"

"Norman. Mike's bound to touch base with him. They're probably in each other's back pockets, now that you rejected them both. There's nothing that unites two former rivals more than a third guy coming on the scene."

"And the third guy would be you?" Hannah asked, noticing his wicked grin and smiling in spite of herself.

"Oh, yes. That would be me. So, do you want to bet, or . . . " The phone rang again, interrupting Ross's sentence and he laughed. "There he is."

"It's not him."

"How can you tell?"

"Look at Moishe," Hannah said, gesturing toward the feline between them.

"What's wrong with him? He's all puffed up and his hair is standing on end."

"Cats do that instinctually when they're angry or frightened. It's a defense mechanism to make them look bigger. Moishe gets like this when Mother calls. He's not infallible, but he gets it right more times than he gets it wrong." She plucked the receiver from the cradle and brought it up to her ear. "Hello, Mother."

"I wish you wouldn't answer the phone like that, Hannah," Delores complained, but Hannah could tell from her tone of voice that her heart wasn't it it. "Carrie just called. She said Norman told her that Ross was still out at your place. Don't you think it's time you went to bed?"

"What a marvelous idea!" Hannah turned to grin at Ross. "I'll tell him you suggested it. I really had no idea you were so liberal minded."

There was a sputtering on the line, a close cousin to the sound of Bill's old Ford when the plugs were dirty. "That's not what I meant and you know it!" Delores finally managed to say. "What are you *doing*, Hannah?"

"We're having coffee, Mother. And then I'm going to bake a cheesecake. But your suggestion sounds like a lot more fun than . . ."

"Cut that out right now, Hannah Louise!" Delores interrupted her.

"Just kidding, Mother."

"Well, it's not funny! I want you to bake that cheesecake now. And then send him straight home. Don't forget that you have to face yourself in the mirror in the morning."

Hannah heard a resounding click and she laughed as she hung up the phone. "I'm a mean person. I gave my mother such a hard time, she hung up on me. A good daughter wouldn't have done that."

"Maybe not, but it feels good once in a while, doesn't it?"

"It sure does!" Hannah turned to give him a grin. "Your five minutes are almost up and Norman hasn't . . ." The phone pealed loudly, drowning out the rest of her sentence.

"That's Norman," Ross said.

"You're probably right." Hannah reached for the phone. "Hello, Norman."

"Hi, Hannah. I figured you'd rather hear from me than my mother."

"You got *that* right!"

"I just wanted to ask . . . I don't have anything to worry about with Ross, do I?"

Hannah stifled the urge to give Norman an earful about privacy, and personal freedom, and sticking his nose into someone else's business, but she didn't. He'd asked her straight out instead of being devious, and she owed him a straight answer. "If you ever do, I'll let you know. How's that?"

"Fair enough," Norman said. "Good night, Hannah. I love you, you know."

"I know," Hannah said, wishing she could return the sentiment, but not wanting to give him false hope. She gently replaced the receiver in the cradle and turned to Ross. "Seems like the whole town's talking about us."

"I figured as much. I hate to say it, but maybe I'd better go. There'll be other times . . . won't there?"

"That's up to you," Hannah said, giving him a playful grin as she headed for the chair by the door to get his coat.

SALLY'S FLOURLESS CHOCOLATE CAKE

Preheat oven to 375 degrees F., rack in the middle position

Hannah's Note: This cake is going to fall in the center. There's just no way around it since there's no flour to hold it up. That really doesn't matter, because it's so delicious. Just be prepared to cover up the crater in the middle with plenty of whipped cream—Sally whips two cups of cream sweetened with ⅓ cup of powdered sugar, spreads it on the top, and shaves some bittersweet chocolate on top of that.

½ cup butter ***(1 stick, ¼ pound)***
8 ounces semi-sweet chocolate chips ***(1 and ⅓ cups—I used Ghirardelli's)***

4 egg yolks ***(save the whites in a separate bowl for later)***
½ cup white ***(granulated)*** sugar
½ teaspoon rum extract ***(or vanilla if you don't have rum)***

4 egg whites ***(the ones you saved)***
¼ cup white ***(granulated)*** sugar ***(you'll use ¾ cup in all)***

sweetened whipped cream to decorate top
shaved chocolate or chocolate curls to decorate top ***(optional)***
sliced or whole berries to decorate top ***(optional)***

Spray an 8-inch Springform pan with Pam or other non-stick cooking spray. ***(An 8½-inch Springform will also work, but a 9-inch is too big.)*** Line the bottom of the pan with a circle of parchment paper ***(wax paper will also work.)*** Spray the paper with Pam or other non-stick cooking spray.

In a small microwave-safe bowl, combine butter and semi-sweet chocolate chips. Melt for one minute on HIGH, stir, and heat for an additional 20 seconds if necessary. ***(Some chocolate maintains its shape even when melted. Stir before you microwave for the additional time.)*** Cover your bowl, or put it back in the microwave, to keep it warm.

In a medium bowl, beat ½ cup of granulated sugar with the egg yolks until they're a light yellow in color. Mix in the rum extract. *(This is easy with an electric mixer, although you can do it by hand.)*

Stir a bit of the egg yolk mixture into the melted chocolate to temper it. Then add the chocolate to the egg yolk mixture and stir until it's well blended.

In a large bowl, using clean beaters, beat the egg whites until soft peaks form. Continue beating while sprinkling in the remaining ¼ cup granulated sugar. Beat until stiff peaks form ***(about ½ minute.)***

Stir just a bit of the egg white mixture into the bowl with the chocolate. Now add the chocolate to the bowl with the rest of the egg whites and gently fold it in with a rubber spatula. Continue folding until the mixture is a uniform chocolate color.

Pour the batter into the cake pan and smooth the top with a rubber spatula. Bake at 375 degrees F. for 35 minutes or until a wooden pick or cake tester inserted in the center comes out dry.

Cool in the pan on a wire rack for 15 minutes. Run a knife around the inside of the rim of the pan, invert the pan on a serving plate, and cool for another 10 minutes. Release the catch on the Springform pan and remove it. DON'T PEEL OFF THE PARCHMENT PAPER UNTIL THE CAKE IS COMPLETELY COOL TO THE TOUCH.

When you're ready to serve, fill in the crater in the center and frost the top of the cake with sweetened whipped cream. If you want it to look fancy, decorate it with chocolate shavings, chocolate curls, and/or a sprinkling of raspberries or strawberries. Slice it and serve it on dessert plates with plenty of excellent coffee.

Hannah's 2nd Note: This is really a type of chocolate soufflé and it's delicious!

Chapter Nine

It was eight-thirty on Monday morning and Hannah was at her wit's end. Moishe, her wannabe movie star, was yowling like a banshee. He'd been expressing his extreme displeasure ever since she'd delivered him to the kitchen of The Cookie Jar and placed him in the crate Eleanor Cox had provided for the week. The crate was large and roomy. Eleanor rescued huskies and malamutes, and these homes away from home were designed to accommodate large-breed dogs. It had a nice, soft pad on the bottom and Moishe had plenty of space to stroll around. Hannah had equipped it with his food and water bowls, his litter box, and even the feather pillow he loved so much at home. Despite all these comforts, Moishe was not a happy cat and he wasn't one to hide his emotions.

Hannah had wracked her brain and tried every trick she could think of to make her pet feel at home. She'd turned the crate so that Moishe could see them working, and put music on the radio so that he wouldn't feel deprived. She'd gone over to reach through the grating and pet him every few minutes, and she'd even resorted to bribing him with a fresh pot of catnip that Lisa had grown in her greenhouse.

Nothing had worked. It was clear that Moishe would complain until he lost his voice and then heaven knew what he'd do!

"Six," Hannah said, shaking her head as her usually accommodating feline roommate tipped over his bowl of water. "But who's counting?" She glanced over at her partner, who was smiling despite the fact that Moishe was vocalizing, and that was putting it nicely, at the top of his lungs. "How can you smile when you have to listen to *that?"*

"Excuse me?" Lisa asked, frowning slightly. "I didn't hear you, Hannah."

It was little wonder, Hannah thought, shaking her head. Just like the teens who listened to music blaring from their earphones, Lisa had probably experienced what Hannah hoped would be a temporary hearing loss. "I said," Hannah got set to repeat herself in a much louder voice. "*How can you smile when you have to listen to that?*"

"Oh, gosh! Sorry!" Lisa apologized as she reached up with both hands to pull two small, bright orange objects from her ears.

"You're wearing ear plugs?"

"Yes. I got them from Herb. They're the kind we use when we go cowboy shooting."

Hannah laughed. It amused her every time Lisa referred to cowboy shooting. It sounded as if her partner went out to shoot cowboys, but the only things Lisa and Herb had in their sights were steel targets. Cowboy shooting was a sport with stages that replicated Wild West settings. Everyone wore period clothing and participants were judged on their speed and accuracy using replicas of guns that had been available during the period.

"I know, we don't actually shoot cowboys," Lisa correctly interpreted Hannah's laugh, "but that's what everyone calls it. When I told Herb that you were bringing Moishe down here and keeping him in a crate so he'd be handy when they needed him for a scene, he figured I'd need earplugs."

Moishe gave another deafening yowl and both Hannah and Lisa reached up to cover their ears. When the sound stopped, Hannah gave an exasperated sigh. "I don't suppose you've got another pair of those?"

"I was a Girl Scout. I come prepared." Lisa reached into her apron pocket and handed Hannah a new pair of earplugs. "Just roll them around in your hands for a few seconds to compress them, and then push them in your ears. They'll expand to fit."

Hannah did what her partner advised and soon both women were working in relative peace. Moishe's yowls, although every bit as loud as they'd been before, had faded by the grace of the bright orange barriers to fit into their auditory comfort zone.

Once nine o'clock approached, Hannah went to the cooler to retrieve the cheesecake she'd baked after Ross had left the previous evening. "I'm going to run over to Mr. Lawrence's trailer to deliver this," she told Lisa. "Have some coffee and relax. We don't open for another hour."

"Do you think he'll stop yowling soon?" Lisa asked, moving closer so that she could hear Hannah's answer.

"Your guess is as good as mine. Try turning out the kitchen lights and going in the coffee shop. He's used to being alone all day and maybe that'll do it."

"You think?"

"Not really, but it's worth a try. And dream up some story about how he's just rehearsing for a singing career in case the S.P.C.A. drops by."

As Hannah approached the huge Winnebago, she was impressed. It was a home on wheels in the true sense of the words, and it must have cost a pretty penny to rent it. The only other motor home she'd seen that approximated the size of the one Dean Lawrence was using as an office was at the Road Deals on Wheels Trade Show she'd attended last year with Andrea and Bill. That particular motor home, the featured item at the show, had cost triple the price of a nice two-bedroom home in Lake Eden.

Hannah supposed she could understand the outlay of money if the big motor home had doubled as a hotel room, but the director of *Crisis in Cherrywood* was comfortably billeted in a luxury suite at the Lake Eden Inn. There was no way he needed an office this large.

Since she couldn't stand here staring at this example of conspicuous consumption all day, Hannah looked for an entrance to the massive mobile home. There were two sets of steps. One was in the rear, but the other set, at the side near the front of the vehicle, had a sign that read, ENTRANCE—RING BELL.

Hannah did as she'd been directed and stood there shivering slightly in the frozen air. The March mornings were crisp and cold, and she hadn't bothered zipping up her parka coat. Until someone invented a zipper that could be operated with one hand, Hannah chose to shiver rather than turn around, go back down the steps, and set her prized cheesecake in the snow in order to zip up her coat.

One of the curtains near the back of the motor home pulled back slightly and Hannah thought she heard faint voices from within. It sounded like a man's voice, and whatever the man said was followed by female laughter. A moment later, Hannah heard the male voice again, much louder this time. "Just wait a second! I'll be right there!"

Hannah's curiosity shifted to high gear, especially since Ross had described his director as a womanizer. She told herself it was none of her business, that he might have been listening to television and that's what she'd heard, but she didn't believe it for a second. There was a woman in Dean Lawrence's Winnebago. She was sure of it. The only thing she didn't know was which woman it was.

A moment later, Dean pulled open the door, greeting her with a smile and a fork held high. "See, Lovey? I've got my fork ready. Just bring it in and set it on my desk."

Hannah was surprised he'd invited her in, especially since the woman had to be somewhere in the immediate vicinity. She set the cake down on the polished desk that sat against the large window, and glanced down the hallway. If she remembered correctly, the motor home she'd seen had the master bedroom in the rear. But there was no way of telling if the director's motor home shared the same design, because the door at the end of the long corridor was closed.

"I really hope you like it, Mr. Lawrence," Hannah said setting the box down on the uncluttered surface.

"It's Dean," he corrected her, lifting the top of the bakery box and gazing down at the cheesecake. "It *looks* perfect, but looks aren't everything. I'm quite a connoisseur, you know. Promise me you won't have any hard feelings if I give you some constructive criticism?"

"Okay, no hard feelings," Hannah said, although she knew it was a promise she couldn't keep. Of course she'd have hard feelings if Dean didn't like her cheesecake!

"Good for you, Lovey. You have no idea how many people can't take criticism, even when it's friendly and for their own benefit. Would you cut me a slice?"

"Of course." Hannah folded down the sides of the box so that she could lift her cheesecake out without damaging it. "I'll need a knife."

"There should be one here somewhere. They took out the kitchen to make a larger space for my office, but they left some things in the cupboards and drawers."

As Dean brushed past her, she jumped slightly. Unless she was imagining things, Mr. Lawrence had just patted her inappropriately! Hannah turned around to glance at him, but he was busily pawing through the contents of the drawers for a knife. Perhaps he had just bumped into her. It was difficult to tell if his touch had been intentional when she was wearing her heavily quilted parka coat.

Even though the Bad Boy Director was making quite a racket, opening drawers and slamming them closed, Hannah heard a door shut at the back of the Winnebago and a faint clanging as someone went down the set of metal steps at the rear of the vehicle. Whoever had been in the master bedroom, if it *was* the master bedroom and hadn't been turned into some sort of a workroom, had exited the back way. That was certainly suspicious. If Dean's early morning visitor had come to see him for business reasons, she should have come out to greet Hannah and enjoy a piece of cheesecake.

Hannah was just inching toward the curtain, hoping to peek out to catch a glimpse of Dean's visitor, when he came back holding a knife and a plate.

"Here you go, Lovey. I found a plate, too. I would have brought another, but I assumed you had to get back to your shop."

"You're right. I do." Hannah cut a slice of the creamy cheesecake and slid it onto the plate. "We're opening in less than an hour."

"I'll see you later then."

Dean reached out to give her a little hug and his hand was overly affectionate. Hannah stepped back. Was that intentional? She couldn't quite decide.

"I'll see you at lunch. And I'll let you know what I think of your cheesecake then. Right now, I have to get back to work myself."

It was a dismissal and Hannah turned to go, even though she really wanted to know what he thought of her creation. Dean was being pretty high-handed, if you asked her, and she wondered if his cast felt the same way. Constructive criticism, indeed! And even more important, had Dean made a pass at her? She just wasn't sure if he had, or hadn't.

As Hannah opened the door to go, she decided to give Dean the benefit of the doubt. The trailer was wide, but not as wide as a regular office. And the area they'd been in was crowded with his massive desk and office equipment. Perhaps it had been difficult to get past a less than svelte woman in the confines of the trailer. Everything that had happened could be perfectly unintentional.

Hannah reminded herself to look on the bright side as she closed the door behind her and hurried down the stairs. Less than two minutes had elapsed since she'd heard Dean's visitor go down the back stairs. If she were very lucky, Hannah might still catch a glimpse of her.

She hadn't been lucky. Dean's visitor had been gone by the time she'd stepped outside. All Hannah had found when she took a slight detour past the back of the Winnebago on her way to her truck were footsteps in the snow. The footsteps were much smaller than most men would leave and the heel mark was a dead giveaway, since the heels on men's shoes were usually only slightly smaller than the overall width. Hannah felt safe in surmising that she'd been correct when she'd identified the laughter she'd heard as female.

When Hannah opened the back door of The Cookie Jar, she found Lisa sitting at the stainless steel work island across from Mike and Norman. Both men had coffee and cookies, and all was blessedly silent from the vicinity of Moishe's crate.

"Moishe gave up?" she asked Lisa, shrugging out of her coat and hanging it on a hook by the back door.

"He negotiated a truce," Norman answered, moving back on his stool so Hannah could see that he was holding Moishe on his lap. "He's just fine as long as someone pays attention to him."

"We tried putting him back in, but he started yowling the minute Norman got him near the cage," Mike informed her.

"It's a crate," Hannah corrected. "A nice big home-away-from-home crate."

"Technically yes, but he thinks it's a cage. Why don't you put on his leash and leave him out?"

Hannah's eyebrows rose in surprise. She couldn't believe that Mike was suggesting something illegal. "Believe me, I'd like to! His yowling drives me crazy, but I'm taking a chance just having him here. I think it's okay as long as he's away from the cookies we bake and serve, but I'm not a hundred percent sure of that."

"Don't worry about it, Hannah. You can forget about the health board."

Hannah's mouth dropped open. "Forget about the *health board*? I can't believe you said that, Mike. The health board has the power to cite me and fine me. And if the inspector's really in a bad mood, they could yank my license and close me down!"

"No, they can't. You're already closed down for the week. What you have here is a private party for the movie cast and crew. And since Moishe is an official part of the cast, he's got a perfect right to be here."

Hannah turned to look at Lisa, who shrugged. "Maybe I'm crazy, but it sounds reasonable to me."

"Me, too," Norman said, giving Moishe a scratch under the chin.

"Our eardrums salute you," Hannah said with a grin, turning back to Mike. "But . . . are you sure I won't get into trouble?"

"I'm sure. Don't forget that I'm the acting sheriff. If I say that it's a private party and health department regulations don't apply, then it's a private party and health department regulations don't apply."

Hannah clamped her lips shut. She suspected that the

power of his new office might be corrupting Mike, but she'd wait until next week to point it out to him.

The first arrivals started to trickle in shortly after they opened at ten o'clock. Hannah met Sophie, the wardrobe mistress, and Honey, the head beautician. Ross had rented Bertie Straub's shop, the Cut 'n Curl, for the week and Honey was using it as her headquarters. Bertie was acting as an advisor on hairstyles of the fifties, and unlike Delores, who didn't want to admit that she remembered the fifties, Bertie didn't seem to mind at all.

As the minutes passed, more members of the crew came in. There was Clark, one of the cameramen, who explained to Hannah that he'd be shooting some footage of Moishe that afternoon, and Coop, the soundman, who'd be there, too. Lars, the head electrician, told Hannah that when it came to the film world, the terminology was different than it was in everyday life. For instance, the men who handled electrical cables were called *grips*. Dom, the assistant director, chimed in to tell her that the people who handled animal actors were called *wranglers* even if the animal in question wasn't a horse, and she would be listed in the screen credits at the end of the film, which were called a *crawl*, as the cat wrangler. That tickled Hannah's funny bone and she chuckled about it all the way back to the counter to get three Old Fashioned Sugar Cookies for Frances, the middle-aged woman who told Hannah that she was the *script girl*.

Hannah was just heading back to the counter for the second time to get Jared, the set decorator, a refill on his coffee when she happened to notice that the swinging door between the coffee shop and the kitchen was inching open. As they watched, an orange-and-white leg poked out and a moment after that, Moishe's head appeared. Hannah was just springing into action to catch her errant feline before he could disturb the cast and crew, when there was a startled yowl and Moishe was pulled back into the kitchen.

"Uh-oh," Hannah breathed. Norman and Mike had offered to take care of Moishe, but he must have gotten away from them. They couldn't cat-sit forever and it was time to figure out a way to keep him confined to the kitchen where he wouldn't bother anyone. She motioned for Lisa to refill Jared's mug, pointed to herself and then to the kitchen door, and hurried to take care of the problem.

"Sorry about that," Mike said, as soon as Hannah came through the door. "He got away from us for a second. We decided we're going to take him out there."

Hannah shook her head. "I don't think that's . . ."

The rest of Hannah's sentence was drowned out by a massive yowl. Moishe had regained his vocal power and he was exercising it to the fullest.

"I don't think he's going to settle for less," Norman observed. "Come on, Big Boy. Let's go."

Without another word to Hannah, Norman picked Moishe up and headed toward the coffee shop with Mike following in his wake. Hannah just stared after them as the door swung closed.

"Catnapped," she said, listening for disaster to break loose. Thirty seconds passed, and then a full minute as Hannah watched the second hand on the kitchen clock. Was Moishe actually going to behave like a well-trained movie cat and not scratch, or yowl, or exercise any of the other bad kitty behaviors he'd perfected over the years? She was listening so intently and concentrating so hard, it came as a shock when there was a sharp knock on the back door. "Coming," Hannah called out and went to open it.

It was Andrea and she was dressed to the nines. Her coat was powder blue suede with white fur around the collar and the hemline, and she wore matching gloves of pale blue leather. Her boots matched her gloves, and the only thing that was missing from the ensemble that Hannah called

Andrea's Princess of Winter outfit was the white fur hat that she usually wore on her head.

"No hat?" Hannah asked, taking her sister's coat and hanging it up on the rack near the back door.

"The dog ate it."

"What dog? You don't have a dog."

"I know. It was Reverend Knudson's dog, Vespers. She got out and Bill spotted her in front of the community center. He put Vespers in the backseat and took her home. It happened a couple of weeks ago."

"And your hat was in the backseat?"

"That's right."

"And Vespers ate it?"

"Well . . . she tore up more than she ate. We couldn't really blame her. I think it was made out of real fur. I'm just glad it didn't make her sick."

Hannah reached out to give her sister a little hug, an unusual gesture from a member of the Swensen clan who weren't known for being demonstrative.

"What was that for?" Andrea asked.

"For being more concerned about Vespers than you were about losing your hat. I'm proud of you, Sis."

"Oh. Well . . . the hat was last season's anyway." Andrea waved off the compliment, but Hannah could tell she was pleased. "How about a cookie for Lake Eden's newest stage mother?"

"Tracey got the part?"

"Yes, and I'm so excited! Mr. Barton called us this morning with the good news. It wasn't just up to him, you know. Mr. Lawrence had to approve her."

"How could he *not* approve her?" Hannah waited until Andrea sat down on a stool at the work island, and then she served her hot coffee and two of their newest experimental cookies. "There was never any doubt in my mind that Tracey would get the part. I saw her audition and she was brilliant."

Andrea looked very proud. "I thought she was brilliant, too. I was ninety-nine percent sure she had it, but I didn't want to count my chickens before they were laid."

"Hatched. Chickens are hatched, eggs are laid."

"That's what I meant to say. I'm just so happy about it, I can't talk straight."

"So when does Tracey start?"

"Her first big scene is Wednesday, but she has to report to makeup today at three. And after that she gets fitted for her costumes. I have to go over to Mr. Lawrence's office at noon to pick up an official script for her. I'll run lines with her tonight so she can practice."

"Run lines?"

"Yes. That's what they call it in the biz. You know, I'll read the line before hers, and she'll respond with her line."

Hannah debated silently for a moment and then she decided she'd better take her sister into her confidence. "You said you're going to Mr. Lawrence's trailer?"

"Yes, at noon."

"Well, be careful."

"Why?" Andrea stopped with the cookie midway to her mouth.

"He has quite a reputation with women."

"How do *you* know? Did he make a pass at you?"

"I'm not sure."

Andrea dropped her cookie back on the napkin. "How can you *not* be sure if somebody made a pass at you? It's not rocket science, you know. They either did, or they didn't."

"I couldn't tell for sure. I was wearing my big parka coat, and he brushed past me in a small space, and . . . never mind. Let's just say a reputable source told me he does that sort of thing, and you'd be smart if you took someone with you, just in case."

"Don't worry about me. I can handle myself around

men. I've never been unfaithful to Bill and I never will be." Andrea tossed her head and a hard look came into her eyes. "I just wish I could say the same for Bill!"

Hannah gulped. Her sister had been sweetness and light just a second ago, and now she looked as if she could spit nails. "What happened?"

"Absolutely nothing and that's the problem."

"I don't understand."

"Bill called me last night and we talked for a long time. I was just getting ready for bed when I realized that I hadn't told him about the car."

"What about the car?"

"Cyril Murphy says it needs new tires on the back, but that's not important. What's important is that I called Bill back in his hotel room, and there was no answer."

"Maybe he was sleeping?"

"Bill's been a cop for too long. Even if he's dead beat, he always wakes up when the phone rings."

"Well . . . maybe he stepped out for a minute to stretch his legs, or something like that."

"At two in the morning?"

"Um . . . that *is* pretty late." Hannah searched her mind for another excuse. "Maybe he couldn't sleep and he went down to the bar for a nightcap."

"The bar closes at one."

"Oh. Well . . . maybe you dialed the wrong number."

"That's what I thought, at first. But then I called the hotel switchboard and I asked them to connect me directly."

"And there was still no answer?" Andrea nodded and Hannah saw her sister's eyes begin to glisten with unshed tears. "Don't jump to conclusions, Andrea. I'm sure there's some explanation."

"That's exactly what I'm afraid of!"

Oh, boy! Hannah said under her breath.

"Well?" Andrea asked, lifting her chin and looking straight into her sister's eyes. "What do you think I should do?"

"There's only one thing *to* do," Hannah replied quickly. "Eat chocolate. Just sit here and try to relax and I'll get you a whole plateful of cookies."

CHERRY CHEESECAKE

Preheat oven to 350 degrees F., rack in the middle position

For the crust:

2 cups vanilla wafer cookie crumbs ***(measure AFTER crushing)***
¾ stick melted butter ***(6 Tablespoons)***
1 teaspoon almond extract

Pour melted butter and almond extract over cookie crumbs. Mix with a fork until they're evenly moistened.

Cut a circle of parchment paper ***(or wax paper)*** to fit inside the bottom of a 9-inch Springform pan. Spray the pan with Pam or some other non-stick cooking spray, set the paper circle in place, and spray with Pam again.

Dump the moistened cookie crumbs in the pan and press them down over the paper circle and one-inch up the sides. Stick the pan in the freezer for 15 to 30 minutes while you prepare the rest of the cheesecake.

For the topping:

2 cups sour cream
½ cup white ***(granulated)*** sugar
1 teaspoon vanilla

21-ounce can cherry pie filling*** ***(I used Comstock Dark Sweet Cherry)***

*** If you don't like canned pie filling, make your own with canned or frozen cherries, sugar, and cornstarch.

Mix the sour cream, sugar, and vanilla together in a small bowl. Cover and refrigerate. Set the unopened can of cherry pie filling in the refrigerator for later.

For the cheesecake batter:

1 cup white ***(granulated)*** sugar
3 eight-ounce packages cream cheese at room temperature ***(total 24 ounces)***
1 cup mayonnaise ***(not Miracle Whip)***
4 eggs

2 cups white chocolate chips ***(11- or 12-ounce bag—I used Ghirardelli's)***
2 teaspoons vanilla

Place the sugar in the bowl of an electric mixer. Add the blocks of cream cheese and the mayonnaise, and whip it up at medium speed until it's smooth. Add the eggs, one at a time, beating after each addition.

Melt the white chocolate chips in a microwave-safe bowl for 2 minutes. ***(Chips may retain their shape, so stir to see if they're melted—if not, microwave in 15-second increments until you can stir them smooth.)*** Cool the melted white chocolate for a minute or two and then mix it in gradually at slow speed. Scrape down the bowl and add the vanilla, mixing it in thoroughly.

Pour the batter on top of the chilled crust, set the pan on a cookie sheet to catch any drips, and bake it at 350 degrees F. for 55 minutes. Remove the pan from the oven, but DON'T SHUT OFF THE OVEN.

Starting in the center, spoon the sour cream topping over the top of the cheesecake, spreading it out to within a half-inch of the rim. Return the pan to the oven and bake for an additional 5 minutes.

Cool the cheesecake in the pan on a wire rack. When the pan is cool enough to pick up with your bare hands, place it in the refrigerator and chill it, uncovered, for at least 8 hours.

To serve, run a knife around the inside rim of the pan, release the Springform catch, and lift off the rim. Place a piece of waxed paper on a flat plate and tip it upside down over the top of your cheesecake. Invert the cheesecake so that it rests on the paper.

Carefully pry off the bottom of the Springform pan and remove the paper from the bottom crust.

Invert a serving platter over the bottom crust of your cheesecake. Flip the cheesecake right side up, take off the top plate, and remove the waxed paper.

Spread the cherry pie filling over the sour cream topping on your cheesecake. You can drizzle a little down the sides if you wish.

Hannah's Note: I've made this cheesecake with other pie fillings including blueberry, apple, raspberry, and even lemon. It's wonderful with any one you choose.

Mother says you have to serve this cheesecake with strong coffee—it's just too rich to eat without something to sip.

Chapter Ten

"I feel *much* better," Andrea said, finishing her last cookie and giving her older sister a half smile. "It's almost as good as rocking Bethany and having her fall asleep in my arms. These are my new favorite cookies, Hannah. What do you call them?"

"Mock Turtles. They've got pecans, caramel, and chocolate, just like the candy."

"That's a great name. They even look like turtles."

Hannah nodded, not mentioning that the candy had been named for the same reason.

"Why does chocolate always make you feel better?"

"I think it's the endorphins, but I don't know for sure. Whatever it is, it works."

"They should set up a chocolate stand in every courthouse, right outside the divorce court."

Uh-oh, Hannah thought, searching desperately for something to say to get her sister's mind off divorce. "Maybe Herb should pass out chocolates every time he writes a parking ticket."

"It might help," Andrea said, squaring her shoulders.

"There's probably a perfectly good explanation and I'll laugh when I hear it. I just don't know what it is yet."

"I'm sure you're right," Hannah agreed, knowing that her sister was still thinking about the unanswered call to her husband in the wee, small hours of the morning.

"Maybe he left a message for me on my voice mail," Andrea reached for her cell phone, the small leather-bound notebook she used to jot down messages, and the expensive pen that fit in a leather loop on the front of the notebook. "I'd better check."

Hannah watched as her sister began to retrieve her messages and write them down. She'd learned to read upside down at an early age, and she knew it was due to innate laziness more than a desire to learn an unusual skill. One of her responsibilities as Andrea and Michelle's big sister had been to listen to them read aloud before bedtime. They'd always sat cross-legged on the foot of her bed, facing Hannah as she'd rested on the pillows propped up against the headboard. It had been easier for her to learn to read upside down, providing the occasional unknown word for them from her comfortable perch, than to get out of bed and walk around to peer at the page over their shoulders.

Mall—Business Cards, Andrea wrote in her perfectly formed script at the top of the small page. Then she paused for a moment, the tip of her pen double-underlining the underline she'd placed at the bottom of the first message.

The pen moved again and Hannah squinted. It was a lot easier to read printing than cursive, but she persevered. *Formula,* the next note read. Unless Andrea had suddenly developed an interest in higher mathematics, Grandma McCann, Bethany's live-in babysitter, must have called to remind her to pick up baby food on the way home.

"Uh-oh!" Andrea breathed, and Hannah watched as the next notation took form. *Three dozen snacks—room mothers' meeting today!* Andrea underlined the word *today* three times for emphasis and then she pressed a button on the phone and lifted it from her ear. "Hannah? I'm in deep trouble. Could you possibly . . . ?"

"Sure, if cookies will do it. How about three dozen or so?"

"That's perfect! But how did you know I needed something?"

"I guess the sister–sister radar must be working," Hannah said with a shrug.

Andrea frowned slightly and Hannah held her breath. Had she remembered their bedtime reading and Hannah's ability to provide a word without getting up? But Andrea gave a little shrug and then she smiled. "You're the best, Hannah. I was going to stop at the Red Owl to pick up some squeezable pimento cheese spread and crackers, but I forgot they'd be closed."

"That's okay," Hannah said, trying not to shudder. Her taste buds lumped squeezable cheese spread in the same category as instant coffee.

Andrea punched another number on her phone and picked up her pen again. She listened for a moment and then she began to smile as the tip of her pen formed a heart on the page.

A moment later, the phone, notebook, and pen were back in Andrea's neatly organized purse and she was smiling from ear to ear. "Guess what happened?"

"You won the lottery."

"No, but it's every bit as good as that. Bill's phone was unplugged! He didn't realize it until he got up this morning, and he was an hour late for his first seminar. He stopped by the desk and chewed them out for not giving him his wakeup call, but they said they did and he didn't answer. They sent a maid up to his room to check it out and she discovered that one of Bill's pillows had slipped down behind the headboard and knocked his phone cord loose in the middle of the night!"

"So you worried for nothing," Hannah said, giving her sister a big smile.

"I guess so! I mean, it's the oldest excuse in the book. You know, *I was home all night. There must have been something wrong with the phone,* but that's exactly what happened. At least that's what Bill told me."

As Hannah watched, Andrea's smile faded and she began to chew on her lower lip, something she hadn't done, to Hannah's knowledge, since Miss Bruder caught her putting on eye shadow in the girl's bathroom in fifth grade.

"What do you think, Hannah?" she asked, looking up at her older sister anxiously. "Am I a fool for believing a tired old excuse like that?"

Hannah didn't even have to think about her answer, since there was only one reply. "Absolutely not," she said.

"But . . . what if Bill's lying to me?"

"What if he is? Do you want to divorce him?"

"No! I love Bill!"

"Then you have to choose to believe him. Maybe he's lying and your trust will be misplaced, but that's a whole lot better than not believing him when he's telling you the truth."

Andrea thought about that for a long moment. "That makes perfect sense. You're a wise woman, Hannah."

"Not really," Hannah said with a smile. "If I were that wise, I'd be independently wealthy, happily married, and Congress would declare me a national treasure. And so far, I'm none of the above."

After Andrea had left with the box of cookies for her afternoon meeting, Hannah sat back down at the work island and lingered over the last few sips of coffee in her mug. She could hear faint conversation and an occasional laugh from the coffee shop, but those sounds were perfectly benign. There were no yowls from her thespian tomcat, not even the slightest mew. As far as she could tell, Moishe was behaving perfectly.

"It's quiet . . . too quiet," Hannah recited the line she'd heard in dozens of grade B cowboy movies. The line always occurred right before the Indians attacked, and even though Hannah knew exactly what was going to happen, those four words still put her on the edge of her seat. She felt like that now, just waiting for Moishe to kick up a fuss. Finally, unable to stand the tension any longer, Hannah got up and headed to the coffee shop to see how her furry friend was doing.

As she pushed open the door, Hannah heard someone speaking in the artificially high voice people tend to use when they're talking to infants. The source of the sound was Sophie, the wardrobe mistress, but there was no baby in sight. The *handsome sweetums* Sophie was addressing was none other than Hannah's cat!

Moishe was holding court at the big round table by the window. He was sitting in the middle of the table, a rumbling, purring centerpiece surrounded by doting admirers. It was no wonder her cat was content. Hannah counted no less than five hands petting him. As she stood there watching, she heard other terms of endearment, *sweety love*, *magnificent fellow*, and *cuddlewuddles* among them. Everyone at the table seemed to be worshipping at the throne of Moishe, and Moishe took it as his due. He was squinting in pleasure and wearing the biggest kitty smile Hannah had ever seen.

"Pushover," Hannah murmured as she passed by the table, but she wasn't at all upset. Moishe was a glutton for affection and it was clear that he was having a wonderful time. As long as the kitty fans kept coming in and the fawning continued unabated, bring-your-pet-to-work week might not be the nightmare she'd envisioned this morning.

Lisa was just passing out the box lunches that Sally had sent for the crew and cast when the bell on the front door tinkled and Hannah looked up to see Dean Lawrence. Lynne was with him, holding his arm, and her college friend looked fabulous in a fifties-style sweater dress. Her hair was fashioned in a pageboy style and Hannah came close to hearing the strains of "Love Me Tender," or "Hound Dog" from a long-dead Elvis as she looked at the sort of girl he would have admired.

"Smell," Lynne said, holding out her wrist, inside up, the way they used to do when they'd gone shopping and sampled everything at the perfume counter. "Bet you ten bucks you don't know this one."

Hannah sniffed and then she laughed. "You lose. It's *Evening in Paris* and my grandmother used to wear it."

"She's absolutely amazing," Lynne explained to Dean. "I think her sense of smell is almost as well developed as her taste buds. That's why she's such a good cook. All she has to do is smell something and taste it, and she knows what's in it."

"Well, I don't know what's in that cheesecake, but it's great!" Dean said, kissing the air next to Hannah's cheek, and then giving her a little squeeze around the waist. "I knew it would be good just looking at it, but I didn't think it would be *that* good."

"He said it was the best he ever tasted," Lynne told Hannah.

"That's right. I'll want two every day, one in the morning and one right after lunch. Can you do that?"

"Absolutely."

"There's something else." Dean leaned closer and looked directly into her eyes. "It's a bit of a challenge."

The warning bells in Hannah's head began to clang. Whenever something was described as a challenge, it was usually impossible to achieve.

"I want to serve cherry cheesecake at the premiere. The only problem is, we're doing champagne and finger food. You know what finger food is, don't you, Lovey?"

"Of course," Hannah said stifling the urge to *plant him a facer*, a Regency English term that she'd picked up while catering coffee and cookies at the Lake Eden Regency Romance Club. *Planting him a facer* meant hitting him in the face and that's what Hannah felt like doing. In addition to his casual touches that bordered on the intimate, which she didn't appreciate, Dean was being very condescending. Just because she lived in a small town didn't mean that she was totally unsophisticated.

"Do you think you can figure out a way to make mini cherry cheesecakes so we can put them on a tray and serve them as appetizers?"

"Maybe," Hannah said, not at all sure she could do it, but willing to try. "It can't be my cherry cheesecake made smaller, though."

"Why not?"

"It won't work. It all has to do with specific gravity." When Dean looked at her blankly, Hannah began to smile. She'd snow him with gobbledygook until his eyes glazed over to get even for implying that she was unsophisticated.

"The cheesecake I baked for you is enclosed in a metal springform, with a lubricated underlay for the carrier ingredients. It's not baked in the traditional slow oven and that means it needs to solidify without granulating. Smaller containers would counter these parameters, and I doubt that experimenting with different media would yield positive results."

"Oh."

Dean's eyes were sufficiently glassy and Hannah decided it was time to back off. "Let's just say that the cheesecake I make for you is special. If I changed the size, I'd have to change the whole recipe."

"I can understand that. I really don't want to share my cheesecake with the general public anyway. Go ahead and bake another kind."

"I'll have something for you to test in a couple of days,"

Hannah promised, hoping that she hadn't bitten off more than she could chew. "If it works out, maybe you can use it in the cocktail scene. That would be a good tie-in with the movie, wouldn't it?"

"In the . . . yes! Yes, it would! The audience would see those little beauties being passed around by the waitresses. And then, when they came out to the lobby after the movie, they'd get to actually taste them! That's a wonderful idea. I'm so glad I thought of it!"

Oh brother! Hannah mouthed as Dean walked away. He'd taken her idea and claimed it as his own in less than twenty seconds. That had to be some sort of a record, even for a director with an ego as big as a double-wide pole barn.

MOCK TURTLE COOKIES

Do Not Preheat Oven—Dough Must Chill Before Baking

1½ sticks chilled butter ***(¾ cup)***
2 cups flour
¾ cup powdered ***(confectioner's)*** sugar
½ teaspoon salt
½ cup chocolate chips ***(I used Ghirardelli's semi-sweet)***
1 egg, beaten
approximately 3 dozen Kraft Caramels ***(the soft kind that's individually wrapped—they're about a half-inch square)***

Cut the butter into 12 pieces and place them in a work bowl. With two forks, mix in the flour, powdered sugar, and salt. Continue mixing until the dough is crumbly.

Hannah's Note: You can also do this in a food processor with the steel blade the same way you'd mix piecrust. It's a lot easier that way.

Melt the chocolate chips in a small microwave-safe bowl ***(I use a glass measuring cup)*** for 40 seconds on HIGH. Stir them to see if they're melted.

(Chocolate chips may maintain their shape until they're stirred.) If they're not melted, microwave them in 20-second intervals until they are.

Add the melted chips to the dough mixture. Stir ***(or process, if you've used a food processor)*** until the chocolate is mixed in and the crumbly dough is a uniform color. Beat the egg in a small cup or bowl and add it to the work bowl. Mix it in ***(or process with the steel blade)*** until a soft, piecrust-type dough results.

Divide the dough into four equal parts. Tear off four pieces of wax paper about a foot and a half long. You'll use these to hold your dough when you roll it out. Turn a piece of wax paper so that the long side faces you and place one piece of dough in the center. Using your hands, roll the dough into a log that's approximately 12 inches long and ¾ inch thick. Do the same for the three remaining pieces of dough.

Wrap the rolls in the wax paper you used to roll them and put them into a freezer bag. Freeze them for an hour or two until firm. ***(Overnight is fine, too.)***

When you're ready to bake, take out the dough and let it warm up on the counter for fifteen minutes. Then preheat the oven to 325 degrees F., rack in the middle position.

Unwrap a roll of dough and cut it into ¾ inch pieces with a sharp knife. Place the pieces cut side down on a greased, or parchment-covered cookie sheet, 12 pieces to a standard-sized sheet.

Unwrap 6 caramels and cut them in half. I find this is easiest if you dip the blades of your kitchen scissors in water and then cut the caramels with the scissors.

Press a half caramel into the center of each chocolate cookie. Be careful not to press it all the way to the bottom. ***(If the dough is still too cold to press in the caramels, let it warm up a bit more and try again.)*** Make sure your caramels are surrounded by cookie dough and won't melt over the sides of the cookies when they bake.

Bake each pan of cookies at 325 degrees F., for approximately 15 minutes, or until firm to the touch. Let the cookies cool for a minute or two on the pan

and then remove them to a wire rack to complete cooling.

When all the cookies are baked and cooled, spread foil or waxed paper under the wire rack containing the cookies and prepare to glaze them. ***(I use extra-wide foil because it's easy to crimp up the edges and make it into a disposable drip pan.)***

Chocolate Glaze:

⅓ cup water
⅓ cup light corn syrup ***(I used Karo)***
1 cup white ***(granulated)*** sugar
1⅓ cup milk chocolate chips ***(8 ounces—I used Ghirardelli's)***

Approximately 6 dozen pecan halves

Measure out the chips and put them in a small bowl so they're ready to add when it's time.

In a saucepan, combine the water, corn syrup, and white sugar. Place the saucepan on high heat, and STIRRING CONSTANTLY, bring the contents to a boil. Boil for 15 seconds, still STIRRING CONSTANTLY, and pull it off the heat.

Dump in the chips, all at once, and poke them down until almost all of them are covered by the hot syrup mixture. Let the saucepan sit on a cold burner ***(or on a pad on the counter)*** for 2½ minutes.

Gently stir the mixture with a whisk ***(a fork will also work)*** until it's almost completely smooth. Be careful not to whisk in air, or you'll get bubbles.

Set the glaze down on a potholder next to your cookies. Spoon a little over the top of each cookie and let it drizzle down the sides. ***(You can also pour it over the cookies, but that's a little harder to do.)*** When you're all through, top each cookie with a pecan half, making sure the nut sticks to the chocolate glaze.

Leave the cookies on the wire rack until the glaze has hardened. This will take approximately 30 minutes. Then eat and enjoy!

Lisa's Note: When I'm in a hurry and don't have time to glaze the cookies, I just sprinkle them with a little powdered sugar, serve them with chocolate ice cream, and call it a day.

Hannah's Note: Norman says to warn any friends with temporary fillings that the caramels in the center of these cookies are chewy.

Another Note: You can store these cookies in a box lined with wax paper in the refrigerator, but take them out at least thirty minutes before you serve them so that the caramel in the center will soften and not break a tooth!

Yield: Approximately 6 dozen very tasty cookies.

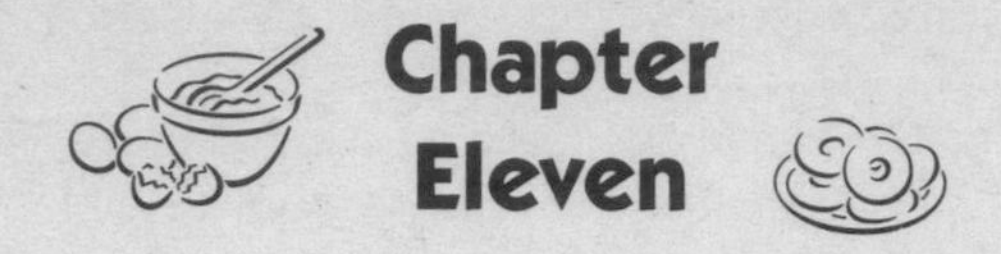

Chapter Eleven

Hannah checked the list of names that Sally had sent along with the box lunches. It was one-thirty, and everyone had been served with the exception of Ross, Burke Anson, and Dean's chauffeur, Connor. Hannah was about to take the remaining lunches back to the walk-in cooler in the kitchen when Ross came in with Burke.

"Sorry we're late," Ross said, coming around the counter to give her a hug, and then standing there with his arm around her shoulders. "Burke and I got hung up on a line rewrite for the scene we're shooting this afternoon."

"Line rewrite?" Hannah asked, picking up on the phrase. She thought she knew what it meant, but she wasn't absolutely certain.

"Small changes," Ross explained, "that don't affect the staging of the scene, or the basic motivation. Burke thought Jody should stammer slightly whenever Amy brought up their father."

"As a clue that Jody killed him?"

"Right. I mean, we're not going to hit them over the head with it, just give a little suggestion of a stammer. Amy's not going to react right then, but later she'll remember and it'll be another almost subliminal indication for her to add to the mix."

"I'll go tell Lynne and Erica what we decided," Burke said, taking his lunch and heading over to the table where Lynne was sitting with Erica James and her mother. Jeanette didn't look happy. Was the strain of corralling her daughter too much for her to handle? Then Hannah noticed someone who looked even unhappier than Jeanette James, and she experienced a jolt of surprise. Norman was positively glaring at Ross. Was it because Ross had his arm around her shoulders? Or was there another reason?

"Uh-oh," Ross said and dropped his arm. "The town dentist looks less than friendly right now. I didn't know he was the jealous type."

"He isn't. Not usually."

"Maybe I'd better take my lunch and go, before he decides to botch up my leading man's caps."

Hannah shot him a sharp look. "Norman would never do that! He's a professional."

"Just kidding," Ross said, but he didn't give her another hug before he walked away to take a chair at Dean's table.

Next in the door was Connor. Hannah knew it was Connor without being introduced because he wore a black chauffeur's uniform. The handsome silver-haired man stepped up to the counter and flashed Hannah a friendly smile.

"Hi, Connor," Hannah said, before he could introduce himself. "I'm Hannah and here's your lunch."

"Nice to meet you, Hannah. I've heard so much about you."

Connor seemed like a nice man, Hannah thought, as he took the box containing his lunch. He was just turning to leave the counter when Dean rushed up to intercept him.

"Connor!" the director stood directly in front of him, blocking his way. "Did you get a signed release from that Henderson woman so we can use the park?"

"No, Mr. Lawrence. I did my best to convince her, but she refused to sign."

Dean's eyes hardened into slits and Hannah could tell he didn't like being denied. "Even after you offered her my incentive?"

"Yes, Mr. Lawrence."

"Cranky old biddy!" Dean muttered. "All right then, I'll just have to raise the stakes. Do it in increments of a hundred until she signs on the dotted line."

Connor nodded and Hannah suspected he'd done this sort of work before. "Yes, Mr. Lawrence. I'll need to know the ceiling."

"Five grand. Six is a deal breaker. If we have to, we can always move to another location. Remind her that we don't really *need* her cooperation. The mayor's already given us the go ahead."

"Is that true, sir?" Connor looked uncertain. "I was under the impression that she controlled the land and its use until her death."

"She does, but I wouldn't expect a woman who's lived on a farm all her life to know the fine points of law. And if it comes down to the wire, who knows? Some of these local yokels who've got a part in that scene might just take things into their own hands. All we have to do is tell them they can't be in the movie because the Henderson woman won't give us permission to use the park."

Hannah did all she could do not to gasp as Dean's words sank in and she realized what he meant. She didn't think he was seriously considering doing away with Winnie Henderson, but he was a callous person to even joke about it!

"Try to buy her cooperation for three," Dean went on. "It's probably more money than she's seen in her whole life. If you can manage that, there'll be a little extra something in your paycheck this week."

"Thank you, Mr. Lawrence." Connor stood there waiting for further instructions.

"Go do it now. You can eat your lunch later. And don't be late for your scene."

"No, Mr. Lawrence."

Connor turned to go, but Dean grabbed his arm. "Did you get the Tattingers?"

Hannah tried not to react as she recognized the name of the famous champagne. She'd tasted it once at an upscale party and actually priced it out at the mall. Since it sold for more than her car payment, she hadn't purchased a bottle.

"Yes, Mr. Lawrence, two bottles. They're in your office."

"Refrigerated?"

"Naturally, sir."

"Good man, Connor. Where did you have to go to find it?"

"A little place called the Wine Cave at the Tri-County Mall."

"Where's that?"

"About forty minutes from here, sir."

"Very good. You've been a busy little beaver, Connor. Remind me to give you some time off when we finish up here. And if there's any champagne left, I'll recork it and save it for you."

"Yes, sir. Thank you, Mr. Lawrence." Connor waited until his employer had gone back to his place at the table, and then he turned to leave.

"Wait a second, Connor," Hannah called him back.

"Yes, Ma'am?"

"It's Hannah. You don't have to *Ma'am* me. Since you're working through lunch, would you like a cup of coffee to go?"

"Yes, I would. Thank you very much."

Hannah filled the largest Styrofoam cup she had and clamped on a lid. "Here you go, the best cup of Swedish Plasma in the country."

"Thanks," Connor said with a chuckle, but he quickly sobered. "I know you heard what Mr. Lawrence said to me and I just want you to know that I like Mrs. Henderson, and there's no way I'm going to cheat her, even if it means disappointing Mr. Lawrence."

"You're a nice man, Connor. And it can't be easy to be nice when you work for Mr. Lawrence."

Connor smiled, but he didn't say a word and Hannah gave him points for that. And then, just because Connor *was* a nice man who worked for a condescending unfeeling director who was the total opposite of nice, she stuck her foot in firmly where it didn't belong. "If you have any trouble convincing Winnie to sign that release form, come and get me. I know her and maybe I can help."

"Mini cherry cheesecakes?" Lisa asked, repeating what Hannah had just told her.

"That's right. He said he needs something that can be passed around on a tray at the premiere. They're doing all finger food."

"So we've got a while to come up with a recipe?"

Hannah shook her head. "All we have is two days."

"But they won't have the premiere until the movie's all finished, and edited, and whatever else they do to it."

"True, but I stuck my big foot in it and that's why we have a time crunch. I suggested that they use the mini cherry cheesecakes in the cocktail scene and then there'd be a tie-in with the premiere."

"That's a great idea! So Mr. Lawrence must have liked it a lot if he's going to do it."

"Oh, he loved it," Hannah said, giving a wry grin. "He loved it so much he stole it."

"Stole it? What do you mean?"

"By the time we were finished talking, he was saying that it was *his* idea."

"That figures," Lisa said, shaking her head. "He isn't the

type to give anyone else credit. I knew he wasn't a nice person five minutes after he sat down at the table."

"How did you know that?"

"I was going around with the coffee carafe and I stopped at his table. I asked if he wanted a refill and he held out his cup. That's all he did, he just held up his cup. He kept right on talking to Mr. Barton and let me give him a refill. And after I did, he just put his cup down in front of him. He didn't even bother to look up or say thank you! Everyone else at the table did, but not him. He thinks he's too big for his own britches!"

Hannah couldn't help it, she laughed. The old-fashioned phrase sounded strange coming from a woman who'd just turned twenty. "You sound like your grandma," she said.

"I know. I've always loved that saying. It makes me think of a smart-mouthed guy running around without pants."

"Lisa!" Hannah was slightly shocked. Her normally very proper and slightly naïve partner had loosened up a lot now that she was married.

"Well, it does. Not that I'd like to see Mr. Lawrence that way!" A little color climbed up Lisa's cheeks and Hannah knew she was about to change the subject to something less embarrassing. "So we need those mini cheesecakes by Wednesday?"

"That's right. Do you have any ideas?"

Lisa looked thoughtful for a moment. "Let me work on it, Hannah. I've seen something like that, and I think my mother used to make them. I'll look through her recipe file and if I don't find it there, I'll ask Dad if he remembers."

"Do you think he might?" Hannah asked, hoping that Jack Herman's memory would come through for them. He'd taken part in an Alzheimer's study and the "cocktail" of three new drugs he'd tested had helped tremendously.

"Maybe," Lisa said, shrugging slightly. "And maybe not.

We'll just have to wait and see. I hope he does, because it makes him so happy when he remembers something."

As Lisa refilled the carafe with hot water and stocked up on tea bags for the tea drinkers who wanted a second cup, Hannah thought about what she'd said. The comment was typical of her kind-hearted partner who saw life's cookie jar half full instead of half empty. Of course Lisa wanted to track down the recipe, but that was less important than making her father happy.

"Hannah?"

Hannah turned from the kitchen counter, where she was restocking one of the serving jars, to see Norman standing just inside the swinging door.

"Do you have a minute?" he asked.

"That's exactly what I've got, one minute. We're out of cookies and Lisa's waiting for these. Just let me carry them out to her and I'll have a lot more than one minute."

"I'll help," Norman said, picking up two of the jars, one containing Molasses Crackles, and the other filled with Boggles. Hannah grabbed the jar with Lisa's White Chocolate Supremes, and the one filled with Cinnamon Crisps, and off they went to the coffee shop.

With both of them carrying, it took only three trips to deliver the cookies. When they came back to the kitchen for the final time, Hannah poured them both a cup of coffee from the kitchen pot, and they sat down on stools at the work island.

"I don't like Dean Lawrence," Norman said out of the blue.

"Neither do I. He's the type of person that makes me appreciate exposure at the city gates."

Norman, who'd looked very serious up to that point, started to laugh. "He must have really gotten to you."

"He did."

"How?"

Hannah ticked the reasons off on her fingers. "He's arrogant, condescending, and callous. He thinks Winnie Henderson is dumb just because she lives on a farm, and he called the people who live in Lake Eden *local yokels*. He steals other people's ideas, he has no respect for anyone, and to top it off, he thinks he's irresistible to women!"

"But other than that, you like him okay?"

Hannah's jaw dropped open and then she giggled, something she hadn't done since seventh grade. Norman was being sarcastic and she'd fallen for it. "You got me, Norman."

"If only I did!" Norman sounded very serious and Hannah's giggles stopped abruptly. "That's one of the reasons I followed you into the kitchen. I need to talk to you in private."

Hannah's early warning system activated. If Ross was right and Norman was jealous, that jealousy might prod him into another declaration. "You're not going to ask me to marry you again, are you?"

"Not today. My ego's had all it can take for the month. This is something different."

Hannah discovered she'd been holding her breath without realizing it and she exhaled quickly. "What is it, Norman?"

"Remember that letter you found in Lucy Richards's desk? The one I said I'd let you read if I ever asked you to marry me?"

Hannah started holding her breath again and this time it was deliberate. Of course she remembered the letter! It had come from the Seattle Police Department and it had just about killed her not to open it. After she'd handed it over, still tightly sealed, Norman had told her it held information about him that might just kill his mother if it were to be made public. And while this information might not put him out of business in Lake Eden, it would certainly change his patients' opinion of him.

"You remember the letter, don't you, Hannah?" Norman prompted.

"Yes. Yes, I do," Hannah managed to say, and a tingle of apprehension ran through her. Was Norman going to tell her his secret at long last?

"Well I didn't let you read the letter before I proposed. And I need to know if that's why you turned me down."

"No," Hannah said, quite honestly. "The letter had nothing to do with my decision. I just chose not to choose right then. I explained all that down at the café."

"Okay, I just had to check. It was really bothering me. I figured if that letter was the only thing standing between fried egg sandwiches at my bachelor kitchen table and happily ever after with you, I'd bite the bullet and publish the darned thing in the *Lake Eden Journal*."

Hannah's eyes widened. "But you said it would just about kill your mother!"

"I didn't mean it literally. It would embarrass her a lot, but I'm pretty sure she'd get over it eventually."

"You'd take a chance like that?"

"Yes, if you'd marry me."

Hannah was silent for a long moment. She knew Norman adored his mother, but he must love her even more. She was tempted, sorely tempted to say yes, but she couldn't.

"Hannah? Should I take that letter to Rod at the paper? I really will do it, you know."

"I know. And that's very sweet, but I can't marry you." Hannah saw Norman's face fall and she softened her response, ". . . at least not yet."

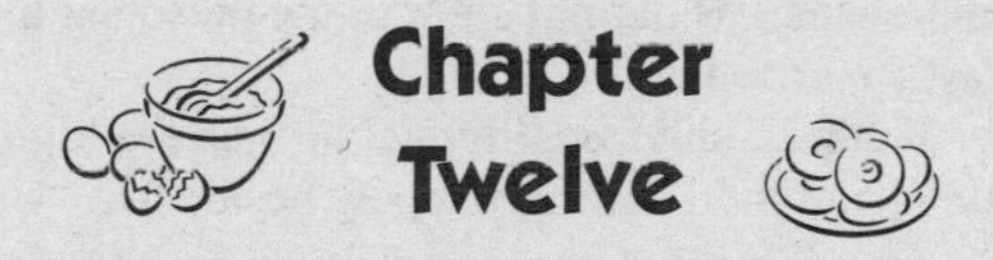

Chapter Twelve

"Ouch!" Hannah yelped, staring down at her pet in surprise. Moishe's ears were back and his fur was beginning to bristle. She might have followed her earlier ouch with something a bit more colorful, but it was Tuesday, Moishe was filming his second scene in *Crisis in Cherry wood*, and she was sitting in a pew at Holy Redeemer Lutheran Church. Even though Moishe's claws were needle sharp and her thighs stung from the punctures, swearing would not have been appropriate.

"He's nervous," Norman said, collecting Moishe from his perch on Hannah's lap. "I'll take him outside and walk him around a little. Just come and get me when they're ready for him."

At first Hannah thought Norman had something in his eye, because he winked at her several times. She was about to ask him what was wrong when she spotted the cause for Norman's wink, her feline's anxiety, and the little puncture marks Moishe's claws had left on her denim clad legs. Delores was approaching, striding hurriedly up the center aisle, and not even the lure of Hollywood fame would keep her cat docile when he caught sight of the person at the top of his Least Favorite list.

"Hello, Mother," she said, giving Norman the high sign to skedaddle, and then patting the pew beside her. "Have a seat."

"Thank you, dear. I know I'm early, but I wanted to see Moishe's scene. I missed out yesterday."

Now this is a fine pickle, Hannah thought, using her father's term to describe a dilemma. She had to think of some way to get her mother as far away from Moishe as possible.

"I'd love to have you watch," Hannah said, clutching onto the first excuse that occurred to her, "but Tracey's going to be disappointed."

"What do you mean? Andrea told me that Tracey's first scene isn't being filmed until later tomorrow."

"That's true, but they're working on her hair and makeup right now down at the Cut 'n Curl. And after that, she's being fitted for her costumes. I just naturally assumed that you'd want to be there, especially since Bill's in Miami and Andrea's dealing with all these stage mother things alone."

"You're absolutely right! Thank you for telling me, dear." Delores rose to her feet with a grateful smile. "Of course she'd never say anything, but with Bill gone and all, she's bound to want someone with her . . . not to mention how much better Tracey would feel with Grandma there."

Hannah watched her mother rush out and she gave a huge sigh of relief. She was free at last, but she'd have to pay the price. Once Andrea figured out what had brought Delores descending on them like a cloud of locusts, she'd owe her sister a whole batch of cookies and then some!

"Incredible!" Clark said, turning to Hannah with a smile. "Just look at that. He's giving me his best profile."

Hannah smiled and nodded. She wasn't sure what else

to do. It was true that Moishe was being amazingly cooperative, holding the poses that Dean called for, and not moving until he said that it was a wrap.

"Only one more to go," Dean said, motioning to Erica, who was waiting in the front pew. "Hannah's going to put him in your lap. When she's out of the scene, pick him up in your arms and take him with you when you walk up to the coffin to view your father. Stand there for a minute looking sad, and then go back and sit down."

Hannah placed Moishe on Erica's lap and waited for the fireworks to start. Moishe didn't like being held by people he didn't know and she hoped the movie company had plenty of insurance. But when Erica picked Moishe up and cuddled him to her chest, something Hannah was sure would earn her a royal slashing with both front and back claws, her cat surprised her so much she gasped out loud.

Instead of lashing out, Moishe gave Erica his best kitty smile, the one where his eyes turned to slits and his cheeks rounded out. And then he let her lug him up to the casket, held in a position that Hannah knew couldn't possibly be comfortable. When she lifted him up so that he could see inside, Moishe licked her cheek, just as if he knew he was supposed to comfort her. Was her cat an actor? Most assuredly! If Moishe hadn't been dreaming dreams of stardom, he would have torn the expensive black silk suit Erica was wearing to shreds.

"I've got a lead, Hannah!" Lisa rushed up to her the moment Hannah came back into The Cookie Jar.

"That's nice," Hannah said, plunking Moishe down on one of the tables and tethering his leash to the leg. "A lead on what?"

"The mini cherry cheesecake appetizers. Dad didn't recall them when I asked him last night, but this morning he remembered that Mom got the recipe from a neighbor, Mary

Hutchinson. She lived across the street from us at the end of the block. But Mary and Marv moved to Iowa and I don't have a forwarding address. Who do you think might . . . ?" Lisa stopped speaking in midthought and began to smile. "Andrea!"

"Yes, Andrea might know. She's sold a lot of houses in Lake Eden and I'm sure the seller has to leave a forwarding address."

"And we can ask her, because she's here right now!"

Lisa motioned toward the door and Hannah turned to see her sister opening it. Andrea looked about as far from happy as anyone could get and for a brief moment, Hannah was puzzled. Then she remembered sending their mother to the Cut 'n Curl to "advise" Andrea on Tracey's makeup and costumes. It had taken less than an hour, but the chickens had come home to roost. Her stylish sister had a frown on her face that looked every bit as rugged as the topography of the Pyrenees. Andrea was loaded for bear and Hannah harbored the unfortunate suspicion that she was Ursa Major.

"Well . . . all right," Andrea conceded, choosing another of the chocolate truffles Hannah had stashed in the walk-in cooler for precisely this type of emergency. "I guess I forgive you, but it *was* a dirty trick fobbing Mother off on me that way."

"I know. It's just that I don't like pain and Moishe was grating the skin on my legs like lemon peel."

"That sounds painful," Lisa said, giving Hannah her next line.

"It was. And I figured maybe Mother would relieve you and you could come over and see Moishe act."

"I just came from the church and Reverend Knudson told me you'd already left. How did Moishe do?"

"He's a natural born actor, at least that's what Dean called him."

"I figured he would be. He's always posing, even when nobody has a camera."

Lisa looked at Hannah and wiggled her eyebrows. Hannah wiggled back in a silent signal that Andrea was calm enough to answer their question.

"We need some information, Andrea," Hannah told her. "And you're the only one who can help us."

"I am?"

"That's right. Do you remember who sold the Hutchinson house, kitty-corner from Lisa's old house?"

"I sold it. It was my first sale as a real estate professional."

"Wonderful!" Lisa gave a relieved smile. "Do you happen to know where the Hutchinsons moved?"

"Someplace in Iowa. Do you need the street address?"

"Yes," Hannah said. "Mary has a recipe for mini cherry cheesecakes and we need it for the cocktail scene in the movie."

"Okay. Just hold on a second and I'll get it for you."

To Hannah's surprise, Andrea took out her cell phone and punched in some numbers. While she was waiting, she took out her pen and her leather-bound notebook and turned to a blank page.

"I'm connected. Hold on," she said to Lisa and Hannah, and then she punched in more information on the phone keypad. There was another wait and then Andrea started to write on the paper. When she was finished, she punched another couple of numbers and switched off the phone, dropped it back in her purse, and handed the page to Lisa. "Here you go. I got the phone number, too."

"How?" Hannah asked, staring at her sister in amazement. "You didn't say a word."

"That's because I wasn't talking to a person. I didn't feel like running back out to the car to get my laptop, so I used my cell phone to connect to the state real estate board's central computer. That's where all the information is stored."

"You can do that?"

"Of course. You really ought to keep up with things, Hannah. Technology's great and you're still stuck in the Dark Ages!"

"Right," Hannah said, looking around her and realizing that her sister had a point. All but one table was filled with afternoon coffee drinkers and at least three out of five people were talking on a cell phone. She counted four laptop computers, and only one person was making notes with a pen.

"At least get a computer. *Everybody's* got a computer. They make life a lot easier."

"Maybe," Hannah said. "I can see where *you* need one, but I'm still not sure about me. I'll make you a promise, though."

"Okay. What?"

"The day that Mother gets a computer, I'll get one too."

"Oh, sure. Like that's going to happen!" Andrea gave a short, little laugh, and then she turned to Lisa. "Go and call Mary now."

"But it's time for me to go around with the coffee carafe."

"I'll do it for you," Andrea volunteered. "Go ahead and make the call. And tell Mary hi from me."

Hannah tried not to show how surprised she was as Andrea got up to don an apron. Her sister had never been this eager to wait on tables before. "You don't have to, you know. I can . . ."

"No, I want to," Andrea insisted, picking up the coffee carafe and bending close so that only Hannah would hear. "I want to find out if that trick you're always talking about really works."

For a moment, Hannah was puzzled, but then she figured it out. "You're talking about the invisible caterer trick?

The one where people keep right on talking, even if it's really private, just as if you're not right there filling up their coffee cups?"

"Yes. Then I'll have some really juicy movie gossip to tell Bill when he calls tonight."

Hannah was amused as Andrea went off to refill coffee cups and gather gossip. She got herself another cup of coffee and sat behind the counter trying to relax. She'd been nervous all day, even though Moishe had been on his best behavior and his scenes had gone off perfectly. It wasn't her cat she was worried about. It was Mike and Norman. And Ross. She thought about Ross, wondering what effect a romance with him would have on the existing triangle she shared with Mike and Norman. Would one more person turn it into a square? Or perhaps a box? It was certainly true that she'd boxed herself in by dating three men!

That brought up another image and Hannah frowned slightly. She'd seen the legendary French mime, Marcel Marceau, perform his routine of a person inside a glass box. Now that her triangle had changed into a box, was she the person inside, trapped there until she chose the right man for her husband?

Chapter Thirteen

Lisa emerged from the kitchen less than ten minutes later. She was waving a piece of paper and wearing the broadest smile Hannah had ever seen.

"You got it?" Hannah guessed, already knowing the answer.

"You bet I got it!" Lisa announced sliding into her chair. "These are just perfect, and they're hardly any work at all. They're made in cupcake papers and they use store-bought vanilla wafers and cherry pie filling!"

Hannah took the paper and glanced down at the title, *Jane's Mini Cherry Cheesecakes*. "Who's Jane? I thought you got this recipe from Mary Hutchinson."

"I did, but she got it from her cousin Jane. What do you think of it?"

Hannah read through one of the easiest and cleverest recipes she'd ever seen. Twenty-four muffin tins were lined with cupcake papers and a vanilla wafer was placed in the bottom. The cheesecake batter was mixed, spooned in on top of the vanilla wafer, and then they were baked. When the mini cheesecakes were cool, they were topped off with three cherries from the can of pie filling and chilled for at least four hours before serving. "That's certainly easy. But are they good?"

"Mary says they're wonderful and everybody always asks her to bring them to parties. The really neat thing is the cherry pie filling."

"Why's that?" Hannah asked, feeling a bit like the straight man in a two-man comedy routine.

"You need three cherries for each little cheesecake and there are exactly seventy-two cherries in a can of pie filling. That means it always comes out even."

"Really?"

"That's what Mary says and she's been making them for a long time. I want to try them now, Hannah. Is that okay?"

"It's fine, but how about the cherry pie filling? We don't have any."

"I already called Florence and she said she'd let me in the back door of the Red Owl. She's doing inventory."

Hannah nodded and Lisa was off in a flash, fairly racing for the kitchen door. When her young partner got enthusiastic about something, she didn't let anything stand in her way. Hannah knew Herb had figured that out early in his relationship with Lisa. When Lisa had made up her mind she wanted to date him, Herb had found himself asking her out. And when Lisa had decided she wanted to marry him, Herb had found himself proposing. Hannah had a feeling their whole marriage would be that way. And she was just as certain that Herb wouldn't mind one bit.

The front door to The Cookie Jar opened and a handsome young man walked in. He was wearing casual clothes, but they fit him perfectly and Hannah had the feeling that they were expensive. She assumed that he was someone from the movie crew she hadn't met and gave him a smile of welcome.

"Hi, Hannah!" the man greeted her. And then he read

the blank expression on her face and laughed. "You don't recognize me?"

Hannah's mind churned as fast as a master butter-maker's tub gone berserk. It was no use. She had no idea who the young man was. She was about to shake her head and admit it when he pointed to the discrete gold stud in one earlobe.

"P. K.?" Hannah guessed, remembering the night engineer from KCOW Television who'd let them watch outtakes from the Hartland Flour Bakeoff.

"It's me. When they made me a feature reporter, I ditched the ponytail and the beard."

"You kept the earring," Hannah commented.

"Yes, but I had to tone it down a little. The diamond was too flashy for the camera. This one's brushed gold."

Hannah got P. K. settled with a couple of cookies and a mug of coffee and then she sat down across the table from him. "So . . . what brings you here?"

"Burke Anson. KCOW sent me out to interview him for my segment of *Night News at Ten*. I do the entertainment news."

"Good for you! But I thought you wanted to direct."

"I do. And I'll get there eventually, now that I'm moving up the ladder. Burke said I could catch him here between scenes. He wants to do the interview at The Cookie Jar if that's all right with you."

"Here?" Hannah was surprised. "Why not on the set?"

"I don't know. Maybe he thought it would be too distracting. He said to meet him here and since I'm the one asking and not the other way around, he gets to call the shots."

"Right." Hannah wondered why she didn't get to call the shots, especially since Burke wanted to use The Cookie Jar for a backdrop without even asking her.

"We'll only use a small corner of the coffee shop, and I'll make sure to mention where we are," P. K. said, practically reading her mind. "It'll be good advertising for your business. And Dee-Dee will do it, too. You know how she gives teasers before the commercials?"

"You mean when she announces what's coming up next?"

"Exactly." P. K. cleared his throat and went into a credible imitation of Dee-Dee Hughes, co-anchor of *Night News*. "*Stay tuned for an exclusive interview with Burke Anson at The Cookie Jar in Lake Eden, right after these words from our sponsors.*"

Hannah laughed. P. K. had mastered Dee-Dee's voice perfectly. "Do you need me to move tables or anything?"

"No, my cameraman and I can take care of that when Burke gets here. What's your take on him anyway?"

"Burke?" Hannah asked, stalling for time. She wasn't about to give P. K. any candid comments he could use on his segment.

"Yeah, Burke. What do you think of him?"

"I really don't know him that well," Hannah said diplomatically and also truthfully. "He's certainly a handsome man."

"That's what my girlfriend says."

"And I heard that he was a good actor."

"I heard that, too. But I also heard that he's not exactly buddy-buddy with Dean Lawrence."

"I haven't heard anything about that," Hannah said, also truthfully.

"Nothing?"

"Nothing," Hannah insisted, shaking her head.

"And you'd tell me if you'd heard?" Hannah shook her head again and P. K. laughed. "I didn't think so. You're a reporter's nightmare, Hannah. You don't gossip."

"I *try* not to," Hannah said. "I wouldn't be in business long if I repeated everything I heard."

As if on cue, Andrea came rushing over with her coffee carafe. "Guess what I just heard! Sophie, she's the wardrobe mistress, told me that . . ."

"Tracey's costumes were just beautiful," Hannah interrupted what she feared was about to be a juicy tidbit. "I know. She told me this morning. Here's an old friend you probably won't recognize, Andrea. It's . . ."

Now it was Andrea's turn to interrupt, "P. K! It's really good to see you again."

"How did you recognize him when I didn't?" Hannah wanted to know.

"The KCOW logo on his company pin. I noticed it that night we watched the outtakes of the Hartland Flour Bake-off. P. K.'s pin has a purple *O* and everybody else's *O* is blue."

"You're right," P. K. sounded pleased. "They gave us pins for Christmas two years ago and somebody goofed on this one. They wanted to send it back and get another one for me, but I said I wanted it because it was different."

Hannah stared at the tiny logo pin and shook her head in disbelief. It was so small, she hadn't even seen it. Andrea had not only seen the pin, she'd also noticed that the color on one of the letters was incorrect. Her sister had amazing powers of observation when it came to clothing and fashion.

"So what are you doing now, P. K.?" Andrea sat down in the chair next to Hannah's.

"I'm the entertainment reporter on *Night News at Ten*."

"I see," Andrea said, flashing Hannah a grateful look. "I haven't watched the news for a while. I'll have to tune in."

"So how do you like having a movie filmed practically in your backyard?"

Andrea laughed. "It's not even close to my backyard, but it's in our mother's store. They're using Granny's Attic for a set."

"Really?" P. K. pulled out a notebook and made a note. "I heard that they were casting some locals. Did anyone you know get a part?"

"We know *everyone* who got a part!" Hannah couldn't resist saying. "This is Lake Eden. It's not that big."

P. K. looked a little sheepish. "True. How about the big parts? Do you know the little girl who was cast?"

Andrea looked at Hannah, and Hannah looked right back. There was a breathless moment where Hannah waited for Andrea to say something, and Andrea waited for Hannah to say something. The silence stretched out for several heartbeats and then they both burst out laughing.

"What's so funny?"

"My daughter!" Andrea said.

"My niece," Hannah replied.

And then both of them started to talk at once, telling P. K. about how he should interview Tracey, and how she was bound to be famous when *Crisis in Cherrywood* hit the theaters.

"Not at all," Burke replied, looking straight into the camera as he responded to P. K.'s question about their exhausting shooting schedule and whether it was taking a toll on the quality of the production. "Our director, Mr. Dean Lawrence, won't let us get by with anything less than our best performance."

Hannah hid a grin. Burke was flattering the Bad Boy director outrageously. So much for the rumor that Burke and Dean didn't get along! She listened to P. K.'s next question, something about their full-dress rehearsals, but before she could hear Burke's answer, Andrea summoned her from the kitchen doorway.

"What's wrong?" Hannah asked when she saw her sister's expression. Andrea looked panic-stricken.

"P. K. wants to interview me next. I said yes, but now I wish I hadn't. What am I going to say?"

"He'll ask you a question. All you have to do is answer it."

"But what if I don't *know* the answer?"

"You're panicking for no reason and it's time to buck up. Come on, Andrea. Don't forget you're a real estate agent."

"You're right," Andrea said, and she squared her shoulders. "I'm a real estate professional and what I don't know, I can make up. They taught us how to do that in real estate college."

"You mean to call something a gourmet kitchen if it's got a spice rack on the wall? And to say a house is cozy if it's small and cramped?"

Andrea's mouth dropped open and then she started to laugh. She laughed so hard, tears rolled down her cheeks. "You really shouldn't say that, Hannah. You're making fun of my chosen profession."

"Well . . . maybe I am. Just a little. But I'll bet you're not nervous anymore."

"Of course I'm nervous. I'm so nervous, I could . . ." Andrea stopped speaking and gave her older sister a wide-eyed look. "You're right. I'm not nervous anymore! How did you do that?"

"You can't be nervous and amused at the same time. They're both powerful emotions and one overrides the other. If your sense of humor kicks in, you lose your case of nerves . . . at least according to the professor who taught the psychology class I took in college."

"Fascinating," Andrea said, giving Hannah a probing look. "What else did he say? Are there any other emotions that cancel each other out?"

"There's another pair that I remember. He said you can't be angry and amorous at the same time."

"Amorous?"

"You know," Hannah said, and then she made little kissing noises.

"Oh, *that* amorous," Andrea said, beginning to grin. "Thanks for telling me, but I think I already knew that. It must have been instinctive."

"You're probably right," Hannah said with a laugh. Her

psychology professor had insisted that particular phenomenon was the secret of any happy marriage.

"All the same, maybe I'd better put it to the test," Andrea said with an impish smile. "Bill can try it out on me, right after he gets home from Miami with Ronni Ward."

"So what do you think?" Lisa asked, presenting Hannah with the tray of Mini Cherry Cheesecakes. "Will Mr. Lawrence like them?"

"They *look* fantastic, and I think that's more important than how they taste."

"Hannah!" Lisa looked positively shocked. "How can you say such a thing?"

"I was thinking about Dean Lawrence, not us. We care how things taste more than how they look."

"Oh, now I understand. And you're right about him. He's a very shallow person. Everything is me, me, me."

"How so?" Hannah asked, agreeing with her young partner completely but wanting Lisa to enumerate her reasons.

"First of all, he just assumes that he's irresistible to women."

"You noticed?"

"I couldn't help but notice. I told you about refilling his coffee and how he kept right on talking and didn't even say thank you."

"I remember."

"Well, that was better than what happened just a couple of minutes ago when I went around with the coffee carafe again."

"What happened?"

"He made a pass and I won't go into detail. Let's just say he doesn't know how to keep his hands to himself. I wasn't expecting it and it startled me so much, I almost poured hot coffee down his collar."

"Maybe you should have."

Lisa giggled. "Maybe you're right. If he ever does it again, I'll figure out a way to let him know it's not appreciated. But there's another thing about him I noticed."

"What's that?"

"He believes that appearance is more important than substance. That's the earmark of a charlatan . . . or a magician. It's all an illusion. And it's all accomplished by misdirected attention. Smoke and mirrors. You know what I mean, right?"

Hannah stared at her partner with new respect. "That sounds right to me. But how do *you* know that?"

"Herb's an amateur magician. He says he's not good enough to take his act public yet, but he's done a few tricks for me, and I think he's simply fantastic. He started practicing in high school, but he never showed anyone until he married me."

It was a new fact about Herb she'd never known, and Hannah added it to the complicated mix that made up her high school classmate. "I had no idea. He really ought to perform at the community center on Halloween."

"I think so, too. He almost did it last year, but he said he wasn't quite ready. Maybe this year."

"Maybe," Hannah said, taking the lesson she'd just learned to heart. Living in a small town was deceptive. Just when you thought you knew everything about everybody, something came along to knock that theory to smithereens.

JANE'S MINI CHERRY CHEESECAKES

Preheat oven to 350 degrees F., rack in the center position

2 eight-ounce packages softened cream cheese ***(room temperature)********
¾ cup white ***(granulated)*** sugar
2 eggs
1 Tablespoon lemon juice
1 teaspoon vanilla
24 vanilla wafer cookies
24 cupcake liners ***(48 if you're like me and you like to use double papers)***
1 can cherry pie filling, chilled ***(21 ounces net weight)***

****** Use brick cream cheese, the kind that comes in a rectangular package. Don't use whipped cream cheese unless you want to experiment—whipped cream cheese, or low-fat, or Neufchatel might work, but I don't know that for sure.***

Line two muffin pans ***(the kind of pan that makes 12 muffins each)*** with paper cupcake liners. Put one vanilla wafer cookie in the bottom of each cupcake paper, flat side down.

Chill the unopened can of cherry pie filling in the refrigerator while you make the mini cheesecakes.

You can do all of this by hand, but it's easier with an electric mixer on slow to medium speed:

Mix the softened cream cheese with the white sugar until it's thoroughly blended. Add the eggs one at a time, beating after each addition. Then mix in the lemon juice and vanilla, and beat until light and fluffy.

Spoon the cheesecake batter into the muffin tins, dividing it as equally as you can. When you're through, each cupcake paper should be between half and two-thirds full. ***(They're going to look skimpy, but they'll be fine once they're baked and you put on the cherry topping.)***

Bake at 350 degrees F. for 15 to 20 minutes, or until the top has set and has a satin finish. ***(The center may sink a bit, but that's okay—the topping will cover that.)***

Cool the mini cheesecakes in the pans on wire racks.

When the cheesecakes are cool, open the can of cherry pie filling and place three cherries on top of every mini cheesecake. Divide the cherry juice equally among the 24 mini cheesecakes.

Refrigerate in the muffin tins for at least 4 hours before serving. ***(Overnight is even better.)*** Then take them out of the tins, carefully remove the cupcake papers, and place them on a silver platter for an elegant dessert at a finger food party.

Hannah's Note: I made these with Comstock Dark Cherry Pie Filling and came up 4 cherries short. Lisa's can of regular cherry pie filling had 72 cherries, 3 for each of her Mini Cherry Cheesecakes.

Hannah's 2nd Note: If you prefer, you can use fresh fruits glazed with melted jelly instead of the canned cherry pie filling. You can also use any other pie filling you like.

Chapter Fourteen

Hannah was sitting at the work island in the kitchen of The Cookie Jar, taking a well-deserved break. She'd just finished making Dean Lawrence's cheesecakes and they were sitting in state in the walk-in cooler, along with the tray of Jane's Mini Cherry Cheesecakes that Lisa had made. Both types of cherry delectables would be thoroughly chilled and ready for delivery to Dean's office in the morning. Hannah would perform that duty. There was no way she would let Lisa come into contact with the seasoned Romeo alone in his fancy Winnebago.

A chuckle escaped Hannah's throat as she thought of what would happen if Lisa delivered the goodies and the Bad Boy Director made another pass at her. There were some in town who might still consider her a blushing bride, but Lisa was far from innocent when it came to dealing with amorous males. According to Hannah's youngest sister, Michelle, who'd been Lisa's classmate at Jordan High, one particular basketball player had ended up benched for a week with a black eye after he tried to get fresh with Lisa on a date. No, Hannah's concern wasn't for her partner. Lisa could and would take care of herself. And her concern wasn't for Dean Lawrence, either. If Lisa was forced to use what Michelle had called her "wicked left hook," he would deserve that and then some. Hannah's concern was for Ross and what it would mean for *Crisis in Cherrywood* if his director got benched for medical reasons.

There was only an hour to go before they could close the shop for the day, and Hannah was anticipating an evening at home with Moishe, a simple dinner of whatever she could find in her cupboards or her refrigerator, and a trial run of a new recipe she'd mixed up while the cheesecakes were baking. It was a type of cookie she knew Lynne would like, modeled after her favorite sandwich, peanut butter and banana on toast. It was the only cooking Lynne had ever done, if you could call toasting bread, spreading peanut butter, and slicing bananas "cooking." They'd eaten so many peanut butter and banana sandwiches while studying together for finals in college that Hannah hadn't been able to look at a jar of peanut butter for a full year after she'd left the campus to return home.

Hannah had just finished the last of her coffee and was preparing to rinse out her mug in the sink when the back door opened and her mother breezed in.

"Hello, Hannah," Delores greeted her eldest daughter. "I have wonderful news!"

"You do?" Hannah took one look at her mother's delighted expression and smiled right back. It was the first time she'd seen Delores look truly happy since Winthrop's abrupt exit from her life.

"We finished early and Jared told us it's absolutely perfect! The nineteen-fifties house is up and running, and I want you to be the first to see it. I value your opinion, dear."

"Thank you, Mother. I'd love to see it," Hannah agreed, pleased that her mother had chosen her for the first viewing. "Just let me ask Lisa to hold down the fort while I'm gone."

A moment later, Hannah was back. She grabbed her coat from the hook by the back door and followed her mother across the parking lot to the rear of Granny's Attic. She wasn't even mildly suspicious until Delores opened the back door of Granny's Attic, and Hannah found Ross Barton waiting for them. Was this another of her mother's matchmaking attempts? Or had she invited Ross by virtue of his writer–producer hyphenate?

"Hey, Hannah!" Ross looked pleased to see her as she came through the back door and into the small narrow room that Delores and Carrie used for storage. "They made me wait in here for you. We're supposed to be the first to see it."

"That's so you an keep us from looking like fools if there's something wrong," Carrie confessed, looking almost as happy as Delores did. "All you have to do is tell us, and we'll fix it before anyone else sees it."

Ross gave both older ladies a warm smile. "I'm sure it's perfect. Can we go in now?"

"Yes, but walk around the side of the building and come in the front way," Delores instructed. "We want you to get the full effect of the porch and then the living room." She gave them a sweet smile. "You will indulge me, won't you?"

"Of course," Ross said, and led Hannah back out the door. They walked, single file, around the side of the building. It wasn't until they rounded the corner to the front that Ross spoke. "I can't believe they got it done so fast. Your mother and Carrie are amazing."

"Amazing," Hannah said, although *amazing* wasn't the word she would have chosen. *Deceptive*, perhaps. Maybe even *conniving* or *scheming*. And if she wanted to tone it down just a bit, *manipulative* was always a safe bet. Delores was definitely up to something, but Hannah wasn't about to get into it now. The less Ross knew about her mother's machinations, the better. She'd have a private chat with Delores later and find out exactly what was going on.

"We had a front porch just like this in Duluth," Ross said, when they opened the door.

"*Everyone* had a front porch like this," Hannah looked around at the addition to Granny's Attic that had been created by the wizardry of Ross's studio carpenters. "There's even a rug by the front door for boots."

"With boots on it. And they're from the right time period. My mother had a pair of boots just like that. She told me she wore them in high school."

Hannah gazed down at the brown suede boots with fur around the tops. If she remembered correctly, those boots had come from her mother's closet. "So there should be a coatrack, or a hall closet, or something like that when we go through the inside door."

"Coatrack," Ross announced as he opened the door to the inside. It was the room that in larger, more expensive houses, would be called a foyer. "It's perfect, Hannah. The coatrack's sitting on a homemade rag rug to catch the drips."

"Of course it is. You're talking about egg money here. Almost every farm wife used her egg money to buy a loom to make rag rugs. They made the rugs from everything you can think of, including burlap sacks and plastic grocery bags. They sold them to the people in town, and the tourists that came through in the summer."

"A cottage industry?"

"Rag rugs, hooked rugs with designs on them, and hand-sewn chair pads for wooden kitchen chairs. Everybody had a craft in the fifties." Hannah stopped at the mahogany door that led to the inside of the house. "Beveled glass, and it's decorated with ferns and . . . is that a letter, or a design?"

"It's a letter *T*, and it's perfect. Amy and Jody's last name is Thompson."

The hallway sported a wooden staircase that Hannah knew led up to nowhere, and two doors that were placed opposite each other. Hannah chose the one on the left, opened it, and stepped inside. It was a fairly small room and the first detail that caught her eye made her smile.

"What's got you so amused?" Ross asked.

"The black panther light on top of the television set. My Grandma Ingrid had one just like it."

"Maybe it *is* your Grandma Ingrid's."

"That's not impossible. Mother's got a lot of her things in storage."

"She's got a green lava lamp, too." Ross pointed to the end table where a lava lamp expurgated its bulbous bubbles.

"The only thing that's missing is a . . . granny afghan!" Hannah burst into delighted laughter as she saw the crocheted wonder draped over the back of the green tweed couch. It was a granny afghan extraordinaire, done in shades of green and blue, surrounded by black borders.

"Perfect," Ross said, gesturing toward the couch that was positioned strategically in front of the television set. "There's room here for three to watch television."

"Two. Nobody likes to sit in the middle of a couch. There's nowhere to rest your elbows."

"Lime green shag carpeting!" Ross exclaimed with a grin. "Your mother and Carrie did a really good job re-creating the nineteen-fifties. They must have done a lot of research."

Not necessarily, Hannah thought, but she didn't say it. If her mother wanted everyone to think she didn't remember the fifties, Hannah wasn't about to call her bluff.

"This is nice and homey." Ross looked around at the ivory wallpaper with little green ivy vines marching down in stripes. "There's even an overstuffed armchair with a pole lamp for reading. If we take out the glass in the window, we can shoot that scene with Tracey reading to Moishe in here."

"It all looks good to me. Let's go see how they decorated the formal living room, since you'll be using it for the cocktail party."

Hannah headed for the set of French doors that separated the small informal family room from the formal living room. The moment she stepped inside the larger space, Hannah knew her mother and Carrie had produced something that was about as close to perfection as anyone could come.

"Gorgeous," Ross pronounced, echoing her emotion.

"Yes," Hannah said, walking around the room in awe. Her mother and Carrie had perfectly re-created the elegant look that had been so popular in expensive homes at the time. The living room floor had a wine red carpet surrounded by a parquet wood border. The drapes were heavy wine-red silk and the walls were covered with ivory flocked wallpaper. There were gilt-edged mirrors in strategic places and several large landscapes in ornate frames.

"The piano's a nice touch," Ross said, heading for the gleaming white baby grand that was positioned by the floor-to-ceiling bookcases. "We'll have someone playing it at the cocktail party."

"No, you won't," Hannah said, lifting the lid to find absolutely nothing inside. "It's just a shell."

"That's okay. We'll mix in the sound later. As long as there's a keyboard, someone can pretend to play."

When they'd finished exploring the formal living room and spotted the desk that would be used for the suicide scene, Hannah and Ross headed back out to the hallway to open the second door.

"It's straight out of *The Student Prince*," Hannah breathed, eyeing the bedroom with its delft blue walls, white curtains, and white furniture. "Is this Amy's room?"

"Yes. See that cushion on the dormer window?"

Hannah nodded. It was the only jarring note in the room. The cushion was bright orange.

"That's for Moishe. Amy bought it so he'd have a spot to sit and watch the birds. Her father threw it in the trash because it didn't match the rest of her room, but Jody retrieved it and gave it back to her on the day of their father's funeral."

"Sounds like a nasty man."

"He was."

Hannah stopped for a moment and then she began to frown. "Who's playing the father in the movie? I haven't met him yet."

"And you won't. The father is done entirely in voice-over. I wanted it that way for impact. We never get to see him, therefore we can't find anything about him to like."

"Interesting," Hannah said.

"I just hope it'll work. It's always a gamble, casting villains. If they overplay the evil, they can be almost comical. And if they're a bit too nice, the audience sympathizes with them. That's why I decided to try a more radical approach. The father appears only in Amy's mind. That should make him larger than life, more menacing, and totally unsympathetic. It also gives me an escape hatch, because it's the father in her mind, not the real father."

Hannah thought about that for a minute, and then she smiled. "It sounds like good reasoning to me. But I'm not a filmmaker and you are."

"I just hope it's not too hokey. If it is, it'll be a simple matter to take out all but the most critical scenes and cast someone quickly."

"When will you know?"

"By dailies on Friday night. Do you want to come out and watch them with me? Sally's got us set up in the bar."

"I wouldn't miss it," Hannah said, thoroughly fascinated by the concept.

"Okay. Let's go tell your mother and Carrie what we think."

"Fine. I think it's fantastic, but you're the producer. What do *you* think?"

"I think it's fantastic, too."

"You really think it's that good?" Delores asked, her eyes sparkling in excitement.

"I do. If I didn't know better, I'd think you'd been dressing sets all your lives."

"Thank you!" Carrie looked just as delighted as Delores did. "We did work very hard on it."

"And you finished it ahead of schedule. Do you know how rare that is in the movie industry?"

Both Delores and Carrie shook their heads and then Delores cleared her throat. "Since you like your sets so much, I have a favor to ask."

"What's that?"

"Invite Hannah out to the inn for dinner tonight. I just know she's not going to eat right."

Really, Mother! You're about as subtle as a ballerina in hip waders! Hannah thought, but she didn't say it. It seemed as if her mother had given up on Norman and Mike as likely candidates for sons-in-law, and was now concentrating all her efforts on Ross.

"My pleasure," Ross said, slipping his arm around Hannah's shoulders and giving her a little squeeze. "And after dinner, I'll have dailies of Moishe for her to see. How about you two? Would you like to join us?"

Delores shook her head. "That's very nice of you, but no thanks. They're having a sale at the mall tonight and I promised Carrie I'd go shopping with her."

"We can go shopping another time," Carrie declared.

"But how about the sale? It's twenty percent off."

"I'd probably buy something I didn't need anyway. And I'm certainly not going to turn down such a nice invitation. Come on, Delores. Let's go see that footage of your grandcat."

"My *grandcat?*" Delores exclaimed, turning to give Carrie a dirty look. "How about Norman? Don't you have to fix dinner for him?"

"Norman can fend for himself tonight. I'm going, Delores. How about you?"

"Oh. Well . . . all right," Delores conceded, looking

none too happy about it as she turned to Ross. "Thank you, Mr. Barton. We'd love to join you for dinner."

"It's Ross. And I'm very glad you're coming." Hannah glanced at Ross in surprise. He sounded as if he actually meant it. "Shall I pick you all up at seven?"

"No need for that," Carrie said, exchanging another look with Delores. "I'll drive and we'll bring Hannah with us."

Hannah choked slightly and covered it with a cough. It was the battle of the mothers and it seemed as if Delores had met her match. Less than two minutes ago, her mother had practically pushed her into Ross's arms, and now Carrie had placed her in the position of co-chaperone.

"That's out of the way for you," Ross said to Carrie. "I'll pick Hannah up at her condo. She has to take Moishe home first."

Hannah was beginning to feel like the ball in a game of *Keep-Away*. It might be exciting, but it certainly wasn't comfortable.

"Norman can take Moishe home," Carrie blithely volunteered her son.

"But I couldn't possibly ask Norman to . . ."

"Nonsense!" Carrie cut off Hannah's objection. "Norman's crazy about Moishe and vice versa. And he'll cat-sit until you get home . . . just so our little kitty star doesn't get lonely."

Ah-ha! Hannah thought. *The custard thickens! Carrie's afraid I'll invite Ross in when he brings me home and she wants Norman there to prevent any hanky-panky.* Of course what Carrie didn't know was that there wouldn't have been any hanky-panky anyway. Hannah had put in a rough day and she was determined to hit the sack early tonight.

Chapter Fifteen

Hannah was beaming like a proud mother when the lights came back up and the screen on Sally's huge television went black. Moishe had been adorable. Even Delores had given a few oohs and ahhs in the appropriate places, especially during the funeral scene when Moishe had licked Erica's cheek to comfort her.

"A born ham," Hannah said in an aside to Ross, but she couldn't seem to stop smiling. She guessed that some cats were born to be actors and others weren't. And she was lucky enough to have a star on her hands.

"He's even better than a trained cat," Ross commented.

"You can train cats?" Hannah asked, but her grin gave her away. She knew there were some cats that were trained to obey commands, but it would never work with Moishe. If he understood what you wanted, he'd do it. If he felt like it. At that particular time. Maybe.

"I'd better get home soon," Hannah said, glancing down at her watch. It was nine-fifteen and the early night she'd promised herself would turn into a late night if she stayed at the inn much longer.

"Just stay for Burke's interview and then I'll take you

home. I want to hear how he handled that reporter. Everybody else is coming in to see it."

"Who's everybody?"

"The whole cast including Dean's wife, Sharyn, and Tom Larchmont. Connor picked them up at the airport at seven and I'm sure they're back here by now."

"Okay," Hannah agreed quite readily. She was eager to meet Lynne's husband and very curious about the type of woman who would marry Dean. Sharyn Lawrence must be as long-suffering as a saint. She wanted to see Burke's interview, too. Since it had been filmed that afternoon at The Cookie Jar, she really wanted to see how her shop looked. "Are they running the interview with Andrea, too?"

"Not until next week. I called the station and the news director said he wanted to intercut Andrea's interview with the ones that they'll be doing later this week of Tracey, Lynne, and Erica. He's going to call it the *Three Faces of Amy*, and it'll run next Friday night."

Ten minutes later, the bar at the Lake Eden Inn was filled with movie people. Ross had introduced Hannah to Tom Larchmont and it was easy to see why Lynne had married him. Tom treated his wife like a porcelain doll, jumping up to get her whatever she wanted and draping an affectionate arm around her shoulders at every opportunity. And even though he was considerably older than Lynne was, he had the body of an athlete and the good looks of a man who had enough money to indulge himself.

Then there was Sharyn Lawrence. Hannah glanced across at the woman who'd married the Bad Boy Director. There was no denying that Dean made the hearts of his actresses beat faster, but his wife had the same effect on the men in the cast and crew. She was petite, barely five feet tall, and she had the wide-eyed look of a child. Her glossy black hair was cut in a gamine style that enhanced the innocent look, but that visual naiveté was completely at odds with her body. Sharyn had a figure that would certainly give Ronni Ward some competition in the Lake Eden Bikini Queen Contest. She was lush and curvaceous from the neck down, and ingenuous and childlike from the neck up. Hannah had spent only moments with Sharyn, but she was left with the impression that Sharyn was too smart and too savvy to put up with any nonsense from her husband. If Dean strayed too far afield while Sharyn was here, Hannah was willing to bet that the fur would fly.

Sally dimmed the lights and Dick put the giant screen in television mode. Chuck Wilson's handsome face filled the screen for a moment and when the camera pulled back, Hannah saw Dee-Dee Hughes, his anorexic co-anchor sitting next to him. Both talking heads were seated at the large, curved desk, an integral part of KCOW's *News At Ten* set, holding sheaves of paper they didn't need since they both used TelePrompTers.

Hannah and Ross watched as the news rolled smoothly along. There had been a robbery on a quiet residential street in Grey Eagle, a fire in a tire store in Browerville, a band concert in Little Falls to benefit a local charity, a near drowning on the banks of the Mississippi when someone's bicycle slid off a path and crashed through the thin ice on the river, and a yard sale in Royalton, where several items, stolen the previous summer, had surfaced. The Skatin' Place in St. Cloud had changed its hours, the Long Prairie Volunteer Fire Department was holding a raffle, and the little town of Sobieski was planning a high school reunion.

The camera pushed in to feature Dee-Dee's perfect face. "Stay tuned for our own P. K. with *The Movie Moment*," she said. "Tonight P. K. will be interviewing a television personality we all know and love at The Cookie Jar in Lake Eden."

"Nice plug," Ross said, patting Hannah on the back.

"It was all his idea. I never would have thought to ask."

Hannah found herself holding her breath as she waited through a slew of commercials for new cars hardly anyone could afford, carpet stores that could install practically overnight, and companies that could give you credit, check your credit, or clean up your credit report. It seemed like forever, but at last Chuck and Dee-Dee were back.

"So tell us who you ran into at The Cookie Jar," Chuck prompted, and the camera moved to the side, where P. K. was sitting a bit removed from the important co-anchors.

"Burke Anson," P.K. said, leaning close as if he were confiding a big secret. "He's the male lead on a new feature that's filming in Lake Eden. It's called *Crisis in Cherrywood.*"

The camera moved to Dee-Dee Hughes. "For the few viewers who don't know who Burke Anson is, why don't you refresh our memory?"

"He's the suntanned Adonis in the Surf 'n Turf commercials," P. K. said. "But for those of you who remember Burke with his surfboard, I've got to warn you that in my interview with him, he's fully dressed."

The camera caught Dee-Dee giving P. K. a petulant look and then the tape of the interview began to run. Hannah smiled as she saw a wide shot with Lisa and the display jars of cookies behind the counter. Their shop looked good, right down to the pictures Norman had taken of their best cookies for the walls. She really ought to have him take more pictures. The Cherry Bomb Cookies would look fantastic, and so would the Mock Turtles. She was just thinking about other cookies she could ask Norman to photograph, when she realized that she wasn't paying any attention to the interview, and she focused on the television again.

"Not at all," Burke replied, looking straight into the camera as he responded to P. K.'s question about their exhausting shooting schedule and whether it was taking a toll on the quality of the production. "Our director, Mr. Dean Lawrence, won't let us get by with anything less than our best performance."

"I heard about the full-dress rehearsals you do the night

before shooting every scene. Someone told me it's not unusual for Mr. Lawrence to run the scene several dozen times. Isn't that hard on the actors, especially when you're not going to shoot the scene until the next day?"

"I don't know. I haven't heard anybody complaining."

"Tell me about the next day. Do you rehearse again, before you actually shoot the scene?"

"Oh, definitely. We rehearse for as many times as it takes to get it right. Then we shoot."

"But most directors don't make you go through the scene that many times, do they?"

"I wouldn't know about that. This is the first feature film I've ever been in. But I firmly believe that Mr. Lawrence is a genius. You should see him when he puts on my costume and does my part for me. It's a great learning experience."

"He puts on your costume and demonstrates your part?"

"Yes, if I can't seem to find my motivation. He does a darn good imitation of my voice, too."

"Do you think he does this because you're a novice? I mean, because you're not a veteran movie actor?"

Burke shook his head. "Oh, I don't think so. He does it for other actors, too."

"How about the actresses?"

"Well, Lynne doesn't really need any help like that. She gets everything right the first time."

"Just let me clarify that, Burke." P. K. turned to face his camera. "Burke is referring to Lynne Larchmont, who plays the female lead in *Crisis in Cherrywood*." P. K. got back in interviewer posture. "You say your director, Dean Lawrence, occasionally puts on the costumes and demonstrates the parts for his actors. Is that right?"

"That's right. It's very helpful."

P. K. gave a little laugh and winked at the camera. "But of course Mr. Lawrence doesn't do this for the women's parts."

"Sure he does. And he looks pretty darn convincing in

drag." There was a stunned silence. It was obvious that P. K. wasn't about to risk a comment after the bombshell Burke had just dropped. But Burke plunged right ahead into even deeper water. "I was just kidding, you know. But Mr. Lawrence can do great voices. He's got Erica's down pat. If he put on her costume and sat down in a dark bar, I bet seven or eight guys would come over and try to hit on him."

Hannah heard several people gasp and she turned to look at Ross. Burke had certainly stepped in every cow pie in Winnetka County and perhaps even in the whole state of Minnesota.

"Idiot," Ross muttered under his breath, staring at the screen. "I hope that reporter's a pro."

"Very funny, Burke," P. K. jumped in, turning to face the camera. "Movie people are always kidding each other like this, folks. But there's no denying that Mr. Lawrence is not only a great director, he's also a great actor. Burke didn't mention it, but there's a cat in the picture. His real name is Moishe and he's got a couple of lines . . . or maybe I should say, he's got a couple of yowls. I wouldn't be surprised if Mr. Lawrence could play that cat better than Moishe himself."

"Smooth," Ross said under his breath. "Now people will remember the cat."

Hannah risked a quick glance at Dean. He was smiling, but it wasn't a friendly smile and Hannah was glad she wasn't Burke right about now.

"Thank you, Burke," P. K. said from his chair on the set. He turned to face the camera. "We've got a treat in store for you next Friday night right after the news. It's an in-depth story about the three actresses playing Amy Thompson in *Crisis in Cherrywood*. We mentioned that Lynne Larchmont plays her as an adult, and Erica James plays Amy as a teenager. What we didn't mention is that the third actress is our very own Tracey Todd from Lake Eden, Minnesota, and she plays Amy as a child."

The news had only five more minutes to run and everyone was silent as Rayne Phillips informed them that the weather tomorrow would be almost the same as it had been today. Then Wingo Jones gave the sports scores and showed a clip of the center from the Little Falls Flyers sinking a basket from the opposite side of the court in the last two seconds to win the game. The credits scrolled much too rapidly for anyone except someone's mother to read, and then the screen went dark and all was silent as the lights came up.

Hannah sneaked a quick glance at Burke. He looked understandably nervous. What he'd said was inflammatory and might even be considered actionable.

"Uh . . . Mr. Lawrence?" Burke said, not daring to call the director by his first name.

"Yes, Burke."

"I'm . . . uh . . . I'm real sorry about that. I'm not used to giving interviews and . . . um . . . I thought it would be funny. You know."

"It *was* funny, Burke. I'm sure people will be talking about it for weeks to come."

"But . . . you're not . . . uh . . . mad, because of what I said and all?"

"Why on earth should I be angry? I just told you I thought it was funny."

"But . . . I think maybe it didn't make you look so good. I mean, with my crack about the dress and the bar and all. I know you don't get dressed up in women's costumes, but I thought it would be really funny . . . at the time, that is."

"And I told you it *was* funny."

Hannah stared at Burke, willing him to quit, but Burke didn't seem to know how to stop. "Then . . . no hard feelings?" he asked.

"No hard feelings." Dean stood up and yawned. "Come along, Sharyn. I'm going up to bed. We have an early call tomorrow. Seven o'clock, my office. I want Erica and her two school chums. They've already been notified."

"Not me?" Burke asked, gulping slightly.

"You're not in that scene, Burke. I'll see you on the set at ten."

Hannah held her breath until Dean walked out the door and then she released it in a long sigh.

"Are you okay?" Ross asked.

"I'm fine. I'm just relieved, that's all. The fallout wasn't as bad as I thought it would be. I expected Dean to keelhaul Burke in Sally's new koi pond."

"Dean wouldn't do that. He's a pro and he knows we need Burke to finish the picture."

"But he was just putting a good face on it, right? I mean, he's mad at Burke, isn't he?"

"I don't know. Dean's lived in Hollywood long enough to know that almost any publicity is good publicity. And Burke mentioned Dean's name and the name of the film several times. Of course Dean didn't *like* the reference to women's costumes, but Burke did say that he was a genius and Dean's bound to like that part of it. It's a mixed bag, but my guess is that Dean'll take it in stride."

"Just one cup of coffee," Hannah said, climbing up the stairs to her condo two hours later. They'd stayed for the late night snacks Sally had put out after the news and chatted with some of the cast and crew. Before they'd realized it, almost two hours had passed and Hannah had told Ross that she had to go home. "And right after your coffee, I have to get to bed. I need to get my sleep tonight."

Ross gave her a teasing grin. "You'd never make it in showbiz. There are nights that I have to deal with only six hours' sleep."

"Six hours' sleep is good. On most nights, I don't get more than five."

"It's been as little as four for me."

"And three for me. And last night, I got only two!"

"Really? But why was that?" Ross asked, breaking the chain of one-downmanship.

"Moishe. He must have been nervous, because he got up to eat every hour on the hour. And then he used his litter-box."

"Why would that keep you awake?"

"His claws screech against the plastic when he covers. And don't ask me what *covers* means."

"I know what it means. My mother had a cat. Do you want me to brace you for the onslaught?"

"Please," Hannah said getting out her key and slipping it in the lock. But when she opened the door, the usual orange-and-white bundle didn't hurtle out to greet her.

"Where's Moishe?" she said, spotting Norman on the couch.

"He went to bed early, right after I fed him. I think he was tired after his scenes today. I hope you don't mind, but I think he's sleeping on your pillow and I didn't have the heart to wake him. And . . . I finished your chocolate fudge ice cream."

Hannah told him she didn't mind about the pillow or the ice cream, and went into the kitchen to put on the coffee. When that was accomplished, she headed to her bedroom to check on her four-footed movie star. Moishe was sleeping the sleep of a well-fed jungle tiger, and from the way he was smacking his lips, he was probably dreaming of mouse body parts. Norman had been right. Instead of falling asleep on the expensive goose-down pillow she'd bought for him, he was on *her* expensive goose-down pillow.

"The pillows are always softer on the other side of the bed," Hannah whispered, and let her minipanther sleep. She was just passing the guest room on her way back to the living room when she noticed that the door was open. That was odd. She always closed it when there were no guests. It wasn't to conserve energy or any of the admirable ecological reasons. It was because Moishe loved to "hunt" the satin butterflies on the new bedspread she'd bought for the guest room. Hannah was about to shut the door when she realized that there was a good-sized lump on her bed, and her eyebrows headed straight toward the ceiling fan the former owner had installed. There was someone sleeping in her bed. She took a step closer and her eyebrows remained on high alert when she recognized her uninvited guest. It was Mike!

Hannah gulped, feeling a bit like Baby Bear who'd come home to find his porridge eaten, his chair recently used, and Goldilocks sleeping in his bed. In her case, it was her ice cream that had been eaten, Norman who'd been sitting on her couch, and Mike who was sleeping in her bed. But all that didn't really matter. It was close enough to prove that fairytales weren't all that wildly exaggerated.

"What are you doing in my bed?" Hannah asked, prompting a bearlike snort and a leap to the feet from the unsolicited sleeper who'd been snuggled up on her new bedspread.

"Hannah! Sorry about that. I started to doze off on the couch and Norman told me to come in here. He said you wouldn't mind."

"Well . . . I guess I don't," Hannah conceded, "but what are you doing here in the first place?"

"I brought the pizza."

"What pizza?"

"The pizza Norman ordered from Bertanelli's. I was sitting there waiting for my pizza when he called in his. Ellie told me they were short a delivery guy, so I figured I'd just bring them both out here and we could eat together."

"Okay," Hannah said, wondering what sort of numbers

that would rack up on the scale of coincidence. "You want some coffee? I just put on a pot."

"Sure. Is Ross here?"

"He's in the living room talking to Norman."

"Great. I have to tell him that the kids are trying to skate on the ice rink at the park."

"What's wrong with that?"

"It's fake ice and it's going to be all marked up by the time they shoot there on Friday."

"Fake ice?" Hannah was surprised. This was the first she'd heard of it, but it made sense to her. It was possible to have a warm spell before Friday that might render the ice rink unusable. "What are they going to do about the snow if the weather warms up?"

"They'll use fake snow. They're going to use it anyway, just to make it look better."

"Okay," Hannah said, too tired to ask the other questions that occurred to her. "If you don't mind, I'm beat and I'm going to bed. Will you tell Norman and Ross?"

Mike looked shocked. "Sure, but you're kicking us out without coffee?"

"I'm not kicking you out at all. Help yourselves to coffee and any cookies you find in the cookie jar. Stay as long as you like, but just don't wake me when you leave. And since you're the official law enforcement officer, would you please make sure that you're the last one out and the door locks behind you?"

"You can be sure of that!" Mike said, putting both hands around her waist to turn her around and give her a gentle nudge toward the bedroom.

Chapter Sixteen

It was ten o'clock on Wednesday morning and Lisa had just opened The Cookie Jar for business. Dean Lawrence had approved the Mini Cherry Cheesecakes enthusiastically, and Hannah had returned to The Cookie Jar to bake and chill another four batches for the cocktail party scene that would be shot that afternoon. Moishe was holding court at the round table by the window, Lisa was waiting on a customer, and Hannah was in the kitchen with Andrea, baking the cookies she'd intended to bake the previous evening.

"All *three* of them?" Andrea stared at Hannah in absolute shock and then she started to laugh. "And you just left them there and went to *bed?*"

Hannah shrugged as she finished shaping another pan of cookies and slid them onto the baker's rack. The timer dinged and she removed the pans that had been in the oven, replacing them with the pans she'd just prepared. "These are new cookies we're going to try out today. They're called All-Nighters."

"Why?"

"Because they're banana and peanut butter. That was

Lynne's favorite sandwich when she was in college and she used to make them every time we got together to cram for finals."

"Not *that* why. The other why."

"What other why?"

"The important why. Why did you just leave them there in your living room?"

"It was easier than trying to get them to leave. And I needed my sleep."

"You mean you actually slept?"

"Like a baby. And that reminds me, how's Bethany?"

"She's great. She smiled at me this morning. Grandma McCann said it was gas, but I know a real smile when I see one. Do you want me to taste one of the All-Nighters and tell you what I think?"

"Absolutely."

Andrea reached for a cookie and took a bite. She chewed and swallowed, and then she smiled. "They're good, Hannah. I've always liked banana and peanut butter. It's a great combination. And that reminds me, do you have a red scarf I can borrow? The kind you wear around your neck when you're skating?"

Hannah hid an amused smile. It was another zinger from the mistress of non sequitur. Andrea probably had a reason for the abrupt change of subject, but Hannah didn't want to ask. Sometimes the explanation took more time than it was worth. "I don't have one. Why do you need it?"

"Mr. Lawrence thought it would add a lot to Tracey's skating scene if she wore a red scarf draped around her neck. He said it would be a great combination with her royal blue coat. And he said the red would make it look as if she's skating even faster when she's on the end for *Crack the Whip*."

"A great combination," Hannah repeated, recalling that Andrea had called peanut butter and bananas a great combination before she'd asked about the red scarf. "Doesn't

Bill have a red scarf? I think I gave him one a couple of years ago for Christmas."

Andrea clapped her hands in delight. "Yes, he does! He wears it with his dress coat and I think it's in his top dresser drawer. Thanks for remembering it, Hannah. It'll be just perfect for Tracey's scene."

"That's today?"

"No, not until Friday. Today they're shooting the classroom scene, where she wins the spelling bee. It's at noon, right before they break for lunch. You'll come, won't you?"

"I wouldn't miss it," Hannah said.

"I think I'll go look for that scarf right now. I have to go home anyway."

"Why?"

"I need to see if Bethany will smile at me again."

Hannah was refilling coffee cups when she noticed Connor motioning to her from the counter. She finished the table she was serving, and then she ducked behind the counter to talk to him. "Hi, Connor. Do you need me?"

"I certainly do. You said to let you know if I couldn't talk Mrs. Henderson into signing that release form. Well, I talked until I was blue in the face, but there's no way she'll do it. She was really nice about it, though. She gave me gooseberry pie and coffee and showed me pictures of her grandchildren."

"But she didn't sign?"

"No. Nothing I said convinced her, not even the money Mr. Lawrence was willing to pay."

"Then I'll give it a try," Hannah promised. "I'll catch her when they shoot the cocktail scene."

"Mrs. Henderson is in the cocktail scene?"

"No, but her youngest daughter is and Winnie's bound to drive in to watch Alice. I think I can convince her."

"Oh, I hope so! Thank you, Hannah. I'll tell Mr. Lawrence that you're going to try. I just hope he doesn't fire me for failing him."

"He won't . . . will he?"

"He's fired me before, but he always hired me back after he got over being mad at me. I'm just afraid that it'll be permanent one of these times. I'm almost sixty and it would be hard to get another job without references from my former employer."

"You're worrying over nothing," Hannah reassured him, reaching into one of the serving jars with napkin-sheathed fingers and handing him two Twin Chocolate Delights. "Eat these cookies. The chocolate will make you feel better."

"But I really should go and find Mr. Lawrence."

"Find him later, after I've talked to Winnie."

"But Mr. Lawrence told me to get right back to him."

"Bad news can wait, especially since that bad news might turn into good news."

Connor considered it for a moment and then he nodded. "You could be right. If Mr. Lawrence doesn't ask me outright, I'll wait to tell him."

Ten minutes later, Connor was smiling and chatting with one of the grips. Hannah's chocolate prescription had done the trick and she was congratulating herself on a job well done when Andrea rushed back in the door.

"Hi, Andrea," Hannah greeted her. "Did you find that scarf?"

"I found it. And I found something else, too."

"What's that?"

"Proof that Bill is cheating on me!"

Klaxons sounded in Hannah's head. Her sister's eyes were blazing with angry fire and it was clear she was fit to be tied. "Come into the kitchen with me and you can tell me all about it. I have to take Moishe back there for a break."

Hannah collected her cat, shifted him to one arm, and grabbed Andrea's arm with her free hand. She rushed her through the crowded coffee shop before anyone could ask what was wrong, and into the confines of the deserted kitchen. She dropped Moishe off in his large dog crate and shut the door, but she didn't release Andrea's arm until her sister was seated on a stool at the work island.

"Eat these!" Hannah ordered, plunking a couple of Chocolate Chip Crunch cookies down on a napkin and shoving them over to her sister.

"But I don't want any . . ."

"Eat them while I get us some coffee," Hannah said, interrupting her sister's protest. "Have I ever steered you wrong with chocolate?"

"No, but . . ." Andrea stopped speaking and sighed. And then she took a bite of the first cookie. It was only after she'd consumed both that she looked up at Hannah with tearful eyes. "It's Bill. He's . . ."

"Have a sip of coffee first," Hannah interrupted her again. "Then I want you to start at the beginning and tell me everything."

Andrea did as ordered. She sipped the coffee, gave another quavering sigh, and then squared her shoulders. "Bill didn't take his new shirt with him. I found it hidden at the bottom of his scarf and hankie drawer."

"Okay," Hannah said, heading to the walk-in cooler for reinforcements. She set the rest of the box of chocolate truffles in front of her sister and got down to business. "Nibble on those while you tell me why the shirt Bill forgot means he's cheating on you."

"He didn't forget it. He didn't not take it on purpose."

Double negative, Hannah's grammatical mind shouted, but she ignored it. This was not the time to correct her sister's speech. "You think Bill deliberately left the shirt at home?"

"Yes! I laid it out on the bed and folded it for him and everything. And then, when my back was turned, he stuffed it in his dresser drawer instead of putting it in his suitcase. And he made sure it was his scarf and hankie drawer, so I wouldn't find out he didn't pack it."

"Okay," Hannah regrouped. "And you think this means he's cheating on you?"

"I *know* it does."

Hannah waited until Andrea had taken another dose of chocolate before she continued. "Exactly how do you know that?"

"The shirt Bill didn't take is the new one I gave him for Valentine's Day. I asked him to think of me every time he wore it and he promised he would."

"But Bill didn't take the shirt."

"That's right. And you know that Bill never promises something unless he means it. That proves he wanted to forget all about me and follow his own agenda in Miami. He's probably out on the beach right now with Ronni Ward and . . ." Andrea stopped as Moishe let out a yowl. "You're absolutely right, Moishe. Bill's probably out there catting around."

But no sooner had the words left Andrea's mouth than Moishe gave another yowl even louder than the first. And then another that was practically earsplitting.

"What's the matter with him, Hannah?"

Hannah walked over to take her cat out of the cage. He wanted to get away from them and back to adoration of his public, but Andrea felt abandoned enough as it was without adding a cat's rejection to the mix. "He's upset," she said, quite truthfully.

"Why?"

"He knows you're upset and you're one of his favorite people," Hannah told her, leaving truth in the dust. "He probably wants to sit in your lap and make you feel better."

"How sweet!" Andrea breathed, holding out her arms. "Give him to me, Hannah."

"Be nice and I'll give you a whole can of tuna when we

get home," Hannah whispered in her mini-tiger's ear. Moishe turned to give her a baleful look, as if a fishy bribe was an insult and he wouldn't dream of misbehaving with someone as upset as Andrea was.

"It's very, very nice of you to care, but I'm much better now," Andrea cooed, stroking Moishe's head. And then she looked up at Hannah. "This is just amazing. I had no idea he liked me this much. Look, Hannah. He's licking my hand."

Hannah smiled and mentally vowed to give her feline a whole canister of salmon-flavored treats in addition to the tuna. And then she got back to the business at hand. "So . . . you found the shirt in Bill's scarf drawer."

"His scarf *and* hankie drawer. He doesn't have a drawer just for scarves."

"Right." Hannah did her best to think of some reason why Bill wouldn't want to take the shirt. "Tell me about the shirt. What kind was it?"

"It was an Armani that I found on sale out at the mall. The salesman told me it was really in right now, and Bill said he absolutely loved it."

Really in tipped Hannah off. She was willing to bet there was more to this story than a simple shirt. "What did the shirt look like?"

"You know. It had two sleeves, and buttons, and a collar, and . . . you know what a shirt looks like."

"Long sleeves, or short?"

"Long."

"Regular collar?"

"That's right. It had one pocket, and it was an absolutely gorgeous color."

"Uh-oh," Hannah said under her breath. They'd come to the crux of it now. "What color?" she asked, narrowing in on what she hoped would explain her brother-in-law's atypical behavior.

"Raspberry."

That set Hannah back a couple of paces. "And raspberry is . . . red?"

"It's a little lighter than red."

Ah-ha! Hannah experienced the sweet thrill of success. "Is it pink?"

"It's not pure pink. It has some blue in it, you know?"

"Not really. Describe the color in more detail."

"Well . . . it's a little bluer than mauve, but much more subdued than cherry. It's really just a shade or two lighter than burgundy."

"I see," Hannah said, doing her best not to chuckle. The shirt Bill had failed to pack was pink and that explained everything. There was no way Bill would wear a pink shirt to a law enforcement convention. With all that testosterone floating around, the chairs and tables were probably growing beards, and any sheriff in a pink shirt would be laughed right out of the hotel . . . especially if he said his wife bought it for him and he'd promised to think of her every time he wore it.

"What?" Andrea asked. "Are you choking?"

"Something must have gone down the wrong pipe. Just let me get a glass of water." Hannah coughed again, doing her best to conceal her mirth as she headed for the sink to run water.

"Well?" Andrea asked, when Hannah came back to the table. "Do you see why I'm so upset?"

"Of course I do. But . . . there may be a very simple explanation. Has Bill ever worn that shirt?"

"No, not yet."

"That's it, then," Hannah said, congratulating herself for saving Andrea's marriage and getting her brother-in-law out of a pickle.

"What's it? I don't understand."

"Bill didn't want to wear it for the first time when you weren't around, especially since he'd think of you and get lonely. It's as clear as the nose on my face." *The nose on my face that's growing longer by the second*, her mind added, but Hannah ignored it.

"I still don't understand."

"Bill didn't wear it because he's saving it for a special occasion."

"Well . . . I guess that makes some kind of sense," Andrea conceded.

"You bet it does. And I'm also sure that when he gets home, Bill's going to take you out to a fancy dinner and wear that shirt."

"You think?"

"I know," Hannah said, making a mental note to call Bill at his hotel in Florida and make sure he knew enough to do just that.

ALL-NIGHTER COOKIES

Preheat oven to 350 degrees F., rack in
the middle position

Hannah's Note: Florence didn't have any bananas (she didn't expect to be open while they were shooting the movie) and I ended up taking one of Edna's shortcuts in this recipe. If you don't like shortcuts and want to do this the original way, use ⅔ cup very ripe, almost all black on the outside, pureed bananas instead of the baby food bananas and banana pudding mix. The other change you have to make is to use 4 cups flour instead of 3½. The dough will be stickier and you'll have to chill it for at least 4 hours in order to make the dough balls. I made these cookies both ways, and Mother was the only one who could tell the difference. (I still think it was a lucky guess.)

1½ cups melted butter ***(3 sticks)***
1 cup white ***(granulated)*** sugar
1 cup firmly packed brown sugar
2 beaten eggs ***(just whip them up with a fork)***
1 teaspoon baking soda
½ teaspoon salt

½ cup baby food mashed bananas ***(I used Gerber's)***
5.1 ounce package banana cream pudding mix ***(NOT sugar-free) (I used Jell-O, 6-serving pkg.)***
3½ cups flour ***(no sifting—pack it down in the cup when you measure)***
1 cup chopped nuts ***(I used salted peanuts)***
2 cups peanut butter chips ***(one 10-ounce package will do just fine)***

½ cup white ***(granulated)*** sugar for later

Melt the butter in a large microwave-safe bowl. Stir in the sugars, beaten eggs, baking soda, and salt.

Measure out ½ cup of baby food bananas and add it, along with the package of dry pudding mix. ***(Make sure your baby food bananas don't have anything else, like cereal, added to them!)***

Mix in the flour by half-cup increments. Add the nuts and then the peanut butter chips. Stir until everything is incorporated.

Roll the dough into walnut-sized balls with your hands. ***(If it's too sticky, chill it for 30 minutes or so, and try again.)***

Put ½ cup white sugar in a small bowl and roll the balls in it. Place the dough balls on a greased cookie sheet, 12 to a standard-sized sheet. Press them down with the heel of your hand, or with a metal spatula sprayed with Pam or other non-stick cooking spray.

Bake the cookies for 10 to 12 minutes at 350 degrees F., or until they're lightly golden in color. Let them cool for 2 minutes on the cookie sheet and then move them to a wire rack to finish cooling.

These cookies freeze well. Roll them up in foil, and place the rolls in a freezer bag.

Michelle asked for this recipe after Lonnie Murphy tasted them at The Cookie Jar. She says she's going to freeze some so he'll have them when he visits her, but she's going to mark the package "Lutefisk Patties" so her roommates won't get into them.

Yield: Approximately 8 to 10 dozen, depending on cookie size.

CHOCOLATE TRUFFLES

6 tablespoons chilled butter ***(¾ stick, 3 ounces)***

12-ounce package semi-sweet chocolate chips ***(two cups—I used Ghirardelli's)***

½ cup firmly packed powdered sugar ***(confectioner's sugar)***

6 egg yolks

1 Tablespoon rum, brandy, flavored brandy, or vanilla extract

Put an inch or so of water in the bottom half of a double boiler and heat it to a gentle boil. Cut the butter in chunks and place them in the top half of the double boiler. Add the chips and then the powdered sugar and set the top half over the bottom half. Put on the cover and let everything melt while you . . .

Beat the egg yolks in a small bowl with a whisk. Whisk until they're thoroughly combined, but stop before they get fluffy or lighter in color.

Stir the chocolate until it's completely melted. It will be thick, almost like fudge. Remove the top half of the double boiler and set it on a cold burner.

Stir several spoonfuls of beaten egg yolk into the chocolate mixture. When that's incorporated, stir in several more spoonfuls. Keep adding egg yolk in small amounts, stirring constantly, until all the egg yolks have been incorporated and the chocolate mixture is smooth and glossy.

Stir in the rum, brandy, or vanilla. Put the lid back on the top of the double boiler and refrigerate the chocolate mixture for 3 hours.

To Decorate Truffles:

finely chopped nuts
powdered ***(confectioner's)*** sugar
chocolate sprinkles
shaved chocolate
cocoa powder
finely shredded coconut

Warning: This next step is fairly messy. If you like, wear disposable plastic food server gloves. You can also lightly grease your hands, or spray them with Pam or other non-stick cooking spray so the chocolate won't stick to your fingers.

Form small balls of chilled chocolate with your hands and roll them in bowls of the above ingredients. You can mix and match, or give all of your truffles the same coating. Place the truffles in ruffled bon-bon papers and store them in an airtight container in the refrigerator.

These are incredibly delicious candies. They're super easy to make, but let's keep that a secret. It can't hurt to let people assume that you went to a lot of trouble, just for them.

Yield: 4 to 5 dozen, depending on truffle size.

Chapter Seventeen

Hannah and Andrea broke into applause when Tracey spelled *onomatopoeia*, a very difficult word for the third-grade girl she was playing. They were standing at the back of the classroom, pretending to be parents who'd come to watch the spelling bee and doubling as extras since Dean Lawrence had decided at the last minute he wanted a few "parents" involved.

He cued Andrea, who was playing Amy's mother shortly before the fatal accident that would claim her life, and she rushed to the front of the room to hug Tracey. They held their pose for a moment and then Dean cued in several of the real third graders, who'd been instructed to look both angry and jealous, and to start whispering to each other.

"Cut," Dean called out, once he'd gotten the shot. "That's a wrap, everybody. We got it in just one shot."

The real third graders took their cue from their teacher and the whole class applauded. Hannah could tell that they were very excited about being in a movie.

Dean caught Andrea's arm as she moved to pass him, and he bent down to address Tracey. "That was perfect,

Sweetheart. You're a fine little actress. And Mommy?" Dean straightened up and took Andrea's hand. "You were every bit as wonderful as I knew you'd be. Now don't forget what I told you, all right?"

"I won't forget," Andrea said, leading Tracey from the room with Hannah following in her wake.

"What did he mean by that?" Hannah asked, as soon as they'd cleared the doorway. "What did he tell you?"

Andrea gave an elaborate shrug, but she didn't meet Hannah's eyes. "Nothing, really. He just said he thought I'd be perfect in that scene as Tracey's mother."

"Because you *are* Tracey's mother?"

"Maybe," Andrea said, leaning forward to re-tie the bow in Tracey's hair. "Okay, honey. Say good-bye to Aunt Hannah. We've got to get you home so we can take off that makeup."

Once Tracey and Andrea had left, Hannah walked back to The Cookie Jar. Andrea had left in such a hurry she'd forgotten she'd promised to give Hannah a ride. That was odd, and so was the comment Dean Lawrence had made as they'd exited the classroom. Could Andrea's doubts about Bill's fidelity have driven her into another man's arms? Hannah didn't think so. She was positive that Andrea loved Bill. But jealousy and doubt could be taking its toll, and a real womanizer would attempt to capitalize on that. The voice she'd heard when she'd delivered Dean's cheesecake this morning sounded a lot like her sister's voice. But certainly she must be mistaken about that.

Hannah put her suspicions firmly out of mind as she passed the park with its empty play equipment. The chains on the swings hung straight down like suspenders holding up a pair of pants, and the gleaming metal slide had a puddle of melted snow at the bend. Tracey's favorite, the Flying Dutchman, Merry-Go-Round, or Whirl-A-Whirl, whatever you cared to call the large circular platform with metal handholds that the children rode as it spun around and around, was perfectly motionless and surrounded by melting bits of snow. The area beneath it, scraped clear of grass by children's feet, was beginning to turn muddy in the noonday sun.

Down at the far end of the park, the skating rink gleamed in the sun. Hannah was amazed that the ice looked so firm until she remembered that it was artificial. If the day kept up its warming trend, all the snow would melt and Ross would have to rely on fake snow as well as fake ice. That wasn't so bad, but Tracey and the other girls would broil in their heavy costumes during the skating scene.

Once she'd passed the circular sidewalk that ringed the park, Hannah crossed the street and walked up Fourth to Main Street. She rounded the corner by the now-defunct Magnolia Blossom Bakery, and found herself glancing in the front plate glass window and remembering how beautifully decorated it had been. Some of those decorations, including the lovely round tables and matching chairs, now graced the coffee shop at The Cookie Jar. Hannah still felt a bit guilty for taking advantage of Vanessa's panicked offer to sell them to her at such a ridiculous price, but she wasn't about to give them up. She'd done the right thing and contacted Gloria Travis, who should have inherited the money Vanessa had spent to buy them, and Gloria had told her to keep everything she wanted and give away the rest.

Lake Eden Realty, the office where Andrea worked, was humming in lonely splendor. The computers were on, the desk lamps were lit, and the fax machine was spewing out paper. The owner, Al Percy, wasn't there and neither was Andrea. Since Ross had rented Main Street for the week, no business except movie business would be conducted.

Her shop looked busy and Lisa must have been waiting for her to arrive, because she opened the front door and motioned to her. Hannah dashed across the street and into

The Cookie Jar, wondering what sort of emergency had reared its ugly head in the forty-five minutes she'd been gone.

"He . . . he wants *what*?" Hannah sputtered, looking at her young partner with dismay. "And by *when*?"

"Hors d'oeuvres, that's what. And he had the nerve to ask me if I knew what they were!"

"That's not the insult you think it is," Hannah informed her. "He asked *me* if I knew what finger food was!"

Lisa gave a startled little giggle, and Hannah knew her good mood had been restored. That was one of the things she loved about her partner. Lisa had a sunny disposition, and even though Dean had introduced a few storm clouds on her horizon, her cheerful nature couldn't remain hidden for long.

"What sort of small bits of appetizing food does he want?" Hannah asked, giving the dictionary definition and earning a smile from her partner.

"He said he'd leave that up to us. The only thing is, everything has to be edible, because he wants the extras at the cocktail party to mingle and munch."

"Mingle and munch?" Hannah repeated, making a face. "That sounds positively inane. I wonder what sort of appetizers they served in the fifties."

"I'll call Marge. The library's got a section of old cookbooks. She can look it up for us."

"Good idea," Hannah said, heading for the pantry to see what supplies they'd need to buy for mingle-and-munch time at the nineteen-fifties house.

Searching the pantry didn't take long, and neither did going through the walk-in cooler. When she came back out to the coffee shop again, Hannah found Lisa just hanging up the phone.

"I've got three," Lisa said, holding up one of Hannah's steno pads. "What do you think of celery sticks stuffed with peanut butter? Everybody served it at parties back then."

"Okay. We've got plenty of peanut butter, but we don't have celery. Put that down on our shopping list. One of us will have to make a quick trip to the Red Owl."

"I'll go," Lisa said, "I'll just call Florence and give her a heads-up, so she'll let me in the back."

While Lisa called Florence, Hannah took the notebook and looked at the other appetizers Lisa had listed. There was something that sounded interesting using olives, crackers, and cream cheese tinted with food dye. They could certainly make those. And there was no reason why they couldn't take the stuffed celery idea and run with it. They could make a second type stuffed with flavored cream cheese, and a third stuffed with Mike's Busy Day Pâté. All three would look nice on a platter.

The last appetizer was the most difficult and it all had to do with the timing. The ingredients were simple enough, just cream cheese mixed with minced onions and a little mayonnaise. The mixture was spread on crackers and the crackers were broiled just before serving so that the cream cheese would puff up. Hannah was sure they could handle that. Delores and Carrie had a toaster oven in their upstairs break room. All it would take was someone to man the toaster oven and they could have hot appetizers at the scene.

"So what's on my grocery list," Lisa asked.

Hannah explained about the three kinds of stuffed celery they could make, and then she read the list she'd made. "Celery, mayonnaise, horseradish, crackers, dried onions, braunschweiger, flavored cream cheese, and a can of tuna."

"Okay." Lisa took the list and headed for the back door, but she turned before she got there. "What's the tuna for?"

"Moishe."

"Because . . . ?"

"He didn't scratch Andrea."

"I see," Lisa said. "I guess I'd better pick up a can of salmon, too."

"Why's that?"

"Because he didn't scratch me, either!"

CREAM CHEESE PUFFS

Hannah's Note: If you're not going to serve these right away, you can mix up the cream cheese part and refrigerate it until it's time to spread it on the crackers.

8-ounce package cream cheese ***(the firm kind, not the whipped)***
2 Tablespoons ***($1/8$ cup)*** mayonnaise ***(We used Hellmann's***)***
3 Tablespoons minced green onion
OR 3 Tablespoons minced dried onion
OR 3 Tablespoons minced shallots
1 beaten egg

A box of salted crackers ***(We used Ritz Crackers and they were great!)***

*** ***Hellmann's Mayonnaise is also known as Best Foods Mayonnaise in some parts of the country.***

Unwrap the cream cheese and put it in a microwave-safe bowl. Nuke it on HIGH for 30 seconds, or until it begins to soften.

Mix in the mayonnaise and stir until the mixture is smooth.

Mix in the onion. ***(If you use green onion instead of shallots or dried onion, you can use up to one inch of the stem.)***

Mix in the beaten egg.

Lay out the crackers on a broiler pan, salt side up. ***(We used a disposable broiler pan so we could trash it at Granny's Attic and we wouldn't have to carry it back to The Cookie Jar.)***

Spread the cream cheese mixture on top of the cracker in a circle that reaches the edges. Mound it slightly in the center. Use about two teaspoons of cheese mixture per cracker.

Position the rack approximately three inches below the coil of the broiler and turn it on HIGH. Broil the crackers ***(with the oven door open to the first latch so the broiler doesn't kick on and off)*** until the cream cheese puffs up and is just starting to turn golden. This should take about 90 seconds if the rack is correctly positioned.

Let cool for a minute or two, so your guests won't burn their tongues. Transfer the Cream Cheese Puffs to a platter and serve.

Yield: Approximately 2 dozen hot and yummy hors d'oeuvres.

Another Note From Hannah: I haven't actually tried this, but I'm willing to bet a dozen of my best cookies that you could also add a quarter cup chopped smoked salmon to the cream cheese mixture.

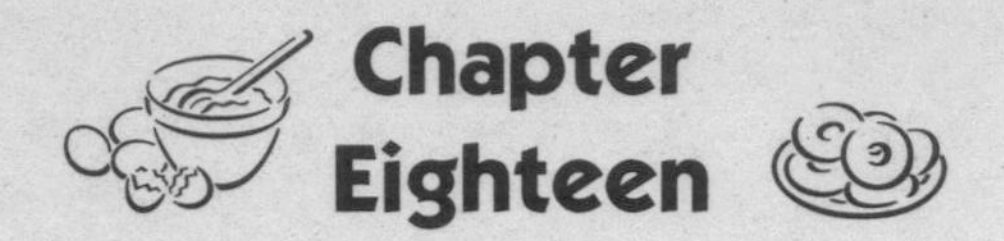

Chapter Eighteen

Hannah had just finished giving instructions to Luanne Hanks, who'd offered to broil the Cream Cheese Puffs. "Michelle will cue Mother and she'll beep you on the intercom when we need a batch. But are you really sure you want to be stuck up here while they shoot the fancy cocktail scene?"

"I'm positive. I don't want to have anything to do with some of those movie people."

Luanne wore a very determined look on her pretty face, and Hannah sensed a story. One of *those movie people* had caused some sort of problem for Luanne.

"Are you talking about any one movie person in particular?" Hannah asked, doing a little fishing.

"Mr. Lawrence. He's a dirty old man, Hannah!"

The *old* classification took Hannah back a little, but then she remembered that Luanne was Michelle's age, only twenty. Dean Lawrence, who was in his forties, would seem old to her. "He made a pass at you?" she asked.

"How did you know?" Luanne looked profoundly shocked. "I didn't tell anybody."

"It was a guess, but I figured it was a good one. From

what I hear, Dean's made a pass at almost every woman in town."

"Even *you?*"

Hannah winced slightly. Luanne didn't have to sound so incredulous. "Yes, even me. He's a frustrated adolescent, Luanne."

"You mean like the high school boys? When all they can think about is girls?"

"Exactly. Dean probably doesn't mean anything by it. It's just a game to him. And maybe they don't mind his behaving like that in Hollywood."

"Lake Eden isn't Hollywood," Luanne retorted, her eyes flashing with anger. "And I don't appreciate grown men acting like high school boys."

"Neither did some of the other women I talked to," Hannah said, thinking about Lisa and how she'd almost poured hot coffee down Dean's neck.

"Well . . . I guess it helps to know it's not just me. And here I was, trying to figure out what I did to make him think I'd say yes when he invited me to his trailer. I thought maybe it was Suzie and the fact I had a baby without being married and all. But it's just the way he behaves with everybody . . . right?"

"Just women. I think the guys in town are safe."

Luanne gave a startled giggle. "Oh, that's funny. Thank you, Hannah. You made me feel a lot better, but I still don't want to get within ten feet of Mr. Lawrence. It's insulting, you know? If he even looks at me crosswise, I'll probably kill him."

"Don't do that. Just come and tell me. We'll organize all the other women and run him out of town on a rail."

"Do we even have a rail?"

"I'm not sure, but if we don't, we'll get one. Besides, he's probably on his best behavior now that his wife's in town."

"I didn't know he was married!" Luanne looked shocked.

"He certainly didn't *act* like he was. That poor woman! She must not know about what he does behind her back."

"What makes you think that?" Hannah asked.

"Because if she knew, she'd either leave him or kill him, whichever one seemed better at the time."

Hannah busied herself by filling the silver trays the movie waitresses would use for the cocktail scene. No one was here yet, but they were due to arrive any minute. As she placed stuffed celery sticks in a giant sunburst around the radish roses that Lisa had made, she thought about all she'd learned in the past several days about the movie business.

Her first revelation had been that movie scenes weren't shot in sequence. Ross had come to Lake Eden to film the "hometown" scenes. Three were with Tracey playing Amy as a child, four were with Erica playing Amy as a teenager, and three were with Lynne playing Amy as an adult. Today's scene, the second to the last in the movie, was the cocktail party. And even though Burke's character would die in the scene they were shooting today, he'd be back tomorrow to play Jody walking arm in arm with Amy down the street.

Tomorrow would be another full day of filming. There would be a scene with Erica in her blue-and-white bedroom, a scene with Burke and Lynne visiting their "father's" grave, and a third scene as they attended their "aunt's" funeral. On Friday they would shoot a scene at the high school with the actor playing Jody as a teenager, the skating scene with Tracey in the park, and the final scene of the movie where an adult Amy, played by Lynne, said good-bye forever to Cherrywood and drove off to return to her husband and family.

Hannah finished the tray of stuffed celery and started to arrange the chilled Mini Cherry Cheesecakes. She'd also learned that there was no good time to deliver cheesecakes to Dean's trailer. After that first morning, when she'd heard someone who'd sounded suspiciously like Erica leave by the rear door, she'd taken the precaution of calling Dean's office before she left The Cookie Jar. But that hadn't helped a speck. Every time she called, she got the answer machine and it was clear that Dean hadn't heard even one of her messages. And each time she'd knocked on the trailer door, she'd heard a female voice and then a muffled curse from the Bad Boy Director. Several minutes later, Dean would open the door looking rumpled and very crabby, Hannah would step in, and then she'd hear the rear door open and close.

So far, in the course of her cheesecake delivery experience, she'd heard five women leaving Dean's Winnebago. She couldn't swear to it in a court of law, but she'd thought about the women's voices she'd heard and come to some tentative conclusions. The first voice had sounded like Erica. There were just too many giggles for anyone else. And the voice on the second morning had sounded a whole lot like Lynne. After lunch, when she'd delivered the second cheesecake, Hannah was almost positive she'd heard Jeanette, Erica's mother. Then there was the voice this morning, the voice that she really hadn't wanted to recognize. She'd denied it at first, but now Hannah had to admit that the woman with Dean had sounded exactly like Andrea. It all tied in with what Dean had said as they'd left the school after Tracey's spelling bee scene. Hannah sent up a silent prayer that she was dead wrong and her sister wasn't involved with the Bad Boy Director.

This afternoon, when she delivered Dean's second cheesecake, Hannah had recognized the woman's voice. She was almost positive that it had been Honey, the head beautician. Even though Sharyn was now in town, his wife's presence didn't appear to be modifying Dean's behavior one bit.

In spite of all this, Dean was a gifted director. Everyone in the cast agreed about that. What Burke had said in his interview was partly true. If Dean wasn't getting the performance he wanted from an actor or actress, he was quick to step in and demonstrate what he wanted them to do. While he didn't actually get dressed up in their costumes, he did occasionally use a hat, or a scarf, or some prop to enhance the illusion.

Only a few people were allowed in to watch the scene that was being filmed, and Hannah breathed a sigh of relief as she spotted Winnie Henderson.

"Hi, Winnie," Hannah said, rushing up to her. "I need to talk to you after all this is over. Will you stop by The Cookie Jar?"

"Sure, but only if you promise not to mention the park. I'm sick and tired of people trying to talk me into signing off so those movie people can use it."

"I can't promise you that," Hannah said truthfully. "But if you listen to what I have to say and you still say no, I'll shut up and I won't say another word about it."

Winnie laughed good-naturedly. "Okay then. That's fair enough. I'll stop by if you save one of those little cherry cheesecakes for me. They look mighty tasty."

"It's a done deal," Hannah agreed, borrowing Andrea's favorite phrase. And then she excused herself and hurried off to check the extra coolers she'd brought to hold the little cheesecakes, in case the ones on the platters began to droop under the lights.

"We're here!" a voice shouted out, and Hannah turned to see Michelle coming in with the cast and crew. Everyone who was in the scene was in full costume, including the extras, and Hannah watched her youngest sister and several other movie people as they helped the extras find their places and coached them on what to do.

They were all ready and waiting to go when Dean strolled in. He moved a few people, stepped back to look at the result, and nodded. While he was giving some last-minute instructions to Burke and Lynne, Michelle came over to stand with Hannah.

"Am I late?" Andrea asked, coming up to join them.

"No, it'll be at least another ten minutes, maybe fifteen," Michelle told her. "Where's Tracey?"

"At home, doing her homework with Grandma McCann. When she's through, they're going to watch a movie."

The three sisters stood there gazing at the scene for a moment. It was strange to see so many Lake Eden people dressed in fancy evening clothes in the middle of the afternoon. Hannah was the first to turn away and as she did, she noticed that both of her siblings were watching Dean Lawrence with identical hungry looks in their eyes.

Hannah shrugged slightly. She guessed she could understand their fascination with the director. He *was* handsome and as long as her sisters were just "window shopping," that was fine with her. Dean looked slightly disheveled and wickedly charming. He would have been right at home in a pirate's costume, ravishing women left and right.

Her attention shifted to a familiar figure who'd just walked in. It was Ross and as far as Hannah was concerned, he was much more appealing than Dean. It was true that he wasn't quite as handsome, but her Grandma Ingrid used to say, *Handsome is as handsome does*, and Hannah thought she was right. Ross was a much nicer person than Dean and he cared about people other than himself.

"Hey, Shelly. Mike and I are here."

Hannah turned to see Lonnie Murphy, Michelle's significant Lake Eden other, standing behind them in full-dress uniform. It was dark blue instead of tan and maroon, the colors of the Winnetka County Sheriff's Department, and there was a patch sewn on the shoulder that read CHERRYWOOD P. D.

Lonnie was smiling and Hannah smiled back. He was the only person who could get away with calling her sister, *Shelly*, a name Michelle absolutely despised. And the fact that Michelle didn't seem to mind at all when Lonnie said it told a lot about their relationship.

Michelle turned and a big smile spread across her face. Hannah was relieved to notice that the look in Michelle's eyes when she shifted her attention to Lonnie was at least a hundred watts brighter than the look she'd given Dean. Michelle had her priorities straight, but did Andrea? Hannah's middle sister was still focused entirely on the Bad Boy Director.

Then something happened that caused Hannah to relax slightly. Sharyn Lawrence stepped onto the set and wove her way through the extras to greet her husband. Andrea stared at her for a moment and then she turned to Hannah.

"That's Sharyn," she said. "She's Dean's wife."

"I didn't know you'd met her."

"I haven't, but who else could it be? Dean said his wife had raven hair."

"You've been talking to Dean about his wife?"

"Not really. He just happened to mention her, that's all. We were talking about Tracey's part in the movie."

Hannah decided to take the bull by the horns. "Was that this morning when I knocked on the door at the Winnebago?"

"Uh . . . yes. Look, Hannah. Nothing happened."

"Then why did you go out the back way?"

"He asked me to. He wanted to avoid any gossip, you know? I mean, since I'm married and all."

That hasn't stopped him in the past, Hannah thought, but she didn't say it. She remained perfectly silent and waited for her sister to get uncomfortable enough to go on with her explanation.

"It's just like I told you, Hannah. Nothing happened!

Dean talked to me about Tracey's part in the movie. He's been just wonderful about advising us."

Again, Hannah remained perfectly silent. It wasn't easy, but the ball was in Andrea's court.

"He said he called me in so early because he needed to talk to me privately. And that's when he told me that he's already chosen his next movie script and I'm perfect for one of the parts."

"You?" Hannah asked, too startled to remain silent any longer.

"Yes, me. And he even offered to fly me to Hollywood for a screen test."

Hannah stared at her sister in absolute shock. "Don't tell me you fell for that old line! My *married* sister who's totally in love with her husband, even though she's momentarily ticked off with him for going off to Miami without her, wouldn't be that naïve . . . right?"

"Of course not! I'm almost certain I'm not star material, and I recognize a line when I hear one. But it really *was* flattering, and I was tempted to say yes for a split second or two."

"But you said no."

"Of course I did. But Dean was very persuasive and now I can understand why so many women would do almost anything he asked them to do."

"I'm just glad you're not one of those women," Hannah said. But before she could say anything else, the assistant director called for quiet on the set.

Some of the prop men hurried up to the set carrying champagne glasses and handed them to some of the guests at the cocktail party. Others didn't get glasses and Hannah assumed that they would be approached by waitresses in the scene with their trays of filled glasses.

"Are they really drinking champagne?" Hannah asked her youngest sister.

Michelle shook her head. "It's cream soda. We'll do a couple of second unit inserts later with glasses being filled with real champagne."

"Like the inserts Clark shot of Moishe?"

"That's right. Excuse me a second, Hannah. Ross needs me."

Michelle rushed onto the set and up to Ross, who'd motioned to her. A second later she headed for the door and came back with Mike in tow.

"Oh, boy!" Hannah said under her breath. Mike was a sight for sore eyes in his full-dress Cherrywood P. D. uniform. Actually, he was a sight for sore eyes in anything he wore, but she didn't want to think about that right now.

Mike, his brass gleaming under the lights, followed Ross and Lloyd, the head prop man, as they led him to an ornate white desk trimmed with gold that sat in the corner of the room. It was a double desk, the kind Hannah had always wanted but wasn't sure why, with room for two people to sit on either side and use it together. Hannah watched as Mike pulled out one of the center drawers and examined what was inside. Then he closed it again, exchanged a couple of words with Lloyd and Ross, and went back out through the living room doorway.

"What was he doing?" Hannah asked Michelle, who'd come back to stand by Andrea.

"He was checking the gun to make sure it was unloaded and Lloyd had removed the firing pin."

"Is that the gun they use in the suicide scene?" Andrea wanted to know.

"That's right."

Hannah started to frown. "But it won't make any noise at all without a firing pin."

"That's right. We'll add the sound of a gun firing in post production."

"Why not use blanks?" Andrea asked.

"Blanks are only safe if your target is a few yards away,"

Hannah answered, remembering the way Ross had described the suicide scene. "Burke has to put the gun right up to his temple."

"So?"

"Blanks have a primer and gunpowder inside a casing. It's sealed with a wad of something that looks like shellac. When the gun's fired, the wad can exit the barrel with enough velocity to kill Burke."

"I didn't know that!" Andrea breathed, shivering a bit.

"A lot of people don't know that. The only reason I know is that Lisa told me."

"How did she find out?" Michelle wanted to know.

"Herb teaches a class in gun safety." Hannah was about to tell them about the television actor who was killed with blanks while pretending to commit suicide on a set, when she saw Delores giving her the high sign. "The Cream Cheese Puffs must be ready. Either that or Mother is trying out for the part of a windmill."

Chapter Nineteen

"I never wanted you to figure it out, but it really doesn't matter anyway. He looked at me right before I shot him and I keep seeing that look in my dreams. It's haunting me and I just can't take it anymore."

Burke pulled out the center drawer and reached for the gun, but before he could grasp it, there was an angry shout from Dean.

"Cut!" Dean shouted again. "What's with you, Burke? You're supposed to make people weep for you! Get up. I'll show you what I want here."

Burke looked very embarrassed as he rose to his feet. "I'm sorry, Dean. I don't know what's wrong, either. I just can't seem to get the motivation right. I know Jody's supposed to be at the end of his rope, but it's just not working for me."

"Why not? He's been dealing with guilt for years and it's taken its toll. He's also sloshed to the gills. All you have to do is sell drunk and guilty."

"I know. We talked about that, and I thought I could do it, but . . ." Burke stopped speaking and sighed. "My back hurts and I just can't seem to get it right."

Dean rolled his eyes at the rest of the cast. "Fine. I'll show you how it should be done."

"Thanks, Dean." Burke moved to the edge of the set and watched as Dean walked toward the desk. But before he got there, the director stopped and turned to his cameramen. "Make this a three-shot. I've got the feeling we're going to need it. The way Burke's going today, I might have to put it on a loop and screen it for him all night."

"That was nasty," Hannah whispered to Michelle.

"And how! Dean's not about to get nominated for the nicest guy in the movie business," Michelle whispered back. "When this scene's over, I'll tell you what he said to me this morning!"

Hannah glanced at Delores and saw she was doing her windmill impression again. Hannah was about to head up the stairs to fetch more Cream Cheese Puffs when Andrea grabbed her arm.

"I'll go," Andrea offered. "I have to make a call anyway. I'll bring the tray back down when this take's over."

"That's fine with me." Once Andrea had left, Hannah turned her attention back to the scene. Dean was getting a glass of cream soda champagne from one of the waitresses and when he turned around to face the camera, she had all she could do not to gasp. He looked glassy-eyed, as if he'd been indulging in strong spirits for hours. The illusion of extreme inebriation was embellished even further as he made his way unsteadily through the crowd to approach the antique partner's desk where Lynne was sitting.

The adult Amy was deep in thought, staring down at the tray of Mini Cherry Cheesecakes that a waitress had left on the top of the desk without really seeing them. Hannah knew Lynne was supposed to be remembering what had happened on the night of her father's suicide.

"Well, how about that . . . it's Li'l Sis," Dean said, stumbling slightly and catching himself on the corner of the desk. "Mind if I sit down?"

"Oh, Jody. You're drunk! You're just as drunk as Dad used to get whenever he threw a cocktail . . ." Lynne stopped and put both hands to her head, as if she could stop the memories from emerging. It was a perfect gesture and Hannah was impressed.

"You're thinking about the night he did it?" Dean asked, slurring his words.

"Yes."

"He was drunk that night, too. And you know what always happened whenever he was drunk."

Hannah watched as Lynne gave a delicate shudder. Her face actually paled and Hannah could see the tears well up in her eyes. "I know, Jody. I remember."

"I couldn't let him do that again, Li'l Sis. No way. You understand that, don't you?"

"Yes," Lynne said and she looked profoundly sad. "It's all right, Jody. Nobody else has to know what happened that . . . "

"But I know!" Dean interrupted, and Hannah almost jumped as he leaned forward over the desktop, coming very close to touching Lynne.

"I'll never tell," Lynne promised, a tear rolling down her cheek. "I promise, Jody. I'll never tell a soul."

"'Course not. Wouldn't expect you to. But that doesn't help a whole lot, Li'l Sis. I never wanted you to figure it out, but it really doesn't matter anyway. He looked at me right before I shot him and I keep seeing that look in my dreams. It's haunting me and I just can't take it anymore."

Dean pulled out the center drawer of the desk and grabbed the gun. He rose to his feet and was raising the revolver to his head when Lynne started to scream. Her scream wasn't audible over the sound of the music and laughter from the merrymakers at the cocktail party. No one reacted in the slightest.

"No!" Lynne sounded positively panic-stricken. "I love you, Jody! Don't do this to me!"

"I'm not doing it to you, Li'l Sis. I'm doing it *for me.*"

Once he'd delivered that line, Dean raised the gun to his temple and squeezed the trigger. The instant the hammer flew forward, there was a loud explosion. The earsplitting blast prompted several screams from the extras, and Hannah stood there staring, barely able to believe what she was seeing. Dean Lawrence, Hollywood's Bad Boy Director, was lying facedown in the tray of Mini Cherry Cheesecakes, his legs slumped against the front of the desk and his arms dangling limply at his sides. There was no doubt in Hannah's mind that he'd suffered the same fate as the character he'd been playing. The fake suicide of the movie had turned out to be all too real. The empty revolver without its firing pin had fired!

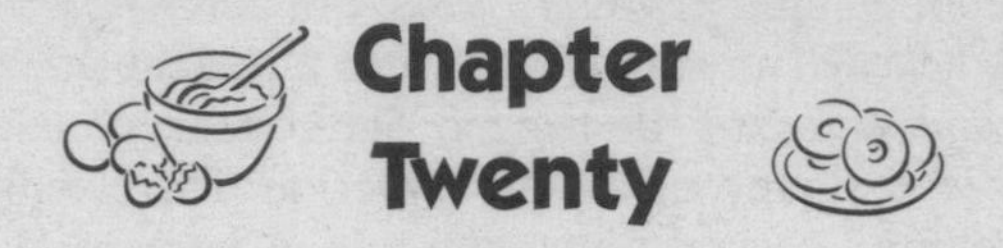

Chapter Twenty

Even if she were so inclined, there was no way Hannah could get close to the mayhem on the set. People were yelling, screaming, pushing, and shoving to get away from the violent scene. Hannah stood where she was, not wanting to move until some sort of order was restored, and stared at the panicking actors and extras.

Was that a blue uniform in the middle of the melee? Hannah tried to see past an opaque lavender silk object that turned out to be Helen Barthel's derrierre. Yes, it was Mike, towering head and shoulders above the diminutive Amber Coombs in her smart little cocktail waitress uniform. As Hannah watched, Mike made his way through the crowd and arrived at Lynne's side. He spoke to her for a moment and Hannah saw him pick up the chair with Lynne still in it, and place it so that she was sitting a few feet away from the desk. A moment later, Mike had commandeered a Japanese silk screen and he moved it in place to block Dean's body from everyone's view.

Hannah was so shocked by what she'd just witnessed, her mind took a strange twist. She'd been planning to add

Jane's Mini Cherry Cheesecakes to her menu at The Cookie Jar, but now that was definitely out. Anyone who had seen the dreadful incident would never be able to look at the cheesecakes without remembering Dean's last effort to play someone else's part and his second-to-final resting place. It was really a shame, because the cheesecakes were very good and they would have looked lovely on a silver tray with a white paper doily and . . .

She was jerked back to the present by a piercing whistle. There was a second whistle, and then a third. And then she heard Mike's voice.

"Stop! Stop right where you are!" he yelled, cupping his hands around his mouth in a makeshift megaphone. "Nobody move a muscle!"

Hannah watched in amazement as everyone did exactly as Mike had instructed. His was the voice of authority, and they needed some authority right about now.

"Let Deputy Murphy through, please," Mike ordered, but in a softer voice. "I want complete quiet while we remove Mrs. Larchmont from the scene. She's had a bad shock and she needs to rest."

There was complete silence on the set. Those who knew what had happened were thankful they hadn't been in Lynne's place, so close to their director's violent death. And those who didn't know weren't about to disobey an acting sheriff's orders.

"As soon as Deputy Murphy leaves with Mrs. Larchmont, I'm going to divide you into groups. The deputies I've called in will escort you to three different locations to be interviewed. Everyone must wait there until a deputy takes his or her statement. Whether you actually witnessed the unfortunate incident or not, we need to interview you. Do you understand?"

There were assenting murmurs and Mike was about to go on when he was interrupted by a question from Lynne.

"Excuse me, but . . . I just have to ask. Dean . . . he's . . . he's dead, isn't he?"

"Yes, Ma'am," Mike answered her. "Just go with Deputy Murphy and he'll take care of everything."

Hannah watched as Tom Larchmont approached Lonnie and asked him a question. Lonnie nodded and Tom joined them as they went out the door.

"I know this may inconvenience some people," Mike went on, "but everyone here will have to be searched before they leave Granny's Attic. It's not that we don't trust you, but it's standard operating procedure with this many witnesses."

There were the predictable grumbles and Mike spoke up again. "If you're good boys and girls, we'll make sure we have coffee at the three locations, and some snacks to tide you over. How's that?"

The grumbles faded and a few people smiled at their acting sheriff. Mike looked pleased as he addressed them again. "Thanks, folks. Let's all cooperate so I can get you home in a timely manner. And just let me add that you are the best-dressed witnesses that the Winnetka County Sheriff's Department has ever interviewed!"

There were a few grins and a couple of tentative chuckles. Hannah couldn't believe it. Mike had done such a good job of covering up the gruesome details that people were feeling much better. Mayor Bascomb, the ultimate politician in Hannah's opinion, had nothing on Mike. If the first man of Lake Eden wasn't careful, Mike might just unseat him someday!

Hannah hung back as Mike and the deputies he'd called to the scene arranged the extras and the movie people into three groups. One group was going to the community center, where Edna Ferguson would provide coffee and snacks. The second group would be held at Hal & Rose's Cafe, and Rose had been alerted. The third group, the group that included the cast, the cameramen, and most of the movie people who'd been working at the scene, would be taken to The Cookie Jar where Lisa was waiting with fresh coffee and cookies.

It took awhile, but at last Hannah had a chance for a private word with Mike. She put all thoughts of how good he looked in the dark blue uniform out of her head and concentrated on asking the right questions.

"Do you think Dean committed suicide?" she asked, speaking softly so that the cameramen, who were loading up their equipment, wouldn't hear her.

"That's one possibility I can't ignore, but I doubt it. Most people who shoot themselves don't do it in front of movie cameras and dozens of actors and extras."

"True." Hannah was glad to learn that Mike had come to the same conclusion she had. "Then it's murder?"

"That's my guess."

"Is there anything I can do to help you?"

"Yes," Mike said, slipping his arm around her waist and pulling her close for a brief hug. "You can forget about investigating this on your own and let me handle it."

Hannah turned the hug into a longer one than Mike had intended. It was partially because she liked to hug Mike and partially because she didn't want to promise something she knew she wouldn't do. "Which witness group am I in?"

"The Cookie Jar group. I'll need you to help me with Mrs. Larchmont. She's a friend of yours, right?"

"That's right. I knew her in college."

"Well, she's very broken up over this whole thing and I don't think we're going to get much out of interviewing her."

"I'm sure you're right. She's bound to be traumatized since it happened right in front of her."

"I had Lonnie take her down to The Cookie Jar. Her husband's with her and that should help. Anything you can say to help calm her down would be good."

"Of course. How about Sharyn Lawrence? What group is she in?"

"She's with Mrs. Larchmont and her husband. I understand he's her uncle?"

"Right." Hannah took a deep breath. She knew she was prying, but it was a question she had to ask. "Did she see the whole thing?"

"No. She told Lonnie she'd just left to get coffee for Dean. He always called for coffee after he finished demonstrating a scene, and she wanted to have it ready for him. She was upstairs in the break room with Luanne and Andrea when it happened."

"Thank goodness!" Hannah said, but her mind was racing. Had Sharyn left just to fetch coffee for her husband? Or had she known the gun would fire and wanted to get as far away as possible?

Mike pulled out his notebook and Hannah took a deep breath. She was about to get interviewed.

"Did you see me check the revolver?"

"Yes."

"Did you see anyone near the desk after that?"

Hannah shook her head. "No, but I was busy filling up trays with appetizers. After I finished, I went to stand with the other people who were watching. There were a lot of people walking around on the set, and I didn't really start looking at the desk until Lynne walked over there and took her place."

"Do you know of anyone who had a reason to want Dean dead?"

Hannah thought for a moment. "No one in particular. He wasn't the easiest man to get along with, but I don't know of anybody who'd actually murder him. And everybody agreed that he was a brilliant director."

"But you knew people who didn't like him?"

"Plenty, including me. Dean could lay on the charm, but he wasn't a nice man. Ask anybody and I think they'll agree with me. If he didn't have everything just the way he wanted it, he could be nasty."

"But you don't think that's a motive for murder?"

"I don't know. Maybe it is. As you said before, you're the detective." Hannah marshaled her thoughts and asked a question. "It's pretty obvious to me that someone switched guns. Do you agree?"

"Of course. They're the same model and manufacturer, but the one I inspected didn't have a firing pin. This one had bullets, and the revolver I checked wasn't loaded."

"Is that the reason you're searching everyone before they leave?"

"That's right. There was only one gun in that drawer, the one that killed Mr. Lawrence. Someone took the prop gun and replaced it with a working, fully loaded revolver. If nobody tries to remove the prop gun from the building, then it's still here."

"And it may have fingerprints on it?"

"It's a possibility."

"Here's another possibility," Hannah said, preparing to throw out a suggestion. "Do you think the bullet was meant for Dean? Or was it for Burke, who was supposed to be acting in that scene?"

Mike laughed and gave Hannah another little hug. "I love the way your mind works. The answer is, it could go either way. Someone who's familiar with Dean's work habits and knew that he usually demonstrated roles for his actors could have set the whole thing up to kill Dean."

"And on the other hand, someone who didn't know Dean's work habits might have set it up to kill Burke?"

"That's right."

"So then we have to treat both Dean and Burke as victims and look at the people who have motives for killing either one of them?"

"Exactly, but what's this *we* stuff?" Mike began to scowl. "I'm the detective here, not you."

"I know that."

"I know you know, but I want you to promise that you won't investigate on your own."

Hannah nodded, but that didn't seem to be good enough for Mike. He was still scowling.

"I want you to promise out loud," Mike insisted.

Hannah hesitated, but then she realized that Mike's wording had given her an out. She gave him the sweetest, most guileless smile she could muster and said, "I promise I won't investigate on my own."

"Okay, 'nuff said." Mike gave her another hug and a push toward the door. "Go back to The Cookie Jar. I'll wait for Doc Knight and then I'll come right over."

Hannah stopped at the door where Rick Murphy was frisking the last of the witnesses. He took one look at Hannah, made sure the last witness was out of earshot, and shook his head. "I don't need to search you, Hannah."

"Yes, you do. Mike said you have to search everyone." Hannah held her arms out to side and let Rick examine her pockets and frisk her for any weapon concealed on her person. "I want Mike to be sure I didn't leave with that prop gun."

Once she was outside on the sidewalk, Hannah started to grin. She'd promised Mike that she wouldn't investigate on her own, and she wouldn't. She'd just nose around and see what turned up, and she wouldn't do that alone either . . . not when she had her two sisters, Norman, Delores, Carrie, and the rest of her extended family to help her!

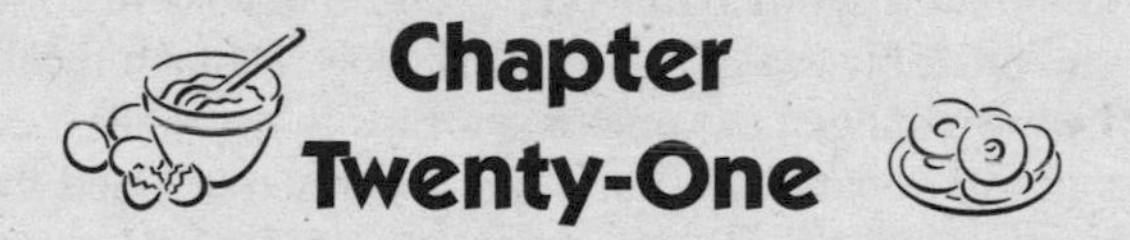

Chapter Twenty-One

When Hannah came in the front door of The Cookie Jar, she found her extended family already organized. Andrea and Lisa were making the rounds with coffee and cookies, while Carrie and Delores were handling hot water for tea and tea bags. They were listening so intently as they waited on the tables that Hannah imagined she could see their ears revolving like Moishe's did when he heard the patter of tiny mouse feet in the space behind the walls.

Sharyn was sitting with Lynne and Tom Larchmont, and she was holding Moishe on her lap. Hannah took in Sharyn's pale face and the tracks of recent tears on her cheeks, and wondered if Dean's wife was truly grief stricken, or whether she was every bit as good an actress as Lynne was. If Sharyn had found out about Dean's infidelities, she certainly had a motive to do away with her husband. And the fact that she hadn't been there when her husband's death had occurred could be either a stroke of luck, or an aversion to witnessing the gory scene.

Hannah's attention turned to Lynne, who looked quite calm despite the trauma she must have endured. It couldn't have been pleasant for her to see her director's death. On the other hand, Lynne had never been squeamish in college and she probably wasn't squeamish now. Hannah recalled that Lynne had been the one to set traps to get rid of the rodents in their apartment building, and she'd emptied them every morning. She'd even kept a record of what she'd called her "kills," posting a tally sheet in the kitchen and marking off every successful snap of the bail. When Ross and Hannah had told her they thought it was a bit cold blooded to keep count, Lynne had just laughed at them. A pest was a pest, she'd said, and she didn't mind exterminating them at all. Perhaps, in light of her college behavior, watching the end result of the gun switch she'd made hadn't bothered Lynne that much at all and her show of horror and grief had been a brilliantly acted ruse.

Then there was Tom Larchmont to consider. Hannah eyed the distinguished, silver-haired man with some suspicion. She was almost certain that Lynne had been one of the early morning visitors to Dean's Winnebago and had left by the rear exit. What if Tom had found out about Lynne's visit to Dean's trailer? Was he the type of jealous husband who'd murder Dean for dallying with his wife?

Hannah was just looking around for Connor, another man she'd labeled as a suspect, when Andrea and Michelle rushed up to her.

"We need a meeting," Andrea said, grabbing Hannah's arm. "Mother and Carrie promised to help Lisa hold down the fort here."

"Let's go to the kitchen," Hannah suggested, but Michelle shook her head.

"We can't. I just talked to Lonnie and Mike's going to be using the kitchen for follow-up interviews. The other detectives are weeding out promising witnesses and sending them to Mike."

"What are those?" Andrea wanted to know.

Hannah was curious. "Did Lonnie tell you what makes a witness promising?"

"I asked him that. He said they're the ones who were in a position to see or hear something potentially important to the investigation, like anyone who was standing close to Dean, or the waitress who put the tray of Mini Cherry Cheesecakes on the top of the desk."

"That would be Amber Coombs," Hannah offered. "Dean told her to put it there, but I don't know why."

Andrea's hand shot up, just as if she were still in school. "I know. I read the whole script. It was so Burke could fall face forward in the cheesecake after he shot himself. Except Burke didn't shoot himself, Dean did. And that's . . . really awful. I wonder if he had any . . . any . . . what's that word, Hannah?"

"Premonition?"

"That's it. I wonder if he had any premonition he'd be the one with his face in the cheesecake?"

All three sisters shivered slightly. It was a reminder of how quickly death could close in on an unsuspecting victim. They shared a moment of nervous silence and then Hannah broke it with a question.

"Are you ready to get down to business?" she asked. And when both of her younger sisters nodded, she went on. "Since Mike has dibs on the kitchen, we'll use my cookie truck."

"That'll get chilly," Andrea objected. "How about running across the street to Lake Eden Realty? I've got the key."

A few minutes later, the three sisters were seated in swivel chairs around Lake Eden Realty's oval conference table. Hannah had brought a thermos of coffee and a bag of her latest creations.

"What are these?" Michelle asked, biting into a cookie.

"Double Flakes."

"*Double* flakes?" Andrea frowned slightly. "I can taste coconut and that's one flake. But what's the other?"

Hannah shook her head. "I'll never tell. Just let me say that it's something you wouldn't expect to be in a cookie." She flipped open the steno pad she'd carried across the street with her and pushed it across the table to Andrea. "Will you take notes?"

"You always ask me to write things down!"

"That's true, but it's because you have such good penmanship. If I take notes, my mind gets ahead of my fingers and I have trouble figuring them out later."

"Okay, I'll do it. But there's a price."

"What is it?" Hannah asked, expecting her sister to demand a whole batch of her favorite cookies.

"I want to know what the second flakes are."

"No, you don't. It's a lot like Mystery Cookies. Once you find out what's in them, you keep eating, and eating, and trying to taste it."

Andrea made a big show of putting down her pen and flipping the steno pad closed. "If you won't cooperate and tell me, then I won't cooperate and take notes. Your unpaid personal secretary just quit."

"Come on, Andrea. It'll just drive you crazy."

"No, it won't. Trust me. Once you tell me, it'll be all over. And then you'll have perfectly legible notes."

Hannah glanced at Michelle, who shrugged. "I think she's got you over a barrel," she said.

"All right," Hannah conceded with a sigh. "I'll tell you. It's instant mashed potato flakes."

"You're kidding! I never would have guessed!" Andrea took another bite, and frowned as she chewed. "Are you sure? I don't taste instant potato flakes."

"I'm sure. I mixed up the dough myself."

"Well, I still don't taste them. Pass me another couple of cookies. Maybe the last one I ate was missing its potato flakes."

Hannah and Michelle sat back and watched as the cookies disappeared one by one. Finally, on the last cookie, Andrea gave a nod. "I think I taste them, but I'm not really sure. You don't have any more, do you?"

"Not here. I'll make you another batch tomorrow."

"That's good enough for me," Andrea said, picking up her pen and then giving a most unladylike burp. "Sorry about that. Now if one of you will pour me another cup of coffee, we can get this show on the road."

"Do you really think Sharyn could have done it?" Michelle asked, watching as Andrea wrote her name on the list of suspects.

"I don't know her well enough to tell," Hannah said. "It all depends on how jealous she was. It also depends on what she knew."

"What do you mean?" Michelle wanted to know.

"If she was the jealous type, but she *didn't* know her husband was entertaining other women in his Winnebago, she'd have no motive to kill him."

"I get it," Andrea said, jotting it down. "And if she wasn't jealous and she didn't care if her husband was entertaining other women in his Winnebago, she wouldn't have a motive, either."

"Correct. For the purposes of this list, let's say she was jealous and she knew. That's a good motive for murder. And now we have to think about the women Dean entertained. They could have spouses or boyfriends who might be jealous enough to kill Dean."

"Well, I'm off the hook," Andrea said, taking another sip of coffee. "Bill's in Miami and everybody knows it."

Michelle's mouth dropped open. "You mean you . . ."

"No!" Andrea interrupted. "But I did go to his trailer to discuss Tracey's part with him. It's a good thing Bill's not in town. He might have gotten the wrong impression and then both of us would be suspects. But Bill's not here and I'm in the clear."

"If Bill's not here, she's in the clear," Hannah repeated, and she started to grin. "If it doesn't fit, you must acquit."

"What?" both sisters asked at once, staring at her hard.

"Sorry. I just couldn't help thinking of O. J.'s trial. That's what the defense said."

"But what does that have to do with . . ."

"Absolutely nothing," Hannah interrupted her youngest sister. "It rhymed so I thought of it, that's all. Let's get back to business here. Can we think of any other women we can link with Dean?"

"Me," Michelle confessed, guilty color rising to stain her cheeks. "He asked me to come to his trailer right after lunch yesterday. I thought he had work for me, but when I got there, he made a pass."

"What kind of a pass?" Andrea asked.

"It was silly, really . . . the sort of thing only a fool would have believed. He put his arm around me and told me I was perfect for a part in his next movie. And he offered to fly me out to Hollywood so I could take a screen test. I guess he thought I'd be so grateful, I wouldn't mind when he tried to kiss me."

Andrea made a strangled sound and covered it with a cough. "Sorry, something was stuck in my throat."

Stuck in your craw is more like it, Hannah thought and immediately felt mean. She poured more coffee for Andrea by way of apology for what she hadn't said, and turned back to Michelle. "So what did you do?"

"I stepped away, and told him I was really flattered that he thought I had talent, but the smart move for me was to stay at Macalester and finish college."

"That was a good way to deal with it," Andrea said, recovering nicely. "But even though you turned him down, Lonnie could still have heard about it. He's got a temper, and he was on the set, and . . ."

"Forget it," Hannah advised her. "Lonnie would have punched Dean's lights out, but he never would have killed him. I think it's safe to assume that he didn't know about the time Michelle spent in Dean's Winnebago."

Michelle looked thoughtful. "You're right. If Lonnie wanted to kill Dean, he'd do it with his bare hands. He'd never switch guns and take the chance that someone else might get hurt. But I just thought of someone else to add to the list."

"Who?" Andrea asked, her pen at the ready.

"Lynne. I know she was in Dean's trailer a couple of times. He mentioned it on the set the other day. And she wasn't happy that he mentioned it, either!"

"Okay. I've got her down. And if Lynne was there, we have to add her husband. His name is Tom, isn't it?"

"That's right," Hannah said. "You'd better add Erica, too. I'm almost positive I heard her giggling that first morning when I delivered Dean's cheesecake. And you'd better put down Jeanette, too."

"Because she'd kill anybody that touched her daughter?" Andrea's pen flew across the paper and then hovered over the motive column she'd drawn next to the column of names.

"That, too," Hannah told her.

"But Jeanette might have another motive for killing Dean?"

"Oh, yes. I think I heard her in Dean's trailer the next afternoon. I'm not positive, but it sounded just like her. I'm surprised Dean didn't ask the rental company to install a revolving door at the back of his trailer."

Andrea laughed. "That's funny. I wonder if there's anyone in Lake Eden that he *hasn't* tried to pick up on."

"Mother and Carrie?" Hannah suggested, expecting a big laugh.

"Maybe Carrie," Michelle answered.

"Not Mother?"

"Not Mother," Michelle said with a grin. "Dean got a little close to her when she was printing out the list of props they collected for him."

"Uh-oh! What did she do?"

"She elbowed him in the stomach."

"Hold on!" Andrea held out her hand palm first in the universal signal for stop and wait. "Did you say Mother *printed out* a list?"

"That's right."

"Then she has a computer?"

"She showed it to me last night," Michelle said. "It's a really nice laptop, a Pentium four, three-gig processor with an eighty-gig hard drive and a seventeen-inch screen. It's got firewire and USB ports, and lots of peripherals . . . scanner, color printer, digital camera, external hard drive backup, you name it."

Andrea gave a low whistle. "Did you hear that, Hannah? Mother got a *computer!"*

"I heard," Hannah said, giving a groan worthy of a hippo mired down in a mud hole.

Michelle glanced from one older sister to the other. "Why is Hannah groaning like that?"

"Because she promised me she'd get a computer when Mother did." Andrea gave a little laugh. "And Mother did."

"Okay, okay," Hannah gave in, although not gracefully. "I'll talk to Norman right after the movie crew leaves and find out what kind to buy."

Andrea's cell phone rang and she put down her pen to answer it. She listened for a minute and then she sighed. "Okay, Lisa. We'll be right there. Thanks for telling us."

"Telling us what?" Hannah asked, already starting to gather up the coffee mugs.

"Mike just came in to interview the promising witnesses. When he noticed that we weren't there, he asked where we'd gone."

"What did Lisa tell him?"

"That we were here, across the street."

"Uh-oh," Hannah groaned. Mike was bound to be suspicious, especially since all three of them had left. "Did he ask Lisa anything else?"

"Yes, he wanted to know what we were doing over here when Lake Eden Realty was closed."

"And what did Lisa say?"

"She said she didn't know, that all you'd done was ask her to mind the shop while you went across the street with us."

"Good girl!" Hannah said, breathing a bit easier. She hadn't asked Lisa to lie for them before they'd left and that omission had been deliberate. There was no way she'd put her young partner in that position. Lisa might agree to bend the truth a bit if it was crucial, but she hated to lie. And even more important, to Hannah's way of thinking, was the fact that Lisa was an extremely unaccomplished liar. No one would ever accuse Herb Beeseman's new bride of having a poker face. Lisa's countenance told the whole story. If she was angry, her eyes blazed and her color was high. If she was nervous, her hands shook and she licked her lips anxiously. If she was sad, her eyes welled up with tears and she sniffled without realizing it. If Hannah had asked her to lie for them, Lisa might very well have done it, but her voice would have trembled and she wouldn't have been able to meet Mike's eyes. Perhaps those two signs of a less than truthful statement might have escaped someone else's notice, but Mike was a master interrogator and there was no way he would have missed it.

"So what do we say when we get back?" Michelle asked.

"We say . . ." Hannah's mind whirled into high gear. She thought for a moment and then she started to grin. "We tell the truth. That's bound to throw him off the track."

"What!" Andrea gasped.

Michelle didn't say anything. She was too shocked to do more than stare at her older sister.

"That's right," Hannah said, visibly warming to her idea. "We tell Mike the truth. We say we were over here talking about Dean's murder and speculating on who might have done it. And then, when Mike wants to know if we questioned any of his witnesses, we tell him the truth and say no. We also add that it's one of the reasons we came over here to talk about the murder."

"Why?" Andrea looked confused.

"Because we knew he wouldn't want any of the witnesses to overhear us talking about Dean. And there were so many people in The Cookie Jar, there wasn't any place for a private conversation."

"Brilliant!" Michelle complimented her.

"It certainly is." Andrea gave a little smile. "And we're not even lying. The only thing we've done is talk about it, and there's no crime in that . . . is there?"

"I don't think so," Michelle said, turning to look at Hannah for the final word.

"I hope not." Hannah handed the thermos to Michelle, took the notebook Andrea handed her, and stuffed it into her saddlebag-style shoulder purse. "So far, all we've done is gossip and if that's a crime, Mike will have to lock up half the people in Lake Eden!"

DOUBLE FLAKE COOKIES

DO NOT preheat oven—dough must
chill before baking

This recipe is from Lisa's cousin, Betty Harnar. Betty's cookies are slightly different than the ones we make at The Cookie Jar, so if you don't like them blame us. If you love them the way the folks in Lake Eden do, please give Betty all the credit.

1 cup melted butter ***(½ pound, 2 sticks)***
3 eggs
1½ cups white ***(granulated)*** sugar
2 teaspoons cream of tartar
1 teaspoon baking soda
½ teaspoon salt
1 teaspoon coconut extract ***(if you don't have it, you can use vanilla)***
1½ cups flour ***(no need to sift)***
2 cups instant mashed potato flakes
1 cup coconut flakes, firmly packed
¾ cup finely chopped pecans or walnuts ***(measure AFTER chopping)***

approximately ½ cup white sugar in a bowl for later

Melt the butter. Set aside to let it cool a bit. Crack the eggs into a mixing bowl and whip them up for a minute. They don't have to be fluffy, just thoroughly mixed. Pour in the sugar and stir it up. Add the cream of tartar, baking soda, salt, and coconut extract. Mix well. Stir in the melted butter and then add the flour. Mix until the flour is thoroughly incorporated.

Measure out two cups of mashed potato flakes and mix them in. Add the coconut flakes. ***(If you're like me and you don't like stringy coconut, chop it up in a food processor with the steel blade before you add it to your bowl.)*** Stir in the chopped nuts and mix thoroughly.

Cover the dough tightly and refrigerate it for at least 4 hours. Overnight is even better.

When you're ready to bake, preheat the oven to 350 degrees F., rack in the center position.

Form balls of cookie dough, 1 inch in diameter, with your hands. Roll the balls in granulated sugar and place them on a greased ***(I used non-stick cooking spray)*** cookie sheet, 12 to a standard-sized sheet.

Flatten them a bit with a metal spatula or the heel of your impeccably clean hand.

Bake at 350 degrees F. for 10 to 12 minutes, or until cookies are golden around the edges. Cool on the cookie sheet for 2 minutes and then transfer the cookies to a wire rack to cool completely.

Yield: Approximately 8 dozen, depending on cookie size.

Mother likes these best as sandwich cookies. I spread one cookie bottom with chocolate frosting and sandwich another cookie on top. (The bottoms should be together, making the cookie sandwiches slightly convex.) Bertie's customers down at the Cut 'n Curl like them best if the sandwich filling is raspberry jam. I think that's because the chocolate melts if they eat them under the hair dryers.

Hannah's Note: You're really supposed to chill this dough, but if you absolutely positively can't wait to bake them, you can. Just be prepared to wet your hands frequently as you roll the cookie balls so the dough won't stick to them.

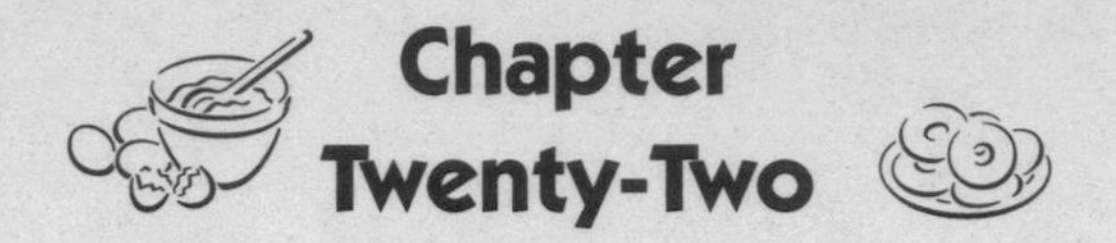

Chapter Twenty-Two

For Hannah, who was beat to the bone, the rest of the afternoon seemed to drag on forever. As the witnesses were released they left the coffee shop one by one, but it was seven o'clock by the time the coffee shop was empty and Hannah waved Lisa out the front door.

Moishe was waiting, tethered to Hannah's favorite round table by the window and she pulled out a chair to sit down. She petted her feline almost automatically as she gazed out the window and waited for Mike to finish his last interview in the kitchen.

Night had fallen and there wasn't any traffic on Main Street. Everyone had gone home and now that six o'clock supper was only a memory, most folks were sitting in their living rooms or their family rooms, watching the latest sitcom. Another group of people, the ones who lived alone, were banded together at the Lake Eden Municipal Liquor Store, where the television set above the bar would be tuned to the Timberwolves as they took on the Miami Heat.

Hannah put her head down on the table and cradled it with her folded arms. She was just thinking about how nice it would be if she could be magically transported to the couch in her own living room when Mike came out of the kitchen followed by the subject of his last interview, Ross.

"Hannah?"

"Huh?"

"Hannah . . . wake up!"

"I'm awake." Hannah looked up at Mike and blinked. "Can I go home now?"

Ross reached down to pat her shoulder. "Come out to the inn for dinner first. I just checked with Sally and she's serving coq au vin until nine."

Hannah glanced at Moishe, who looked every bit as tired as she felt and made a unilateral decision. "No thanks, Ross. Moishe and I are heading straight home. I don't know when I've been so tired."

"That's my fault," Mike said, reaching out to pat her other shoulder. "I should've taken those last couple of witnesses out to the station so you could go home."

"S'okay," Hannah said, slurring her words just a bit. The hard work she'd done and the sleepless nights she'd experienced had taken their toll. She was seriously considering turning out the lights and sleeping right there in the coffee shop rather than driving all the way home.

Hannah was barely awake enough to notice as Ross and Mike stepped back from the table. She heard their voices, but they must have moved away toward the back of the shop because she couldn't make out what they were saying. They were probably talking about her, but she was simply too tired to care. She shut her eyes, nestled close to her purring cat, and drifted back off to sleep.

When Hannah opened her eyes again, she thought she was seeing triple. Three pairs of eyes were staring down at her. Then she realized that Norman had joined Mike and Ross, and she sat up, blinking. "Sorry about that. Guess I fell asleep."

"I guess you did," Mike chuckled as he handed Moishe to Norman. "Come on, Hannah. Ross is going to bring you your coat and things, and Norman's going to drive you home."

"But I don't need anybody to . . ."

"Yes, you do," Mike cut off her protest. "You're tired and you could fall asleep on the road. I'd drive you myself, but I've got to get down to the station to file my reports. And I've got a briefing scheduled with Lonnie and Rick."

Mike had said the magic words and Hannah woke up fast. He must have found out something if he had to brief Lonnie and Rick. This was a perfect time to pump him for information. Norman had taken Moishe back to the kitchen for one last trip to the litter box, and Ross had gone with him to get Hannah's coat and purse. Hannah's short nap had revived her, and she knew she'd never have a better chance to find out what Mike knew. "So you learned something from your interviews?" she asked.

"A couple of things. Number one, Miss Larchmont wants to direct."

Hannah came close to laughing out loud. "Of course she does. There isn't an actor or actress alive who *doesn't* want to direct."

"But she's going to get the chance now that Dean's dead. I interviewed Ross and he said he's going to give her a shot at it."

"Oh," Hannah said and then she was silent. That put a new light on it. But had Lynne known she'd get the opportunity to direct if something happened to Dean? That was the important question. "Anything else?"

"The wardrobe mistress . . . what's her name?"

"Sophie."

"That's right. Sophie said that Miss Larchmont and her husband were arguing in their room last night."

"What about?"

"She doesn't know. She was passing by and she heard angry voices, but she didn't stick around to listen. She told me she decided it was none of her business and walked on down the hallway."

Right, Hannah thought, but she didn't say it. She'd find out what had really happened from Sophie tomorrow.

"I don't know if that means anything, but we'll add it to the mix," Mike said. "And then there's the set decorator."

"What about him?" Hannah asked, seriously doubting that Jared would have had anything to do with Dean's murder.

"One of the witnesses saw him close to the desk right before the first take."

"That may or may not be important," Hannah said, but she made a mental note to write it down in her shorthand notebook just as soon as she could. "Jared could have been rearranging something on the desk top."

"Maybe, but it's something I have to check out. And so far that's about it. Nobody remembers, for sure, who went near the desk. It's like you told me at Granny's Attic. People didn't pay any attention to the desk until the actors went over there."

"Did you watch all the tapes? Maybe one of the cameramen caught someone fiddling with the desk drawer."

"What tapes?"

Hannah stared at Mike in surprise. "I thought you knew. Dean taped all of his rehearsals."

"Nobody told me!" Mike looked thoroughly astounded.

"That's probably because they thought you knew. From what I heard, it was standard operating procedure. They taped it all, including the rehearsals where Dean played someone else's part."

"Thanks for telling me, Hannah," Mike said, flipping open his notebook and jotting it down. "I'll check with the head cameraman in the morning. Is there anything else you think I should know?"

Hannah shook her head. Mike looked very grateful for

the information she'd given him and this was the time to ask her most important question. "How about the search at Granny's Attic? Did you find the prop gun?"

"No."

"But the killer couldn't have taken it with him. They searched everyone, didn't they?"

"Even Mayor Bascomb, and he wasn't too happy about that."

"I'll bet he wasn't!" Hannah said, giving an amused grin as she pictured their mayor, a man who was accustomed to giving the orders, being ordered to stand in line with everyone else to be searched by a sheriff's deputy.

"So . . . either the prop gun's still there and you haven't found it yet, or the killer took it with him and left early, without sticking around to witness the result of his switch."

"You're right. And if the killer left early, he must have gone out the back way. Nobody came past me and I was standing right there by the front entrance waiting for my cue." Mike stopped talking and his eyes narrowed. "It sounds to me like you're thinking about investigating."

"Absolutely not."

"You promise?"

"You bet. I promise you that I won't investigate."

Mike was still staring at her and Hannah wondered if he smelled a rat. She'd told the truth the way she saw it, narrowly construed. He opened his mouth to ask another question, one Hannah hoped wouldn't be too probing, when fate intervened in the form of Norman with her coat and her purse.

"Here you go, Hannah," Norman said, handing over her parka coat and her shoulder purse. "Ross had to run back out to the inn. Somebody beeped him and he said it was important. He told me to tell you he'll touch base with you later tonight or first thing tomorrow morning."

"Okay," Hannah said, pushing aside a little twinge of

disappointment that Ross hadn't come to tell her so himself.

"If you're ready, I'll load Moishe."

"I'm ready," Hannah said, standing up and letting Mike help her into her coat. The little nap she'd taken had done her a world of good. She wasn't at all sleepy, but she certainly was ravenous and she could hardly wait to get home and make something to eat.

Twenty-five minutes later, as Hannah climbed the stairs to her condo, she sniffed the air. Unless she was hallucinating, someone was having Chinese food for dinner. She turned to Norman, who was right behind her, and asked, "What do you smell?"

"Chinese. Somebody's having hot and sour soup, kung pao chicken, house special chow mein, pork fried rice, scallops with fresh mushroom, shrimp and snow peas, and one duck's web plain, without the special soy sauce."

There was a yowl from the cat in his arms and Norman laughed. "I think the Big Guy knows all about that last menu item."

"He does. Whenever I order take-out Chinese, I always get one duck's web without the special soy sauce for him. He loves to chew on it and chase it around on the kitchen floor."

"So I heard. That's why I ordered all that stuff, and asked your sisters to pick it up on their way here. I hope you don't mind."

"Mind?" Hannah's stomach gave a mighty growl. "I don't mind at all. You may have saved my life."

"If you're tired, we'll leave," Michelle offered, gathering up the white boxes that sat on Hannah's big, round coffee table, closing the lids, and preparing to stash them in Hannah's refrigerator.

"Actually . . ." Hannah paused to take stock of her mental state. "I'm not tired anymore. I think I got about twenty minutes' sleep waiting for Mike to finish interviewing Ross, and it took the edge off."

"Sometimes a twenty-minute nap is all you need," Andrea said. "I read it in one of my parenting magazines." She stopped and began to frown. "You've got to promise not to tell Tracey I said that. I have enough trouble getting her to bed at a reasonable hour as it is."

You mean Mrs. McCann has trouble getting Tracey to bed, Hannah thought, but she remained silent. There was no way she'd take such a nasty shot at her sister.

"Of course now that Mrs. McCann is living in to take care of Bethany, I don't have that problem," Andrea went on, almost seeming to read Hannah's mind. "Do you think I'm a bad mother for not staying home to take care of my daughters?"

"No!"

"Of course not."

"Never."

They all spoke at once, hotly denying that suggestion. All three of them knew that Andrea wasn't cut out to be a stay-at-home mom. She was a consummate social being who needed the stimulation of other people to be happy and fulfilled.

"Good." Andrea was smiling again as she opened the small white bag that sat in the center of the table and passed out fortune cookies. "Let's all read our fortunes out loud. You go first, Michelle."

Michelle broke her fortune cookie in half and drew out the folded strip of paper inside. "*Aim for the stars to reach the moon.*"

"That's almost profound," Norman said, cracking his

cookie open. "Mine says, '*Helping others is its own reward.*' How about you, Andrea?"

"*True beauty is like the night.*" Andrea wore a puzzled expression when she looked up from the strip of paper. "What does that mean?" Everyone shrugged and she gave a little laugh. "That's what I thought. They must have left out a couple of words. What's yours, Hannah?"

"I don't really like fortune cookies." Hannah pushed hers over to Norman. "I'll trade you for your almond cookie."

"Deal." Norman said, handing over his almond cookie. "If you're up to it, Hannah, we want to talk some more about Dean's murder. I've got some ideas."

"Fine with me," Hannah said, reaching for her purse. She got out the steno book they'd used earlier at Lake Eden Realty and shoved it across the table to Andrea.

"You're sure you're not too tired?" Michelle looked concerned.

"I'm positive. I couldn't sleep through that racket anyway."

All four of them turned toward the kitchen, where Moishe was trying to spear the duck's web with his claws and drag it out from behind the garbage can. He yowled every time he failed, but he didn't stop trying.

"So what did you get out of Mike?" Norman asked after crunching a bite of his fortune cookie. "Ross said you talked to him while we were in the kitchen."

"Lynne wants to direct and Ross is going to give her the chance now that Dean's dead. That's another motive for her, Andrea."

"Got it," Andrea said, flipping the notebook open to the list of suspects and adding a second motive for Lynne. "Anything else?"

"Mike didn't know that Dean taped all his rehearsals. I told him and he said he'd check the tapes in the morning."

"Then I'd better call Clark." Michelle got out her cell phone and punched in a number. "He's in charge of collecting all the tapes. I can always run out to the inn and screen them if you think they're that important."

Hannah nodded. "Good idea. You'd better call Mother and tell her where you're going. She'll worry if you stay out at the inn too late."

"No, she won't. She told me to come and go as I please."

Andrea exchanged glances with Hannah. "That doesn't sound like the Mother we know and love," she said.

"I know. She also told me she'll have dinner with me, but she has her own plans after dinner every night this week."

Hannah started to frown. "I wonder what plans she could have. There aren't any club meetings. They all canceled their activities until the movie company leaves town." She turned to Norman. "Are the mothers going somewhere together at night?"

"No. Except for the night they went out to dinner with you and Ross, my mother's been home watching television."

"Then what's Mother doing?" Andrea looked worried. "You don't suppose it's another man, do you?"

"It's possible, I guess," Hannah conceded.

"But right after Winthop? I mean . . . wouldn't you think she'd wait?"

"For what? Old age to set in?"

Andrea's mouth dropped open, but Michelle and Norman started to laugh. They laughed so contagiously that Andrea had to join in, and eventually so did Hannah.

"Do you want to know what else I found out from Mike?" Hannah asked when the laughter had died down. There were nods around the round table and she picked up the thread of their former conversation. "Mike said his deputies searched everyone who left Granny's Attic, but they didn't find the prop gun. They also made an initial search of Granny's Attic and it wasn't there, either."

"But it has to be!" Andrea exclaimed. "Guns don't just vanish."

"You're right, they don't. And they'll search again tomorrow. But there's also the possibility that whoever switched the gun left early and took the prop gun with him."

"Winnie Henderson," Norman said.

"What?"

"I saw her driving down Main Street after they'd already started shooting. I know her daughter was in that scene and I thought it was odd she'd leave before it was over."

"Got it," Andrea said, writing it down. "What else?"

"There's the question we didn't get around to discussing this afternoon." Hannah took a bite of her cookie. As far as she was concerned, her almond cookies were a lot better than the commercial kind.

"What question is that?" Norman asked.

"Whether the killer actually meant to murder Dean. Or if his intended target was Burke."

"That's good, Hannah!" Michelle sounded very impressed. "You're absolutely right and I bet no one else will even think of it. We're probably light years ahead of the official investigation."

"No, we're not. I mentioned it to Mike."

There was silence for a moment while the other three stared at her incredulously. It made Hannah so uncomfortable, she started to try to explain. "I know I probably shouldn't have said anything, but he *is* the investigating officer. And I was really rattled. It happened at Granny's Attic right after the murder and . . ."

"That's okay," Norman soothed her. "It isn't supposed to be a contest."

"True," Andrea said, "although it seems like it most of

the time." She turned to Michelle. "Don't you think it seems like a contest?"

"I think it does," Michelle agreed. "But what we've all got to keep in mind is that it doesn't really matter who catches Dean's killer as long as someone does."

Norman reached out to squeeze Hannah's hand again. "Michelle's right. And besides, we have your fortune to consider."

"My fortune?"

"I saved it for you when I ate your cookie. It says *Redhead with big mouth is still better detective than tall man in uniform.*"

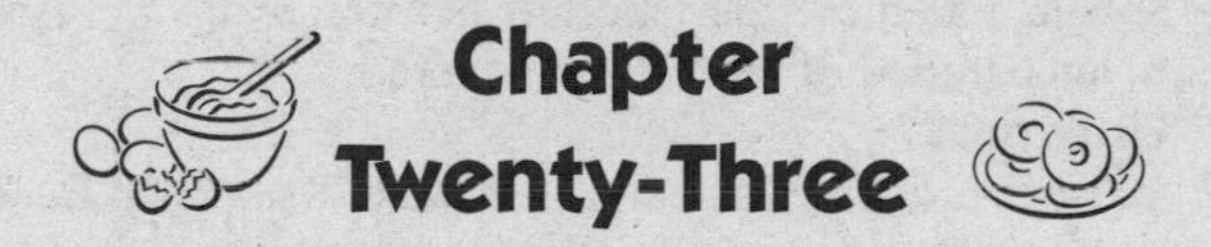

Chapter Twenty-Three

"I think I should have changed places with Norman. I could have driven Michelle out to the inn and helped her go through the tapes."

"You said you thought it would be boring," Hannah reminded her sister.

"I'm changing my mind about boring. It's not that bad and at least it's safe."

Hannah didn't say a word as Andrea pulled over to the side of the gravel road that led past the Henderson farm. Her sister was right. What they were about to do was far from safe. Winnie had a shotgun and she wasn't afraid to use it. And Winnie didn't take kindly to intruders.

"Why are we doing this, again?" Andrea asked as she got out of her Volvo and pocketed the keys. She had driven to their destination after they'd decided that Hannah's cookie truck was too easy to identify.

"We're doing this because Norman said he saw Winnie driving down Main Street only minutes before the incident at Granny's Attic. And I saw Winnie earlier, watching Alice waltz around on the cocktail party set."

"So she was there and she left before Dean . . . " Andrea's voice trailed off and she shuddered.

"That's right."

"And because she left early, she wasn't searched. And that means she could have switched the revolvers and taken off with the prop gun. And nobody would be the wiser."

"You got it."

Andrea gave a deep sigh as she trudged up the one-lane road to the farm. They could see the house in the distance, gleaming alabaster white in the bright, cold rays from the halogen yard light.

"I wish I'd worn boots," Andrea groused, glancing down at her sneaker-clad feet. "The ground's still frozen and the bottoms of my feet are cold."

"It'll be warm in the barn."

"You're right. I forgot that barns were heated."

Hannah didn't bother to correct her sister. Strictly speaking, Andrea was right. Barns were heated. They were kept warm by herding in all the cattle, keeping them together in a closed space, and utilizing their body heat. When it came to barns in the winter, BTUs stood for Bunched Together Until Summer.

"Are you sure this is a good idea?" Andrea asked, stepping over a frozen rut in the road.

"It's probably a bad idea, but somebody's got to do it." Hannah eyed the farmhouse again. "I don't see any lights on in the house. Do you?"

"No, it's dark. Winnie's probably been in bed for hours. She told me once that she gets up at five. Can you imagine getting up that early?"

"Oh, yes."

"Of course you can. I forgot that you get up early, too."

Hannah didn't say anything. Now wasn't the time to give Andrea any grief about sleeping in. As they walked closer, Hannah noticed that Winnie's sedan and her pickup truck were parked in the driveway. The house was perfectly silent, and the only things moving were the shadows from wispy clouds scuttling across the moon.

"Why don't we tell Mike what we know and let him look for the gun?" Andrea suggested, not for the first time.

"I told you before. Mike can't get a search warrant on speculation alone. And he can't search anywhere without a warrant. If we don't do it, nobody will."

In the pale, blue light of the moon overhead, Hannah could read her sister's expression. Andrea was seriously considering that option.

"Don't even think about backing out now," Hannah told her sternly. "You're the one who told us that Winnie hid her valuables in the barn."

"Yes, but I didn't know I'd have to come out here and look for them! What if Alice made up the whole thing? Lots of kids fib when they're in grade school."

Hannah knew her sister was trying to bail out, but they'd come too far to give up now. Andrea had gone to school with Alice Henderson and she'd told them about what Winnie's youngest daughter had brought to class for Show and Tell. Hannah was pretty sure Alice's story was accurate. It sounded like something Winnie would do. "But Alice showed you the gold medallions Winnie won for her prize cows, didn't she?"

"Yes, but maybe Winnie didn't keep them hidden in the barn. Alice could have fibbed about that."

"Why would she fib?"

"I don't know. And I guess maybe she didn't. The plastic bag with the medallions smelled a lot like . . . you know . . . the kind of smell you'd smell in a barn."

"Let's just hope Winnie still uses the barn for a safe. And we can also hope she stashed the prop gun there and hasn't gotten rid of it already. It's a long shot, but we have to look."

"I wish it wasn't *we*," Andrea muttered, taking a deep breath as they stepped up to the front of the barn. "How are we going to get inside, again?"

Hannah explained for the third time that evening. "The door slides to the side and it's got a counterweight. I'll pull it open just far enough for you to slip inside. If I open it up all the way, it'll probably make a loud screeching noise. Most farmers don't grease the barn doors on purpose. It's like a burglar alarm."

"Smart," Andrea said.

"And a lot cheaper than hiring an alarm company. Once you're inside, I'll let the big door close and you'll use your flashlight to walk to the small door and unlatch it."

"Right. There's just one thing."

"What?"

"Aren't the cows going to see me when I come in?"

"I don't know. Why?"

"Well, what if they don't like me and they start doing what they do in *Away in a Manger*."

"Huh?"

"You know . . . when the cattle are lowing. What's lowing anyway?"

"That would be mooing." Hannah thought fast. If her sister suspected that the cows would be awake, she might refuse to go inside the barn. "I don't think you have to worry about any mooing, or lowing, or whatever. The cows are probably sleeping. They get up early, you know."

"You're right. I saw that commercial where the rooster wakes them." Andrea stopped and took a deep breath. "Okay, Hannah. I'm as ready as I'm ever going to be."

"Watch out for the trench by the door. That's for the run-off when they clean the barn."

"Run-off?"

"Never mind. Just step carefully, that's all. The minute you're inside, I'll go stand by the small door."

Hannah used every muscle she had to push open the

heavy door so her sister could slip inside. Once Andrea was safely past the trench and she'd snapped on her flashlight, Hannah let the door close and tromped around the side of the barn to the smaller door. There she waited. And waited. And waited. She was about to go back and try to force open the big door again when she heard Andrea draw back the latch, and the smaller door opened.

"What happened to you?" Hannah asked, frowning at the sight of her sister in the moonlight. Andrea had several globs of hay stuck in her hair and even more on her pants and jacket.

"One of the cows woke up and lowed at me, and I got scared and fell down. I didn't fall in anything really . . . um . . . messy, did I?"

Hannah turned on her Maglite and surveyed the damage. *Messy* didn't begin to cover it. There was something on the back of Andrea's pants that Hannah didn't even want to try to identify and more of the same was stuck to the back of her hair.

"Hannah?" Andrea prompted, looking slightly sick. "It's not that bad, is it?"

"It's not that bad," Hannah said, lying through her teeth, and breathing through her mouth while she was at it. Whatever Andrea had fallen in was pungent. "Let's search the bullpen and get out of here so you can get cleaned up."

"*Bullpen*? How do you know Winnie's hiding place is in the bullpen?"

"I figured it out from what you told us. You said Alice told the class she had to climb over a rail to get it, and it was in a box on the wall of a big pen. All the farmers around here keep their bulls penned up when they're in the barn."

"How do you know so much about farms, anyway?"

"I spent a lot of time on Grandma and Grandpa Swensen's farm. I used to love going out to the barn with Grandpa and hand-feeding silage to the cows."

"I don't remember that."

"Of course not. You were just a baby and you stayed in the house with Grandma." Hannah stepped inside the barn and shut the door. "Walk down the center aisle, Andrea. That way we'll avoid the muck."

"What's . . . never mind," Andrea said, obviously thinking better of the question she'd been about to ask. "I see two pens way down there at the end. One's empty and the other has a cow in it."

"That's a bull," Hannah pointed out as they got closer.

"How can you . . . never mind," Andrea said again, deciding she preferred to be zip for two with her questions. "I'll check the empty pen and you can check the other one."

Hannah smiled. She'd expected no less. "Go ahead. I'll wait to see if you find anything before I tackle the bullpen."

As they walked down the center aisle of the barn, Andrea let her flashlight play over the cows. "They've all got signs hanging above their places," she said. "Look, Hannah. This black-and-white cow is Daisy. And this brown one is Buttercup. And here's Petunia, and . . . drat!"

"There's a cow named *drat?*"

"No. I was reading the names and I forgot to look where I was going. I almost stepped in some dirt."

There was no way Andrea could get any dirtier, but Hannah didn't want to remind her of that. She just grinned and followed in her sister's wake to the very rear of the barn.

The empty pen didn't take long to search. Andrea lifted the lid on the wooden box, checked for contents, and came rushing back out again. "There's nothing there. You're up," she announced.

"*We're* up," Hannah corrected her. "I'll go in, but I need you to distract the bull."

"How am I supposed to do that?"

"Talk to him, pet him on the head, give him a cookie,

whatever. Just keep him focused on you while I climb in and check the box."

"I don't have any cookies."

"Yes, you do," Hannah reached into her pocket and pulled out a bag of day-old cookies. She'd grabbed them from her cookie truck along with her Maglite before they'd left the condo.

"What kind are these?"

"Assorted. Lisa emptied what was left in the serving jars. Just keep trying until you get to one the bull likes. And then feed it to him slowly, to give me time to get in, check the box, and get back out."

"Okay, I guess." Andrea started to move to the front of the pen, but she stopped and turned back to Hannah. "I can't talk to him if I don't know his name. And there's no nameplate on his pen."

Hannah thought fast. "Call him Larry."

"His name is Larry?"

"Absolutely," Hannah said, crossing the fingers on her left hand to negate the lie.

"Winnie told you that?"

"You bet," Hannah said, crossing the fingers on her right hand.

"And you remembered?"

"Of course." Hannah was running out of fingers and she gave Andrea a little shove toward the front of the pen. "Hurry up. We haven't got all night."

"Hi, Larry," Andrea said, in the same tone of voice Hannah had heard her use with Bethany. "Are you hungry? I bet you are. Just look at what I've got for you! Try an Old Fashioned Sugar Cookie. It's got colored sugar on it and you're really going to like it."

Hannah was beginning to have second thoughts. Andrea didn't sound very confident. To tell the truth, Hannah wasn't very confident, either. She knew nothing about Winnie's bull.

Some bulls were gentle and complacent, but others were aggressive and mean. Hannah wouldn't know what type of bull Winnie had until she got into the pen with him. And by then, it would be too late to do anything about it.

"Don't you like sugar cookies, Larry? Okay, they're not my favorites, either. Let's try a Chocolate Chip Crunch Cookie. That's got cornflakes in it and I'll bet you like cornflakes for breakfast. Or maybe Winnie doesn't give you cornflakes. How about oatmeal? I think I see one of Hannah's Oatmeal Raisin Crisps."

Hannah tested the gate. It wasn't locked. She could step in at any time. She did her best not to think about the dire consequences that could follow her action, but her mind continued to drown her in a cascade of scenarios. The bull would attack her, pin her to the rails, and gore her. That was the first scenario. The second scenario had the bull turning on Andrea and attacking her instead of Hannah. But if that happened, Hannah would still be in danger because Bill would attack her the minute he got back from Florida. The third scenario was a little less ugly but equally scary. The bull wouldn't attack anyone, but he'd start bellowing, and Winnie would come out with her shotgun and shoot both Hannah and Andrea. There was also a fourth scenario and Hannah liked that one the best. The bull would fall in love with Hannah's cookies, become her mascot at The Cookie Jar, and sit beside Moishe on one of the tables by the front window, sniffing cookies the way Disney's Ferdinand had sniffed flowers.

"Hannah!" Andrea's voice roused her from the last and most ridiculous scenario. "What are you waiting for? Larry likes Peanut Butter Melts and I've only got two left!"

"Okay," Hannah said and opened the gate to the pen. She slipped inside, went straight to the box on the wall, and opened it. "Jackpot," she breathed, pulling out a plastic bag. But it was far too light to include a gun, even a prop gun. They'd struck out and put themselves in danger for nothing!

"Hurry, Hannah. I'm on the last cookie and Larry doesn't like anything but peanut butter."

"Okay. I'm almost through." Hannah exited the bullpen without incident and made sure the gate was securely latched behind her. She was just preparing to give Andrea the bad news when all the lights in the barn went on.

"Freeze, you varmints! I've got you covered six ways to Sunday!"

Hannah glanced toward the door to see Winnie heading toward them, a shotgun cradled in her arms. She was about to raise her arms in surrender and advise Andrea to do the same when she realized that Winnie wasn't wearing her glasses.

"Down," she hissed, pushing her sister down in the hay. "Follow me. We'll hug the side wall of the barn and crawl out."

"But . . . won't Winnie see us?"

"She can't see a thing without her glasses and she's not wearing them. Just follow me. It won't be pretty, but we'll make it."

Truer words were never spoken. By the time they'd crawled through the feed trough that ran along the outside of the stanchions, Hannah and Andrea were covered with liquids and solids that would give a microbiologist a nice workout.

The smaller door was standing open and Hannah raised her head to check on Winnie's whereabouts. "Run!" Hannah hissed, grabbing her sister's hand and pulling her through the open door.

Both sisters were breathing hard by the time they arrived at the Volvo. Andrea used her remote to open the door, and she was about to slide into the driver's seat when she looked down at herself. "Yuck!"

"And another yuck for me," Hannah said, realizing that she was just as filthy as Andrea. Do you have any blankets in the trunk?"

"Of course I do! I have two thermal blankets. They're part of my Minnesota Winter Driver Survival Kit. Bill puts it together and he doesn't let me take it out of the trunk until June."

"Smart man," Hannah said, recalling that they'd once had a blizzard in May. "You take one blanket and I'll take the other. We'll sit on them so we won't get your upholstery dirty."

"What is this stuff, anyway?" Andrea asked, popping the trunk and taking out the blankets.

"It's muck. Drive straight to my place and we'll take showers."

"A shower would be good, but I don't have any clean clothes with me."

"Michelle left a pair of jeans and a sweatshirt the last time she stayed over. You can use those."

"But . . . maybe I should just go home."

"And let this muck dry on you? Don't be silly, Andrea. Cow pies are like plaster. Once they set, nothing less than a flamethrower can dislodge them."

"Cow pies?" Andrea turned to her sister in shock. "Are they the same as muck?"

"Pretty much. At least in our case."

"Well, why didn't you say so in the first place?! Hang on and we'll be at your place in less than ten minutes!"

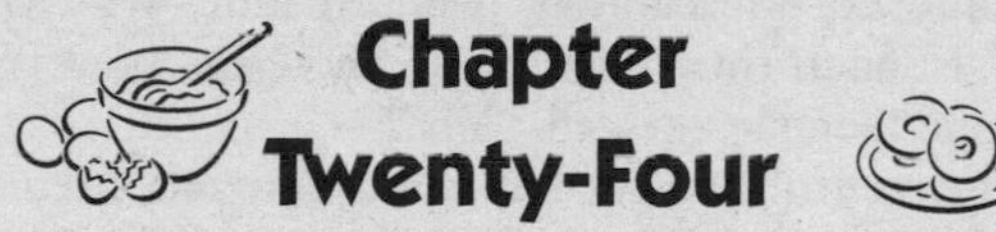

Chapter Twenty-Four

"You look like you've been through the wars," Lisa said when Hannah came into the kitchen of The Cookie Jar the next morning.

"That about covers it." Hannah headed to the sink to wash her hands.

"Where's Moishe?"

"Home sleeping. He doesn't have any scenes today."

"I bet he'll miss all the attention he gets when he's here."

"I don't think so," Hannah replied, reaching for the soap. "When I told him he didn't have to come to work with me today, he licked my hand and then he burrowed under the blankets and hid at the bottom of the bed."

"He must have needed a day off. And speaking of days off, I think you should have taken one. Were you out late last night investigating?"

Hannah shook her head as she lathered up. "I don't investigate."

"You don't?"

"Absolutely not. Only an investigator can investigate. I'm just a small-town snoop."

Lisa laughed. "Still arguing over semantics with Mike?"

"No." Hannah rinsed her hands, thought about it for a minute, and then she nodded. "Yes."

"Let me see if I've got this right. You promised Mike you wouldn't investigate, but you didn't promise him that you wouldn't snoop?"

"Something like that."

"That's my partner!" Lisa crowed, well pleased with her ability to figure it all out. "So where did you snoop last night?"

Hannah dried her hands and headed for the work island. Lisa was mixing up a batch of Boggles, and the recipe for Cinnamon Crisps was next in line on the recipe holder. "Andrea and I did a little B and E."

"Breaking and entering?" Lisa looked shocked when Hannah nodded. "Where?"

"Winnie Henderson's barn." Hannah headed off to the walk-in cooler to get the butter and the eggs. Once she'd carried them back to her workstation, she gathered the dry ingredients from the pantry and arranged everything in order. She was ready to start mixing the dough when she realized that Lisa was still staring at her. "What?"

"Why?" Lisa countered.

"Why what?"

"Why did you and Andrea break into Winnie Henderson's barn?"

"Winnie left the dress rehearsal early, so she wasn't searched. She's familiar with firearms, and a couple of her husbands had nice gun collections that might have included revolvers that resembled the prop gun. She didn't want Dean to use the park for the skating scene, and Dean was the kind of guy who wouldn't take no for an answer."

"And that's a motive?"

"It's a pretty good one. Winnie could have figured that a real suicide on the set would shut the movie down. Then Ross and his company would leave town."

"Makes sense," Lisa said, getting out another of the large stainless steel mixing bowls they used and grabbing the next recipe on the rack. "You can ask her some probing questions when she comes in at noon."

"Winnie's coming here?"

"That's what she said when she called this morning. She apologized for not coming in yesterday, but she had to rush home to meet the vet."

Hannah thought about that for a moment. Winnie had cattle, horses, several dogs, some cats, and a flock of chickens. With that many animals, it was certainly possible that one of them had required medical attention. The excuse was reasonable, but that didn't necessarily mean it was true. "What was wrong?"

"The bull had some sort of intestinal upset and it made him really ornery. Winnie said he's usually pretty good-natured, but not yesterday. It took Winnie, the hired man, and four of the neighbors to subdue him so the vet could give him a shot of antibiotics."

Hannah felt her stomach drop down to her knees and come slowly back up again. She'd gone into the pen with a sick, ornery bull and he could have gored her six ways to the center. Her sister had handed that same sick, ornery bull homemade cookies and heaven only knew what that had done for his intestinal problem.

"The good news is the bull's fine today. Winnie said that when she went out to the barn this morning, he was as quiet as a lamb. That shot the vet gave him must have worked."

Forget the shot, Hannah said under her breath. *My money's on the five Peanut Butter Melts that Andrea fed him.*

Winnie slid onto a stool at the work island and accepted the mug of coffee that Hannah poured for her. "I sure can use some wake-me-up," she said. "I kept hearing noises in the barn last night."

"Really?" Hannah asked, placing two mini cherry cheesecakes on a napkin in front of Winnie and hoping she looked more innocent than she felt.

"That's right. I could have sworn somebody was in there, but when I checked, everything seemed okay. 'Course I couldn't see much without my glasses."

"What happened to your glasses?"

"I knocked 'em on the floor when I jumped out of bed and I couldn't find 'em until this morning." Winnie took another sip of her coffee. "I apologize for not getting here yesterday, but I had an emergency. Did Lisa tell you about Larry?"

"Larry?"

"My bull. The grandkids named him."

Hannah had all she could do not to laugh out loud. The bull's name was Larry, so she hadn't been lying after all! It couldn't be a coincidence. She must have heard Winnie mention it and it had stuck in her mind. "Yes, Lisa told me. I'm glad Larry's better now."

"Guess you're not going to try to talk me into letting them use the park."

"Why not?"

"Use your head, girl! Now that their big-shot director is dead, they'll be packing up and leaving town." Something in Hannah's expression must have tipped her off, because Winnie cocked her head and stared at Hannah curiously. "Won't they?"

"I don't think so. At least that's not what I heard last night. Most of the important scenes have already been filmed, and there are only four to go. Lynne Larchmont is going to direct those."

"You mean they still want to use the park?"

"That's right. I hope you'll let them use it, Winnie."

Winnie gave a deep sigh. "I said they could use it if they

didn't move the statue my brother made of the first mayor, but that highfaluting director wanted it out of the way. He said it would ruin the shot. He wanted to move it clear over by the bandstand. I figured for sure they'd break it and Arnie put a lot of work into making it. It's the only thing of his I got left."

"Maybe they don't have to move it that far. How would you feel about it if they just hoisted it up out of camera range?"

"You mean . . . they could just pick it straight up and leave it dangling in the air while they did whatever they had to do?"

"That's exactly what I mean."

Winnie considered that for a minute and then she shrugged. "I don't know what to say. Would I still get the money?"

"I'll have to check for sure, but I think so."

"Well just between you and me, it would sure come in handy right now. Elmer Petersen over in Eagle Bend's selling off twenty head, and he's got a couple of Jerseys I wouldn't mind mixing in with mine. They're good producers according to Betty Jackson over at the dairy."

"So you'll agree if you get the money?"

Hannah was wise enough not to say a word as Winnie thought it over. The seconds ticked by so slowly it seemed that time had stopped, but finally Winnie gave a little nod. "I'll sign that paper if they swear they'll just lift up the statue and put it right back down again when they're through. No moving it anywhere. Just up and back down. And I'm going to be right there to make sure they do it right."

"I'll call Ross and find out if it's a deal," Hannah promised, refilling Winnie's coffee cup and then heading for the phone.

"Hi, Hannah," Ross said, answering on the first ring of his cell phone. "I was just about to call you."

"Well, I beat you to it. I'm sitting here with Winnie Henderson and she's going to sign that release form to use the park as a location, with some stipulations."

"What stipulations?"

"Dean was going to actually move the statue somewhere else and then put it back again. Winnie wants it lifted up in the air, held there by a crane or something, and then put right back down again."

"We can do that," Ross said. "We'd have to use a crane to lift it anyway."

"She wants to be there to make sure you do it right, and she also wants the . . . hold on a second," Hannah covered the mouthpiece with her hand and turned to Winnie. "How much did Dean promise to pay you if you signed the release?"

"Five thousand. And it was Connor doing the promising."

"Okay, I'll tell him that." Hannah turned back to the phone again. She was feeling a bit like an agent and she wasn't sure whether she liked the role or not. "Winnie says Connor promised to pay her five thousand dollars if she signed. Is that okay?"

"That's fine. We allotted six thousand in the budget."

Hannah frowned slightly. "I heard Dean tell Connor that five thousand was as high as he could go."

"Then Dean must have had plans for that other thousand. He was a whittler, Hannah. A lot of the guys who make the big bucks are."

"What do you mean?"

"They nickel and dime the production companies. It's like a guy who earns a hundred thousand dollars from a big corporation and steals pens and paper to use at home. He could buy his own, but it makes him feel good to put one over on the company."

"And Dean did that?"

Ross laughed. "All the time. He just about drove our accountant crazy. You know those cheesecakes you delivered to his trailer? He charged the budget a hundred dollars for paper plates and plastic forks, and Michelle told me they cost less than ten dollars at the Red Owl."

"Oh, boy!" Hannah breathed, shaking her head. "That really *is* cheap, especially because if he'd asked me, I would have provided them free of charge."

"That wouldn't have made any difference to Dean. He loved to pad his vouchers for out-of-pocket expenses. It was just the way he did business."

Another reason somebody might have killed him, Hannah thought, but she didn't say it. Since Tom Larchmont was the moneyman, she'd add it to his motive later. "Shall I tell Winnie it's a go, then?"

"Only if you have dinner with me out at the inn tonight."

Hannah laughed. "That's extortion."

"No, it's desperation. I need to spend time with someone who doesn't have a personal agenda and who isn't directly involved with the movie."

"In other words, you need a friend?" Hannah guessed, reading between the lines.

"That's exactly right. Ask Winnie if I can meet her at her house in an hour with the money and the release form. I'll hang on."

"Ross wants to know if he can meet you in an hour at your place with the money and the papers," Hannah reported, covering the phone with her hand.

"Fine by me, but tell him to bring Connor along. I don't know this feller you're sweet on, but I spent a lot of time with Connor when he was trying to get me to sign that paper. He was as polite as he could be and he ate three slices of my gooseberry pie. Haven't seen anybody do that since my second-to-the-last husband died."

Michelle rushed into The Cookie Jar at eleven-thirty, right before the noon rush, and handed Hannah a package.

"Here," she said, puffing a little. "Clark showed us how to make a copy of the important footage and we left on the time codes."

"Thanks, Michelle. I'll go over to Andrea's and watch it."

"Better not. Dean's murder is on the tape, and it's not something Tracey should see."

"Okay. I guess I'll have to run home after lunch then."

Michelle shook her head. "I've got a better idea. Why don't you use Dean's trailer? I've got a key and you can use his screening room . . . unless that'll creep you out?"

"It won't creep me out," Hannah said, jumping at the chance to get a better look at Dean's trailer. If she had time, she might even do a little snooping to see if she could find any other motives for his murder.

"Well, it would creep me out, especially if I had to go in alone. But I won't be alone. You'll be with me."

"You want to watch the tape again?"

"No, that's just an excuse. I want to help you do what you're *really* going to do in Dean's trailer."

"You mean . . ."

"That's right," Michelle interrupted her. "I want to help you snoop through Mr. Big-Shot Director's things."

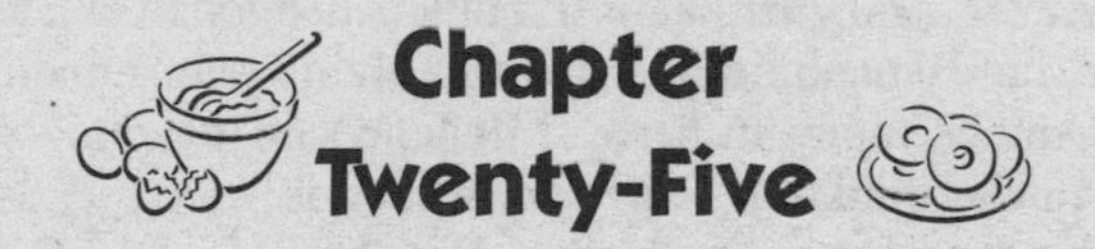

Chapter Twenty-Five

Hannah glanced around uneasily as they ducked through the trees in the vacant lot and emerged in front of Dean's Winnebago. She tried to squelch the feeling, but it wouldn't go away.

"What's the matter?" Michelle asked, noticing her big sister's nervous expression. "You look jumpy."

"I am. And I don't know why."

"Is it because we're going to snoop?"

"I don't think so. Heaven knows I've snooped before! Maybe it's because we don't have to break in and it's not the middle of the night."

Michelle laughed as she climbed the steps and unlocked the door. "Come on, Hannah. I've got a perfect right to be here. Ross asked me to pick up Dean's shooting script and look for any changes he indicated for the skating scene we're shooting tomorrow afternoon. Frances was supposed to drive over here to get it, but Lynne needed her for something else."

Hannah stood back as Michelle opened the door, and then the two sisters stepped inside. The interior smelled musty, as if the owner had left it untouched for an extended period, but Hannah figured that was all in her imagination.

"It smells funny in here," Michelle said, echoing what Hannah was thinking. "I wonder what it is."

"This could have something to do with it." Hannah plucked a crumpled sock from the top of a bookcase and held it up for Michelle's inspection.

"Dean's. I recognize the pattern. It looks like argyle, but it's really his initials arranged in a design all over. His wife told me she gets them from a place in Beverly Hills that makes socks to order."

"Dean might have been a genius, but his personal habits could have used some work." Hannah picked up the other sock, which was lying smack dab in the middle of the aisle that led down the center of the trailer. She put both socks in a plastic bag she found on top of his desk and turned to her youngest sister. "Do you think we should save these for Sharyn?"

"It seems a little silly now that he's dead. I mean, what's she going to do with them? And it's not like she doesn't have a whole drawer full of others just like them at home. Let's toss them. It's quicker and easier." Michelle used two fingers to gingerly pick up a grungy handkerchief from the desk chair. "And let's add this to the bag."

Once Hannah had relegated the bag to the wastebasket next to Dean's desk, she followed Michelle down the hallway toward the rear of the trailer. As they progressed, the bad smell grew stronger and Hannah coughed slightly.

"Yuck," Michelle commented as she passed a closed door. "That smell seems to be coming from the bathroom."

"Maybe I'd better check it out," Hannah offered. Her mother had accused her of being a dead body locator and she didn't want Michelle to share that reputation. And while it didn't exactly smell as if anyone had died in the Winnebago water closet, something definitely reeked.

"Go ahead, Hannah." Michelle agreed so fast, Hannah

knew her youngest sister had hoped she wouldn't have to step into the small, smelly room. "Just holler if you need me. I'll be right out here."

Hannah put her hand on the doorknob and hesitated. The smell was familiar, but she couldn't quite place it. She had just turned the handle and was getting ready to inch open the door when the reels spinning in her memory banks came up with triple red sevens. "Skunk!" she exclaimed.

"Skunk?"

"Definitely skunk. Is there a window in the bathroom?"

"I'm almost sure there is."

"Then it must have crawled in through the bathroom window."

"Do you think it's still in there?"

"I don't know," Hannah said with a shrug.

"Do you think we should try to rescue it?"

"Absolutely not, if we want to have anything to do with people for the rest of the day. I'm fresh out of tomato juice at The Cookie Jar."

Michelle looked confused. "What does tomato juice have to do with it?"

"If you pour it all over, it's supposed to get rid of the skunk smell."

"Does it work?"

"I don't know and I really don't want to try it . . . at least not now. Let's keep the door closed and count ourselves lucky."

"But . . . how about the skunk? What if it's stuck? And scared?"

Hannah turned to smile at her sister. Michelle was a true animal lover. "When we're through here, you go out the back way and prop open the door. I'll hold my nose, open the bathroom door, and run outside."

"And we'll leave the back door open so it can get out?"

"Absolutely. We can have someone come over here to check later, after the smell dissipates."

"That sounds like a plan. You know, now that I know for sure that the smell is skunk, it doesn't bother me quite so much." Michelle stopped and started to frown. "I wonder why Frances didn't mention it."

"Mention what?"

"The skunk smell. I guess she didn't come in to clean this morning, now that Dean is dead."

"Are you talking about the Frances I know?"

"That's right, Frances Newman. She cleaned up in here every morning before Dean came in."

"But . . . Frances told me that she was the script girl. And when I asked her what she did she said she was in charge of continuity on the set, and noting little differences between the takes so the editor would know which one the director liked best, and . . ."

"That's all true," Michelle interrupted, "but they don't call them script girls anymore. The real title, the one on the credits, is *Continuity Coordinator*."

"Then why did Frances tell me she was a script girl?"

"Because that's what it was called when she started in the biz, and she still thinks of herself that way."

"How about cleaning Dean's Winnebago? That isn't part of her job description, is it?"

"No. It was an extra job Frances took on when Dean asked if anyone wanted to make a little money on the side. He paid her twenty-five dollars a day to make sure his trailer looked good when he came in every morning. She said it never took her more than an hour and Dean paid her in cash."

Hannah thought about that for a moment. "I should probably talk to Frances. She might know more about Dean's life than anyone else in the company."

"I'm sure she does. From what I understand, she's been cleaning for him since they started filming two months ago."

Hannah had an unwelcome thought. "There wasn't anything *personal* going on between Frances and Dean, was there?"

"I don't think so. And even if there was, Frances couldn't have killed him. I saw her take up her position by the door, and the only time she left it was when Dean called her over to give her a note. She didn't go anywhere near the desk, Hannah. I know that for a fact."

"Okay, that leaves her in the clear," Hannah said, putting a mental line through Frances's name only seconds after she'd imagined writing it on the roster of suspects she kept in her head.

"This way," Michelle said, leading Hannah down the center hallway of the trailer and opening the door to a room just beyond Dean's office. "This is the screening room. Take a chair and I'll put in the tape."

While Hannah was waiting for her sister to ready the electronic equipment, she took note of her surroundings. The room was messy and that substantiated her belief that Dean had been a slob. There were paper plates on the coffee table from the cheesecake he'd served to whoever had screened footage with him, and no one had bothered to put them in the wastebasket. That wasn't so bad, but Hannah spotted one of her distinctive bakery boxes and she was sure there was part of a cheesecake inside. By now it would be twenty-four hours old and it had been sitting out all this time. Hannah felt like putting it in Dean's refrigerator, but it seemed silly since he was no longer around to eat it.

"Okay. We're all set." Michelle grabbed the remote control and took the chair next to Hannah. "Here we go."

Hannah stared at the big-screen television as the tape began to run. She saw Mike check the gun—they'd even captured that on tape—and she saw Burke walk over to the desk. Burke pulled out the drawer, made sure the gun was inside, and walked away. Several other people milled around in that area, but as far as Hannah could see, no one else touched the drawer except Lloyd, the prop man, who came over to check it after Burke.

Hannah made a mental note to quiz Lloyd to see if he'd noticed anything unusual about the gun in the drawer. He hadn't taken it out to check the firing pin, but there might have been something not quite right, something that hadn't made him suspicious until now, in retrospect.

One other person was a possibility and that was Jared, the set decorator. He'd gone over to straighten the flowers that sat on the desk and stood in front of it, effectively blocking the camera's view of the drawer. Perhaps he hadn't touched the drawer. Hannah had no way of knowing, but he'd had the opportunity and that was enough to make him a suspect.

Hannah watched as Lynne took her place in the desk chair and Burke entered the scene. The first take was awful, as were the second and the third. It was exactly the way Dean had described. Burke couldn't act his way out of a paper bag. Hannah knew Burke's character was supposed to be drunk, but Burke slipped several times and forgot to slur his words. He also looked more pained than guilty and Hannah remembered that he'd said his back was hurting him.

"Brace yourself," Michelle said as Dean started to demonstrate the scene. "Camera two does a close-up and it's not fun to watch."

It was a clear warning from the baby sister who hadn't minded watching an autopsy on educational television. Hannah took it to heart and did what she always did when a particularly frightening or gory scene appeared on television or in the movies. She peeked through her fingers.

This whole device of peeking through her fingers might look silly to other people, but it worked for Hannah. Just seeing her own fingers in front of the scene was a constant reminder that it wasn't really happening and she was really in a movie theater or in her own living room. Of course in this case, it *had* really happened. And her fingers didn't work quite so well.

When the scene was over, Hannah drew a deep breath and looked over at her sister. Michelle was just lowering her hand and she gave a sheepish smile. "Sorry. You told me to do that when I was a kid, and I still do it."

"So do I," Hannah admitted, and then she got back to business. "Okay, who did you notice?"

Michelle ticked them off on her fingers. "Lynne, but she didn't touch the drawer, at least not when the camera was running. Burke, who did touch the drawer and even pulled it out to make sure the prop gun was there."

"If it *was* the prop gun when he checked," Hannah pointed out.

"Yes. I should probably ask around and find out if Burke has any background with revolvers."

"Good idea. Who else?"

"Lloyd. He checked the drawer before filming started."

"Was that part of his job?"

"Yes. He always checks a scene right before they shoot it to make sure the important props are in the correct position."

"Anyone else?"

"Only one and that's not for sure. Jared went over to rearrange the bouquet on the desk. He stood in front of the drawer and he could have pulled it out without us noticing."

"Very good!" Hannah said, smiling at her baby sister. "And that's it?"

"That's all I saw.

"Me too, except for me."

"You?"

"Dean had me replace the tray of mini cherry cheesecakes right before the final take. I blocked the drawer with my body, and I could have switched the revolvers without anyone noticing."

"But you didn't!"

"Of course not. The important thing is that I could have. You didn't even notice me because you didn't suspect me. What you have to remember is that when you're working on a crime like this, you can't overlook anybody."

Michelle sighed deeply. "You're right. I should have mentioned you even though I knew you didn't do it. I guess that's why I'm the helper and you're the detective."

"I'm not a detective. I'm a snoop." Hannah reached out to give her sister a pat on the shoulder. "And speaking of snooping . . . let's go through Dean's things and see what we can dig up."

The first room they searched was the largest room in the trailer, the one at the end of the hallway. Hannah opened the door and gave a smug smile. She'd been right. It was the master bedroom and Dean hadn't changed it. The large bed it had been designed to accommodate was the focal point of the room, and the only concession to office work was a conversational grouping of four barrel-backed chairs around an octagonal coffee table.

"So what did he use this room for?" Hannah asked, almost certain that she knew the answer to her own question.

"Private rehearsals. If one of the actors was having trouble with a scene, Dean would bring them here to go over it. But I'm pretty sure he used it for other things, too."

"Right. You start with the closet and see if there's anything of interest in there. I'll check the coffee table and the little chest of drawers by the bed."

Hannah went through the coffee table quickly. There were a few magazines, a couple of books, and several yellow legal-size pads. A ceramic holder was filled with an assortment of pens and pencils, and a couple of decks of cards were tossed into a basket with a bridge score pad. Unless someone had gotten completely bent out of shape over a rubber of bridge and killed Dean in retaliation, she hadn't found a thing.

"How are you coming?" Hannah asked, aiming her question at the closet.

"Fine. I'm almost through."

"Me too." Hannah headed over to the small dresser, but all it contained were CDs for the sound system. Hannah paged through them. There were show tunes, blues, movie soundtracks, and some pop classical. It was quite apparent that they were carefully generic, and Hannah suspected that they'd come with the Winnebago and were meant to appeal to anyone who rented the giant vehicle.

"I didn't find anything interesting," Michelle said, emerging from the closet just as Hannah shut the dresser drawer.

"Neither did I. Let's go search the rest of the trailer."

Fifteen minutes later, they were still searching and they were down to the last room. Both sisters thought that Dean's office might contain clues, but what they dug up was a big fat zero. Then Michelle began going through Dean's file cabinet and she let out a whoop as she hit pay dirt.

"Look at this," she said, shoving a file across the desk to Hannah, who'd seated herself behind Dean's massive work surface to go through the contents of the drawers. "It's Connor's employment file."

"And that's important?" Hannah asked, opening the file. The first page was a standard personnel questionnaire, the kind every large corporation asks applicants to fill out before their initial interview. "This looks pretty standard to me."

"Take a closer look. Do you see what Connor listed as his last job, the one right before Dean hired him."

Hannah glanced a little farther down on the page and found the section Michelle had indicated. "Chauffeur and bodyguard for a family named Dickinson in Iowa. He drove the wife to social events. What's so unusual about that?"

"Nothing in itself, but take a look at the wife's name."

"Emily?" Hannah asked, beginning to frown. "Mrs. Emily Dickinson?"

"Exactly. And that must have made Dean curious, because he hired a private detective firm to check with Connor's former employers. The answer he got is on the next page."

Hannah gasped as she turned the page and studied the investigator's report. Connor was stretching the truth even more than the image in a funhouse mirror, but she had to admire the attempt. There was a kernel of accuracy in what he'd written and it was very clever. He *had* protected Emily Dickinson and driven her, or at least her books, around to social events. Connor had been a library aide at Iowa State Prison and he'd been in charge of the carts that were wheeled around to the cellblocks.

"Well?" Michelle asked.

"It certainly gives him motive, especially if Dean was going to fire him. And it fits in with what Connor told me about how he couldn't use Dean as a reference." Hannah thought back to the tape they'd watched and shook her head. "I didn't see Connor on the tape, did I?"

"I don't think so. I know I didn't."

"Would it be possible for him to be there and not get on the tape?"

"Absolutely. They didn't tape everyone."

"Do you remember if Connor was on the set yesterday?"

"I didn't see him, but I'll check with Ross. He always notices who's there and who's not."

Hannah shook her head. "Never mind. You've got enough to do. I'll check with Ross when I see him tonight."

"Tonight?" Michelle asked with a grin. "What's tonight?"

"Ross is taking me out to the inn for dinner."

"All right!" Michelle gave a pleased smile. The smile lasted for several seconds and then it turned into an impish grin. "Do Norman and Mike know you're going out to dinner with Ross?"

"No, and don't tell them. I don't need anybody to cat-sit."

"Cat-sit?"

"That's right. Moishe's perfectly all right alone. I don't think I can take another late night gathering at my place."

Michelle gave her a perfectly blank look. "What's this about cat-sitting and late night gatherings?"

"I'll tell you on the way back to The Cookie Jar. Are we finished in here?" Hannah waited until Michelle nodded and then she pushed back Dean's desk chair. "Pick up your tape and the shooting script, and head for the hills. I'll let the skunk out and join you."

Less than two minutes later, Hannah came barreling out the back door. She took the steps at a running jump and landed next to Michelle with a thump.

"Did you see the skunk?" Michelle asked.

"I saw it, all right. When I opened the bathroom door, there it was trying to jump back out the window. It was really scared and it's going to be glad to get back outside."

"Do you think it'll find its way out all right?"

"I don't know why not. I shut all the other doors so the only thing that's open is the back door."

"Good. I wonder why it went in there in the first place."

"Maybe it was attracted by the other skunk."

Michelle looked confused. "What other skunk?"

"The two-legged one that used the trailer for an office."

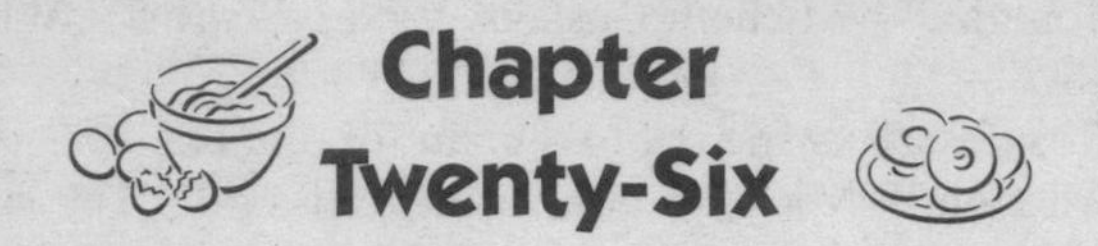

Chapter Twenty-Six

"You look great!" Ross said, stepping inside and giving Hannah an approving hug. "I really like that outfit."

"Thank you." Hannah shut her mouth firmly, following the advice her mother had drummed into her head from little on. *When a man compliments you, don't argue with him. Just say a polite thank-you.* She didn't explain that she'd run next door to Beau Monde Fashions in a panic right after Ross had asked her to dinner, and she'd begged Claire to pick out something to make her look irresistible. She failed to mention that the outfit had put a crater in her budget even with her generous business-next-door discount. And she bit back her inclination to repeat Claire's remark about how the new dress would hide the extra ten pounds around her waist and make the parts of her anatomy that most men noticed look lush and curvy.

"Hi there, Big Guy." Ross walked over to greet Moishe, who immediately started to purr. Hannah watched as her feline made a fool of himself by rolling over for a belly rub, and she started to grin. The feline vote was in on Ross and he was a definite winner. To date, her four-footed roommate had given his unqualified approval to all three of her suitors. Hannah suspected that Moishe would give the same unqualified approval to any man who called him "Big Guy" and rubbed his belly, including the condo maintenance man.

"I'll just get my coat, then," Hannah said, heading for the bedroom. She really hated to break up this feline–human love fest, but her stomach was growling and she'd heard that Sally was featuring boeuf Wellington tonight. Since it was one of her favorite entrées, Hannah was eager to get out to the inn and order just in case Sally ran out.

Hannah took her best dress coat from the closet, the one she wore only when the moon turned azure. The coat was black and not cat-friendly. She'd brushed it before she'd put it away, but as she watched, several orange-and-white hairs floated through the air and settled on one sleeve. Hannah brushed them off with her hand, but she knew full well that it was an exercise in futility. There would be several hundred more by the time she walked through the living room and went out the door.

"I turned on the animal channel for him," Ross said, as Hannah reentered the living room. "Is that all right?"

Hannah glanced at the set and saw that they were rerunning a documentary she'd watched about penguins. "It's perfect. Moishe gets upset when birds fly, but it doesn't bother him at all when they waddle."

Once she'd tossed Moishe a half-dozen salmon-flavored treats to keep him occupied, Hannah locked the door behind her and walked down the steps with Ross to the garage. She expected to see his rented sedan parked in her other parking spot, and she stopped short as she caught sight of the vehicle that was taking them out to the inn. "That looks just like Dean's limo," she said.

"That's because it *is* Dean's limo. We rented it for him as part of his contract. Since we've got it for another week, I figured we might as well use it tonight."

"Do you want me to drive?" Hannah gave a little laugh. "I've got some experience as a chauffeur. When the regular driver broke his leg, I had to drive the limo for Lisa and Herb's wedding."

Ross gave her a quick hug. "You're an amazing woman, Hannah Swensen! And I don't have a doubt in my mind that you could double as a chauffeur. But we already have one, so we get to ride in back."

"You hired a chauffeur just for tonight?"

"No, we already had one. Connor is driving. We paid his salary as a provision of Dean's contract. I told Connor he could keep the money and go back home, but he wanted to stay on and work."

"I see," Hannah said, and she thought she did. Connor was probably hoping to use Ross as a reference for future employment.

Connor jumped out as they approached and opened the rear door for Hannah. Once she was seated, he went around the car and opened the other door for Ross. "Straight out to the inn?" he asked Ross.

"Could we drive past Dean's trailer first?" Hannah asked, before Ross could answer.

"Of course. But why?"

"When Michelle went to pick up the shooting script, I went with her. We think there was a skunk in there." Hannah heard a muffled cough from the front seat and she suspected that Connor was coughing to cover up a laugh. "We left the back door open so it could get out, and I need to make sure someone closed it and locked it."

"They did," Connor said from the front seat.

"You're sure?"

"Yes. I drove Mrs. Lawrence and Mr. Larchmont there this afternoon, right before I took them to the airport. They asked me to come in with them while Mrs. Lawrence picked up some things that she wanted. When we left, I made sure both doors were locked."

"Did you smell the skunk?" Hannah asked.

"All three of us smelled it. We just didn't know what it was. Mrs. Lawrence thought maybe the sewer was backed up."

"Obviously a city girl," Ross said to Hannah in an undertone.

"And Mr. Larchmont thought that the gas on the stove might be on."

"Obviously a city boy," Ross added.

"I checked the stove, and the gas was shut off."

"Thanks, Connor." Ross leaned back and put his arm around Hannah's shoulders. "Since you're sure everything is locked up tight, let's go out to the inn and I'll buy dinner for both of you."

Hannah pushed aside a little twinge of disappointment as Connor joined them at the table. She'd wanted to talk to Connor anyway and she should be glad that he was sitting right across from her in one of Sally's private booths. It was silly to resent the fact that she wasn't alone with Ross, when she wasn't entirely sure she *wanted* to be alone with Ross.

"So who did it?" Ross asked, turning to her.

"What do you mean? The police are investigating and I wouldn't dream of interfering with an official . . ."

"Of course you wouldn't, but you don't have to give me the standard party line," Ross interrupted the speech Hannah had used countless times at The Cookie Jar. "I know you always investigate."

"I never investigate," Hannah corrected him. "I leave that sort of thing to the trained professionals. But I can't really help it if people tell me things, and I put two and two together, can I?"

"Of course you can't. So let's get back to my original question. Who do you think killed Dean?"

"I don't know. Almost everybody who knew him seems to have a motive."

Connor gave a short laugh. "You're right. And if you haven't done so already, you'd better add me to your list of suspects."

"Why?" Hannah asked, wondering if Connor's reason would match the one they'd already thought of.

"Because Dean fired me right after I talked to you on Wednesday morning. I told him you were going to talk to Winnie after the cocktail party scene at Granny's Attic, but that didn't make any difference to him. He made me turn in my keys. Then he told me to clear out of my room at the inn and go home."

"But you didn't leave," Hannah pointed out.

"That's right. I was hoping that after you convinced Winnie to let him use the park, he'd hire me back. It's not like he hasn't done this sort of thing before. Dean is . . ." Connor stopped and swallowed hard. "Dean *was* a little hotheaded. He'd fly off the handle over something minor and apologize for it the next day. I learned to stick around after he fired me, because he always hired me back when he cooled off."

It was time to play hardball and Hannah was no stranger to that sport. "And Dean had you over the barrel. He knew that without references, it wouldn't be easy for you to get another job. And he knew about your background, too. That meant he could be as abusive as he wanted and you had to stand there and take it."

"True," Connor said, "except for one thing. I already had another job lined up this time around."

"You did?" Hannah's tone clearly indicated her surprise. "What job?"

"Mrs. Henderson's stockbroker."

Hannah's jaw dropped open and she attempted to conceal the sudden descent of her chin by making a comment. "I didn't know Winnie had investments!"

"She doesn't, at least not as far as I know. I'm talking about *stockbroker* in the original sense of the term. Each year Mrs. Henderson auctions off her prizewinning cattle. And each year she gets far less than she should for such magnificent animals. I told her I'd handle the cattle auctions for her and my salary would come from the extra profit we'd make."

There was no way Hannah could hide her smile. It seemed as if Winnie had attracted yet another man with her gooseberry pie. She just hoped that Connor was as honest as he seemed and his time in prison had nothing to do with a conviction for fraud, or embezzlement, or . . .

"Since you're Winnie's friend, you probably want to know why I was in prison," Connor said, leaning across the table to lock eyes with Hannah. "It doesn't sound good and I'm the first to admit it. I almost killed the guy who beat up my baby sister and left her for dead."

Hannah thought about that for a moment and then she reached out to pat Connor's hand. "I'd probably be tempted to do the same to anyone who hurt Michelle."

"Thanks, but just knowing that should shoot me to the top of your suspect list. I was really angry with Dean and I admit that I thought about landing a few punches. I controlled my anger by driving out to Winnie's farm, but she wasn't home and I don't have any way of proving where I was when the revolver was switched."

Ross spoke up, "Maybe not, but you do have a way of proving where you weren't. And that wasn't anywhere near Granny's Attic or the set."

Both Hannah and Connor turned to look at Ross. They'd been so intent on their conversation, they'd almost forgotten he was sitting in the booth with them.

"I had Frances make a list of everyone who came in the door," Ross said, "and your name isn't on it. You weren't there so you couldn't have done it."

Connor looked very pleased to hear that. "Then . . . I'm off the suspect list?"

"That's right. And you don't have to worry about anyone else holding your prison record over your head. Michelle gave me the personnel file Dean kept on you, and I shredded it."

Hannah started to smile. She was proud of her baby sister. Maybe Michelle shouldn't have absconded with Connor's personnel file, but it had all turned out right in the end.

"Now, how about dessert?" Ross continued, turning to Hannah. "Sally's got a terrific lemon torte, and she told me you gave her the recipe."

"I did. My Grandma Ingrid used to make it and I haven't had it for ages."

"This might be the night for memories," Ross said, capturing Hannah's hand under the table.

"Perhaps," Hannah said, doing her best to downplay the tingles that ran from the top of her head to the tip of her toes, and concentrate on something that was supposed to be more important . . . solving Dean's murder.

When Hannah emerged from the dining room and turned down the hall that led to the ladies' room, she found Amber Coombs waiting for her.

"Thank goodness!" Amber said, giving a sigh of relief. "I thought you'd never leave that booth!"

"You were waiting for me?"

"Yes. Sally said you were investigating . . ."

"I'm not really investigating," Hannah broke in. "I leave that up to the . . ."

"Professionals," Amber supplied the word before Hannah could say it. "That's what you always say, but we all know better. I talked to Sally and she said to tell you what I overheard when I delivered coffee to Mr. Lawrence's office on Wednesday morning."

Hannah motioned toward the door of the ladies' room. "Step into my office and tell me all about it."

The ladies' room at the Lake Eden Inn was spacious. Sally had placed several chairs around a round table opposite the sinks and the mirrors, and there was even a phone on the wall. Hannah had spent too many minutes thinking about how that phone might be used. She'd come up with several scenarios, including a woman on an unpleasant date who might use it to call a taxi and leave before her escort could become any more unpleasant.

"Have a chair," Hannah said, taking a quick peek in the other room to make sure they were completely alone and then sitting in the chair directly opposite the teenage waitress she was now beginning to think of as her informant. "Why did you take coffee to Mr. Lawrence's trailer?"

"He forgot to pick up the thermos Sally had at the desk for him. And since I was scheduled to work breakfast and I had a car, Sally asked me to run it into town for her."

"Okay," Hannah said, pulling her shorthand notebook from her purse and flipping it to the right page. "What time did you get to Mr. Lawrence's trailer?"

"Eight-thirty. I was listening to KCOW radio and Kelly was just about to bang the gong for the half-hour when I pulled in and parked."

Hannah jotted down the time and decided not to ask about the gong. Jake and Kelly were the half-comedy, half-news team who hosted KCOW's *News at O'Dark-Thirty*, and they could get a bit strange. "What happened next?"

"Well, I got out of the car with the thermos and the first thing I heard was yelling. It was coming from the trailer and I recognized Mr. Anson's voice."

"Are you absolutely positive it was Mr. Anson?" Hannah asked, her pen poised over the page.

"Oh, I'm sure. And I saw him leave a couple of minutes later, so that proves it."

That was good enough for Hannah and she jotted down Burke Anson's name. "And Mr. Lawrence was in his trailer at that time?"

"Oh, yes. He was yelling, too. That's why I waited to knock on the door. I didn't want to go inside in the middle of a fight."

"A wise decision," Hannah said, hoping that Amber had overheard something useful. "So you sat in your car and waited?"

"That's right. But I did something I'm a little ashamed of. I left the door open a little so I could listen."

"Of course you did!"

"But I know I shouldn't have done that. I was eavesdropping on a private conversation and that's never nice."

"Of course it's not, but I don't think you could find a single person in Lake Eden who wouldn't have done exactly what you did." Hannah stopped to give Amber an encouraging smile. "And you had a good reason for listening."

"I did?"

"Absolutely. You had to know when Dean and Burke stopped yelling so that you could deliver the coffee."

"That's right." Amber smiled right back. "I really like the way you think, Miss Swensen."

Hannah glanced down at her notebook. "All right. While you were sitting in your car waiting for them to end their altercation, what did you hear?"

"Mostly it was just yelling at each other about who did something. You know how that goes."

"I probably do, but tell me anyway."

"Mr. Anson was saying, '*I know you did it, Dean!*' And

Mr. Lawrence was saying, '*You're crazy. I had nothing to do with it.*'"

"Did you ever find out what they were arguing about?"

"Not really. It just went back and forth after that and each time it got louder. Mr. Anson kept telling Mr. Lawrence to remember last Tuesday, and Mr. Lawrence kept saying that he had nothing to do with it."

Hannah jotted down *Last Tuesday* with a question mark. "And they never mentioned what happened last Tuesday?"

"Not once. But something must have, Miss Swensen. They were sure hot under the collar about it. The only other thing that Sally thought you might want to know is what Mr. Anson said right before he stormed out of Mr. Lawrence's trailer."

Hannah leaned forward, her pen poised to record something of great import. "What did he say?"

"If I find out you did it, you're going to pay!"

"Okay, Amber." Hannah jotted down Burke's final threat and returned the notebook to her purse. "Thanks a lot for telling me."

After Amber left, Hannah just sat there for a minute, thinking about what she'd learned. The fight between Burke and Dean was interesting, but it didn't shed any real light on Dean's murder. Burke certainly hadn't switched the prop gun for a real one, not when he was about to hold it up to his own head and pull the trigger. It had to be someone else, perhaps another person who was involved in whatever had happened the previous Tuesday. She'd ask Ross about that and if Ross didn't know, she'd ask Michelle to quiz the other members of the crew about it.

LEMON CREAM TORTE

Preheat oven to 250 degrees F.,
rack in the middle position
(Not a misprint—two hundred and fifty degrees F.)

Hannah's Note: Try to choose a day when the humidity is low to bake this. Meringues don't crisp up as well if the air is too humid.

Meringue:

4 egg whites ***(reserve the yolks in a bowl for the filling)***
1 cup white ***(granulated)*** sugar
½ teaspoon vanilla extract

Cover a cookie sheet with parchment paper. ***(You can use brown parcel-wrapping paper, but parchment works best.)*** Draw two 8-inch diameter circles on your paper, using a round 8-inch cake pan as a guide. Spray the paper with Pam, or other non-stick cooking spray, and sprinkle it lightly with flour.

Beat the egg whites until they are stiff enough to hold a soft peak. Add ⅔ cup of the sugar gradually, sprinkling it in and beating hard ***(on high speed with an electric mixer)*** after each sprinkling. Pour in the

vanilla extract and sprinkle in the rest of the sugar ***(1/3 cup.)*** Mix it in very gently ***(on low speed with an electric mixer),*** or fold in with an angel food cake whisk until the meringue is smooth.

Spoon half the meringue neatly into one of the 8-inch circles. Smooth the top—it should be about 3/4 inch thick. Spoon the remaining meringue into the second circle and smooth the top.

Bake at 250 degrees F. for one hour, or until slightly golden on top and the surface is hard when touched.

Cool completely on the cookie sheet on a wire rack.

When the meringues are cool, gently loosen them by peeling off the paper. Put them back on the paper loose, and move them to a cool, dry place. ***(A dark cupboard is fine—The refrigerator is NOT FINE.)***

Filling:

4 egg yolks
1/2 cup white ***(granulated)*** sugar
3 Tablespoons lemon juice
2 teaspoons lemon zest ***(finely grated peel—just the yellow part)***

½ cup whipping cream
2 teaspoons vanilla extract
¼ cup white ***(granulated)*** sugar ***(you'll use ¾ cup total in the filling)***

Beat the egg yolks with ½ cup sugar until smooth. Add the lemon juice and zest.

Cook in the top of a double boiler, over gently boiling water, until the egg yolk mixture is smooth and as thick as mayonnaise. ***(That's a little thicker than gravy and takes about 3 minutes or so.)*** Move the top part of the double boiler to a cold burner and let the mixture cool while you complete the rest of the recipe.

Pour the vanilla into the cream. Whip the cream just until it holds a peak. Don't overbeat. Beat in the remaining ¼ cup sugar. Slowly stir the whipped cream mixture into the warm lemon mixture until you have a light, smooth sauce. ***(Lick the spoon—it's yummy!)*** Cover it and refrigerate the sauce until you're ready to serve.

To assemble, get out the meringues and the lemon filling. Decide which meringue looks best and set that aside for the top. Place the other meringue on a cake plate.

Spoon half of the lemon filling over the top of the meringue on the cake plate. Spread it with a rubber spatula so it's almost out to the edge.

Put the best-looking meringue on top. Spoon the rest of the lemon filling on top of that meringue and spread it out with a rubber spatula.

To serve, cut pie-shaped wedges at the table and transfer them to dessert plates. This is a light, sugary but tart, totally satisfying summer dessert.

Yield: Serves 4 to 6 people ***(unless you invite Carrie—she always has thirds).***

Another Note From Hannah: This dessert is certainly yummy, but it's not gorgeous. When Sally serves it at the Lake Eden Inn, she slices it in the kitchen because the meringues tend to crumble. Then she puts it on a beautiful dessert plate or in a cut glass dessert bowl, tops it with a generous dollop of sweetened whipped cream, and places a paper-thin lemon slice on top to make it look fancy.

Chapter Twenty-Seven

"Why are you smiling like that?" Delores asked.

Her mother's question yanked Hannah out of the contented daydream she'd slipped into after finishing the baking and back to reality, where she was sitting across from Delores in the kitchen of The Cookie Jar. Since telling her mother that she'd been thinking about Ross, the fun they'd had the previous evening, and the possibility of more fun in the future might encourage her matchmaking matriarch much too much, Hannah pretended she hadn't heard. "What did you say, Mother?"

"Why were you smiling like that?"

"Smiling like what?"

"Like the cat that got into the cream pot."

Hannah's ears perked up. It was another Regency expression from the mother who'd been spouting them left and right for the past few weeks. In less time than it took to mix up a batch of Oatmeal Raisin Crisps, Delores had used three Regency expressions and the cat and the cream pot counted as the fourth. She'd said *high in the instep* to describe someone who was snooty, she'd called the new sweater she'd bought *all the crack* to mean that it was fashionable, and she'd explained that one of her customers had *suffered an attack of the megrims* when she went into a severe depression over her daughter's divorce. Hannah was used to hearing Regency expressions for a day or two after a meeting of the Lake Eden Regency Romance Club, but the meeting this month had been canceled so that the members could try out for parts in the movie.

"What's with all this Regency-speak?" Hannah asked, answering a question with a question in an effort to throw off her mother's game.

"It's just so much more colorful, isn't it?" Delores also answered a question with a question, and mother and daughter began to volley.

"Do you really think so?" Hannah lobbed the question ball right back over the net. She must have landed a good one, because her mother didn't reply. "So how many Regency expressions do you think you know?"

"Hundreds, I'm sure," Delores answered, not even trying for a return.

Hannah felt the thrill of victory. She'd served and scored on that last question. But just as she was relishing her win, a dire thought crept into her mind. Delores had a computer, and she was using a lot of Regency expressions. Had her mother found another Englishman who piqued her interest, perhaps someone she'd met in some international chat room on the Internet? Delores had already shown that she wasn't such a good judge of character when it came to handsome Englishmen who liked to dance.

"Mother?" Hannah started out tentatively, but only after she'd replenished her mother's supply of German Chocolate Cake Cookies.

"Yes, dear."

"Michelle says you've got a new computer."

"Yes, I do. Norman helped me order it and he hooked it all up for me."

"Why didn't Norman tell me?"

"Because I asked him not to. I was going to surprise you the next time you came over, but I forgot to tell Michelle that it was a surprise. It's an amazing machine, dear, much better than a typewriter."

"So," Hannah proceeded gingerly down the path she'd chosen, "you use it for word processing, then?"

"That's right. And Norman installed a mail program for me."

A mail program. Hannah digested that bit of information and then she went for another bite. "You're connected to the Internet?"

"Not yet. Norman says to wait until the cable company has a special on their high-speed line. That's when you can get free installation. He told me I wouldn't be happy with a dial-up connection. It's just too slow."

"I see," Hannah said, relaxing slightly. Delores wasn't connected to the Internet, and that meant she couldn't be having a cyber romance with a handsome, ballroom dancing Englishman she'd met online. "Is that mail program Norman installed for later when you have e-mail?"

"No, it's for snail mail. I learned how to make labels and I'm keeping our master address list of customers for Granny's Attic. Would you believe that Carrie and I were hand-addressing all our sale notices? Now all I have to do is print out labels, and we can just stick them on."

"That's a real time-saver." Hannah still wasn't completely satisfied. Nothing Delores had told her explained her mother's sudden obsession with Regency terms. "Have you been doing a lot of reading lately?"

"Not as much as I'd like, dear. Running Granny's Attic is a full-time job, even with all three of us. And after I get home, it's all I can do to grab a bite to eat, switch on my laptop, and work for a couple of hours."

"Work?" Hannah zeroed in on her mother's last statement. "What are you working on?"

Delores glanced at the clock on the wall. "Oh, just a little hobby of mine. You wouldn't be interested. I'd better run, dear. I left Carrie at the shop all alone. She'll need my help."

"But you're not open for business," Hannah pointed out.

"I know, but there are still things to do." Delores stood up, shrugged into her coat, and headed for the door. "Inventory, straightening up, things like that. Later, dear."

Hannah stared at the door that closed behind her mother, but there were no answers written on the white paint that covered the wood. Delores had a secret and she was guarding it carefully. Hannah figured that it would come out sooner or later, but in the meantime her curiosity was killing her.

"Hannah?" Lisa pushed open the swinging door that separated the kitchen from the coffee shop and glanced in at her partner. "Mike's here to see you and I told him I'd check to see if you were busy. He says he needs to ask you some questions."

"What a coincidence!" Hannah said with a grin. "I'd like to ask him some questions, too."

"Shall I go out and lead the lamb to the slaughter?"

"Yes, but I wouldn't put it quite that way to the lamb."

"Don't worry. I won't." Lisa went through the swinging door, but she turned around to stick her head back into the kitchen again. "If we're betting on who gets the most questions answered, my money's on you."

"Thanks, Hannah." Mike picked up the mug of coffee that Hannah had poured him and took a big gulp. "This would be a whole lot easier if Bill hadn't gone to that convention. I'm working a double shift most days."

"Filling in for Bill as acting sheriff, plus heading up Dean's murder investigation?"

"That's right. I got four hours' sleep last night and I considered myself lucky."

If you'd just swallow that silly pride of yours and let me help you, you'd get more sleep, Hannah thought, but of course she didn't say it. She also didn't commiserate too much. She'd had less than four hours' sleep herself, but she wasn't about to tell Mike the identity of the person with whom she'd had a late date!

"I know what you're thinking."

"You do?" Hannah felt a little tingle of alarm. Had Mike heard about her dinner with Ross?

"You're thinking that if I'd accepted your offer to help with the investigation, I wouldn't be so overworked."

"Mmm," Hannah said, settling for the most noncommittal reply she could come up with on short notice.

"It's not that I don't *want* your help. I do. It's just that I can't ask for it. You know?"

"Not really."

"Winnetka County Sheriff's Department regulation four-eighteen, subsection *B* says, *No civilian shall be recruited into an official investigation without insurance, bonding, compensation commensurate with duties, and deputization.*"

"Is that a word?"

"Commensurate? Yeah, it means . . ."

"Not that," Hannah interrupted him. "I know what *commensurate* means. I was talking about *deputization*. I don't think it's a word."

"It must be a word. They used it in the official department regulations."

Hannah bit her tongue rather than say what was on her mind. Mike had a lot to learn about regulations and the overworked secretaries who usually wrote them for their bosses. A mistake in word usage could multiply from county to county, and from state to state, until it was as rampant as gophers running wild on a golf course.

"I was really tempted to deputize you, but I thought it would be overstepping my bounds as acting sheriff."

"You silver-tongued devil, you!" Hannah murmured under her breath, smiling despite herself. If Mike had deputized her, she would have worked her sleuthy fingers to the bone for him. But he hadn't. And he'd only mentioned it because he was trying to sweet-talk her into giving him the information she'd gathered.

"So what did you find out?" Mike asked, validating Hannah's conjecture.

"Not much," Hannah said, but she knew she had to give him more than that so he'd give her something in return. "From what I've heard nobody liked Dean all that much."

"Who do *you* like for the murder?"

"At first I liked Connor. He had a good motive, but it turns out that he couldn't have done it. He wasn't at Granny's Attic that afternoon."

"Right. His name isn't on Frances's list. Who else?"

Hannah drew a big breath of relief. Since Mike had eliminated Connor, he hadn't bothered to run a background check. Connor's prison days would remain his secret unless he chose to tell someone. "I thought maybe Sharyn had found out about Dean's extracurricular activities and lowered the boom. I even entertained the thought that Tom Larchmont might have done away with Dean because he was a lousy husband for his niece, Sharyn."

"Nope. I cleared them both. They alibi each other, and an independent third party swears they never left their chairs between takes."

Hannah made a mental note. There was no need to ask Sophie about the fight she'd overheard between Tom and Lynne since Mike had cleared Tom. "How about Lynne, herself? She was certainly in a position to switch the revolvers."

"She was, and she was my prime suspect when Ross told me that she wanted to direct. But I searched her myself right after the murder and she didn't have the prop gun anywhere on her."

Anywhere on her? Hannah bit back an amused chuckle. Lynne was a gorgeous leading lady and she couldn't blame Mike if he'd enjoyed his search just a little more than he should have. "So who do *you* like for Dean's murder?"

"Jared's a possibility."

"Jared? Why do you think he did it?"

"Remember when I told you someone saw him straightening some flowers on the desk?"

"I remember."

"Well, he had the opportunity to switch the revolvers. I watched the tapes of the rehearsals and one of the cameramen caught Jared blocking the drawer with his body. If he'd had another working and loaded revolver, he could have switched them."

"I agree," Hannah said, "but why would he do that? As far as I know, he didn't have a grudge against Dean. And even if Burke was the intended victim, Jared doesn't have a reason to want him dead, either."

"Maybe he does and we just don't know about it yet."

"You could be right," Hannah said. "I'll ask around about him and see what I can dig up. In the meantime, why don't you concentrate on your other suspects."

"Okay," Mike said, giving a weary sigh. "I'll go back to work and you can go back to your baking."

"I'm all through. Have a couple of my new cookies and tell me what you think."

Mike bit into a cookie and his frown disappeared. "These are good, Hannah. Do you have a name for them yet?"

"Not yet."

"I think you should call then Angel Kisses. They're light and sweet."

"Good idea. Have another."

Mike finished four more cookies and when he turned to go, he was smiling, especially when Hannah pressed a bag of Angel Kisses in his hand and told him to share with his deputies.

When the door closed behind him, Hannah popped a cookie into her own mouth. Mike had gotten such a lift from the chocolate, he was all fired up and ready to catch Dean's killer. Maybe a dose of her own medicine would work to inspire her, too.

ANGEL KISSES

Preheat oven to 275 degrees F., rack in the middle position
(That's two hundred seventy-five degrees F., not a misprint.)

3 egg whites ***(save the yolks in the refrigerator to add to scrambled eggs)***
¼ teaspoon cream of tartar
½ teaspoon vanilla
¼ teaspoon salt
1 cup white ***(granulated)*** sugar
2 Tablespoons flour ***(that's ⅛ cup)***
approximately 30 Hershey's Kisses, unwrapped ***(or any other small chocolate candy)***

Separate the egg whites and let them come up to room temperature. This will give you more volume when you beat them.

Prepare your baking sheets by lining them with parchment paper ***(works best)*** or brown parcel-wrapping paper. Spray the paper with Pam or other non-stick cooking spray and dust it lightly with flour.

Hannah's note: These are a lot easier to make with an electric mixer, but you can also do them by hand with a copper bowl and a whisk.

Beat the egg whites with the cream of tartar, vanilla, and salt until they are stiff enough to hold a soft peak. Add the cup of sugar gradually, sprinkling it in by quarter cups and beating hard for ten seconds or so after each sprinkling. Sprinkle in the flour and mix it in at low speed, or fold it in with an angel food cake whisk.

Drop little mounds of dough on your paper-lined cookie sheet. If you place four mounds in a row and you have four rows, you'll end up with 16 cookies per sheet.

Place one Hershey's Kiss, point up, in the center of each mound. Push the candies down, but not all the way to the bottom. ***(You don't want the chocolate to actually touch the parchment paper.)*** Drop another little mound of meringue on top of the candy to cover it up.

Bake at 275 degrees F. for approximately 40 minutes, or until the meringue part of the cookie is slightly golden and dry to the touch.

Cool on the paper-lined cookie sheet by setting it on a wire rack. When the cookies are completely cool, peel them carefully from the paper and store them in an airtight container in a dry place. ***(A cupboard shelf is fine, just NOT the refrigerator!)***

Yield: 3 to 4 dozen cookies with a nice chocolate surprise in the center.

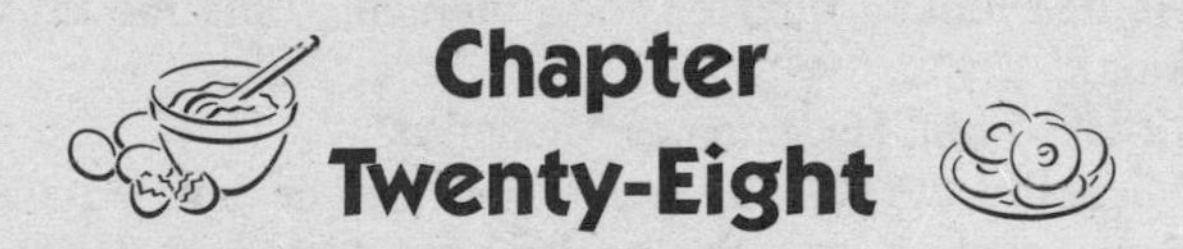

Chapter Twenty-Eight

It was a noon meeting of the sisters and it was taking place in the small coffee room at Bertie Straub's Cut 'n Curl beauty parlor. Thankfully the owner, the biggest gossip in Lake Eden, was watching Honey apply Tracey's makeup and the sisters had the coffee room all to themselves.

"Did you ever see so many flamingos in your life?" Andrea asked, glancing around at the flamingo lamp standing in a corner, the wastebasket with a rather rotund pink flamingo painted on the side, the wallpaper with bright pink flamingos flapping their wings and marching in parallel lines around the room, and the mirror peppered with flamingo decals in various hues of pink.

"Bertie said this place used to be called The Flamingo Hair Salon before she bought it," Hannah explained. "She threw out a lot of the decorations, but she saved some for back here."

"The seller didn't want to take the decorations with her?"

"I guess not. Maybe she figured they'd compete too much with the real thing."

Andrea looked puzzled for a moment. "She moved to Florida?"

"That's right. Here comes Michelle."

Michelle, the last to arrive for their designated rendezvous, rushed into the back room. She pulled out a white vinyl-covered chair with a pink flamingo painted on the back. The chair was old and there were cracks in the flamingo, with yellow foam stuffing peeking through them. "I've never been back here before," she said, sitting down at the pink Formica-topped table.

"That's a blessing," Andrea quipped, pulling out her dark glasses and putting them on.

"Why did you do that?" Hannah asked her.

"To tone down the pink. The only thing that's not a flamingo in here is that."

Hannah and Michelle looked where Andrea was pointing. It was a wicked-looking machine standing in the corner, with wires hanging down from a metal hood.

"What is it?" Michelle asked.

"I think it's an old-fashioned permanent wave machine," Hannah told her. "They used it to do marcelled hair."

"What's marcelled hair?"

"A marcel was a hairstyle back in the nineteen-thirties. They also called it a finger wave. You know what a wave is, don't you?"

Michelle nodded. "Dad's hair was wavy when he put hair oil on it. Mother liked it that way."

"But Dad didn't," Andrea broke in. "He said it felt greasy."

"So did a marcel. The waves were all perfectly lined up and they were sharp and even all over the head. Think about the early pictures you've seen of Joan Crawford and Mae West. They wore marcelled hair."

"How did the machine work?" Andrea wanted to know.

"See those metal rods hanging down on cords from that

hood?" Both of her sisters nodded and Hannah continued her explanation. "I'm not a hundred percent positive, but I think the operator wound hair around those metal rods. The wires led to the power source and when the operator turned on the machine, electricity heated the hair and curled it."

Andrea looked shocked. "But that would be dangerous! I wonder if anybody was ever electrocuted."

"I don't know. That was way before my time."

"I can ask Mother about it," Michelle offered.

"I wouldn't if I were you," Andrea warned.

Hannah nodded her agreement. "That was way before her time, too. And you know Mother doesn't like to be reminded of her age."

"I know *that*. I just thought I could ask her if she ever came in here when she was a little girl and if she ever saw anyone actually using . . . " Michelle stopped and sighed. "You're right. Better not."

"Let's get down to business," Andrea suggested. "I have to take Tracey over to wardrobe when Honey's done with her makeup."

Michelle turned to Hannah. "I found out about Jared."

"What's all this about Jared?" Andrea asked, grabbing the steno pad Hannah had placed on the table and flipping to the suspects page. "He's not even on here."

Hannah handed her a pen. "We were waiting for you to write him down. Michelle and I watched the tape from the dress rehearsal and Jared was one of the people who had the opportunity to switch the revolvers."

"What's his motive?" Andrea asked, jotting down Jared's name.

"He doesn't have one," Michelle answered quickly. "And he didn't do it, either."

"How do you know that?" Hannah asked her.

"Because once Jared finished straightening the flowers on the desk, he walked over and took the chair next to

Honey. He sat there with her until the gun went off, and he was still with her when they were all ushered out by the deputies and searched."

"So he never had the opportunity to get rid of the prop gun?" Hannah asked, catching on immediately.

"That's right. I checked it out with Honey and she substantiates everything Jared told me."

"Well, that lets Jared out," Andrea said, crossing his name off the list. "Is there anybody else I don't know about"

"There's Lloyd," Michelle said.

"Lloyd," Andrea repeated, her pen poised over the suspect column. "Shall I write him down? Or will I just have to cross him out again right away?"

"Write him down," Michelle said.

And at the very same time, Hannah said, "Don't bother to write down his name. Lloyd's in the clear."

"You cleared him?" Andrea wanted to know.

"No, Mike did. He told me about it this morning. Lloyd didn't have any time to get rid of the gun. Mike watched him go over to the desk and check the drawer, and then he came right back to where Mike was standing so they could finish their discussion about guns."

"Opportunity to switch, but no opportunity to hide the prop gun," Andrea summarized. "Okay, who else did we eliminate?"

"Connor," Hannah told her.

"How did we do that?"

"He didn't have the opportunity. Frances wrote down the names of everyone who came in the door at Granny's Attic for the dress rehearsal, and Connor wasn't on her list."

"Oh, good!" Andrea said with a smile. "I like Connor. Besides, I've talked to him a lot and I'm a pretty good judge of character. He's just not the type to do anything violent."

Michelle and Hannah exchanged glances, but they remained mum. Let Andrea have her illusions. The secret of Connor's past wasn't theirs to tell.

"We're down to practically nobody," Andrea told them, glancing at the list. "And I guess I should cross off Winnie's name since we didn't find the prop gun in her barn."

Hannah reached out to still her sister's hand. "Not quite yet. We only searched in one place and that gun could have been anywhere on her property. She could even have thrown it in the lake on the way home."

"You mean . . . you think Winnie did it?"

"No, but she certainly had the motive. Everyone in town knew she couldn't stand Dean, and she was bound and determined to stop him from filming at the park because he was going to move her brother's statue."

"Wait a second," Andrea said, looking confused. "I thought she agreed to let Ross move the statue."

"No, all they're going to do is lift it with a crane and shoot the scene under it. Then they'll lower it right back down again in exactly the same spot. That was the whole point. Dean wanted to put the statue in another location while he shot the scene, and move it back again when he was through. Winnie didn't want it moved twice."

"I guess that makes sense." Andrea said. "That statue's been sitting there for years, and she was probably afraid it wouldn't hold up if they had to move it twice."

Michelle looked a little sad. "If Dean had been satisfied with just lifting it up and shooting under it the way Lynne is going to do, Winnie might have signed the release form right away. But Dean had to have everything exactly his way. He was just as stubborn as Winnie. The only way two people that stubborn can reach a compromise is for one of them to back down."

"Or wind up dead," Hannah pointed out, turning to Andrea. "And that's why you shouldn't cross out Winnie's name. Logically, she's still a suspect . . . however illogical that seems."

* * *

Hannah smiled as someone knocked on the back door of The Cookie Jar. It was probably Norman. He'd called this morning and asked if he could take her to watch Tracey's big skating scene.

"Are you ready to go?" Norman asked, stepping inside when Hannah opened the door.

"Just let me get my coat. Mother and Carrie left about ten minutes ago and they said they'd save us a seat." Hannah grabbed her parka coat from the hook by the door, and Norman held it as she put her arms into the sleeves. "Thanks," she said, turning around to face Norman. Being this close to him was nice, a little like warming herself in front of a blazing fireplace on a cold winter's afternoon, or snuggling up in a warm afghan with a good book.

"What?" Norman said, noticing her bemused expression.

"I was just thinking how much I missed you."

"But I've been right here."

"That's true, but I haven't been." Hannah put her arms around his neck and gave him a hug and a kiss.

"That was nice," Norman said, leading her out the door to his waiting sedan. "Maybe you should not be here more often."

The Lake Eden Municipal Park looked like the circus had come to town. Since the skating scene was supposed to take place at a Winter Carnival–type affair, warming tents were set up around the outer perimeter of the park. The tents were heated and between takes, the extras could crowd into them to warm up. It was a bit colder than it had been the preceding two days, but this afternoon it had warmed up to a balmy forty degrees. That was rather pleasant for March, but standing for hours in the snow or on the frozen ground could drain body heat even from a hardy Minnesotan who was wearing insulated boots.

As they made their way through the crowd of people, Hannah spotted Eleanor and Otis Cox, each holding a leash attached to one of their huskies. Next to them were the First Couple of Lake Eden, Mayor and Mrs. Bascomb, and Hannah began to like Stephanie Bascomb much better when she saw her bending down to pet the dogs. "What a crowd! It looks like everyone in town is here!"

"They put out a call for more extras this morning on KCOW radio. I heard it when I was driving out to the new house."

"Why did you go out there?" Hannah asked.

"I wanted to make sure they installed the countertops when they said they would. You wanted black granite, didn't you?"

"Right," Hannah said. The moment the word left her lips she thought better of it, but it was too late. "I thought the black would look nice with the light oak cabinets. But really, Norman . . . you should have ordered what you wanted."

"I want what you want," Norman said, putting an end to that discussion. And then he slipped his arm around her shoulder and gave her a little hug as they walked over to join the mothers.

"You have no idea how difficult it was to save these chairs!" Delores said, greeting them with a complaint. "I put down my purse to show it was taken, but people kept asking me to move it."

"Thank you so much for saving them, Mother." Hannah knew it was time for compliments. Her mother always complained in an effort to gain her gratitude. "I've been on my feet all morning and I don't think I could have stayed on them for another minute. By the way, these are for you and Carrie."

Delores smiled as she took the bag. "Cookies? How sweet of you, dear! What kind are they?"

"They're called Mock Turtles and you'd better eat them right now. It's like a refrigerator out here and these cookies have caramel in the center. You could break a tooth if they got too chilled."

"More business for me," Norman said, causing the three of them to laugh. But Hannah noticed that her mother and Carrie each took a cookie immediately.

"Excuse me for just a minute," Hannah said, getting up from her chair. "I see Frances over there and I need to ask her a question."

"About the murder?' Delores wanted to know.

"In a way, but only indirectly. I'll be right back."

Frances was standing in front of the statue, obviously guarding it from curious onlookers. She was a substantial woman with curves that were apparent even under her bulky parka, and she had curly brown hair and wire-framed glasses. Despite her jeans and boots, Frances looked like she should be passing out signup forms at a P.T.A. meeting and she reminded Hannah of a painting she'd once seen, titled, *Everyone's Mom*.

"Hi Frances," Hannah said, coming up to stand beside her. Winnie's brother's granite likeness of Ezekiel Jordan, the first mayor of Lake Eden, had been wrapped in furniture pads and tied with twine. It resembled a badly wrapped package on Christmas morn, something a child might have done all by himself. "You got stuck guarding Ezekiel?"

"Ross told me to stand here and make sure no one touches the statue. He promised Mrs. Henderson he wouldn't let anyone lay a hand on it until after the crane picked it up and put it back in place. What's the deal with her anyway? Is she crazy?"

"I think she's just protecting a family treasure. Her brother sculpted the statue years ago and placed it here. Then he gave the land to the city for a park, but Winnie has control of it until her death. Her brother never married and now that he's gone, the statue is his only legacy. Winnie feels an obligation to keep it safe from harm."

"I guess that makes sense." Frances glanced around her nervously and leaned a little closer to Hannah. "Do you think she killed him?"

"Who are you talking about?"

"Mrs. Henderson. Do you think she switched the guns and killed Dean?"

"I don't think so. Winnie's a pretty straightforward person. If she'd wanted to kill Dean to keep him from moving her brother's statue, she would have taken a stand right here and shot him when he tried to do it."

"That's exactly what Michelle told me. I was just wondering, that's all."

"Who do *you* think switched the guns?"

"I don't know. I didn't think anyone hated Dean that much. I mean, he could be a real pill, but he never actually hurt anyone that I know of."

"So you never found anything when you cleaned his office."

"Like what?"

"Like hate mail, or evidence that someone was blackmailing him, or any compelling reason someone might have to want him dead?"

Frances shook her head. "No, nothing like that. I've gone over and over it in my mind, Hannah, and I don't think anyone hated him enough to kill him. Everyone knew what he was and they accepted that, because he was such a genius. They made allowances. Live and let live, you know? And all those women he *coached* in his trailer? They didn't expect to be his one and only."

"How about his wife? Sharyn expected to be his one and only, didn't she?"

"Of course she did. And not one single person in the company would have told her she wasn't. We all liked Sharyn and we were loyal to Dean."

"Everyone?"

"I think so. If anyone wasn't, I don't know about it." Frances glanced around her again to make sure no one was near enough to overhear their conversation. Presumably she was getting ready to impact some tidbit of great secrecy. "It's like this, Hannah. I don't think Dean was the target. I really believe someone was trying to kill Burke."

"Who?"

Frances shrugged. "I don't know, but I'm almost sure it wasn't anyone connected with the movie."

Stalemate, deadlock, logjam, gridlock, Hannah's mind gave her all the synonyms for the impasse she seemed to have encountered. Frances didn't have any information she hadn't heard before, but Hannah decided to ask a few more questions anyway and see what came up. "Tell me about Burke. Was he well liked?"

"Well enough. None of us knew him before he signed on, but he seemed nice enough. He had a big part, but he didn't have his nose in the air, and he was really nice to the little people."

"Little people?"

"People like grips, script girls, P. A.'s, and everybody who's hourly and not salaried. A lot of actors don't bother being polite to the people who can't do them any good, but Burke was nice to everybody."

"So you liked him?"

"I did. That's why I can't imagine anyone trying to kill him. He was naive, and fun, and really grateful when you went out of your way to do something nice for him."

"Do you think everybody in the crew feels the way you do about Burke?"

"I think so. It's like this, Hannah . . . killing Burke would be like killing the Easter Bunny. And that would *really* be a crime!"

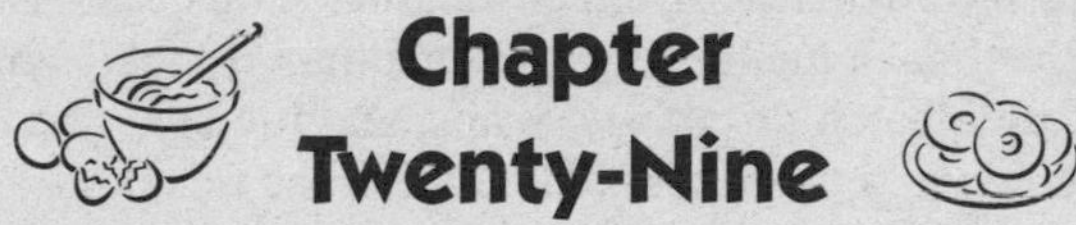

Chapter Twenty-Nine

"Hannah? Wait a minute!"

Hannah swiveled around as a hand grabbed hers and she came face to face with Winnie Henderson. "Hi, Winnie. Are you here to check on the statue?"

"Yes, and I like that gal that's guarding it. She doesn't look like she takes any prisoners."

Hannah laughed. Frances must be the master of multiple looks, from *Everybody's Mom* to *Female Prison Guard*. "I'm glad you're relaxing about it. Did you see the crane Ross rented?"

"I already inspected it," Winnie said, glancing back at the bright red piece of heavy equipment. "Never seen anything like it before. Says *50-Ton Hydraulic Boom Truck* on the side. I don't think Arnie's statue weighs anything close to that much."

"Probably not, but I'm sure Ross didn't want to take any chances." Hannah did her best to remember the phone conversation she'd heard Ross make. It was all about what kind of crane he needed to rent and he'd mentioned overhead cranes, bridge cranes, gantry cranes, jib cranes, and boom trucks. It must have been a guy thing, because Ross and the representative from Minnesota Crane and Hoist had agreed on something in less time than it took Hannah to mix up a batch of Orange Snaps, and the crane had arrived at noon. "I heard him talk to the crane rental place on the phone, and he said something about how it was better to overestimate than underestimate."

"Better safe than sorry," Winnie put her interpretation on it.

"That's right. Would you like to watch the taping with us? Tracey's been practicing her skating every night after school. She's going to fly off the end while they're playing *Crack The Whip* and she wants it to be perfect."

"You don't have to worry about that little gal. She'll be perfect. She can do anything she sets her mind on. Reminds me of me, when I was that age."

Hannah started to grin. Somehow she couldn't imagine Winnie as a little girl.

"I know that's hard to imagine," Winnie said, guessing Hannah's thoughts, "but I wasn't always old. And thanks for inviting me to sit with you, but I'd better keep an eye on that crane man to make sure he does his job right."

Hannah shifted a bit on the metal chair. It was a good thing she had a cup of hot coffee to warm her up, because they'd turned on the wind machine to make Tracey's red scarf flutter in the breeze and all that air blowing across the flat surface of artificial ice in the skating rink had kicked up the wind-chill factor and then some.

"Cold?" Norman asked, noticing that she was shivering.

"Yes."

"More coffee?" He gestured toward the tent the movie company had set up to provide hot drinks for the cast, crew, and extras.

Hannah shook her head. She'd already had two large cups of coffee and any more would necessitate a trip to the nearest ladies' room. "No thanks. I don't want to have to leave during Tracey's scene."

"Leave? But why would you have to . . ." Norman stopped and thunked the side of his head with his gloved hand. "Never mind. I get it. I'll try another way to warm you up that doesn't involve liquid."

Hannah smiled as Norman slipped his arm around her shoulders and pulled her close. They'd been dating long enough for her to notice that he was always toasty warm, even in the coldest weather. It probably had something to do with his metabolism, and she wished she had inherited whatever gene he had that she didn't have.

"Here we go," Norman said, gesturing at the skating rink with his other hand. The boom crane operator had moved the truck behind the coffee tent to hide it from view and he was currently attaching a harness to the statue of the first mayor. "Looks like old Ezekiel is about to rise."

"If Winnie's brother had known this would happen, he could have sculpted a statue of Lazarus," Hannah quipped, and she was gratified when Norman laughed.

It took only moments to secure the harness and hook it to the cable that was attached to the boom. Hannah watched, along with everyone there, as the boom operator began to lift the statue. The only sound was for the powerful motor that drove the hydraulic winch. Everyone was perfectly silent, fascinated by the spectacle, as Ezekiel Jordan's granite likeness rose from the ground.

"Stop! No!"

Hannah heard a faint voice over the roaring of the motor and she turned to see Winnie heading for the statue at a dead run. Something must be terribly wrong.

Without really planning what she was about to do, Hannah jumped to her feet and set out for the statue from the opposite direction. She had less space to cover and she passed the statue on the fly and managed to intercept Winnie several feet from her goal.

"Winnie!" Hannah panted, holding the small farmwoman so she couldn't get away. "What's wrong?"

"That danged fool's taking the base! I said they could move the statue, not the base!"

"But the base is part of the statue," Hannah did her best to explain. At the same time, she moved Winnie away from the rising statue and back toward the coffee tent. "Come with me. I'll get you a cup of coffee."

"But they *can't* move the base!" Winnie insisted.

"They have to move the base. It can't be in the shot. Ross explained it all to me. They're going to sweep the snow over the bare spot on the ground, and no one will even know there was a statue there."

"But . . . if they cover the ground with snow, how'll they get it back in the right place?"

"I asked the same thing." Hannah loosened her hold on Winnie since the older woman seemed much calmer now. "Michelle told me they're going to put down a piece of cardboard the exact size as the base of the statue and sweep the snow over that. Then, when they're all through shooting, they'll sweep the snow off and have the crane operator put the statue back down on the cardboard."

"Oh. Well . . . that should work." Winnie looked much more relaxed as she accepted the cup of coffee from Hannah.

"Come on back and sit with me," Hannah urged, grabbing a chair that someone had left unattended, and leading Winnie back to the area where Delores, Carrie, and Norman were waiting.

Everyone held their breath as the sculpted image of Lake Eden's first mayor hovered, swaying slightly on its tether, as high as a two-story house above them. Winnie watched the statue for longer than most, but at last she lowered her gaze and drew a deep breath. "Guess everything's okay with Arnie's statue."

"Of course it is," Hannah reassured her, and the mothers and Norman added their own words of encouragement before their attention was drawn to the wooden warming house at the far end of the skating rink.

"It's that new lady director," Winnie said, nudging Hannah as Lynne appeared. "Looks like she can skate just as good as the kids."

Hannah watched as her old college friend glided across the rink and stopped in the center.

"Thank you all for coming out today," Lynne said, and since there was no way anyone's voice would carry over the sound of the crane's motor and the whine of the wind machine, Hannah realized that she must be using a clip-on microphone. "I know it's cold and there's coffee and hot chocolate over there in the red striped tent. Feel free to help yourselves. We've already shot some crowd scenes and we'll be shooting more when the action on the rink starts."

Lynne motioned with her hand and seven young girls came out of the warming house, with Tracey bringing up the rear. "These are our little stars for this scene. They're going to skate out to the middle of the rink and play *Crack The Whip*. As the new girl in town, not yet accepted as one of the crowd, Tracey's character will be on the end. On the fifth complete revolution, the girl who's holding Tracey's hand will let go and Tracey will end up crashing into the snowbank in front of the green-and-white tent."

Hannah, along with everyone else, turned to look at the snowbank where Tracey would be landing. It looked slightly different than the rest.

"If you've noticed that the bank of snow looks a little different, it's because it's made out of foam that's been painted to look like hard-packed snow. The fall will look horrible on camera, and Tracey will scream and pretend to break her arm, but that'll be acting and she won't actually be hurt at all."

There were murmurs from the audience, and then someone shouted out a question Hannah didn't hear.

"One of our extras asked about saying *walla-walla*. That may sound silly to some of you, but if a crowd of people says it over and over again at different times and in different voices, it sounds as if people are talking to each other. You don't have to say *walla-walla* today. We're not picking up crowd noises. They'll be added later in postproduction and some of the dialogue will be dubbed."

Hannah was impressed. Lynne was doing a good job of explaining what they should do.

"When the action starts, I want everyone to look as if you're having a wonderful time at the winter games in the park. And when the impromptu game of *Crack The Whip* begins, you can smile and even applaud as the girls twirl around. When Tracey veers off and heads for the snow bank, I'd like to see some expressions of alarm and fear for her safety. And finally, I need you to look horrified when she crashes into the icy snow and breaks her arm."

"This is pretty exciting," Winnie said, turning to Hannah with a smile. "I didn't know that moviemaking was so much fun."

It wasn't when Dean was in charge, Hannah felt like saying, but she didn't. Lynne was much better at public relations than her predecessor.

"Is everyone ready?" Lynne asked, and there were nods and a few shouts of assent. "All right, then. Let's see if we can do this in one take. Tracey? Costume, please."

Tracey turned and skated for the wooden warming house that sat on the far end of the rink. When she got there, she went in and closed the door, but not before Hannah had spotted Honey, the makeup person, and the wardrobe mistress, Sophie, waiting for her.

Hannah looked around and noticed that one cameraman

had taken up his position in the spot vacated by the statue, another was up on a platform at the far end of the rink, and Clark, the cameraman Hannah had met, was walking the perimeter of the rink with a Steadicam on his shoulder.

"Places please, girls!"

At that instruction from Lynne, the six girls still on the rink skated toward the center. Lynne arranged them at intervals, changing their positions a few times. Once everything and everyone looked the way she wanted them to look, Lynne called out to Tracey. "Ready, Tracey?"

"Ready," Tracey replied, opening the door to respond and then shutting it again.

"Lights!"

Hannah was surprised as the bright outside lights that had been mounted on poles surrounding the rink came on. It was broad daylight, but perhaps they were needed.

"Cameras!" Lynne waited a beat, and then she gave the final call. "Action!"

That was the cue for the girls and they began to play on the ice. One practiced spins at the far end of the rink, another skated backward, two girls joined hands and made slow circles in an imitation of the figure skaters they'd seen on television, and another two girls clasped crossed hands and skated as fast as they could around the perimeter of the rink. This went on for several minutes.

"Cut!" Lynne said at last. "Next scene! Action!"

The two girls who were skating slow circles headed to the middle of the rink. One of them motioned to the girl who was skating backward and she went over to get the girl who was practicing her spins. When they'd lined up at the center of the rink, the last two girls joined the line. There was some good-natured kidding and lot of smiles as they joined hands and began to play *Crack The Whip*.

"Cue Tracey!" Lynne said.

A moment later, Tracey opened the door to the warming house. She was dressed in a royal blue coat with a red satin lining, and Bill's red scarf around her neck. She had a royal blue knit cap on her head, and blue pom-poms on her figure skates. Instead of bulky snow pants, Tracey was wearing ski pants with stirrups that fit under the soles of her feet and kept her pant legs from pulling up. Her outfit was fashionable, what a rich little girl might wear to skate at the Rockefeller Plaza rink, and it contrasted sharply with the rest of the girls who wore parka jackets and snow pants.

Tracey, who seemed unaware of the contrast, began to smile as she saw the girls playing at the center of the rink. She skated out and approached the girl on the end, obviously asking if she could play. The girl exchanged glances with several other girls and then she nodded. Tracey happily joined the line.

The line began to revolve in a circle at the center of the rink. Tracey looked as if she was having a wonderful time as the line revolved faster and faster around the largest girl, the pivotal point at the head of the line. Tracey was on the other end, the place with the most torque.

The girls skated faster and faster, and Hannah counted the revolutions. She saw other people in the crowd doing the same and she heard Winnie and Norman counting them off aloud. As Tracey faltered slightly at the end of the fourth revolution and almost lost her balance, everyone in the crowd looked concerned.

The fastest revolution of all was the fifth and Tracey barely managed to hang on as the end of the line whipped past the coffee tent. The blue-and-white tent was next in line and everyone could see that Tracey was tiring and she was bound to stumble soon. She hung on by what looked like the skin of her teeth past the yellow-and-white tent, and Hannah glanced around at the crowd as her niece neared the green-and-white tent, the spot where she was slated to fall. Everyone was staring at Tracey with alarm, just as Lynne had wanted. Hannah knew the feeling. Although Andrea had told her that Tracey had practiced this stunt with the same girls, her actual friends, at least two dozen times, she was alarmed, too!

As the green-and-white tent came into Tracey's view, she wobbled alarmingly, tried to right herself, and made a real effort to hang on. That was when her real best friend, Karen Dunwright, dropped Tracey's hand and let her crash into the snow bank.

There were gasps from the crowd and a few actual screams as Tracey fell spectacularly. She landed on her arm and Hannah could see her eyes fill with pain and surprise as it twisted under her. She gave a faint whimper and then everyone was silent, waiting to see what would happen.

"Cut!" Lynne shouted, despite the fact that she was miked. "Are you okay, Tracey?"

"I'm fine, thanks." Tracey got up and smiled at the crowd. Then she swung her arm over her head to show that she'd sustained no injury and everyone there applauded.

Hannah turned to Winnie. "I think Tracey has a career waiting for her in show biz. I really thought she'd hurt herself, didn't you?"

But Winnie didn't reply. She was staring up in absolute horror as something fell from the bottom of the statue.

The cameraman who taken the statue's place shouted out an invective that Hannah wouldn't have said in front of Tracey or Bethany, and rubbed his head. Then he looked up and jerked his camera several feet back and into the crowd.

There was another shout, something about the statue falling apart and raining debris, and everyone reacted. Lynne skated toward the girls and rushed them inside the warming house, the people who were close to the falling debris headed for cover, and whatever was falling continued to rain down from above.

"Wow!" Hannah said, wondering if the cameras were still running. Winnie had been right about moving the statue. It was disintegrating before their very eyes. She turned to tell Winnie she was sorry for even suggesting that they move her brother's granite tribute to the first mayor, and she was surprised to see that Winnie's chair was empty. Why had Winnie left when their chairs weren't even close to the debris falling from the bottom of the statue?

Finally the rubble stopped falling, and some brave soul ran out onto the ice to pick up a piece that had fallen. Hannah watched as Doc Knight, who'd been watching the taping from the side of the rink, grabbed the piece from the man who'd fetched it from the ice.

"What is it, Doc?" Lynne asked, skating back to Lake Eden's local physician after having delivered the girls into the capable hands of Sophie, Honey, and Andrea.

Doc Knight shrugged. "Looks like a fibula."

"You mean a leg bone?"

"That's right."

"From some animal?"

Doc Knight took his time about answering, and the crowd waited. They were so quiet Hannah thought she could hear them breathe.

"No," Doc finally said. "It sure looks human to me."

Chapter Thirty

"Winnie? Are you here?" Hannah knocked on the door of the farmhouse. When there was no answer, she turned around to face Mike and Norman. "I think she's here, but she's afraid to answer."

"You're probably right," Mike said.

"Try again," Norman suggested. "And tell her who you are this time."

"Winnie? It's Hannah." Hannah knocked on the door again. "Open up. You know we need to talk to you."

"I'm coming," came a faint voice from within, followed by a shuffling of feet. "All right, all right. Hold on while I get this lock off."

It seemed to take awhile, but at last Winnie unlocked the door. She stood there in the fading light of the day, looking very small and very alone. "So did you come to arrest me?"

"No," Mike answered for all three of them. "Should I?"

"Maybe. Come in and have some coffee. I've got a pot going in the kitchen."

She always was a good hostess, Hannah thought as she followed Winnie into the large farmhouse kitchen and took a chair at the round oak table that dominated the room. "Why did you run off like that, Winnie?"

"You know why. Doc must've figured out those bones are human by now."

"That's right, he did," Mike confirmed it. And then he turned to give Hannah a warning glance. His message was loud and clear. She should let him handle this. It was his job.

"Well, let's have coffee before you haul me off to jail," Winnie said, pouring four cups from the blue-and-white speckled pot that sat on the old wood stove. "Anybody take cream and sugar?"

"Just black, thanks Winnie," Hannah responded.

"Me, too," Norman added.

"Black's fine with me," Mike said, watching as Hannah and Norman picked up their cups and sipped.

Hannah held in a chuckle. Like a king with an official food taster, Mike wasn't about to sip the coffee until they'd tried theirs. She figured he'd wait at least a minute to make sure Winnie hadn't put anything lethal into the brew. What he didn't know was that Winnie's brew was lethal all by itself. It was strong Norwegian coffee made the old-fashioned way. Winnie washed the pot on Saturday night and made it fresh on Sunday morning. Then it sat warming on the old wood stove until the whole pot had been consumed. When there were only used grounds in the bottom, Winnie added more water and several tablespoons of new ground coffee, and brewed another pot. By the time Saturday night rolled around and it was time to wash the pot, it was at least half-filled with spent coffee grounds, some of them pressed into service at least a dozen times.

Hannah took another sip of her coffee. Thank goodness it was only Friday! She'd once had Winnie's coffee on Saturday afternoon and it was strong enough to knock out a mule!

At last Mike raised his cup and took a sip. Hannah

watched closely and she gave him points for not choking. His eyes watered a bit, but that was to be expected from a first-timer tasting Winnie's coffee. Then he did something Hannah hadn't expected from someone not born and raised in Lake Eden. He cleared his throat, gave Winnie a smile, and said, "This coffee'll peel the paint right off the walls!"

Winnie gave a little smile and Hannah could tell she felt slightly better. Everybody in town said that Winnie's coffee could peel the paint off the walls, and that was a compliment. Hannah held her breath, waiting for Mike to put down his cup and start asking questions. He'd once told her that he had two favorite techniques he used to interrogate suspects. One technique was intimidation, and the other was to use a sympathetic approach.

"Why don't you tell me about those human bones and maybe we can work something out," Mike said, and Hannah gave him a grateful look. She was glad he'd decided to be sympathetic rather than intimidating.

"Guess I'd better do that," Winnie said, taking the chair across from Mike. From the way she was sitting, stiff and poised on the edge of the wooden seat, Hannah knew the story they were about to hear would be painful for her to tell. She took a sip of her own coffee and then she sighed.

"It's like this," she said. "My second husband used to beat on me every time he got a snootful. I was smart enough not to keep any liquor in the house, but he went down to the Municipal on Saturday nights. There was nothin' I could do to keep him here on the farm. Lord knows I tried."

Hannah frowned slightly, but she didn't interrupt to ask the question that had occurred to her the moment that Winnie mentioned her second husband. If she had the chronology of succession correct, his name was Red and he'd left one morning to buy a pack of cigarettes and never come back.

"Anyways, the night my first boy was born it was a Saturday and Red was down at the Municipal. I knew I had some time, but I called my brother Arnie, he lived in town, and asked him to go fetch Red so he'd be home to take me to Doc Knight's."

"Go on," Mike encouraged her.

"Well, Red didn't want to come home that early, but Arnie got tough with him and brought him out here. Red wouldn't let Arnie in. He told him to go home and slammed the door in his face. But Arnie was afraid to leave me alone with Red when he was drunk, so he walked around the house and looked in the window. By the time Arnie got to the kitchen window, Red was already slapping me around pretty good."

Hannah felt sick just hearing about it and one glance at Norman told her he felt the same. She glanced at Mike. He was managing to keep his emotions in check, but she saw him swallow hard.

"What did you do when your husband slapped you?" Mike asked.

"I took it for a couple of minutes, but then I fought back. I thought he might hurt the baby. Hitting with my hands didn't do any good, so I looked around for something else I could use. I always kept a coffeepot on the stove, a big one about twice the size of the blue-and-white one I got now. It had two handles like this one, see? And it was full of coffee."

Winnie pointed to the handle on the back of her current coffee pot, and the wire bail that was attached to both sides near the top. "You need two handles when you got a big pot. You hold the top one in one hand and tip the pot up with the handle on the back, just like I did when I poured your coffee."

"Which handle did you grab that night?" Mike asked her.

"The one on top. And I swung it around and hit him right in the face. The coffeepot went flying and he went down hard on the kitchen floor. When he made to get up again, I knew he was probably gonna kill me, so I grabbed the spider that was setting on the stove and hit him again."

"Spider?" Mike asked, looking very confused.

"It was just like this one," Winnie said, getting up to fetch a large, black, cast-iron skillet, the kind you could use to fry two chickens at once. "It's heavy, see?"

Mike lifted the skillet. "You're right. It's got to be ten pounds at least, maybe more."

"Well I wasn't sure that would keep him down for good, so I hit him again on top of the head. And by the time Arnie had bashed in the glass and come right in through the window to help me, I'd hit him another couple of times for good measure."

"What did your brother do?"

"He checked to see if Red was a gonner, and he must have been because he just left him there. And then he scooped me up in his arms and drove me straight to Doc Knight's office."

"Not the hospital?"

"We didn't have one then. Doc's office was like a clinic. He had a couple of beds and he lived in the back, so he was always there."

"And you had the baby?"

"I did, but not until Doc got me all stitched up. I was cut pretty bad from the ring Red wore when he went to the Municipal. It had these sharp edges, just in case he got in any fights."

Hannah took another sip of her coffee to quell the sick feeling in her stomach. What kind of man would attack his pregnant wife? The coffee didn't help, she still felt sick, and she swallowed hard.

"Anyways, right before Doc knocked me out, Arnie got me alone for a minute. He told me not to worry, and he'd take care of everything. And that's what he did. I didn't find out until I came home with the baby, but Arnie went back and rolled Red's body in this big rug we had in the kitchen. He cleaned up the whole place so nobody would know what happened, and then he dragged Red out to his car and drove him over to the garage he used for a studio. I guess he must've chopped him up or something. Arnie never would tell me that part. But when he was dying, he told me he hid Red's body in the base of that statue he made for the park."

Hannah and Norman gulped in tandem even though they'd already figured out the end of the story. It was still horrifying. But Mike seemed unfazed. Perhaps he'd heard even worse tales than this when he'd been a detective on the police force in Minneapolis.

"So what did you tell everybody about where Red was?" Mike asked.

"I said he went out for a pack of cigarettes and never came back. Nobody ever asked me any more about it. They all figured he left me because he didn't want to take care of a wife and a baby. So are you gonna arrest me now? Or what?"

"What," Mike said, earning a smile from Hannah. "There's no reason to arrest you, Mrs. Henderson. It sounds to me like it was self-defense."

"But I killed him, all the same!"

"What do you think?" Mike turned to Norman, and Hannah came close to gasping out loud. For a cop who always went by the book, this was quite a divergence.

"Justifiable homicide," Norman said, jumping in quickly with his vote. "How about you, Hannah."

"It's certainly not murder. You killed him, but you were protecting your baby's life."

"Okay," Mike said, smiling at Winnie. "As long as Doc Knight substantiates the injuries you described, this matter is concluded."

"You mean . . . you're not taking me to jail?"

"That's right. Now here's a hard question and I want you to answer it honestly. Did you switch those revolvers so that Dean Lawrence would die and keep his hands off that statue?"

Winnie's mouth fell open and she looked as if a little puff of air from one of Bertie's handheld hairdryers could knock her over. When she recovered, she shook her head vigorously from side to side. "I was already planning out what to do to keep him from moving that statue, and murder had nothing to do with it!"

"What were you planning to do?"

"I was gonna chain myself to that statue, lock it with a padlock, and throw away the key. I figured by the time somebody got bolt cutters, it would be too dark to shoot it anyway."

"Then you never thought about switching the revolvers?"

"'Course not! It could've been that young surfer in those commercials that got himself killed, and I got nothing against him. Or it could've been anybody that picked up that gun and was fooling around with it."

"Okay," Mike said, snapping his notebook closed and putting it in his pocket. "That's what I thought, but I had to ask. It's part of my job."

"A person's got to do their job." Winnie looked very relieved once she saw that Mike believed her. "Are you gonna tell everybody that I killed Red?"

"I can't see any reason to do that. It was over years ago."

"But . . . how about those bones? Everybody knows they're human by now." Winnie's expression was a curious blend of elation and worry.

"I'm open to suggestions," Mike said, and turned to look at Hannah. "What do you think I should say?"

"That they're really old? Like fossils, or something like that?" Hannah grasped at straws.

"It won't work," Norman said. "They look too new. But why don't you say that Winnie's brother was leveling the ground to landscape the park and he found some Indian bones in the pile of rocks and debris he was hauling away. He knew he should put them back, but he didn't know exactly where they came from."

Hannah began to smile as she took over the fabrication. "That's a great idea! Arnie didn't want to go to the authorities with the bones. He was afraid they'd stop him from working on the park and donating the land to the city. So he bundled up the bones and gave them a decent burial in the base of the statue he sculpted for the park."

"And he didn't tell anybody about it until he was dying and that's when he confessed it all to me," Winnie added.

"Sounds good," Mike agreed, pushing back his chair. "You folks can stick around and drink more coffee with Mrs. Henderson, but I've got Mr. Lawrence's killer to catch."

Winnie showed Mike out and when she came back into the kitchen, she was smiling. "Well, doesn't that make a body feel good? All these years I've been worrying about being a criminal, and I'm not."

"Maybe not quite yet," Hannah said, grinning right back, "but if you don't wash out that coffeepot soon, Mike could lock you up for making paint thinner without a license."

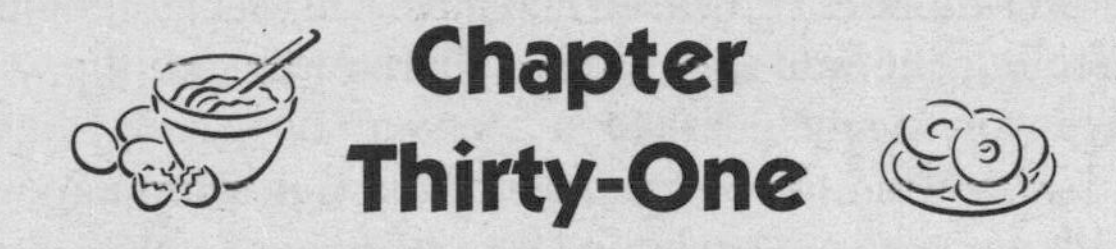

Chapter Thirty-One

It was Saturday afternoon and Hannah was standing at the back of a classroom in Jordan High, waiting for Burke Anson to play a much younger version of himself. Disaster had struck without warning when the young actor who'd been hired to play Jody at fifteen came down with laryngitis and could do no more than squeak. Burke had offered to play the teenage Jody as long as Honey could *age him down*. Hannah had known the term from college and the time she'd spent hanging out in the *green room*, another show-biz term for the backstage room that actors used to relax and wait for their cues. *Aging down* meant applying makeup so that an actor would look younger, and *aging up* was making an actor look older.

The classroom was stuffy and Hannah had all she could do not to yawn. She'd been out late last night, watching footage of the film with Ross and the cast at the inn, and that was when Lynne had asked her if she'd play the high school English teacher in today's classroom scene.

Hannah had her fingers crossed that Burke would be able to pull off his role in less than a dozen takes. Lisa had recruited Herb to help her at The Cookie Jar and they'd both told Hannah to go ahead and have fun, but she couldn't help feeling she was shirking her share of the work.

"Are you ready?" asked a teenage boy, and Hannah turned, expecting to see one of Jordan High's sophomores. But although she'd been hailed by a teenager's voice, it was Burke who was standing next to her.

"Did you just say something?" Hannah asked, hardly daring to believe her ears.

"Yes. Are you ready, Miss Bowman?"

Hannah answered the question with a smile and a nod. This might work out after all. Burke certainly looked like a teenager, and his voice was absolutely perfect. Now if he could only act like a teenager, they'd be through with the scene in no time at all.

"Places," Lynne called out and Hannah walked to the front of the room. She had only one speech, but Lynne had told her that it was important because it set the tone for the whole scene.

"Lights . . . and action!"

Lynne cued Hannah, and Hannah delivered the lines in her best schoolmarm voice. "All right, class. I have papers to grade at the table in the back, so for the remainder of the period I want you to study *Mending Wall* by our own poet laureate, Robert Frost. If you have trouble understanding any of the allusions, ask Jody. If the last test is any indication, he has a better understanding of Frost's work than any other student in this class."

Hannah picked up the sheaf of papers on her desk and walked, in her gray tweed suit and sensible shoes, to the table at the rear. The moment she had cleared the last desk at the back of the rows, students began to lean over in the aisle and whisper.

Lynne waved her to her chair at the table and Hannah sat down. She spread out her papers and pretended to be engrossed in grading them, her red pencil moving over the paper and making a checkmark and an occasional comment, but she knew she'd be present only in the wide master shot and no one could actually see what she was doing. She, however, could still see the class and the quiet but threatening interaction between Jody and the rest of the students.

"Think you're so smart, huh?" the boy with the yellow shirt hissed.

The girl in the pink sweater set nodded. "Yeah, you drove up the curve, you creep!"

The insults went on in hushed voices, and the boom mike picked them up. Jody looked defensive, and then nervous, and finally about to jump out of his skin as the other students taunted him.

"Come on, guys!" he said in a low voice, glancing back at Hannah. "I didn't mean to ace that test."

"What'cha got going with Miss Bowman, huh?" the boy in the yellow shirt, who'd started it all, moved over to stand between the table at the back and Jody's desk. Hannah couldn't see it, but she'd read the script and she knew the boy cuffed Jody on the back of the head.

At that point, Lynne motioned to Hannah and she got up to stand at the side of the room. The master shot was finished and they'd already shot several minutes of her at the table, pretending to grade papers. As Lynne had explained it, they'd intercut the footage so that Miss Bowman appeared to be oblivious to the harassment of her best student.

"Cut it out!" Jody hissed, glancing back at the table. But when he saw that the boy in the yellow shirt was blocking his teacher's view, he started to tremble. "I don't have anything going with Miss Bowman. She's our teacher, that's all."

"That's what you say, and maybe it's right. But you're teacher's pet, aren't 'cha?"

The boy cuffed Jody again and he started to shake even more violently. Hannah felt her heartbeat speed up, even though she knew everyone in the scene was acting.

"So . . . let's talk about this test we're having next Friday. You're gonna sit next to me and give me the answers."

"That would be cheating!"

"No, that would be smart. If you don't do it, I'll find you after school and beat you into meatloaf. Got it?"

"But . . ."

The boy threw a punch that seemed to hit to Burke's head. It didn't. It missed by several inches, but it would look as if it had on camera. And even though Burke hadn't been touched, Hannah saw tears spring up in his eyes.

"Next to me," the bully warned. "And anytime I ask, you give me the answer. If you let me down, I'll make sure my dad finds something wrong with your dad's work. Got it?"

Burke dipped his head in a nod and Hannah saw the anguish on his face. He knew it was wrong and he didn't want to do it, but he believed the bully's threats.

"That's good. You're gonna be my ticket to an *A* in this class. And if you tell anybody about his conversation we're having, I'll make sure your cute little sister isn't so cute anymore. Got it?"

Burke nodded again, and Hannah resisted the urge to run into the scene and slap the bully silly. She was still resisting when the bully swaggered back to his seat.

"Cut," Lynne called, "and that's a wrap, folks. You were perfect Burke! I don't know anyone who could have played it better."

The high school students started to applaud and so did the cameramen and the rest of the crew. The applause grew and Burke took a bow. "Aw shucks," he said, still in character and blushing to the roots of his hair. "That's real nice of you guys."

Hannah watched the young actor with something approaching awe. He had been magnificent. She'd never dreamed that he was such a fine actor. No wonder Ross hadn't been worried when they'd cast a relative unknown. Burke had more talent than most of the leading men in Hollywood.

"Wrap party at seven at the Lake Eden Community Center," Lynne announced. "I expect to see everyone there, because this film is now officially . . . in the can!"

"Not tonight, Moishe," Hannah said, giving her famous feline a pat and a handful of triangle-shaped treats that were supposed to taste like fresh tuna. "I'm going to the wrap party and you're going to watch the animal channel. There's a great feature on bats, and right after that they're showing *Frogs of North America* again."

Moishe purred and licked her hand. It wasn't his usual way of saying good-bye and Hannah knew he was glad to be staying home with the creatures behind the glass screen, the full food bowl in the kitchen, the pristine litter box in the laundry room, and Hannah's best feather pillow in the bedroom.

"Okay. How do I look?" Hannah asked, swirling around for the cat, who was clearly more interested in his triangular tuna treats than in her appearance. He did close one eye in a wink, though, and Hannah interpreted that to mean that he approved of her midnight blue sweater and skirt. She'd even squirted on some of the perfume one of her college roommates had given her for Christmas, and with the hammered gold necklace Michelle had brought back from a college art fair, Hannah figured she could hold her own with anyone in Lake Eden.

Dress coat or parka coat? Hannah pondered that decision for a brief moment, but fate took it out of her hands. Her parka coat was lying on the chair near the door and her dress coat was back in her bedroom closet. Expediency won, Hannah shrugged into her parka coat, and a moment later she was rushing down the stairs to her cookie truck.

"Gorgeous," Ross said, taking Hannah's coat and hanging it on the rack. "I love that color with your hair. Come with me. I've been waiting for you to arrive."

Hannah could believe that. Ross had been standing by the front door of the community center to usher her in, and she'd just barely resisted the urge to ask him how long he'd been there. Having a man wait for her arrival was certainly flattering to a woman's ego, and Hannah was smiling as she walked down the stairs to the banquet room.

One look and Hannah was impressed. Ross had hired a firm from Minneapolis to cater the event, and they'd gone all out. The large banquet room was decorated with flowers and candles, and food tables draped in pristine white had been set up around the perimeter. Formally clad waiters and waitresses manned the food stations, and there was a live five-piece band playing for dancing at the far end of the room.

"Would you care to dance?" Ross asked. "Or would you like to inspect the food tables?"

Hannah turned to give him a look and Ross laughed. "Never mind. It was a silly question. Follow me. We'll go see what the caterers have on the menu."

They had anything and everything on the menu, as Hannah soon discovered. There was a table with caviar, which Hannah avoided like the plague, and another with cheeses and a variety of crackers. Pâté and toast rounds were on a third table, and shrimp wrapped in bacon on a fourth. Cracked crab wrapped in flaky sheets of filo dough were next, and another table held a variety of fruit cut into bite-sized pieces, each speared with its own food pick. There were hot little sausages in tiny buns, and miniature sandwiches on tiny croissants. Smoked salmon commanded a whole table, along with a round silver platter of pumpernickel triangles decorated with cream cheese rosettes.

Part of one wall was taken up by what Hannah called "hot carts" containing meat sliced to order. There were beef roasts, ham, turkey, roasted chicken, and baked salmon, all aromatic and succulent. The meat was carved by chefs in white aprons and toques, and served as dinners with baked potatoes loaded with your choice of toppings, herbed dinner rolls, and sides of creamed spinach, green beans, creamed corn, or all three.

The next food section contained the display that interested Hannah the most. One look, and she was impressed. The caterer had provided colorful Italian ices for the party.

"Pretty fancy," Ross said, eyeing the assortment of ices that dominated the first two tables. There were coconut ices in real coconut shells, orange ices in oranges that were cut in half and hollowed out, lemon ices and peach ices in a similar presentation, and banana ices that were shaped like bananas and served in a miniature bunch of three. Hannah especially admired the pineapple ices that were served in hollowed out rounds of pineapple.

The usual array of desserts filled the tables that remained. There were pies, cakes, tarts, cookies, and sweet treats in puff pastries. Hannah was about to call *Uncle*, and give in to her urge to try the pineapple ice in its pineapple round, when Ross moved up behind her and put his arms around her waist.

"Eat first and then dance? Or dance first and then eat?"

"Dance first," Hannah said. The siren call of the desserts was strong, but she was enjoying the feeling of being in Ross's arms even more.

What a diet! she thought as he led her to the dance floor in the center of the dining room. I could name it the Dance Diet and rent out handsome men to whirl overweight women away at mealtime as an alternative to eating. It would work with men, too. Most guys would give up a meal to dance with a gorgeous woman. And then, as Ross took her into his arms and they began to move to the slow, romantic music, the new diet craze she'd just invented became the furthest thing from her mind.

"Thanks for snagging a table!" Hannah said, sitting down with a sigh. "It feels so good to be off my feet."

Michelle laughed. "I didn't think you were ever going to stop dancing."

"Neither did I." Hannah slipped off one shoe and glanced at the bottom. "I thought for sure I'd need them resoled by now."

"Ross, Mike, Norman, Lloyd, and Clark. And after that it was Mike, Ross, Norman, and Burke."

"You're in charge of my dance card?" Hannah asked with a laugh.

"No, Mother is. She's keeping track of your partners."

"That figures." Hannah picked up the pitcher of water on the table and poured herself a glass.

"I was watching Burke dance with you and the expression he was wearing was priceless. I wish I had a picture."

"I didn't notice. What did he look like?"

"Like he was the only boy in the world and you were the only girl."

"You're kidding!" Hannah was surprised, not only by the observation but also by her baby sister's use of such dated song lyrics. "But we talked while we were dancing and Burke didn't say anything in the least bit romantic."

"I know. He danced with me and we talked about the film. And then Mother cornered me to ask what was going on. That's exactly how she put it, that whole *only boy and only girl* thing. I thought she was imagining things until I saw him dancing with you."

Now that Michelle's use of the old song lyric was explained, Hannah looked out at the dance floor. She spotted Ross dancing with Honey and experienced a totally unwarranted twinge of jealousy. Reminding herself that no promises had been exchanged or even offered, she quickly suppressed it and resumed her search for Burke.

Burke was dancing with Carrie, one of the least likely candidates for a romantic liaison. Not only was Norman's mother over thirty years older than Burke was, she was also . . .

Hannah searched for the right word, couldn't find it, and settled for something close. That word was *ordinary*. Norman's mother was a perfectly nice, ordinary woman, but not someone Burke, a talented young Adonis with his whole life before him, could possibly be interested in pursuing.

"See what I mean?" Michelle asked, also spotting Burke and Carrie. "He looks like he's about ready to propose."

"Would that be a decent or an indecent proposal?" Hannah asked with a grin.

"Either one would do. It's really strange, Hannah. Burke makes it look really intimate to anyone who's watching, but they're probably talking about the weather."

Hannah watched for a minute in utter amazement. "How does he *do* that?"

"Who? And what's he doing?" Andrea asked, rushing up to the booth.

"Burke," Michelle explained. "He looks like he finds every woman he dances with irresistible."

Andrea sat down next to Michelle and shrugged. "That's what Lisa said. Herb was starting to get a little hot under the collar until Lisa told him that all the time they were dancing, they were talking about target shooting."

"So Burke knows about guns?" The wheels in Hannah's mind were spinning.

"I guess. Lisa said he won a couple of trophies for shooting, and he got a job as a spokesman for an outdoor outfitter. Maybe he'll have to go back to the commercials now that he didn't get that part."

"What part?" Michelle asked, and Hannah could tell she hadn't known Burke was up for another part after *Crisis in Cherrywood*.

"This part." Andrea pulled a folded copy of *Variety* from her purse and read a section out loud. "*Burke Anson of Surf 'n Turf fame may have a BEEF with Halsey Productions because something's definitely FISHY.*" Isn't that cute? They're using food terms because he was in that restaurant commercial."

"Cute," Hannah said, not believing it for a minute. "Go on."

"*Slated for the lead in* Remember Last Tuesday, *Anson was given the CHOP in favor of Derek Pullman, who decided to CLAM up and refused to give us a comment. When queried about the last-minute change, a spokesman for Halsey said that Anson had earned the reputation for being difficult on his current project,* Crisis in Cherrywood."

"Remember Last Tuesday," Hannah breathed. "It's a movie title!"

Michelle just shook her head. "No wonder I couldn't find anyone who knew what happened last Tuesday! So that's what Amber overheard Dean and Burke arguing about!"

"If that isn't a motive, I don't know what is," Hannah pointed out. "Burke must have been convinced that Dean was the one who said he was difficult. What date is that paper?"

Andrea looked down beneath the green-and-black banner. "It's Wednesday. They mail it from L.A. and I just got it today."

"Burke wouldn't have to wait to find out from *Variety*," Michelle pointed out. His agent would have called him right away. Burke could have taken the call and then rushed right off to confront Dean in his office. I'm sure he thought

Dean wrecked his career by tagging him with the *difficult* label. That's the kiss of death, you know."

"But Amber said Dean denied everything," Andrea argued. "She heard Dean tell Burke that he didn't do it."

Hannah gave a short laugh. "It's pretty obvious Burke didn't believe him. He must have thought Dean was getting even for that awful interview he gave on KCOW television."

"But didn't Dean say he wasn't mad about that? That he thought what Burke said on television was funny?" Andrea asked.

"He said it, but I was there and I didn't believe him for a second. I don't think anybody did. It was pretty clear that Dean was only pretending to be amused to save face."

"Do you think Dean told the producers of *Remember Last Tuesday* that Burke was difficult to work with?" Andrea wanted to know.

Michelle shrugged. "It could have happened that way. Most of the producers know each other and they compare notes. It doesn't really matter whether Dean did it or not, as long as Burke was convinced he did."

"*That's* why Burke was so lousy in the scene," Hannah felt a current of excitement as the light dawned. "He's a great actor. We all know that. And a great actor can play a lousy actor."

Andrea stared at Hannah for a moment. "You're right. It's why he said his back hurt and he couldn't seem to get the motivation right. He wanted Dean to demonstrate the suicide and pull the trigger on the real revolver."

"He's a stone cold killer," Hannah said, shivering slightly. "He stood there watching, only a few feet away, and he knew exactly what was going to happen."

"So shall we tell Mike?" Michelle asked.

"Not yet. It's all supposition at this point. We don't have any proof." Hannah turned to Andrea. "Can you locate Sally and ask her if Burke got any calls in his room on

Wednesday morning? I'm sure she's around here someplace."

"I'm on it," Andrea said, rushing off.

"And can you think of an excuse to find out who Burke's agent is?" Hannah asked Michelle. "We can always call and ask when Burke was notified that someone else got the part."

"No problem. Somebody's bound to know. What are you going to do?"

"I'm going to find Mother and get the keys to Granny's Attic. We know that Burke didn't have that prop gun on him when he left the building, so it's just got to be hidden there somewhere."

Hannah searched in vain for her mother. She'd seen her only minutes ago, but Delores seemed to have vanished. She even checked the ladies' room, but the only person there was Winnie Henderson, who was standing in front of the mirror brushing her hair.

"Hi, Winnie," Hannah said. "I'm glad you came to the party."

"Connor brought me. He said the caterers cost more than one of my prize heifers and I owed it to my taste buds to come and eat."

Hannah's stomach growled. With all this excitement she'd forgotten to eat. "Sounds like a good idea to me. Have you seen Mother?"

"I saw her about ten minutes ago. She was just leaving."

"Leaving?" Hannah glanced at her watch. "But it's only eight-thirty."

"Oh, she's coming back. She just ran down to Granny's Attic to make sure they were careful when they loaded the sewing machine on the truck."

"What sewing machine?"

"The one they had on the living room set. You must have seen it. It was all the way in the corner, right next to the desk where you-know-what happened."

Hannah remembered the sewing machine. The top had been down, with the sewing head tucked inside, and it had been covered with a large crocheted doily.

"Your mother was pleased as punch to sell it, 'specially because it went for a fortune."

"It did?" Hannah was puzzled. "I thought that model was mass-produced by Sears, or one of the other big mail-order chains in the fifties."

"You're right, but that young actor from the film paid close to a thousand dollars for it. He's having it shipped back to California."

Now Hannah was even more puzzled. Why would Burke pay that much for a common sewing machine? Then her mind kicked into high gear and the truth dawned. Burke would pay through the teeth if he'd hidden something inside that perfectly ordinary sewing machine, something like the prop gun!

But why hadn't the deputies found the gun when they'd searched Granny's Attic? Hannah considered that for a moment and came up with a possible explanation. The sewing machine had looked exactly like a table with a false front and two small drawers on either side. What if the deputies had searched the drawers but hadn't realized that the sewing head swiveled up from a hollow below, where there would be plenty of room to hide a revolver?

"Holy cow!" Hannah gasped, taking Daisy, Buttercup, and Petunia's breed in vain. She knew where Burke had hidden the prop gun and she had to get it before it headed off on a moving van for California!

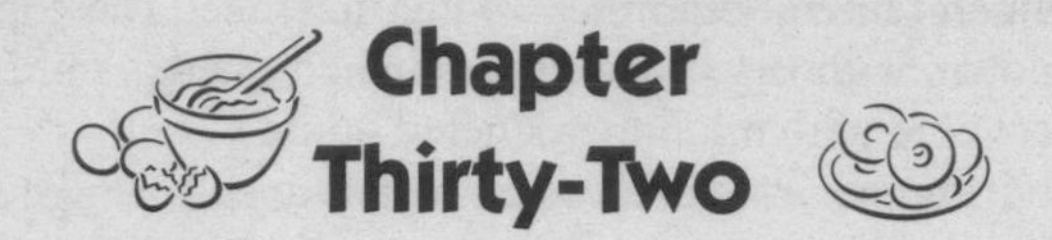

Chapter Thirty-Two

A light, lazy snow was falling as Hannah drove to Granny's Attic. There weren't quite enough snowflakes to keep her windshield wipers from squeaking against the glass, but the snowfall was a bit too much not to use them. She was about to turn into the alley when she saw the taillights of a semi idling in back of Granny's Attic. Rather than drive in behind it, Hannah went around the block and entered the alley from the other way, effectively blocking the semi. Expecting to hear an angry shout from the driver when she got out of her much smaller truck, Hannah heard nothing but the powerful motor idling. She'd gotten here just in time. The driver must be inside with Delores, getting ready to load Burke's sewing machine.

Hannah raced for the back door, almost slipping on the blacktop in her dress shoes. She hadn't wanted to take the time to get her boots and it was a good thing she hadn't or she might not have caught the semi. "Mother!" she called out as she opened the back door and hurried past the section her mother called "Trash or Treasures," the unsorted items that might or might not be valuable.

"In here, dear," Delores sounded surprised. "We're just filling out some paperwork for a shipment."

"Stop!"

"What was that, dear?" Delores sounded even more surprised and she looked surprised, too, as Hannah burst into the large main room of Granny's Attic, the room that was still decorated as a living room set.

"I need to look at that sewing machine, Mother!"

"You mean the one that Burke bought?"

"That's right. Where is it?"

"Over there," Delores pointed to a large crate sitting on a dolly near the door. "You can't look at it now, dear. It's all crated up."

Hannah turned to the driver. Do you have a crowbar?"

"Got one in the truck."

"I'll need to use it. I have to uncrate that sewing machine and inspect it. It may contain evidence in a murder investigation."

The driver, a large man who looked like he could handle a sledgehammer as well as a crowbar, stepped back a pace. "No way I want to have anything to do with a murder!"

"Then help me uncrate that sewing machine and you can go."

"But how about the guy on the other end? He's not gonna be happy when that sewing machine he bought doesn't get delivered."

"Oh, I don't think he'll mind," Hannah said. "If I'm right about what's inside that crate, he won't be there to receive it anyway."

"Ready?" Hannah said, lifting the lid the driver had loosened with his crowbar before he'd left and propping it up against the nearest wall. "Did you see them crate it, Mother?"

"They did it the day Burke bought it."

"When was that?"

"Thursday afternoon. He came in with two carpenters from the crew to crate it for him."

"It looks like it's wrapped in furniture pads and then taped," Hannah said using the scissors her mother handed her to cut the tape.

"It's also secured on the inside. I watched Burke do it. He wrapped a strap around the top so it wouldn't open or twist on the hinges, and he taped the drawers so they couldn't bang open and closed during transit."

"And he did it himself," Hannah noted, unwrapping the pad and letting it fall to the bottom of the crate.

"Yes. I did think that was a little unusual, but then he told me why."

"What did he tell you?"

"He said he knew he had to have that sewing machine the moment he set eyes on it. His mother died when he was only ten, you know, and she had one just like it. Every year, before school started, they used to go shopping for material so she could sew new shirts for him. He still has several of them. They're keepsakes. And now he has a replica of the sewing machine, too."

"Right," Hannah said, not believing the story of the dead mother and the shirts for an instant. "So that's why he offered you so much money for it?"

"That's what he said. I pointed out that old Sears machines weren't worth even half of what he offered, but he said he didn't care, that he wanted that particular model. He said he was buying it in honor of his mother and he'd think of her every time he saw it. And he was also buying it because it was on the set and he wanted a memento of his very first movie."

"Oh, brother!" Hannah breathed, wondering how her mother could have swallowed such a line. But then she reminded herself that Burke was a superlative actor and if he'd told her the same story, she probably would have fallen for it, too. It was entirely possible that Burke's mother had owned a Sears sewing machine. Hundreds of thousands of women had. And it was also possible that Burke remembered that you could lift the lid and drop something inside to hide it from view. There was plenty of room around the sewing head to conceal an object the size of a revolver.

"So what did you find?" Delores asked.

"Nothing yet." Hannah couldn't pull out the drawers. The crate was built too snugly around the machine. But she didn't worry about that because the deputies probably checked those. "I'm going to cut the strap and lift up the lid. If I'm right, that's where Burke hid the prop gun after he put the real revolver in its place."

"Wait," Delores advised, opening a drawer and pulling out a pair of gloves. "Put these on. You don't want to destroy any fingerprints."

"Good thinking, Mother," Hannah said, "but fingerprints don't prove anything in this case. Everyone on the set saw Burke practice taking the prop gun out of the drawer right before the first take. He got his fingerprints on it then. And since he was using the real gun when he convinced Dean that he was having trouble doing the scene, his fingerprints are on that, too."

"So he was only pretending he'd lost his motivation for the scene?" Delores asked.

"That's my theory. And if I find the prop gun stuck in this sewing machine, I can prove it."

Hannah held her breath as she cut the strap and lifted the lid. She felt around in the largest space between the bottom of the sewing machine head and the sewing platform and she began to smile.

"You found it?" Delores asked, interpreting her daughter's smile to mean success.

"Oh, yes. Now all I have to do is . . . " Hannah stopped speaking and worked to extricate the gun. "Yes. Here it is!"

"So Burke just said he loved my sewing machine because he needed it to get rid of the evidence?"

"I'm afraid so, but at least it didn't work. Let's get back to the party and tell Mike what happened. He can arrest Burke."

Delores looked worried. "I just hope Mike can catch him in time."

"What do you mean?"

"When Burke danced with me earlier, he asked me to supervise the loading of the crate because he was leaving tonight. He said he had to drive back out to the inn, pack up his things, and catch a midnight flight out of Minneapolis."

"A flight to where?"

"Somewhere in Europe. He told me he was taking a little vacation now that the movie was over. That's why he made arrangements with the moving company to store the sewing machine until he got back."

Hannah glanced at her watch. If Burke was taking an international flight, he had to arrive at the airport at least two hours in advance. That meant he had to leave the inn less than thirty minutes from now to make it on time.

"I need your help, Mother," Hannah said, shrugging into her coat and pulling on her gloves. "Call the sheriff's station, tell them it's an emergency, and have them patch you through to Mike's cell phone. Tell him Burke killed Dean and I found the prop gun to prove it."

"Right away, dear. Where are you going?"

"Out to the inn. Tell Mike to meet me there just as fast as he can, and I'll try to hold Burke until he arrives."

Sixteen minutes later, Hannah barreled down the circular drive of the Lake Eden Inn. She'd probably broken the winter land speed record for the gravel road that wound through the trees to the inn, and every spring in her truck could testify to that fact. The leftover cookies that Lisa bagged every night and Hannah stored in her truck to use as samples now decorated the floorboards in the rear. Hannah knew because she'd heard them hit the sides of the truck when she'd taken the turns. One errant Oatmeal Raisin Crisp, centrifugally challenged by the sharp bends she'd taken just adjacent to the inn's parking lot, had whizzed past her ear and was now sitting, slightly the worse for wear, on the passenger seat.

As Hannah approached the loading zone, four head-in spaces next to the entrance that were reserved for arriving and departing guests, she heard a car motor start. A second later, taillights went on and Hannah spotted Burke's rental car, a sporty, bright yellow Toyota. She rolled down her window, zipped into the vacant space to the left of his car, and shouted out, "Hi, Burke!"

"Hi, Hannah. What are you doing out here?"

Hannah thought fast. "Mother told me you were leaving tonight, and I wanted to say good-bye."

"'Bye, Hannah. It's been a real pleasure knowing you. Your cookies are the best I've ever had."

"Thanks." Hannah glanced at the gravel road, but she didn't see approaching headlights. Somehow she had to keep Burke talking until Mike got here.

"I have to run, Hannah. I've got a plane to catch. I'm going to London to do another commercial."

"No you're not!" Hannah shouted out. "Not until you answer some questions for me."

Burke gave her a boyish grin, the same grin that set the hearts of every female between sixteen and sixty beating faster than normal. "That sounds serious. Don't you know you shouldn't be serious on a night like tonight?"

"Why not?" Hannah stalled for time.

"This is a night for celebrating. The movie's going to be a huge success, your niece is going to be the toast of the silver screen, and your cat will be famous. What could be better than that?"

"Not much," Hannah said, "except maybe the lead in *Remember Last Tuesday*."

"What was that?"

Burke looked totally confused by what she'd just said, and Hannah would have sworn he'd never heard the movie title before if she hadn't known better. "*Remember Last Tuesday* is the major motion picture that would have made you a star . . ." Hannah paused and let that sink in, ". . . except Dean Lawrence made a phone call and kept you from getting the part."

"What are you *talking* about?"

Burke still looked baffled and it was disconcerting. For a brief second Hannah wondered if she could be wrong, but then she reminded herself that Burke was a very talented actor who could play any part, including innocent.

"Dean was angry about that interview you gave and he found a perfect way to get even. All it took was a couple of words to his important director friends, and your career was down the drain."

Burke gave her a tight smile. "I don't know if you're crazy, or if you had too much to drink at the wrap party. Whatever it is, I think you'd better go home and sleep it off."

About time! Hannah thought as she heard a siren in the distance. Mike was coming and she didn't have to stall much longer. Within seconds, he'd pulled up on the other side of Burke's car and was rolling down his window.

"What's going on here?" Mike asked, looking at Hannah and then Burke.

"I want you to arrest Burke," Hannah said, hoping that Delores had given him a satisfactory explanation. "He killed Dean."

Burke laughed long and hard, and then he turned to Mike. "That's the third time she's said that and I don't know what she's talking about. You'd better take her home and sober her up. She's got some ridiculous idea that I'm a murderer."

"Is that right?" Mike addressed Hannah.

"That's right. Dean wrecked Burke's career and Burke got even by switching the revolvers. He stood right there and let Dean demonstrate the suicide and he knew the gun would go off."

"Isn't that the craziest story you've ever heard?" Burke was joviality personified as he beamed at Mike. "I don't know where she gets her ideas, but I think she ought to try writing a movie script." He pulled up his coat sleeve and made a big show of checking his watch. "If I don't leave now, I'm going to miss my plane."

"You can't leave!" Hannah protested, glancing over at Mike. "Tell him he can't leave, Mike."

Mike shook his head. "Sorry, Hannah. It's an interesting theory, but I don't have enough evidence to hold Burke." Mike turned to the actor and said, "You're free to go."

Burke gave a little wave and put his car in reverse. He was about to back out of the parking spot when Hannah grabbed the prop gun and aimed at him. "Stop or I'll shoot!" she yelled.

"Hannah! Where did you get that revolver?" Mike looked shocked.

"From the sewing machine at Granny's Attic." Hannah answered, and then she turned to Burke again. "I'm a good shot, so don't fool around with me. Get out of the car with your hands up, or I'll shoot."

"No, you won't," Burke said with a nasty laugh. "That gun doesn't have a firing pin."

"Gotcha!" Hannah said. And then she watched as the smug look on Burke's face disappeared. "The only way you could know that is if you hid the prop gun in the sewing machine right after you switched revolvers. And you know what *that* means!"

Burke stepped on the gas, but Mike was quicker and his squad car shot back to block Burke's exit. At the same time, a second squad car arrived with Lonnie Murphy at the wheel and his brother, Rick, riding shotgun. Literally. Rick had his department-issued twelve-gauge pointed at the driver's side window of Burke's yellow Toyota.

"Read him his rights and take him in," Mike told his deputies and he stood by to watch them do it. It was only after they'd cuffed Burke, loaded him into the backseat of the squad car, and were pulling away that he walked over to Hannah's cookie truck and leaned down to talk to her through the open window.

"Did you know all along that the revolver I had was the prop gun?" she asked.

"Sure I did. Your mother told me all about it."

"I don't understand. If you knew how Burke killed Dean and you knew that we'd found the prop gun, why did you wait to arrest him?"

"I wanted a little extra insurance, and we got it. Burke admitted in front of both of us that he knew the gun in the sewing machine didn't have a firing pin."

"And you were afraid that without that admission, Burke might convince a jury that he was innocent?"

"It's possible. Don't forget that he'll be playing the part of a lifetime." Mike leaned through the window and touched his lips to Hannah's. "I've missed you, Hannah."

"Because you were busy working on the murder investigation and I wasn't with you?"

"Yup." Mike moved forward and kissed her again, a little more deeply and a lot longer. "Guess I should've deputized you after all," he said.

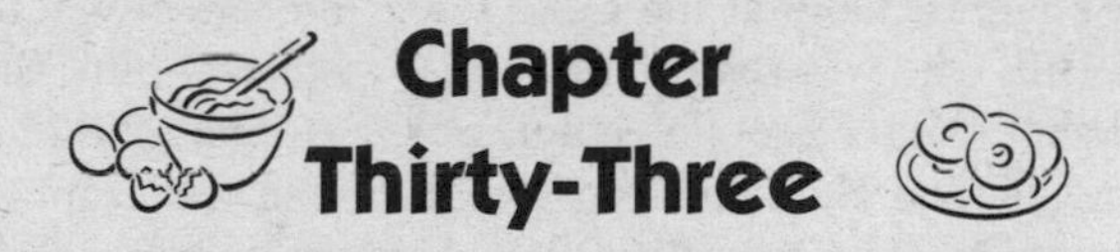

Chapter Thirty-Three

Hannah glanced in the mirror as she fastened the pendant Ross had given her around her neck. The red stones in the miniature cherries sparkled brightly in the sun that was streaming in her bedroom window and flashed scarlet streaks against the wall. Ross had presented her with the pendant the previous night, right before he'd left for the airport and his flight to California. "Think of me every time you wear it," he'd told her. "If *Crisis in Cherrywood* makes it to Cannes, I'll send you a ticket."

Then he'd pulled her into his arms and kissed her, and Hannah had been spared a reply. Of course she wanted to go to Cannes. Who wouldn't want to go to Cannes? But wanting and actually going were two different things. She'd thought about it for hours after Ross had left, imagining what it would be like to be an important producer's date at a gala movie premiere.

It seemed as if she'd just fallen asleep when the phone had rung this morning. It was Andrea and she'd sounded on top of the world when she'd invited Hannah to join them for a family brunch. It would be the usual crowd and Norman would pick her up. And now Hannah was sitting at

Sally's largest table at the Lake Eden Inn, directly across from Bill, who was resplendent in his raspberry pink shirt.

"I should have brought sunglasses," Norman said under his breath, and Hannah hid a grin. Norman was right. On the linear brightness scale, Bill's shirt was only a point or two short of eye-popping. Mike, who was sitting on Hannah's other side and had overheard Norman's comment, stifled a chuckle with his napkin.

Hannah smiled at Norman and then she turned to smile at Mike. On past occasions she'd resented the fact that she was always seated between them. She'd even made cracks about being the filling in a Mike and Norman sandwich. Today she didn't mind at all. She'd upset their equilibrium by going out with Ross and it was time to reassure them. Ross was like an exotic dessert, a diversion to tingle the taste buds and make her savor her own life with a more discerning palate. He was like a baked Alaska flambéed with fine brandy, flashy and exciting, but not something you'd serve with an ordinary supper of meat and potatoes. Mike and Norman were more like . . . cookies. Cookies were something you could have every day without ever tiring of them.

The smile on Hannah's face grew wider. If she had to choose their cookie types, Norman would be an Old-Fashioned Sugar Cookie, one of her very favorites. You couldn't go wrong with an Old-Fashioned Sugar Cookie. It was perfect for any occasion and at any time of day.

Mike was different, and Hannah gave it some thought. She finally decided that he'd be a Black-and-White Cookie, perfectly shaped and gorgeous to look at. It was sweet on the outside, and darker and more intense once you got past the powdered sugar.

"Hannah?" Andrea raised her from her mental dessert game. "Come up to the buffet with me. I want you to show me which bar cookies you brought."

Hannah made her excuses and got up to join Andrea at the dessert table. She pointed out the Ooey Gooey Chewy Cookie Bars she'd made in honor of the fact that Dean's killer was behind bars, but Andrea simply nodded.

"I knew which ones they were," she said. "I just wanted an excuse to talk to you alone."

Hannah took a deep breath and prepared for bad news. Andrea and Bill had been smiling throughout the brunch, but that could have been for their mother's benefit. "What is it?"

"Ronni Ward got engaged and she's getting married next month!"

"That's great news! When did this happen?"

"Last week in Miami. Remember when Lisa was trying to make me feel better and she said that maybe Ronni would meet another fitness instructor and they'd do exercises together?"

"I remember."

"Well, that's exactly what happened. Ronni met a personal trainer from The Cities and they're going to open a studio together. Isn't that just wonderful?"

"It certainly is." Hannah swiveled around as someone tapped her on the shoulder. It was Michelle and she looked a bit dazed. "What's wrong, Michelle? You look as if a strong wind could blow you over."

"That's because it *could* blow me over. Lonnie just told me that he entered me in the Miss Winnetka Beauty Contest."

"He did it without asking you first?" Andrea asked the critical question.

"That's right. He said he knew I was the prettiest girl in the county and he wanted everybody to see how beautiful I am. Is that crazy, or what?"

"Crazy in love," Hannah offered, grinning a little. "That's very sweet, and you don't have to worry about it. If you get chosen as a finalist, you can always turn it down."

"I *was* chosen as a finalist. Lonnie just told me. And I *can't* turn it down."

Andrea began to frown. "Why not?"

"Because Mother signed the papers agreeing I'd be a contestant."

"Can she *do* that?" Hannah recovered enough to ask.

"Oh, yes. The rules say that if you're under twenty-one, a parent can sign the forms for you."

"Oh, boy!" Hannah muttered. "When is the contest?"

"In June. It's part of the Winnetka County Fair. And I'm not going to college this summer, so I don't have that for an excuse. I'm stuck, and I don't know how to get out of it. But at least I'm not alone."

"What do you mean?" Andrea asked.

"I'm not the only one Mother signed up. She entered you and Tracey in the Mother-Daughter Look-Alike Contest, and she entered Bethany in the Beautiful Baby contest."

"Oh, for Pete's sake!" Andrea said, but she didn't look too upset.

Hannah burst out laughing. "I'm going to have fun at the fair this year. I can hardly wait to see both of you up there on stage."

"Don't laugh too hard," Michelle warned.

"Why not?"

"Mother signed you up to judge the baked goods at the fair."

"That's fine with me. It sounds like fun." Hannah smiled, but her smile turned into an anxious look as Michelle burst out laughing. "What?"

"Don't crow yet. She also volunteered you for the Lake Eden Historical Society Booth."

"That's not so bad. I don't mind passing out literature for the Historical Society."

"It's not literature this year."

"It's not?"

"No, they're doing a fund-raiser. Have you ever seen the

type of booth where a lady in a fancy silk dress and a parasol sits over a tank of water?"

Hannah gasped. Surely Mother wouldn't do that to her! "Are you talking about the kind of booth where people try to hit a target with a baseball and dunk the lady?" she asked.

"That's right. You're in the booth from two to four on Saturday afternoon. According to Mother, that's a heavy traffic period. And Bill says to tell you that Norman and Mike have already signed up with a coach to take pitching lessons!"

OOEY GOOEY CHEWY COOKIE BARS

Preheat oven to 350 degrees F., rack in the middle position

For the Crust:

½ cup white ***(granulated)*** sugar
¾ cup flour ***(not sifted)***
⅓ cup unsweetened baking cocoa*** ***(I used Hershey's)***
¼ teaspoon salt
½ stick melted butter ***(¼ cup–⅛ pound)***

For the Filling:

2 cups milk chocolate chips ***(I used Ghirardelli's)***
3 cups miniature marshmallows ***(pack them down in the cup)***
1½ cups flaked coconut ***(pack it down when you measure it)***
1 cup chopped nuts ***(I use either pecans, or walnuts)***
1 can sweetened condensed milk ***(14 ounces)***

****** You can find unsweetened baking cocoa in the baking aisle of your grocery store. Make sure***

you get an American brand—some of the others are Dutch process and they won't work in this recipe. Also be careful not to get cocoa mix, the kind you'd use to make hot chocolate or chocolate milk.

Mix the sugar, flour, cocoa, and salt together in a medium-sized bowl. Drizzle the melted butter over the top of the bowl and mix it in with a fork. When the butter is incorporated, the mixture should resemble small beads. ***(You can also do this in the bowl of a food processor, using chilled butter and the steel blade.)***

Spray a 9-inch by 13-inch cake pan with Pam ***(or other non-stick cooking spray)*** and dump the crust mixture in the bottom. Gently shake the pan to distribute evenly and then press it down a bit with a metal spatula.

Sprinkle the chips evenly over the crust layer. Sprinkle the marshmallows over that. Sprinkle the flaked coconut on next and then sprinkle on the chopped nuts. Press it down again with the metal spatula. Pour the sweetened condensed milk evenly over the top.

Bake the bars at 350 degrees F. for 25 to 30 minutes, or until the bars are nicely browned on top.

Let the bars cool on a rack. When they're cool, cut them in brownie-sized pieces.

WARNING: DON'T REFRIGERATE THESE COOKIE BARS WITHOUT CUTTING THEM FIRST—THEY'RE VERY DENSE AND SOLID WHEN CHILLED.

A Note From Edna Ferguson, the Queen of "Cheat" Recipes: If you want a shortcut for the crust, just buy a chocolate cake mix and use half of it, dry, mixed with the melted stick of butter. (Keep the rest of the cake mix in an airtight bag and you can use it the next time you bake them.)

Kids really love these cookie bars, especially the name.

Index of Recipes

Baking Conversion Chart

These conversions are approximate, but they'll work just fine for Hannah Swensen's recipes.

VOLUME:

U.S.	*Metric*
½ teaspoon	2 milliliters
1 teaspoon	5 milliliters
1 tablespoon	15 milliliters
¼ cup	50 milliliters
⅓ cup	75 milliliters
½ cup	125 milliliters
¾ cup	175 milliliters
1 cup	¼ liter

WEIGHT:

U.S.	*Metric*
1 ounce	28 grams
1 pound	454 grams

OVEN TEMPERATURE:

Degrees Fahrenheit	*Degrees Centigrade*	*British (Regulo) Gas Mark*
325 degrees F.	165 degrees C.	3
350 degrees F.	175 degrees C.	4
375 degrees F.	190 degrees C.	5

Note: Hannah's rectangular sheet cake pan, 9 inches by 13 inches, is approximately 23 centimeters by 32.5 centimeters.

It's Tri-County fair time and Lake Eden, Minnesota, is buzzing with more than mosquitoes. Hannah Swensen, owner of The Cookie Jar, is hot on the trail of a killer whose perfect carnival prize would be getting away with murder . . .

It promises to be a busy week for Hannah Swensen. Not only is she whipping up treats for the chamber of commerce booth at the fair, she's also judging the baking contest, acting as a magician's assistant for her business partner's husband, trying to coax Moishe—her previously rapacious feline—to end his hunger strike, and performing her own private carnival act by juggling the demands of her mother and sisters.

With so much on her plate, it's no wonder Hannah finds herself on the midway only moments before the fair closes for the night. As the lights click off, she realizes that she's not alone among the shuttered booths and looming carnival attractions. After hearing a suspicious thump, she goes snooping only to discover Willa Sunquist, a student teacher and fellow bake contest judge, dead alongside an upended key lime pie. But who would want to kill Willa and why? Before long Hannah is sifting through motives and a list of suspects that include a high school student Willa flunked, the hot-blooded brothers of a disqualified beauty contestant, a rodeo cowboy, a baking competitor who failed to win her yearly blue ribbon, and the college professor Willa was dating.

As fair week draws to a close, Hannah cranks up the heat, hoping that the killer will get rattled and make a mistake. If that happens she intends to be there, even if it means getting on a carnival ride that could very well be her last . . .

Please turn the page for an exciting sneak peek at Joanne Fluke's KEY LIME PIE MURDER coming next month in hardcover!

Hannah felt a bit like a salmon swimming upstream as she headed for the Lake Eden Historical Society booth. It was never easy bucking a crowd. Everyone seemed to be streaming toward the exit in a giant wave. She doubted that the bag with Moishe's Paul Bunyan Burger was still where she'd left it, but she had to find out.

"Excuse me," Hannah said, resisting the urge to elbow three high school boys walking with their girlfriends six abreast. But they didn't even notice her, so Hannah stepped aside to let them past. This happened more times than she could count as she treaded water in the sea of humanity and darted forward against the surge of boisterous fairgoers whenever she saw an opening.

"Aren't you leaving?" someone shouted out, and Hannah turned to see Carrie passing her.

"Yes, in a second. Did I leave . . ." Hannah's voice trailed off. It was too late. Carrie had passed her in the opposite directly and she couldn't possibly hear Hannah's question.

" 'Bye, dear," Delores hailed her. Hannah's mother and her two companions, Bernie "No-No" Fulton and Wingo Jones, were being carried along on a tide of humanity that was heading for the turnstile at the exit. If there'd been any doubt in Hannah's mind about the identity of the person who'd contacted the Triple A pitcher and invited him to visit the dunking booth, it was now erased.

" 'Bye, Mother," Hannah shouted back. No sense in asking Delores if her takeout burger bag was still at the booth. Her mother was already several booth-lengths away and there was no way Hannah could make herself heard over the din of the crowd.

Hannah considered her options. It was obvious that the Lake Eden Historical Society booth was closed since she'd seen both her mother and Carrie leaving. Finding the bag with Moishe's burger was unlikely, but she'd come this far despite the aggravation of opposing human traffic, and she might as well finish her quest.

She made good progress for several more feet and then things came to a standstill. There was no way she could paddle upstream any longer. Hannah accepted the inevitable and moved laterally, heading for a handy booth where she could wait out the rush.

The Tri-County Dairy booth beckoned and Hannah flattened herself against the shuttered front. She found an anchor of sorts, a giant milk bottle carved from wood and painted white. She held on as the crowd surged past her, hoping that no one would bump into her and knock her from her feet. She'd wait until the foot traffic had thinned, and then she'd set out for the historical society booth again.

Over the next several minutes, Hannah called hello to at least two dozen people she knew and the lights flickered several more times. At last the crowd thinned out and Hannah set off for her mother's booth. It didn't take long to get there and she met only one or two people walking rapidly in the direction of the gate.

By the time Hannah arrived, panting slightly, the lights had flickered on and off again. She was too late. The wooden shutters that served as counters were raised and padlocked shut. Hannah walked around to the side, where the dunking stool was located, and gave a dejected sigh. These counters were also locked into place, tightly shuttering the booth for the night. She should have known the futility of coming all the way back to the booth. If her mother or Carrie had found the bag when they were closing, they would have thrown it away.

"Trashed," Hannah muttered, wondering how she was going to explain this to Lisa and Herb. But then she realized what she'd said and looked quickly around for the nearest trash container. If no one had emptied the trash yet, Moishe could be feasting on hamburger tonight.

A fifty-gallon drum painted red and labeled TRASH in big black letters stood only feet from the side of the booth. Hannah set her key lime pie on the ground next to the trashcan, glad that she'd found a bakery box to put it in, and peeked inside the receptacle. There was a white bag right on top and it certainly looked like the one she'd left on the counter.

Hannah sent up a silent plea for luck and good fortune, and then she opened the bag, hoping that it didn't contain any gross leftovers. She was almost afraid to look, but she did. And then she grinned from ear to ear. There was Moishe's Paul Bunyan Burger, still neatly wrapped in wax paper that was stamped with the green and white logo of the Burger Shack.

Hannah tucked the bag inside her shoulder bag purse and picked up the pie box again. She'd accomplished her mission and now it was time to get back to the gate to meet Mike before he fell asleep on the bench and someone locked her in for the night.

As she walked, Hannah began to feel uneasy. Everyone else had left and the only noise was the sound of her own footfalls. The thump of her rubber soles hitting the dirt was deafening in the surrounding silence, and she resisted the urge to tiptoe. There was something very unnerving about being alone on the midway at night.

She was just passing the Family Farms Association booth when everything went black. Hannah came to a standstill and reached out to steady herself against the mechanical bull. Rather than just a saddle and a mechanism that bucked and swiveled, this bull looked like a real Brahma bull and cost five dollars to ride.

For a moment Hannah just stood there gripping the bull's ear, feeling even more apprehensive and wondering how she was ever going to find her way to the gate in the darkness. There were occasional flashes of heat lightning way off in the distance, but that provided no real illumination. She could hear a low rumbling, barely audible. Thunder? Whatever it was, it added to Hannah's growing apprehension.

She told herself not to panic. She'd just wait for her eyes to adjust and pick her way to Mike, lifting her feet high so she wouldn't trip over any ropes or cables. She was about to set out when there was a hollow clunk, as if someone had thrown the lever on a transformer, and a long string of dim lights went on overhead.

If Hannah hadn't been so nervous, she might have chided herself for borrowing trouble. Of course they had nightlights on the midway. It was a safety precaution and it probably served to discourage kids from climbing the fence and sneaking in after hours.

Although the lighting was by no means bright, now she could make out the rectangles of the shuttered booths and the looming, almost menacing shapes of the carnival rides. Hannah shivered even though the night was hot and her skin felt slick with moisture. It wasn't good being here alone. It wasn't good at all.

As she made her halting way forward, Hannah kept to the center of the path, her eyes scanning the shadows for movement. Every bad horror movie she'd ever seen flashed through her mind and she thought about what she might use for a weapon if someone or something emerged from the darkness. There was her shoulder bag purse. It was heavy enough to knock someone off balance, especially if she swung it in an arc. The key lime pie she was carrying could be used to render someone temporarily blind. It was a terrible waste of a first-place-winning dessert, but if push came to shove, she wouldn't hesitate to use it. If she took it out of the box and shoved the sticky meringue right in an assailant's face, it would take him a minute or so to wipe it from his eyes. By that time she'd be well on her way to the gate to alert Mike.

Hannah walked on, but her mind was in turmoil. The old adage against borrowing trouble was warring with the advice to be prepared. The Boy Scout motto won, hands down. She stopped at the next trashcan she passed and removed the pie, tossing the bakery box on top of the refuse the evening's fairgoers had left behind them.

Now she had a purse and a pie to use in her defense. Hannah gave a little sigh. Somehow that didn't seem like much. For the very first time in her life, she wished that she were wearing a pair of Andrea's stiletto-heeled shoes. Then she could slip one off and do real damage to anyone or anything that threatened her. Of course that was silly. If she'd been wearing a pair of her sister's stilettos, she wouldn't be in this position in the first place. There was no way she could walk in heels that high, much less fit into shoes that were four sizes too small for her.

She'd just passed the Tri-County Volunteer Fire Department's Red Hot Ring-Toss booth when she heard a noise that couldn't be explained by the nonexistent wind, or any small furry creature that made the fairgrounds its home. It was the sound of something heavy striking something composed of flesh and bone. Hannah wasn't sure how she knew that, but she did. And her blood ran cold.

"Is someone there?" she called out before she'd had time to consider the wisdom of speaking. And then she did, and she wished she could call back her words. Now the person who'd struck the blow she'd heard knew that he wasn't alone on the midway. And he also knew approximately how far away and in which direction she was.

Open mouth, insert foot, Hannah thought, but she didn't stand still to think about it. She knew she had to get away fast and that's exactly what she proceeded to do. But as she scurried away, her brain wasn't idle. She was almost certain the sound she'd heard had come from a booth across the path and around the corner, no more than three booths from where she'd been standing. If she remembered the layout of the midway correctly, that was where the shooting gallery was located.

But it hadn't been a gunshot. Hannah was sure of that. She tried to forget about the heavy object striking flesh and bone and considered what other things might produce a sound like it. It could have been someone kicking a hollow rubber ball with considerable force. Or someone striking a ripe melon with a baseball bat. Or a sledge hammer hitting . . . Hannah gave a little shiver. She didn't want to think about this now. Whatever it was, it was ominous. Right now she had to get as far away from the shooting gallery as possible!

Heart pounding hard and her senses on full alert, Hannah scuttled down the line of booths, keeping to the shadows and doing her best to move quickly, carefully and silently. One misstep and he'd know where she was. She'd just reached the end of the row of booths when she heard a second thunk. Whoever it was hadn't moved and that meant he hadn't heard her. Hannah took advantage of the moment to dart around the corner, putting even more distance between them.

She was at the side of the Strong Man Booth, where fairgoers could win a Strong Man badge if they pounded a mallet onto a metal bed with enough force to make a ball scoot all the way up the vertical shaft to ring the bell at the top. Hannah took refuge behind several bales of hay placed there as a makeshift barrier to keep observers from getting too close to the prospective Strong Man and the mallet.

All was silent, perfectly silent. Hannah resisted the urge to slap at a mosquito that landed on her cheek and remained motionless. She crouched there for long minutes that seemed like hours, wondering if whatever or whoever she'd heard could hear her breathing or the rapid beating of her heart.

Was it safe to move yet? Hannah wasn't sure so she didn't. Instead she swiveled her head slowly, examining her surroundings and committing every shape and shadow to memory. Mike had told her that trick, not long after they'd first met. He said cops on a stakeout got tired after a while and thought they saw things that weren't there. He examined everything at the start so that his mind would sound an internal alarm if anything in his visual pattern changed.

As Hannah huddled there, trying to make as small a configuration as possible, her mind spun through the possibilities. Someone was here on the deserted midway with her. The noise she'd heard proved that. She didn't think it was another late fairgoer rushing toward the exit and tripping over a rope or a stake. If that had happened, she would have heard groaning, or cries for help. She supposed it could have been a carnival worker locking up a little late, or coming back to secure something or other he'd forgotten. But if it had been a carnival worker, he would have answered her when she called out. This person was up to no good. His silence proved that.

Hannah drew her breath in sharply. The Strong Man mallet was gone. When she'd walked past the booth earlier in the day, it had been on a chain next to the vertical shaft. The chain was still there. She could see it on the ground, glistening slightly in the dim glow from the string of lights.

Had they locked the mallet inside the booth for the night? Or had someone taken it, used it to hit someone else, and was in the process of bringing it back so that no one would know . . .

And there he was! And it was too late to run! Hannah did what any strong, courageous, modern Minnesota-born woman might have done in the same circumstance. She shut her eyes and attempted to become one with the hay.

Of course it didn't work. There was no way she was going to huddle here waiting for him to find her and whack her with the mallet, too. Not only that, if she did escape his notice, she wanted to be able to give the authorities a good description.

Hannah opened her eyes, inched toward the side of the hay bale and risked a peek. But the light was too dim. All she saw was a shadowy figure bending over the chain to reattach the mallet. She pulled her head back and listened for the sound of footfalls coming her way. She was almost positive that he hadn't spotted her, not unless he was a sideshow attraction and he had eyes in the back of his head. Still, it was better to be safe than sorry and she readied the pie for action.

Long moments passed as she listened intently, alert for the slightest sound. She imagined that her ears swiveled independently like little satellite dishes, the way Moishe's ears did when he heard a mouse in the walls. The hair at the base of her neck prickled in apprehension and she made her breathing shallow and almost inaudible. Except for the far-off sound of a dog barking in a neighboring farmyard, the muted swoosh of cars on the highway, and the faint rumble of thunder in the distance, all was deathly quiet.

And then she heard it. He was moving again. She had the key lime pie in a death grip, ready to hurl it at the slightest provocation, but the sound grew fainter with each passing heartbeat. He was moving away from her, running away from her hiding place. He hadn't seen her! She was safe!

But where had he gone? The moment Hannah thought of it, she stood up and moved to the front of the booth. Her eyes scanned the midway for movement and found none. Had she been too slow? But then she spotted him disappearing around the side of the Tilt-A-Whirl.

It was safe for her to go now and Hannah knew what she should do. She should head straight for the gate where Mike was waiting for her. She should tell him what happened, and he could take over from here on out. He'd hammered that point home often enough. He was the detective, and she was not. If she thought something was wrong, she should tell him and he would take care of it. Her caution should win out over her curiosity.

Hannah leaned against the booth to let her breathing return to normal and her heartbeats slow to a reasonable rate. The moment she told Mike, he'd turn on the bright lights and investigate. But what if the sounds she'd heard had been perfectly innocent and nothing at all was wrong? She'd look like a first-class fool in front of a man she admired and could possibly even love.

There was only one thing to do. Perhaps it was the wrong thing, but that had never stopped her before. Hannah straightened up, stretched to relieve her cramped muscles, and headed off toward the shooting gallery. She'd check it out first, before she raised the alarm. And if she was right and something was wrong, she'd head for the gate and sound the alarm immediately.

The sounds seemed magnified as Hannah headed down the row of booths. A slight breeze picked up and she almost jumped out of her skin as the plastic flags fluttered over the booths. They sounded as loud as the flock of crows that used to land in her grandfather's cornfield, the ones her Grandma Ingrid refused to chase off because she was partial to crows. Hannah's every instinct told her she was heading into trouble, and she was likely to discover something she didn't want to find. She knew she should turn tail and run for Mike, but instead she forged ahead, each footstep deliberate and even, drawing her inevitably closer to the shooting gallery. She was like Moishe who still occasionally pushed the cold water lever in the shower, even though he'd gotten drenched several times in the past.

When she arrived at the shooting gallery, Hannah took a deep breath. It was show time. She was convinced it would be either, or. Either she'd find something horrible, or she'd find nothing at all. In the dim light from the single string of lights high overhead, the teddy bear prizes lined up in rows inside the glass front of the booth seemed to be staring at a point just around the corner. Hannah rounded the corner, stopped short, and felt herself assume the same glassy-eyed stare. Someone was sprawled out in the dirt. It was a woman, Hannah could tell because she was wearing a dress. And she was perfectly motionless.

Hannah's mind spun. This was the time to go after Mike, but of course she couldn't. What if this poor woman was injured and in need of immediate help. She knew CPR. She could even fashion a tourniquet if she absolutely had to.

Her need to help another human being in trouble drew her forward. The woman was facedown in the dirt, and Hannah was about to reach for her wrist to feel for a pulse when she saw the back of her head. This caused her to step back without taking her pulse or touching her. No aid she could give would make a particle of difference. This woman was quite dead and Hannah hoped that it had been quick. Blunt force trauma didn't make for a kind demise.

The woman's skirt pulled up a bit in back, a result of the way she'd fallen, and Hannah reached out to tug it down. It wouldn't make any difference to her now, but there should be dignity in death. And once she'd fixed the woman's skirt and straightened up again, Hannah had an awful realization.

"No!" Hannah gulped. She took one halting step closer and the pie dropped from her nerveless fingers. She'd seen and admired this dress before, no more than an hour ago!

Hannah stared down at the bits of meringue and key lime pie filling that were scattered on the ground. She couldn't just stand here. She had to get moving and go after Mike. He needed to know about this.

"Hannah?"

Mike's voice rang out loud and clear, as if she had summoned him by mental telepathy. But she wasn't sure she believed in things like that. It must be a coincidence, a wonderful coincidence. And if she could only find her voice, she could answer him.

"Where are you, Hannah?"

"Here," Hannah answered, finding her voice at last. Of course her answer wouldn't do him much good. *Here* could mean anywhere. Her one-word answer wasn't descriptive enough. On the other hand, Mike was the head detective at the Winnetka County Sheriff's Department and he ought to be able to figure it out.

"Where's here?" Mike asked, and his voice sounded closer.

Hannah had the insane urge to tell him he was getting warmer. It was almost as if they were playing her favorite childhood game, the one where someone leaves the room, the group hides something, the person comes back in, and the group directs them to the hidden object by telling them whether they're warmer or colder.

But this is no game, Hannah's mind told her. *It's all too real and you have to answer him.* She took a deep breath and did what her mind had suggested. "I'm around the side of the shooting gallery," she said.

"You sound weird. What's the matter?"

Hannah opened her mouth to answer, but she was too busy wondering how he could run and ask questions at the same time. He didn't even sound winded! She certainly couldn't do it, but then she was at least twenty pounds overweight, and she'd been about to add to that total by ordering a deep-fried, cookie-battered Milky Way until he'd caught her standing in front of the booth.

"Hannah? I asked you what was the matter?"

Hannah sighed. He'd be here any second and then he could see for himself. But he'd asked and his question deserved an answer. "Dead," she said.

"Someone's dead?" Mike asked, rounding the corner with the speed of an Olympic hopeful. "Who?"

"Willa Sunquist," Hannah identified the victim for him before her legs gave way and she sank down to the ground to stare back at the glass-eyed teddy bears.